THOMAS LOVE PEACOCK
Nightmare Abbey
The Misfortunes of Elphin
Crotchet Castle

Thomas Love Peacock at 72. From a contemporary photograph.

THOMAS LOVE PEACOCK
Nightmare Abbey
The Misfortunes of Elphin
Crotchet Castle

Edited with an Introduction and Notes
by CHARLES B. DODSON

HOLT, RINEHART AND WINSTON, INC.

*New York Chicago San Francisco Atlanta
Dallas Montreal Toronto London Sydney*

Copyright © 1971 by Holt, Rinehart and Winston, Inc.
All rights reserved
Library of Congress Catalog Card Number: 74-169972
ISBN: 0-03-083025-7
Printed in the United States of America
1234 065 123456789

CONTENTS

INTRODUCTION

Thomas Love Peacock (1785–1866) was a civil servant, poet, novelist, and opera critic who is most often remembered (apart from being a novelist) as an intimate friend of Shelley. He was born in Weymouth, Dorsetshire, in 1785, the only child of a London glass merchant. His father died a few years later, and by the time he was five his mother had moved to her parents' home at Chertsey, a village on the Thames some twenty miles from London. There Thomas grew up in the house of his grandfather, a retired navy captain. His mother, for whom he had a deep and abiding affection, encouraged his interest in books throughout his life until her death when Peacock was almost fifty.

Peacock received his only formal education at a nearby school which he attended from ages six to twelve, but for the rest of his life he read avidly and widely, especially in English and in the classical literatures, but also in French, Italian, and Welsh, and in the popular subjects of the day.

After leaving school he took a job briefly as a clerk in London. The next several years were spent in voluminous reading and in excursions and walking tours through England, Scotland, and Wales. In 1808–1809, following an unsuccessful courtship, he served as secretary aboard a warship, which he called a "floating inferno." By this time he had started in earnest on a literary career.

His interest in poetry had begun early; in 1800 he had written a prize poem, "Is History or Biography the more Improving Subject?" Other poems appeared between 1804 and 1812 on such subjects as the English landscape and the pleasures of melancholy. They were largely as conventional in manner as in matter and are no longer read, although the earliest, *The Monks of St. Mark,* anticipates the often boisterous humor of the novels, as do two farces, composed between 1811 and 1813 but never staged.

Peacock first met Shelley in 1812. Their friendship grew steadily and continued after Shelley left England for good in 1818. As a friend of the Shelleys, Peacock had been a pained observer of the breakup in 1814–1816 of Shelley's marriage. He favored Harriet over Mary Godwin, and Mary, understandably enough, conceived a dislike for him that lasted until long after Shelley's death. Although he disapproved of Shelley's abandonment of Harriet and adultery with Mary, he refused to condemn Shelley openly for it and after Harriet's suicide in 1816 counseled Shelley to legalize his relationship with Mary. When Shelley drowned in 1822 Peacock became, with Byron, his executor. His diligence and loyalty in this capacity finally won Mary's trust.

Perhaps his intimacy with Shelley led Peacock to realize that fame as a poet lay beyond his grasp. In any event, a few years after meeting Shelley he turned to the novel. His observation of the eccentric enthusiasts who gathered around Shelley had stimulated his sense of the ridiculous and ultimately provided a basic ingredient in his novels. "I was sometimes irreverent enough," he later recalled of a visit to Bracknell in 1813, "to laugh at the fervour with which opinions utterly unconducive to any practical result were battled for as matters of the highest importance to the well-being of mankind." Over a period of forty-five years he produced seven novels which satirized the intellectual, scientific, political, and literary enthusiasms which he believed his age had substituted for the time-tested qualities of moderation and common sense.

The first of the novels, *Headlong Hall,* was published in 1815 (dated 1816). After this he published only two more volumes of verse, *Rhododaphne* (1818) and *Paper Money Lyrics* (1837), although he included a number of lyric and short narrative poems in his novels. *Melincourt* appeared in 1817 and *Nightmare Abbey* in 1818. In the same year he began his employment, which was to last for thirty-seven years, with the East India Company, having won his position through competitive examination. Here he worked with James and John Stuart Mill, succeeding the former to the responsible position of Examiner in 1836. For several years during his India House period he dined weekly with Jeremy Bentham, the founder and chief apostle of Utilitarianism.

Shortly after his initial appointment he proposed marriage, by letter, to Jane Gryffydh, whom he had first met on a tour of Wales in 1809 and whom he had last seen eight years before. She accepted. Their courtship had been unorthodox, but their marriage was affectionate and successful though marred by misfortune—the early death of one of their four children resulted in Jane's becoming an invalid until her death in 1851. A daughter, Mary, later made an unfortunate marriage to George Meredith; both she and another daughter did not survive their father.

After the publication of *Maid Marian* in 1822 Peacock's literary production began to fall off, undoubtedly due to family affairs and increasing responsibilities at the India House. *The Misfortunes of Elphin* appeared in 1829, followed two years later by *Crotchet Castle*. For the next thirty years he published little except some miscellaneous essays and other short pieces. From 1829–1836 he was music critic for two London papers. In 1861 his final novel and last major work, *Gryll Grange,* was published, having first appeared serially in *Fraser's Magazine.* He died in 1866 at his country house.

II

Crotchet Castle, Peacock's sixth novel, appeared anonymously (as did all his novels) in 1831. One of the characters was suggested to him as early as January 1829 when a Lombard Street banker and his clerk absconded, leaving over £100,000 in debts. Peacock nicknamed the banker Touchandgo and published a poem about him in the *Globe and Traveler* of January 24, 1829. The banker became Timothy Touchandgo in *Crotchet Castle,* and the clerk became his "factotum" Roderick Robthetill. Peacock was still writing or revising the novel as late as December 1830, as we learn in Chapter XVIII, where Peacock quotes the *Morning Chronicle* of December 20.

Crotchet Castle pre-eminently displays the characteristics of what has come to be called the Peacockian novel.[1] The setting is rural, largely in and around the country estate of a host whose main interests are eating and listening to his guests' opinions. For the most part, the details of everyday life are omitted—for example, it seems unnecessary that the characters earn a living.[2] Plot is scanted, although there is a romantic subplot ending happily. There is little narration; instead dialogue is the primary vehicle for the satire. Both the dialogue and the narration may be interrupted by passages of verse, and at the drop of a hat—or the passing round of a bottle—the characters are liable to break into a rousing drinking song or a sentimental ballad. Action usually takes the form of slapstick comedy, but even this will often turn out to be an illustration of some foible of society personified in one of Squire Crotchet's eccentric guests or discussed over the bottle. Characterization is important, but most of the characters are purposely left one-dimensional, so that each can represent some fad, theory, or eccentricity of the day. The characters thus exist only as spokesmen for ideas, and in this respect they resemble the characters of allegory. It is seldom necessary that we even know what they look like. Another typically Peacockian characteristic is the use of devices often associated with verse satire, such as burlesque, parody, or the mock-heroic. Still other ingredients are the omnipresent dinner table (food and drink are always taken seriously in Peacock's novels), frequent allusions to both contemporary and classical subjects, a liberal sprinkling of quotations, much learned and epigrammatic conversation, outrageous puns, a pervading tone of irony, gaiety, and good humor, and a highly Latinate prose style.

---

[1] Or *tale* or *romance* or *anatomy*, all of which terms have been applied to it. Peacock himself would have preferred his own conveniently vague term *comic fiction*.

[2] Lady Clarinda, it is true, makes much of Capt. Fitzchrome's meager income; yet even he has the leisure to wander about the countryside, sketching, sightseeing, and wooing her.

A few of the more significant techniques deserve elaboration. Peacock flouts many of the conventional devices of fiction, but perhaps nowhere so obviously as in his scanting of plot—at a period when Scott's exciting narratives were setting the pattern for success in fiction. The main functions of plot in *Crotchet Castle* are to provide interludes in the dialogue and to provide a semblance of the real world for the setting—as in the attack on Dr. Folliott in Chapter VIII. Individual incidents are carefully devised to fit the characters and to emphasize their crotchets; none of the other eccentrics, for example, would become as upset over Squire Crotchet's nude statues of Venus as would Dr. Folliott (Chapter VIII), for nudity in art is of no concern to one whose sole interest is poisons, steam navigation, transcendentalism, or co-operative societies. But it is a subject about which Dr. Folliott, as a cleric, a conservative, and an upholder of all things beautiful and moral (i.e. Greek), would naturally have strong opinions. Perhaps the best illustration of the unimportance of plot for its own sake occurs in the one section of the novel that relies fairly heavily upon plot—the unfolding of the Chainmail–Touchandgo love story (Chapters XII–XVI). Here, in the midst of telling Captain Fitzchrome about his new-found love, Mr. Chainmail casually interrupts his excited narrative to recite the long ballad of the diving friar. In another type of novel this breach of logic and narrative coherence would be annoying, but it is the sort of playfulness we expect from Peacock.

What little narration there is often displays some of the techniques of verse satire, showing that Peacock's long apprenticeship as a poet had not been wasted. The description of Squire Crotchet's coat of arms provides a superb example of burlesque:

> Crest, a crotchet rampant, in A sharp: Arms, three empty bladders, turgescent, to show how opinions are formed; three bags of gold, pendent, to show why they are maintained; three naked swords, tranchant, to show how they are administered; and three barbers' blocks, gaspant, to show how they are swallowed. (Chapter I.)

Two fine examples of the mock-heroic occur in Chapter XVI,

when Mr. Chainmail, that champion of the knightly tradition of twelfth-century England, uses a poker and the bottom of a chair as a sword and buckler and tilts against the bumpkin Harry Ap-Heather; and in Chapter XVIII, when the guests reel out of Chainmail Hall armed with lances and halberds to repulse the rioters spawned by an age of machinery. The ironic tone pervading the novel is most stinging when Peacock describes through Lady Clarinda the activities of the squirearchy as represented by Sir Simon Steeltrap (who, as "a great preserver of game and public morals," is thus epitomized in a phrase suggestive of zeugma, a device frequent in verse satire):

> By administering the laws which he assists in making [Lady Clarinda relates], he disposes, at his pleasure, of the land and its live stock, including all the two-legged varieties, with and without feathers, in a circumference of several miles round Steeltrap Lodge. He has enclosed commons and woodlands; abolished cottage-gardens; taken the village cricket-ground into his own park, out of pure regard to the sanctity of Sunday; shut up footpaths and ale houses, (all but those which belong to his electioneering friend, Mr. Quassia, the brewer;) put down fairs and fiddlers; committed many poachers; shot a few; convicted one third of the peasantry; suspected the rest; and passed nearly the whole of them through a wholesome course of prison discipline, which has finished their education at the expense of the county. (Chapter V.)

This passage, and the description of Squire Crotchet's coat of arms quoted above, are reminiscent of the epigrammatic qualities and syntactic economy of Pope's heroic couplet. Parody is used to ridicule the ideas of Coleridge, Southey, and the Utilitarians. Peacock also makes use of a favorite device of the verse satirist, anticlimax; one example occurs during the Thames excursion: "At Oxford, they walked about to see the curiosities of architecture, painted windows, and undisturbed libraries" (Chapter IX).

Any study of Peacock's fictional technique in *Crotchet Cas-*

tle and the other novels must take into account his prose style. There is little appreciable difference between the style of the dialogue and that of the narrative passages. The characters in their pedantry speak as coherently and correctly as if they were reading a prepared speech. Peacock doubtless felt that the absurdity of their ideas would be self-evident without the addition of solecisms or vulgarities of expression. Furthermore, with three minor exceptions, there are no "low" characters in the novel, so there is little occasion for any but the easy (if slightly formal) modulations of reasonably literate Englishmen of his time, as evidenced in the novels of Trollope, for example. Peacock's style in *Crotchet Castle* is essentially the same as in his other novels, for it was mature when he began his career as a novelist and altered very little as he grew older.

Peacock's sentences are often very long and either periodic or balanced, and they are always carefully sculptured. The periodic sentence which begins the novel is a *tour de force,* as is the long and delicately balanced sentence which follows it. Other sentences echo the cadences of the King James Bible: "They left him mingling his tears with the spring and his lamentations with its murmurs" (Chapter XV).

Peacock's vocabulary is highly Latinate, as a few quotations selected at random will show:

> Mr. Mac Crotchet had derived from his mother the instinct, and from his father the rational principle, of enriching himself at the expense of the rest of mankind, by all the recognized modes of accumulation on the windy side of the law. (Chapter I.)

> The schemes for the world's regeneration evaporated in a tumult of voices. (Chapter VI.)

> . . . the only palpable fragment among its minutely pulverised atoms, and which is still resplendent over the portals of its cognominal college. (Chapter IX.)

Another peculiarity is Peacock's frequent use of archaisms which stand out because of both their unfamiliarity and their

Latin origins. These are not simply long yet reasonably common words; instead they are rarities or coinages like "inesculent," "eximious," "peirastically," "conterminal," "asseverated," "vaticinate," and "excubant." Moreover, Peacock often uses such words in a strictly etymological sense. The general meaning of "digladiations" in the following passage is "arguments" or "contentions":

> Mr. Mac Quedy and the Reverend Doctor Folliott had many digladiations on political economy: wherein, each of his own view, Dr. Folliott demolished Mr. Mac Quedy's science, and Mr. Mac Quedy demolished Dr. Folliott's objections. (Chapter X.)

According to the etymology of the word, to digladiate is to rend asunder (with swords); thus it is logical for Peacock to say that the two gentlemen *demolished* each other's positions. Many of these unfamiliar Latinisms occur in the dialogue of Dr. Folliott, but Peacock uses them in descriptive or narrative passages as well. Peacock's vocabulary is not exclusively learned, however; he sometimes mixes high and low diction to good effect, as when, upon seeing Miss Touchandgo and Mr. Chainmail together, Harry Ap-Heather "fixed on her a mingled look of surprise, reproach, and tribulation; and, unable to control his feelings under the sudden shock, burst into a flood of tears, and blubbered till the rocks reechoed" (Chapter XV). Similarly, in the passage describing the Crotchet family's talent for making money (quoted above), the unexpected occurrence of the simple Anglo-Saxon word "windy" following a number of Latinate words gives a humorous effect.

Another example of Peacock's interest in language is the etymological significance of the names of some of his characters. Thus the history of Dr. Folliott's surname is traced through three languages (Chapter I), and we are informed that the name of Skionar, the transcendental poet, is an acronym on the Greek words meaning "a dream of shadow" (Chapter II). Other characters also have names which fit their eccentricities, ranging from Mr. Eavesdrop and Mr. Chainmail to the less apparent Mr. Henbane.

Peacock delights in puns, sometimes rather weak and obvious—"What was Jacquerie in the dark ages, is the march of mind in this very enlightened one" (Chapter XVIII)—but usually clever and sometimes quite elaborate. As Squire Crotchet's guests dine on delicious salmon, Mr. Mac Quedy comments that salmon, like men, are inherently the same everywhere but that education differentiates one man from another. This provides Dr. Folliott with a pun on schools for people and schools of fish:

> Education! Well, sir, I have no doubt schools for all are just as fit for the species *salmo salar* as for the genus *homo*. But you must allow, that the specimen before us has finished his education in a manner that does honour to his college. (Chapter IV.)

More subtle is the following:

> *Mr. Crotchet:* Hermitage [a heady wine first produced by monks], Doctor?
> *Dr. Folliott:* Nothing better, sir. The father who first chose the solitude of that vineyard, knew well how to cultivate his spirit in retirement. (Chapter IV.)

Perhaps the most elaborate pun in the novel, however, occurs when Mr. Chainmail speaks of flourishing "the oaken graff of the Pinder of Wakefield" (Chapter XII). This is probably an allusion to the Elizabethan play *George a Greene, the Pinner of Wakefield* (attributed to Robert Greene). According to the *Oxford English Dictionary* a pinder or pinner is "an officer whose duty it is to impound stray beasts"; a graff is a branch, but it has also meant stylus or pencil. Peacock is therefore making a complex pun on the poet Pindar, the office of pinder, the symbol of that office, and the writing instrument of a poet.

The allusiveness of Peacock's style is apparent everywhere in *Crotchet Castle,* from the reference to the wells of Scamander in the opening sentence to the battle of Camlan in the Conclusion. The allusions range through a variety of subjects, including geology; philosophy; the works of Shakespeare, Pope, and other English authors, as well as French, Italian, German, Latin, and Greek literature; the Bible and the Book of Common Prayer; science; ancient and modern history; mythology; art and music; and contemporary events and politics. He also quotes extensively from authors both ancient and modern, both famous and obscure. These allusions and quotations are skillfully woven into his text or used as epigraphs at the beginning of chapters, and they are always germane; they occur with such regularity that they are organic rather than obtrusive. Remove them and what is left is not Peacock.

It is difficult to describe the total effect of Peacock's prose style. If it frequently smells of the lamp, it is also redolent of good English beef, French wine, and the Welsh countryside. It can be alternately playful and serious. It combines weighty erudition with the epigrammatic tang of the proverb, and a learned allusion can occur cheek-by-jowl with an outrageous pun. In it both straight-faced irony and Chaucerian drollery find a home. Witty and concise, it is yet neither coy nor terse. Even when it takes on the sculptured fullness of Ciceronian periods it still flows smoothly and does not become clogged or cluttered. When it is pedantic it is so in order to satirize pedantry—perhaps even its own. In short, it can be described as was Peacock's examination for his position at the India House: "Nothing superfluous and nothing wanting."

England in 1831 was a fertile ground for a satirist, especially one so prejudiced as Peacock. The industrial revolution was expanding rapidly, and Disraeli's two nations had begun to emerge—"all hunger at one end, and all surfeit at the other," as Dr. Folliott puts it. Parliament, largely controlled by a reactionary squirearchy which also enforced the laws it made, was still unreformed and the rotten borough system was at its worst. A mad king had been succeeded by a dandy and then by a nonentity. Religious dissent was becoming increasingly strident and the discoveries of geologists increasingly disturbing. Various types of scientism and intellectual absurdity were frequently excused in the name of progress. Faction was rampant, and in Peacock's view faction and reason were incompatible. The patriarchal god in every camp was materialism, and the middle class, which identified progress with success, were its priests (except for the Ap-Llymrys and Harry Ap-Heather, all of the characters in *Crotchet Castle* are members of the middle class, as was Peacock). It was against the icons of this class that Peacock directed his satire.

If one idea preoccupied most Englishmen of Peacock's time, it was the cult of progress. Any well-informed communicant could point to England's continuing accomplishments in science, in business, in literature, in government, in education. The new scientific and technological discoveries being made almost daily increased his profits at the factory and his comfort at home (little matter that the wages and working conditions of the common laborer were unconscionably bad and his living conditions worse). More novels were being written and more people were able to buy them than ever before; but much of what was written was intellectually and artistically worthless. Social progress was evident in the emancipation of the colonial slaves and the Catholics, yet serious flaws in the electoral system remained uncorrected. More of the population was literate than ever before; but its education was in facts and technology, not in the humanities, and the universities still catered largely to the Establishment. The true believer overlooked or explained away the shortcomings of progress: to join in the ranks of the "march of mind" became an end in itself, and quantity was often substituted for quality—"everything for everybody, science for all, schools for all, rhetoric for all, law for all, physic for all, words for all, and sense for none," as the Johnsonian Dr. Folliott says. Most of the subjects dealt with in *Crotchet Castle* relate directly or indirectly to the cult of progress, and to understand Peacock's satirical aims we must understand his concept of this phenomenon. To him it was a sort of intellectual cancer, a promising and potentially useful idea which had gone out of control and had become self-perpetuating, until what should have been its goal—the betterment of the whole man, not just his material condition—had been forgotten. Throughout *Crotchet Castle* we see that the popular outcry for progress is mere enthusiasm and its manifestation is irresponsible innovation, two phenomena which are as distasteful to Peacock as they were to Pope and Swift; they are false progress, for they obscure the light of reason and reduce life and man to a series of formulas as Mr. Mac Quedy does laughter.

But Peacock is not an encrusted Tory appalled by any idea that threatens the status quo. Some of his most vigorous satire is directed against serious abuses defended by the Tories: enclosure, the repressive game laws, rotten boroughs, and the economic imbalance between the haves and the have-nots. Similarly, the novel shows little tolerance of the Whig insistence on educating the mind instead of the man (Brougham, the "learned friend," was a Whig). And we must remember that Mac Quedy voices Benthamite views and that *Crotchet Castle* rejects such Benthamite enthusiasms as the Useful Knowledge Society, paper money, and industrialism. Thus the question of Peacock's adherence to one faction or another, in this or in his other novels, is irrelevant. In an 1861 letter in which he looked back over his career, Peacock said, "In the questions which have come within my scope, I have endeavoured to be impartial, and to say what could be said on both sides. If I have not done so, it is because I could find nothing to say in behalf of some specific proposition." When Peacock examines the popular concepts of social, political, and educational progress he does so as neither reactionary nor radical but as a man who wants to conserve what needs to be conserved and change what needs to be changed, as long as the demands of reason, common sense, and humanitarianism are met.

III

Nightmare Abbey, which appeared in 1818, is the third of Peacock's novels and has been the most popular. Whereas the satire in *Crotchet Castle* is primarily social and political, the satire in *Nightmare Abbey* is mostly literary. As Peacock said in a letter to Shelley, his purpose was "to bring to a sort of philosophical focus a few of the morbidities of modern literature, and to let in a little daylight on its atrabilarious complexion." One type of "morbidity" was the Gothic novel, which beginning with Horace Walpole's *The Castle of Otranto* (1764) had become a highly popular form. The other type also had its beginnings in the eighteenth century in, among others, the writings of Gray and the "Graveyard School" of poetry, had been augmented by translations of Schiller and Goethe, and had reached new heights in the amazing popularity of the misanthropic, brooding, melodramatic "Byronic hero" found in Byron's *Childe Harold's Pilgrimage, Manfred,* and such verse tales as *Lara* and *The Corsair.*

This morbid strain of romanticism (quite different, of course, from the strain developed by Wordsworth) had actually absorbed and replaced the Gothic, as explained in *Nightmare Abbey* by Mr. Flosky: "That part of the *reading public* which shuns the solid food of reason for the light diet of fiction," he says, "lived upon ghosts, goblins, and skeletons . . . till even the devil himself . . . became too base, common, and popular, for its surfeited appetite. The ghosts have therefore been laid, the devil has been cast into outer darkness, and now the delight of our spirits is to dwell on all the vices and blackest passions of our nature, tricked out in a masquerade dress of heroism and disappointed benevolence. . . ."

The novel ridicules the excesses of melancholic romanticism aginst a backdrop of the trappings and machinery of the Gothic novel: hidden doors, secret passages, mistaken identities, mysterious goings-on, an apparent ghost (which turns out to be a sleepwalking servant). Nightmare Abbey itself contains the requisite deserted wings and ruinous towers, and is located in a properly bleak and remote area. But many other characteristics of the Gothic novel are consciously omitted. There are no usurped heritages or strawberry birthmarks. The stilted dialogue of the true Gothic novel is replaced by the lively repartee of the Glowrys and their guests, as we would expect in a Peacock novel. And perhaps most important, the appallingly diabolical villain of the Gothic novel has been modulated into the ridiculous and ineffectual Scythrop Glowry.

In spite of its title and setting, then, *Nightmare Abbey* is not primarily a satire on Gothic literature, though it can be read with pleasure as such. What gives the novel its real substance is the way Peacock unites his setting with plot and character to ridicule what he called in a letter "the darkness and misanthropy of modern literature." The misanthropy abounds in the persons of the Glowrys and Messrs. Toobad, Listless, Cypress, and Flosky, the latter also providing much of the darkness in the form of incomprehensible metaphysical double talk, as the dismayed Marionetta finds out in her unsuccessful interview in Chapter VIII.

"A gloomy brow and a tragical voice," says one of the characters, "seem to have been of late the characteristics of fashionable manners: and a morbid, withering, deadly, antisocial sirocco, loaded with moral and political despair, breathes through all the groves and valleys of the modern Parnassus. . . ." To make life imitate art seems to be a guiding principle of Scythrop Glowry. He has, we are told, "a strong tendency to the love of mystery, for its own sake; that is to say, he would employ mystery to serve a purpose, but would first choose his purpose by its capability of mystery." He sleeps with an extravagantly Gothic novel under his pillow, spends much of his time in brooding isolation indulging melodramatic fantasies, and even believes that he and Marionetta should drink each other's blood "as a sacrament of love" in the manner of the lovers in a popular Gothic tale.

Typically Byronic too is his despair over the current dismal state of the world, an opinion he voices to the delight of the pessimistic Mr. Toobad in a lengthy catalogue of ills at the end of Chapter III. His frustrated romancing first of Marionetta and then of the mysterious Stella provides many opportunities for him to display the exaggerated melancholy and misanthropic posturing of the Byronic strain of romanticism. His vacillation between the two women and his inability to choose either one, ultimately resulting in his rejection by both of them, constitute one of Peacock's finest achievements in the novel, the contrast between the idealistic zeal of Scythrop's "great designs for the emancipation of mankind" and his inability to manage even his own life.

Ferdinando Flosky, "a very lachrymose and morbid gentleman," is one of the best of Peacock's many caricatures of Coleridge. In him Peacock means to join the excesses of Byronism with the obscurity of transcendental philosophy, the results being, in Flosky's words, "as fine a mental chaos as even the immortal Kant himself could ever have hoped to see." The alliance as it is developed in the novel is tenuous and actually misrepresents the preponderant tone and content of Coleridge's work. But in the obscurity and cant of transcendental metaphysics Peacock saw an intellectual kinship with the irrationality of the morbid strain of romanticism he was ridiculing in *Nightmare Abbey*. Peacock admirably weaves together his satire of both in the delightful scene between Flosky and Marionetta in Chapter VIII.

Peacock had said in a letter to Shelley, "I think it necessary to 'make a stand' against the 'encroachments' of black bile [peevish melancholy and misanthropy]. The fourth canto of *Childe Harold* is really too bad. I cannot consent to be *auditor tantum* of this systematical 'poisoning' of the 'mind' of the 'reading public.' " The result is Mr. Cypress, whose brief appearance in Chapter XI constitutes the most brilliant parody of Byron and the Byronic manner in all of English literature. Mr. Cypress is on the point of leaving England, because, he says, "I have quarrelled with my wife; and a man who has quarrelled with his wife is absolved from all duty to his country." (Peacock's readers would immediately recognize the allusion to Byron's scandalous separation from his wife and self-exile to Italy.) Most of the remainder of his dialogue consists of paraphrases of some of the more morbid stanzas from the fourth canto *Childe Harold's Pilgrimage,* all carefully footnoted by Peacock. At the end of the chapter he sings one of the few songs in the novel, "There is a fever of the spirit," which captures the very essence of the Byronic attitude. It should be noted, however, that Mr. Cypress—and indeed the picture of Byronic romanticism that pervades the novel—is based on the public's concept of Byron and "Byronism." It was widely assumed that the attitudes and life histories of Childe Harold, Manfred, Lara, and similar characters were one and the same with Byron's, an impression that Byron's own behavior did little to contradict. But modern scholarship has shown that in many ways the "real" Byron, if he is to be found anywhere in his writings, emerges in the letters and the satires. It is ironic that in satirizing the popular but erroneous conception, Peacock has helped to perpetuate it. In any event, Byron evidently did not resent the satire, for upon reading *Nightmare Abbey* he sent Peacock a rosebud, which Peacock is said to have treasured for the rest of his life.

Although as *Crotchet Castle* shows it is hazardous to search for spokesmen for Peacock among the characters in his novels, the most likely candidate in *Nightmare Abbey* is Mr. Hilary. He is the character who most frequently and articulately voices criticism of the tone of modern literature. In Chapter VII, for example, he protests against those "morbid spirits" who "see nothing but faults" in life and in man "because they are predetermined to shut their eyes to beauties. . . . Misanthropy is sometimes the product of disappointed benevolence," he continues, "but it is more frequently the offspring of overweening and mortified vanity, quarrelling with the world for not being better treated than it deserves." Mr. Hilary also follows Peacock's habitual practice of measuring modern literature by classical standards; not unexpectedly, Hilary finds modern literature wanting:

> The contrast it presents to the cheerful and solid wisdom
> of antiquity is too forcible not to strike any one who has
> the least knowledge of classical literature. To represent
> vice and misery as the necessary accompaniments of
> genius, is as mischievous as it is false, and the feeling
> is as unclassical as the language in which it is usually
> expressed. (Chapter XI.)

We have dwelt at length on the ridicule of melancholy romanticism—"black bile"—in *Nightmare Abbey*. But, as in all his novels, Peacock's satiric vision is wide-ranging. Many other topics come in for their share of comment, among them several of Peacock's favorites: university education, marrying for money, the Lake Poets and their politics, paper money, blue-nose Bible Societies, and the repressive policies of the Tory government. Moreover, it is well to remember that interspersed with the literary and topical satire, there are many passages of fine and often boisterous comedy. Among the first that come to mind are the descriptions of the love-smitten Scythrop "reading" Dante with the book upside down and of Diggory Deathshead, whose cheerful countenance was such a disappointment to Mr. Glowry and whose conquest of Mr. Glowry's maids "left him a flourishing colony of young Deathsheads to join chorus with the owls, that had before been the exclusive choristers of Nightmare Abbey." There are also Fatout's humorous confusion over the word "mermaid" and the slapstick chain reaction when the assembled company see a "ghost" in Chapter XII. One of the best instances of sustained comedy includes the whole of Chapter XIII, when Mr. Glowry discovers Stella and, to the mortification of Scythrop, Stella and Marionetta discover each other. This is one of several scenes in which, in the handling of dialogue, movement, and entrances, we see the results of Peacock's abiding interest in the drama; the whole sequence is as well realized and carefully paced as a scene from the pen of a skilled comic playwright.

A great deal has been written about the resemblance of Scythrop to Shelley. That Peacock had Shelley in mind when he drew the character there can be no doubt. Scythrop's passionate nature, his interest in the Gothic and in science, his early refusal by Emily Girouette, his pamphleteering, his "passion for reforming the world," and of course the love triangle in which he ultimately becomes involved—all of these details have their counterpart in Shelley's own life and were well known to Peacock. Other similarities have been elaborated in biographies of both men. But it is important to remember that Scythrop is a fictional character first and last; *Nightmare Abbey* is a novel, not a biography. Peacock seems to have taken great pains, in fact, to make Scythrop significantly different from the real Shelley in important respects. Scythrop lives at home; he is an only child; his college days were quite convivial, and he remains a thoroughgoing tippler. Moreover, there are several significant differences in the love triangles. Unlike Shelley's wife Harriet, Marionetta is little more than a coquette. Although Stella (Celinda Toobad) does provide Scythrop the kind of intellectual companionship that Shelly found in Mary Godwin, for whom he left his wife, Peacock gives her a physical appearance and mercurial temperament very different from Mary's. Even more important is the fact that unlike Shelley, Scythrop is quite incapable of making a choice between the two. Peacock did indeed play an important role in the resolution of this painful event in Shelley's life, and the outcome had its effect on Peacock's relationship with all three of the principals. But it should be clear that this aspect of the novel is no more or less biographical than is any novel in which an author uses his acquaintances and his own observations and experiences as source material for his fiction. Shelley, who could not have helped recognizing Scythrop and his quandary, saw no reason to take offense. His remarks in a letter to Peacock convey his pleasure over the work and provide a concise summation of its accomplishment: "I am delighted with *Nightmare Abbey*. I think Scythrop a character admirably conceived and executed; and I know not how to praise sufficiently the lightness, chastity, and strength of the language of the whole. It perhaps exceeds all your works in this. The catastrophe is excellent. I suppose the moral is contained in what Falstaff says—'For God's sake, talk like a man of this world' . . . ."

IV

Peacock's papers provide no record of the precise dates of composition of *The Misfortunes of Elphin*. Published in 1829, it shows closer kinship in form to *Maid Marian* (1822) than to the other novels. Like *Maid Marian* it is based on legendary materials and thus is set in the past. More important, Peacock completely eschews his typical procedure of gathering together a group of humorous eccentrics in a country estate and letting them talk at each other over food and drink. Instead the novel uses conventional narrative method with its descriptive passages and reported speeches.

One of Peacock's main interests in *The Misfortunes of El-phin* is in recounting Welsh history and legends, and he is said to have prided himself on the fact that *The Misfortunes of El-phin* was studied by historians and scholars. But part of his interest in Wales was doubtless as much personal as scholarly. He had first visited Wales in 1809, where he met the girl who eventually became his wife.

Widespread interest in Welsh history and legends had grown up in the eighteenth century as a part of the general interest in England's folkways stimulated by such works as Bishop Percy's *Reliques of Ancient English Poetry* (1765). A number of sources were available to Peacock, but he depended upon them only for the barest outlines of his novel and characters. The discovery of Taliesin was recounted in Edward Davies' *Mythology and Rites of the Druids* (1809), but Peacock omitted most of the supernatural element from this and the other legends he drew upon. The triads which he uses throughout the novel, and the figure of Prince Seithenyn, were found in the pages of a periodical, *The Cambro-Briton*. Seithenyn's responsibility for a disastrous flood is taken from the legendary materials, but the embankment itself, the details of his character, and the later incidents in which he is involved are Peacock's invention. The works of Ross of Warwick and Giraldus Cambrensis, the only one of his sources he mentions in the novel, provided the picture of Arthur's court. Most of the songs are based on those in *The Myvyrian Archailogy of Wales* (1801); Peacock evidently translated the Welsh originals, with the help of his wife, retaining the basic point and subject while producing what amounts to a new poem in English. Of the fourteen songs in the novel, however, it is the delightfully skeptical and ironic "War-Song of Dinas Vawr," entirely Peacock's own creation, which has always been considered the best.

In the novel Peacock weaves together the legendary materials in a series of relationships of his own devising: the romance of Taliesin and Melanghel, the connection of Taliesin and Seithenyn, and Taliesin's part in the recovery of Guinevere are all supplied by Peacock. Indeed, the novel might well have been titled *The Fortunes of Taliesin,* for if any character fills the

function of protagonist it is he, Elphin being of decidedly secondary interest and Seithenyn, by far the most memorable
character, appearing in only six of the novel's sixteen chapters.

The latter is surely one of the more memorable characters
of all literature, deserving an honorable place at the same table
with Gargantua and Falstaff, other notable drunkards from the
pens of two of Peacock's favorite authors. From his bleary-
eyed greeting of Elphin and Teithrin in the second chapter
("you are welcome all four") to his appointment as Arthur's
second butler (in charge of the liquor supply) in Chapter XVI,
he is quite irresistible. He steals every scene in which he
appears, and all of the other characters—even Taliesin, his admirable character and his function as the "hero" notwithstanding—are uninterestingly conventional in comparison. Probably
only Falstaff himself can exceed him in displays of vinous logic;
thus to Elphin:

> we will not quarrel for three reasons: first, because you
> are the son of the king, and may do and say what you
> please, without anyone having a right to be displeased:
> second, because I never quarrel with a guest, even if he
> grows riotous in his cups: third, because there is noth-
> ing to quarrel about; and perhaps that is the best reason
> of the three; or rather the first is the best, because you
> are the son of the king; and the third is the second, that
> is, the second best, because there is nothing to quarrel
> about; and the second is nothing to the purpose, because,
> though guests will grow riotous in their cups, in spite
> of my good orderly example, God forbid I should say,
> that is the case with you. (Chapter II.)

But Seithenyn provides more than humor in the novel. His
speech justifying the neglect of his duty as Lord High Commissioner of the Royal Embankment is a parody of the current
Tory opposition to Constitutional reform and thus contributes
to the satiric comment on the nineteenth century that runs
through the novel:

> "Decay," said Seithenyn, "is one thing, and danger is
> another. Every thing that is old must decay. That the

embankment is old, I am free to confess; that it is somewhat rotten in parts, I will not altogether deny; that it is
any the worse for that, I do most sturdily gainsay. . . .

It is well: it works well: let well alone. Cupbearer, fill.
It was half rotten when I was born, and that is a con-
clusive reason why it should be three parts rotten when
I die." (Chapter II.)

In *The Misfortunes of Elphin,* as in his other novels, Peacock thus mixes romantic stories with ironic commentary on
human nature in general and, often, on nineteenth-century life
in particular. Many of Peacock's favorite targets from his other
novels and occasional writings are here as well: paper money,
universal education, mysticism, enclosure of common lands by
the landed gentry, political self-serving and irresponsibility,
technology, blue-nose societies. A basic procedure is to describe the sixth century in such a way as to denigrate, with
pointed irony, the nineteenth; the people of the sixth century,
we are reminded,

had no steam-engines, with fires as eternal as those of
the nether world, wherein the squalid many, from infancy to age, might be turned into component portions
of machinery for the benefit of the purple-faced few.
They could neither poison the air with gas, nor the
waters with its dregs: in short, they made their money
of metal, and breathed pure air, and drank pure water,
like unscientific barbarians. (Chapter VI.)

Peacock, however, is no primitivist. The nineteenth century
may be guilty of vice and folly, but, he seems to say, this does
not mean that the people of Elphin's time therefore are all virtuous and reasonable. For example, Rhûn's "bard of all work,"
a self-server "who was always willing to go to any court with
any character, or none," is no different from the standard de-
piction of Wordsworth and Southey in *Crotchet Castle* and his
other novels. Peacock is careful to show in the persons of
Maelgon Gwyneth and Melvas that the philosophy of "the
right of might" had strong adherents in the sixth century. Nor

must we forget that the ironic "War-Song of Dinas Vawr" is "the quintessence of all the war songs that ever were written, and the sum and substance of all the appetencies, tendencies, and consequences of military glory."

Some readers may find the mixture of the romantic and ironic in the novel disconcerting. It may appear that Peacock could not decide whether to write a fanciful and nostalgic "historical" romance about a favorite country in the manner popularized by Scott, or whether to write a satire on human nature; for the result is neither wholly one or the other. (In both *Nightmare Abbey* and *Crotchet Castle* the satiric element clearly predominates, the marriages at the end of the latter notwithstanding.) This split purpose in *The Misfortunes of Elphin* may account, at least in part, for its general lack of popularity (copies of the first—and only—edition remained unsold forty years after publication). That Peacock was not completely comfortable in writing *The Misfortunes of Elphin* is hinted by the fact that for no apparent reason he shifts from reported speech to his preferred method, dramatic dialogue, in Chapter XIV, the last chapter to contain extensive dialogue.

Peacock returned to the contemporary setting and the "conversation" method in his last two novels. But in spite of its departures from Peacock's typical method, *The Misfortunes of Elphin* remains a delight in itself. It is also indelibly Peacockian in its interest in eating and drinking, the echoes of older literatures and of Shakespeare, the satiric comment on nineteenth-century manners and institutions, the frequent songs, the learned vocabulary, the idealization of simple rural life, the interest in picturesque scenery, and the pervading urbanity and irony of its tone. It is true that many of these characteristics are less noticeable than is usual, due to the emphasis upon medieval legends. But like his other novels, *The Misfortunes of Elphin* will continue to be read and enjoyed as long as there are readers, who, like Peacock, enjoy indulging their sense of the ridiculous in human nature and human institutions.

Oshkosh, Wisconsin   Charles B. Dodson
June 1971

Textual and Bibliographic Note

The present text of all three novels is that of the Halliford Edition of Peacock's *Works* (London and New York, 1924–1934), which in turn is based on the latest editions that Peacock is known to have seen through the press. I have silently corrected a few errors that managed to slip by the Halliford editors.

Notes followed by [P] are by Peacock; the others are the present editor's. Each novel begins with a facsimile reproduction of the title page of the first edition.

The standard edition of Peacock's complete works is the Halliford, edited in ten volumes by H. F. B. Brett-Smith and C. E. Jones (see above). It was reprinted in 1967. David Garnett's edition of the novels (London, 1948, reprinted 1963) contains helpful notes. The standard biography is still Carl Van Doren's *Thomas Love Peacock* (1911, reprinted 1966), although the lengthy "Biographical Introduction" in Volume I of the Halliford edition contains additional material. The early critical studies by A. Martin Freeman (*Thomas Love Peacock, A Critical Study,* New York, 1911), J. B. Priestly (*Thomas Love Peacock,* New York, 1927), and Jean-Jacques Mayoux (*Un Epicurien Anglais,* Paris, 1933) are still useful, as is Jack B. Ludwig's "The Peacock Tradition in English Prose Fiction" (unpublished dissertation, UCLA, 1953); but all have been superseded by Carl Dawson's excellent *His Fine Wit: A Study of Thomas Love Peacock* (Berkeley and Los Angeles, 1970). Lionel Madden's brief *Thomas Love Peacock* (London, 1967) can be highly recommended as a concise and judicious introduction to Peacock's life and works.

NIGHTMARE ABBEY:

BY

THE AUTHOR OF HEADLONG HALL.

There's a dark lantern of the spirit,
Which none see by but those who bear it,
That makes them in the dark see visions
And hag themselves with apparitions,
Find racks for their own minds, and vaunt
  Of their own misery and want. Butler.[1]

LONDON:

PRINTED FOR T. HOOKHAM, JUN. OLD BOND-STREET;
AND BALDWIN, CRADOCK, AND JOY,
PATERNOSTER-ROW.

1818.

MATTHEW. Oh! it's your only fine humour, sir. Your true melancholy breeds your perfect fine wit, sir. I am melancholy myself, divers times, sir; and then do I no more but take pen and paper presently, and overflow you half a score or a dozen of sonnets at a sitting.

STEPHEN. Truly, sir, and I love such things out of measure.

MATTHEW. Why, I pray you, sir, make use of my study: it's at your service.

STEPHEN. I thank you, sir, I shall be bold, I warrant you. Have you a stool there, to be melancholy upon?

BEN JONSON:
Every Man in his Humour.
A. 3. S. 1.

---

1 Title page: a composite; Peacock also follows the nineteenth-century practice of quoting only as accurately as is convenient. The passages are from *Hudibras*, Part I, Canto 1, ll. 505–506; Part III, Canto 3, ll. 19–20; *Satire upon the weakness and misery of man*, ll. 71–72, 172–174.

NIGHTMARE ABBEY

Chapter I

Ay esleu gazouiller et siffler oye, comme dit le commun proverbe, entre les cygnes, plutoust que d'estre entre tant de gentils poëtes et faconds orateurs mut du tout estimé.—RABELAIS, *Prol. L. 5.*[1]

NIGHTMARE ABBEY, a venerable family-mansion, in a highly picturesque state of semi-dilapidation, pleasantly situated on a strip of dry land between the sea and the fens, at the verge of the county of Lincoln,[2] had the honour to be the seat of Christopher Glowry, Esquire. This gentleman was naturally of an atrabilarious[3] temperament, and much troubled with those phantoms of indigestion which are commonly called *blue devils*.[4] He had been deceived in an early friendship: he had been crossed in love; and had offered his hand, from pique, to a lady, who accepted it from interest, and who, in so doing, violently tore asunder the bonds of a tried and youthful attachment. Her vanity was gratified by being the mistress of a very extensive, if not very lively, establishment; but all the springs of her sympathies were frozen. Riches she possessed, but that which en-

---

[1] "I have made bold to choose to chirp and warble my plain ditty, or, as they say, to whistle like a goose among the swans, rather than be thought deaf among so many pretty poets and eloquent orators" (Urquhart and Motteux translation).

[2] Located in east central England and bounded on the east by the North Sea, Lincoln once contained extensive fens, or swamps.

[3] Melancholy and ill-tempered.

[4] Despondency, depression (from the apparitions supposedly seen in *delerium tremens*).

riches them, the participation of affection, was wanting. All that they could purchase for her became indifferent to her, because that which they could not purchase, and which was more valuable than themselves, she had, for their sake, thrown away. She discovered, when it was too late, that she had mistaken the means for the end—that riches, rightly used, are instruments of happiness, but are not in themselves happiness. In this wilful blight of her affections, she found them valueless as means: they had been the end to which she had immolated all her affections, and were now the only end that remained to her. She did not confess this to herself as a principle of action, but it operated through the medium of unconscious self-deception, and terminated in inveterate avarice. She laid on external things the blame of her mind's internal disorder, and thus became by degrees an accomplished scold. She often went her daily rounds through a series of deserted apartments, every creature in the house vanishing at the creak of her shoe, much more at the sound of her voice, to which the nature of things affords no simile; for, as far as the voice of woman, when attuned by gentleness and love, transcends all other sounds in harmony, so far does it surpass all others in discord, when stretched into unnatural shrillness by anger and impatience.

Mr. Glowry used to say that his house was no better than a spacious kennel, for every one in it led the life of a dog. Disappointed both in love and in friendship, and looking upon human learning as vanity, he had come to a conclusion that there was but one good thing in the world, *videlicet,* a good dinner; and this his parsimonious lady seldom suffered him to enjoy: but, one morning, like Sir Leoline in Christabel, "he woke and found his lady dead,"[5] and remained a very consolate widower, with one small child.

This only son and heir Mr. Glowry had christened Scythrop,[6] from the name of a maternal ancestor, who had hanged himself

---

[5] Part II, line 4. Coleridge wrote *rose,* not *woke*.

[6] From the Greek σκυθρωπός, "of a sullen countenance." Scythrop is modeled in some respects on Shelley as a young man. The character so amused Shelley that he called the study at the villa where he wrote *The Cenci,* "Scythrop's Tower."

one rainy day in a fit of *tædium vitæ*, and had been eulogised by a coroner's jury in the comprehensive phrase of *felo de se;*[7] on which account, Mr. Glowry held his memory in high honour, and made a punchbowl of his skull.[8]

When Scythrop grew up, he was sent, as usual, to a public school, where a little learning was painfully beaten into him, and from thence to the university, where it was carefully taken out of him; and he was sent home like a well-threshed ear of corn, with nothing in his head: having finished his education to the high satisfaction of the master and fellows of his college, who had, in testimony of their approbation, presented him with a silver fish-slice, on which his name figured at the head of a laudatory inscription in some semi-barbarous dialect of Anglo-Saxonised Latin.

His fellow-students, however, who drove tandem and random[9] in great perfection, and were connoisseurs in good inns, had taught him to drink deep ere he departed.[10] He had passed much of his time with these choice spirits, and had seen the rays of the midnight lamp tremble on many a lengthening file of empty bottles. He passed his vacations sometimes at Nightmare Abbey, sometimes in London, at the house of his uncle, Mr. Hilary, a very cheerful and elastic gentleman, who had married the sister of the melancholy Mr. Glowry. The company that frequented his house was the gayest of the gay. Scythrop danced with the ladies and drank with the gentlemen, and was pronounced by both a very accomplished charming fellow, and an honour to the university.

At the house of Mr. Hilary, Scythrop first saw the beautiful Miss Emily Girouette.[11] He fell in love; which is nothing new.

---

[7] Suicide.

[8] Drinking from a skull has come to be associated with the Gothic strain of romanticism. Byron once offered a skull full of Burgundy to his guests, and at Eton Shelley drank from a skull in hopes of calling up a ghost. When Edward Trelawny cremated Shelley, he refused Bryon's request that he preserve the skull, fearing that Byron would make a drinking cup out of it.

[9] From "random tandem," three horses driven tandem fashion.

[10] *Hamlet*, I.ii.

[11] Corresponds to Shelley's first "Harriet," his cousin, Harriet Grove. Her treatment of Shelley, and his reaction, roughly parallel that

He was favourably received; which is nothing strange. Mr. Glowry and Mr. Girouette had a meeting on the occasion, and quarrelled about the terms of the bargain; which is neither new nor strange. The lovers were torn asunder, weeping and vowing everlasting constancy; and, in three weeks after this tragical event, the lady was led a smiling bride to the altar, by the Honourable Mr. Lackwit; which is neither strange nor new.

Scythrop received this intelligence at Nightmare Abbey, and was half distracted on the occasion. It was his first disappointment, and preyed deeply on his sensitive spirit. His father, to comfort him, read him a Commentary on Ecclesiastes, which he had himself composed, and which demonstrated incontrovertibly that all is vanity. He insisted particularly on the text, "One man among a thousand have I found, but a woman amongst all those have I not found."[12]

"How could he expect it," said Scythrop, "when the whole thousand were locked up in his seraglio?[13] His experience is no precedent for a free state of society like that in which we live."

"Locked up or at large," said Mr. Glowry, "the result is the same: their minds are always locked up, and vanity and interest keep the key. I speak feelingly, Scythrop."

"I am sorry for it, sir," said Scythrop. "But how is it that their minds are locked up? The fault is in their artificial education, which studiously models them into mere musical dolls, to be set out for sale in the great toy-shop of society."

"To be sure," said Mr. Glowry, "their education is not so well finished as yours has been; and your idea of a musical doll is good. I bought one myself, but it was confoundedly out of tune; but, whatever be the cause, Scythrop, the effect is certainly this, that one is pretty nearly as good as another, as far as any judgment can be formed of them before marriage. It is only after marriage that they show their true qualities, as I know by bitter experience. Marriage is, therefore, a lottery, and the less choice and selection a man bestows on his ticket the

ascribed to Emily and Scythrop, though Harriet did not marry until a year after she broke off her relationship with Shelley.

12 Ecclesiastes 7:28.
13 Harem.

better; for, if he has incurred considerable pains and expense to obtain a lucky number, and his lucky number proves a blank, he experiences not a simple, but a complicated disappointment; the loss of labour and money being superadded to the disappointment of drawing a blank, which, constituting simply and entirely the grievance of him who has chosen his ticket at random, is, from its simplicity, the more endurable." This very excellent reasoning was thrown away upon Scythrop, who retired to his tower as dismal and disconsolate as before.

The tower which Scythrop inhabited stood at the south-eastern angle of the Abbey; and, on the southern side, the foot of the tower opened on a terrace, which was called the garden, though nothing grew on it but ivy, and a few amphibious weeds. The south-western tower, which was ruinous and full of owls, might, with equal propriety, have been called the aviary. This terrace or garden, or terrace-garden, or garden-terrace (the reader may name it *ad libitum*), took in an oblique view of the open sea, and fronted a long tract of level sea-coast, and a fine monotony of fens and windmills.

The reader will judge, from what we have said, that this building was a sort of castellated abbey; and it will, probably, occur to him to inquire if it had been one of the strong-holds of the ancient church militant. Whether this was the case, or how far it had been indebted to the taste of Mr. Glowry's ancestors for any transmutations from its original state, are, unfortunately, circumstances not within the pale of our knowledge.

The north-western tower contained the apartments of Mr. Glowry. The moat at its base, and the fens beyond, comprised the whole of his prospect. This moat surrounded the Abbey, and was in immediate contact with the walls on every side but the south.

The north-eastern tower was appropriated to the domestics, whom Mr. Glowry always chose by one of two criterions,—a long face, or a dismal name. His butler was Raven; his steward was Crow; his valet was Skellet. Mr. Glowry maintained that the valet was of French extraction, and that his name was Squelette. His grooms were Mattocks and Graves. On one occasion, being in want of a footman, he received a letter from a person signing himself Diggory Deathshead, and lost no time in securing this acquisition; but on Diggory's arrival, Mr. Glowry was horror-struck by the sight of a round ruddy face, and a pair of laughing eyes. Deathshead was always grinning,— not a ghastly smile, but the grin of a comic mask; and disturbed the echoes of the hall with so much unhallowed laughter, that Mr. Glowry gave him his discharge. Diggory, however, had staid long enough to make conquests of all the old gentleman's maids, and left him a flourishing colony of young Deathsheads to join chorus with the owls, that had before been the exclusive choristers of Nightmare Abbey.

The main body of the building was divided into rooms of state, spacious apartments for feasting, and numerous bedrooms for visitors, who, however, were few and far between.

Family interests compelled Mr. Glowry to receive occasional visits from Mr. and Mrs. Hilary, who paid them from the same motive; and, as the lively gentleman on these occasions found few conductors for his exuberant gaiety, he became like a double-charged electric jar,[14] which often exploded in some burst of outrageous merriment to the signal discomposure of Mr. Glowry's nerves.

Another occasional visitor, much more to Mr. Glowry's taste, was Mr. Flosky,[15] a very lachrymose and morbid gentleman, of some note in the literary world, but in his own estimation of much more merit than name. The part of his character which recommended him to Mr. Glowry, was his very fine sense of the grim and the tearful. No one could relate a dismal story with so many minutiæ of supererogatory wretchedness. No one could call up a *raw-head and bloody bones*[16] with so many adjuncts and circumstances of ghastliness. Mystery was his mental element. He lived in the midst of that visionary world in which nothing is but what is not.[17] He dreamed with his eyes open,

---

[14] A Leyden jar (named for the Dutch city where it was invented), i.e., a precursor of the battery.

[15] A corruption of Filosky, quasi Φιλοσκιος, a lover, or sectator, of shadows. [P] [Coleridge]

[16] *Hudibras,* Part III, Canto 2, l. 682.

[17] *Macbeth,* I.iii.

and saw ghosts dancing round him at noontide. He had been in his youth an enthusiast for liberty, and had hailed the dawn of the French Revolution as the promise of a day that was to banish war and slavery, and every form of vice and misery, from the face of the earth. Because all this was not done, he deduced that nothing was done; and from this deduction, according to his system of logic, he drew a conclusion that worse than nothing was done; that the overthrow of the feudal fortresses of tyranny and superstition was the greatest calamity that had ever befallen mankind; and that their only hope now was to rake the rubbish together, and rebuild it without any of those loopholes by which the light had originally crept in. To qualify himself for a coadjutor in this laudable task, he plunged into the central opacity of Kantian metaphysics, and lay *perdu*[18] several years in transcendental darkness, till the common daylight of common sense became intolerable to his eyes. He called the sun an *ignis fatuus;*[19] and exhorted all who would listen to his friendly voice, which were about as many as called "God save King Richard,"[20] to shelter themselves from its delusive radiance in the obscure haunt of Old Philosophy. This word Old had great charms for him. The good old times were always on his lips; meaning the days when polemic theology was in its prime, and rival prelates beat the drum ecclesiastic[21] with Herculean vigour, till the one wound up his series of syllogisms with the very orthodox conclusion of roasting the other.

But the dearest friend of Mr. Glowry, and his most welcome guest, was Mr. Toobad, the Manichæan Millenarian.[22] The twelfth verse of the twelfth chapter of Revelations was always in his mouth: "Woe to the inhabiters of the earth and of the

[18] Lost.

[19] Will-o'-the-wisp.

[20] I.e., about ten people; see *Richard III*, III.vii.

[21] *Hudibras,* Part I, Canto 1, ll. 11–12.

[22] John Frank Newton, crackpot astrologer, vegetarian, eccentric practitioner of the back-to-nature philosophy, and friend of Shelley who believed that man had degenerated from a past golden age. Toobad's "Manichæanism" consists in his belief in the opposing dualism of Good and Evil, his "Millenarianism" in his belief that Evil will eventually be "cast down."

sea! for the devil is come among you, having great wrath, because he knoweth that he hath but a short time." He maintained that the supreme dominion of the world was, for wise purposes, given over for a while to the Evil Principle; and that this precise period of time, commonly called the enlightened age, was the point of his plenitude of power. He used to add that by and by he would be cast down, and a high and happy order of things succeed; but he never omitted the saving clause, "Not in our time:" which last words were always echoed in doleful response by the sympathetic Mr. Glowry.

Another and very frequent visitor, was the Reverend Mr. Larynx, the vicar of Claydyke, a village about ten miles distant; —a good-natured accommodating divine, who was always most obligingly ready to take a dinner and a bed at the house of any country gentleman in distress for a companion. Nothing came amiss to him,—a game at billiards, at chess, at draughts, at backgammon, at piquet, or at all-fours[23] in a *tête-a-tête,*—or any game on the cards, round, square, or triangular, in a party of any number exceeding two. He would even dance among friends, rather than that a lady, even if she were on the wrong side of thirty, should sit still for want of a partner. For a ride, a walk, or a sail, in the morning,—a song after dinner, a ghost story after supper,—a bottle of port with the squire, or a cup of green tea with his lady,—for all or any of these, or for any thing else that was agreeable to any one else, consistently with the dye of his coat,[24] the Reverend Mr. Larynx was at all times equally ready. When at Nightmare Abbey, he would condole with Mr. Glowry,—drink Madeira with Scythrop,—crack jokes with Mr. Hilary,—hand Mrs. Hilary to the piano, take charge of her fan and gloves, and turn over her music with surprising dexterity,—quote Revelations with Mr. Toobad,—and lament the good old times of feudal darkness with the transcendental Mr. Flosky.

[23] *Draughts:* checkers; *piquet:* a card game similar to pinochle; *all-fours:* a card game for two players in which four of the cards are especially important.
[24] I.e., any activity not unbecoming a clergyman.

Chapter II

SHORTLY AFTER the disastrous termination of Scythrop's passion for Miss Emily Girouette, Mr. Glowry found himself, much against his will, involved in a lawsuit, which compelled him to dance attendance on the High Court of Chancery.[1] Scythrop was left alone at Nightmare Abbey. He was a burnt child, and dreaded the fire of female eyes. He wandered about the ample pile, or along the garden-terrace, with "his cogitative faculties immersed in cogibundity of cogitation."[2] The terrace terminated at the south-western tower, which, as we have said, was ruinous and full of owls. Here would Scythrop take his evening seat, on a fallen fragment of mossy stone, with his back resting against the ruined wall,—a thick canopy of ivy, with an owl in it, over his head,—and the Sorrows of Werter in his hand.[3] He had some taste for romance reading before he went to the university, where, we must confess, in justice to his college, he was cured of the love of reading in all its shapes; and the cure would have been radical, if disappointment in love, and total solitude, had not conspired to bring on a relapse. He began to devour romances and German tragedies, and, by the recommendation of Mr. Flosky, to pore over ponderous tomes of transcendental philosophy, which reconciled him to the labour of studying them by their mystical jargon and necromantic imagery. In the congenial solitude of Nightmare Abbey, the distempered ideas of metaphysical romance and romantic metaphysics had ample time and space to germinate into a

[1] London court for the trying of civil cases, notorious for its long delays.

[2] Henry Carey, *Chrononhotonthologos, The Most Tragical Tragedy That Ever Was Tragediz'd by Any Company of Tragedians* (1734), I.i.

[3] The stone, the ruin, and the owl are conventional trappings of the melancholy "graveyard" strain of Romanticism which Peacock is satirizing in the novel. Goethe's *Sorrows of Young Werter* (1774, 1787) is a partially autobiographical novel of unrequited love and exaggerated emotion culminating in the hero's suicide.

fertile crop of chimeras, which rapidly shot up into vigorous and abundant vegetation.

He now became troubled with the *passion for reforming the world*.[4] He built many castles in the air, and peopled them with secret tribunals, and bands of illuminati, who were always the imaginary instruments of his projected regeneration of the human species. As he intended to institute a perfect republic, he invested himself with absolute sovereignty over these mystical dispensers of liberty. He slept with Horrid Mysteries[5] under his pillow, and dreamed of venerable eleutherarchs[6] and ghastly confederates holding midnight conventions in subterranean caves. He passed whole mornings in his study, immersed in gloomy reverie, stalking about the room in his nightcap, which he pulled over his eyes like a cowl, and folding his striped calico dressing-gown about him like the mantle of a conspirator.

"Action," thus he soliloquised, "is the result of opinion, and to new-model opinion would be to new-model society. Knowledge is power; it is in the hands of a few, who employ it to mislead the many, for their own selfish purposes of aggrandisement and appropriation. What if it were in the hands of a few who should employ it to lead the many? What if it were universal, and the multitude were enlightened? No. The many must be always in leading-strings; but let them have wise and honest conductors. A few to think, and many to act; that is the only basis of perfect society. So thought the ancient philosophers: they had their esoterical and exoterical[7] doctrines. So thinks the sublime Kant, who delivers his oracles in language which none but the initiated can comprehend. Such were the views of those

---

[4] See Forsyth's *Principles of Moral Science*. [P] [Shelley's dedication to political and moral reform was lifelong. He applies this phrase to himself in the Preface to *Prometheus Unbound* (1818–1819).]

[5] Written (in German) by the Marquis of Grosse, translated by P. Will, 1796.

[6] Members of an imaginary secret society; see *The Memoirs of Prince Alexy Haimatoff* (1813), by Thomas Jefferson Hogg (a close friend of Shelley).

[7] According to the Greek satirist Lucian (ca. 115–200 A.D.), Aristotle classified his own works thus, i.e., those writings (esoteric) intelligible only to a select group as opposed to those (exoteric) intelligible to the public.

secret associations of illuminati, which were the terror of superstition and tyranny, and which, carefully selecting wisdom and
genius from the great wilderness of society, as the bee selects
honey from the flowers of the thorn and the nettle, bound all
human excellence in a chain, which, if it had not been prematurely broken, would have commanded opinion, and regener-
ated the world."

Scythrop proceeded to meditate on the practicability of re-
viving a confederation of regenerators. To get a clear view of
his own ideas, and to feel the pulse of the wisdom and genius
of the age, he wrote and published a treatise, in which his meanings were carefully wrapt up in the monk's hood of transcendental technology, but filled with hints of matter deep and
dangerous, which he thought would set the whole nation in a
ferment;[8] and he awaited the result in awful expectation, as a
miner who has fired a train[9] awaits the explosion of a rock.
However, he listened and heard nothing; for the explosion, if
any ensued, was not sufficiently loud to shake a single leaf of
the ivy on the towers of Nightmare Abbey; and some months
afterwards he received a letter from his bookseller, informing
him that only seven copies had been sold, and concluding with
a polite request for the balance.[10]

Scythrop did not despair. "Seven copies," he thought, "have
been sold. Seven is a mystical number, and the omen is good.
Let me find the seven purchasers of my seven copies, and they
shall be the seven golden candle-sticks with which I will illumi-
nate the world."

Scythrop had a certain portion of mechanical genius, which
his romantic projects tended to develope. He constructed models
of cells and recesses, sliding panels and secret passages, that
would have baffled the skill of the Parisian police. He took the

---

[8] In 1812 Shelley had written his *Address to the Irish People* and
*Proposals for an Association of those Philanthropists Who, Convinced
of the Inadequacy of the Moral and Political State of Ireland to Produce
Benefits Which Are Nevertheless Obtainable, Are Willing to Unite to
Accomplish Its Regeneration.* Shelley expected a strong reaction, but the
pamphlets were ignored by both the government and the Irish patriots.

[9] Ignited a fuse leading to a charge of explosives.

[10] I.e., the balance of the cost of publication.

opportunity of his father's absence to smuggle a dumb carpenter into the Abbey, and between them they gave reality to one of these models in Scythrop's tower. Scythrop foresaw that a great leader of human regeneration would be involved in fearful dilemmas, and determined, for the benefit of mankind in general, to adopt all possible precautions for the preservation of himself.

The servants, even the women, had been tutored into silence. Profound stillness reigned throughout and around the Abbey, except when the occasional shutting of a door would peal in long reverberations through the galleries, or the heavy tread of the pensive butler would wake the hollow echoes of the hall. Scythrop stalked about like the grand inquisitor, and the servants flitted past him like familiars. In his evening meditations on the terrace, under the ivy of the ruined tower, the only sounds that came to his ear were the rustling of the wind in the ivy, the plaintive voices of the feathered choristers, the owls, the occasional striking of the Abbey clock, and the monotonous dash of the sea on its low and level shore. In the mean time, he drank Madeira, and laid deep schemes for a thorough repair of the crazy fabric of human nature.

Chapter III

MR. GLOWRY returned from London with the loss of his lawsuit. Justice was with him, but the law was against him. He found Scythrop in a mood most sympathetically tragic; and they vied with each other in enlivening their cups by lamenting the depravity of this degenerate age, and occasionally interspersing divers grim jokes about graves, worms, and epitaphs.[1] Mr. Glowry's friends, whom we have mentioned in the first

---

[1] *Richard II*, III.ii.

chapter, availed themselves of his return to pay him a simultaneous visit. At the same time arrived Scythrop's friend and fellow-collegian, the Honourable Mr. Listless.[2] Mr. Glowry had discovered this fashionable young gentleman in London, "stretched on the rack of a too easy chair,"[3] and devoured with a gloomy and misanthropical *nil curo*,[4] and had pressed him so earnestly to take the benefit of the pure country air, at Nightmare Abbey, that Mr. Listless, finding it would give him more trouble to refuse than to comply, summoned his French valet, Fatout, and told him he was going to Lincolnshire. On this simple hint, Fatout went to work, and the imperials[5] were packed, and the post-chariot was at the door, without the Honourable Mr. Listless having said or thought another syllable on the subject.

Mr. and Mrs. Hilary brought with them an orphan niece, a daughter of Mr. Glowry's youngest sister, who had made a runaway love-match with an Irish officer. The lady's fortune disappeared in the first year: love, by a natural consequence, disappeared in the second: the Irishman himself, by a still more natural consequence, disappeared in the third. Mr. Glowry had allowed his sister an annuity, and she had lived in retirement with her only daughter, whom, at her death, which had recently happened, she commended to the care of Mrs. Hilary.

Miss Marionetta Celestina O'Carroll[6] was a very blooming and accomplished young lady. Being a compound of the *Allegro Vivace* of the O'Carrolls, and of the *Andante Doloroso* of the Glowries, she exhibited in her own character all the diversities of an April sky. Her hair was light-brown; her eyes hazel, and sparkling with a mild but fluctuating light; her features regular; her lips full, and of equal size; and her person surpassingly

---

[2] Probably modeled on Sir Lumley Skeffington (1771–1850), playwright and fop, who had a reputation for indolence. He was a good enough friend of Shelley that in 1816 Shelley consulted him on the propriety of marrying Mary immediately after Harriet's suicide.

[3] Pope, *Dunciad, I* V.342.

[4] An "I don't care" attitude; see Horace, *Odes,* Book I, No. 28.

[5] A type of trunk designed to be carried on the top ("imperial") of the carriage.

[6] Shelley's first wife, Harriet Westbrook.

graceful. She was a proficient in music. Her conversation was
sprightly, but always on subjects light in their nature and
limited in their interest: for moral sympathies, in any general
sense, had no place in her mind. She had some coquetry, and
more caprice, liking and disliking almost in the same moment;
pursuing an object with earnestness while it seemed unattainable, and rejecting it when in her power as not worth the trouble of possession.

Whether she was touched with a *penchant* for her cousin
Scythrop, or was merely curious to see what effect the tender
passion would have on so *outré*[7] a person, she had not been
three days in the Abbey before she threw out all the lures of her
beauty and accomplishments to make a prize of his heart. Scythrop proved an easy conquest. The image of Miss Emily
Girouette was already sufficiently dimmed by the power of
philosophy and the exercise of reason: for to these influences,
or to any influence but the true one, are usually ascribed the
mental cures performed by the great physician Time. Scythrop's romantic dreams had indeed given him many *pure
anticipated cognitions*[8] of combinations of beauty and intelligence, which, he had some misgivings, were not exactly realised
in his cousin Marionetta; but, in spite of these misgivings, he
soon became distractedly in love; which, when the young lady
clearly perceived, she altered her tactics, and assumed as much
coldness and reserve as she had before shown ardent and ingenuous attachment. Scythrop was confounded at the sudden
change; but, instead of falling at her feet and requesting an
explanation, he retreated to his tower, muffled himself in his
nightcap, seated himself in the president's chair of his imaginary secret tribunal, summoned Marionetta with all terrible for-
malities, frightened her out of her wits, disclosed himself, and
clasped the beautiful penitent to his bosom.

While he was acting this reverie—in the moment in which
the awful president of the secret tribunal was throwing back his

[7] Extravagant.
[8] William Drummond, *Academical Questions* (1805), p. 352. Peacock knew the book and found it a convenient source for criticism of
transcendentalism and Kantian metaphysics.

cowl and his mantle, and discovering himself to the lovely culprit as her adoring and magnanimous lover, the door of the study opened, and the real Marionetta appeared.

The motives which had led her to the tower were a little penitence, a little concern, a little affection, and a little fear as to what the sudden secession of Scythrop, occasioned by her sudden change of manner, might portend. She had tapped several times unheard, and of course unanswered; and at length, timidly and cautiously opening the door, she discovered him standing up before a black velvet chair, which was mounted on an old oak table, in the act of throwing open his striped calico dressing-gown, and flinging away his nightcap—which is what the French call an imposing attitude.

Each stood a few moments fixed in their respective places—the lady in astonishment, and the gentleman in confusion. Marionetta was the first to break silence. "For heaven's sake," said she, "my dear Scythrop, what is the matter?"

"For heaven's sake, indeed!" said Scythrop, springing from the table; "for your sake, Marionetta, and you are my heaven, —distraction is the matter. I adore you, Marionetta, and your cruelty drives me mad." He threw himself at her knees, devoured her hand with kisses, and breathed a thousand vows in the most passionate language of romance.

Marionetta listened a long time in silence, till her lover had exhausted his eloquence and paused for a reply. She then said, with a very arch look, "I prithee deliver thyself like a man of this world."[9] The levity of this quotation, and of the manner in which it was delivered, jarred so discordantly on the high-wrought enthusiasm of the romantic inamorato, that he sprang upon his feet, and beat his forehead with his clenched fists. The young lady was terrified; and, deeming it expedient to soothe him, took one of his hands in hers, placed the other hand on his shoulder, looked up in his face with a winning seriousness, and said, in the tenderest possible tone, "What would you have, Scythrop?"

Scythrop was in heaven again. "What would I have? What

[9] *Henry IV, Part II,* V.iii.

but you, Marionetta? You, for the companion of my studies, the partner of my thoughts, the auxiliary of my great designs for the emancipation of mankind."

"I am afraid I should be but a poor auxiliary, Scythrop. What would you have me do?"

"Do as Rosalia does with Carlos, divine Marionetta. Let us each open a vein in the other's arm, mix our blood in a bowl, and drink it as a sacrament of love. Then we shall see visions of transcendental illumination, and soar on the wings of ideas into the space of pure intelligence."[10]

Marionetta could not reply; she had not so strong a stomach as Rosalia, and turned sick at the proposition. She disengaged herself suddenly from Scythrop, sprang through the door of the tower, and fled with precipitation along the corridors. Scythrop pursued her, crying, "Stop, stop, Marionetta—my life, my love!" and was gaining rapidly on her flight, when, at an ill-omened corner, where two corridors ended in an angle, at the head of a staircase, he came into sudden and violent contact with Mr. Toobad, and they both plunged together to the foot of the stairs, like two billiard-balls into one pocket. This gave the young lady time to escape, and enclose herself in her chamber; while Mr. Toobad, rising slowly, and rubbing his knees and shoulders, said, "You see, my dear Scythrop, in this little incident, one of the innumerable proofs of the temporary supremacy of the devil; for what but a systematic design and concurrent contrivance of evil could have made the angles of time and place coincide in our unfortunate persons at the head of this accursed staircase?"

"Nothing else, certainly," said Scythrop: "you are perfectly in the right, Mr. Toobad. Evil, and mischief, and misery, and confusion, and vanity, and vexation of spirit, and death, and disease, and assassination, and war, and poverty, and pestilence,

---

[10] From the *Horrid Mysteries* (see above, p. 12). Carlos narrates: "Her [Rosalia's] hand was still armed with the dagger. She bared my arm and opened a vein, sucking the blood which flowed from the orifice in large drops; and then wounded her arm in return, bidding me to imbibe the roseate stream, and exclaimed: 'Thus our souls shall be mixed together.'"

and famine, and avarice, and selfishness, and rancour, and jealously, and spleen, and malevolence, and the disappointments of philanthropy, and the faithlessness of friendship, and the crosses of love—all prove the accuracy of your views, and the truth of your system; and it is not impossible that the infernal interruption of this fall down stairs may throw a colour of evil on the whole of my future existence."

"My dear boy," said Mr. Toobad, "you have a fine eye for consequences."

So saying, he embraced Scythrop, who retired, with a disconsolate step, to dress for dinner; while Mr. Toobad stalked across the hall, repeating, "Woe to the inhabiters of the earth, and of the sea, for the devil is come among you, having great wrath."

Chapter IV

THE FLIGHT of Marionetta, and the pursuit of Scythrop, had been witnessed by Mr. Glowry, who, in consequence, narrowly observed his son and his niece in the evening; and, concluding from their manner, that there was a better understanding between them than he wished to see, he determined on obtaining the next morning from Scythrop a full and satisfactory explanation. He, therefore, shortly after breakfast, entered Scythrop's tower, with a very grave face, and said, without ceremony or preface, "So, sir, you are in love with your cousin."

Scythrop, with as little hesitation, answered, "Yes, sir."

"That is candid, at least; and she is in love with you."

"I wish she were, sir."

"You know she is, sir."

"Indeed, sir, I do not."

"But you hope she is."

"I do, from my soul."

"Now that is very provoking, Scythrop, and very disappointing: I could not have supposed that you, Scythrop Glowry, of Nightmare Abbey, would have been infatuated with such a dancing, laughing, singing, thoughtless, careless, merry-hearted thing, as Marionetta—in all respects the reverse of you and me. It is very disappointing, Scythrop. And do you know, sir, that Marionetta has no fortune?"

"It is the more reason, sir, that her husband should have one."

"The more reason for her; but not for you. My wife had no fortune, and I had no consolation in my calamity. And do you reflect, sir, what an enormous slice this lawsuit has cut out of our family estate? we who used to be the greatest landed proprietors in Lincolnshire."

"To be sure, sir, we had more acres of fen than any man on this coast: but what are fens to love? What are dykes and windmills to Marionetta?"

"And what, sir, is love to a windmill? Not grist, I am certain: besides, sir, I have made a choice for you. I have made a choice for you, Scythrop. Beauty, genius, accomplishments, and a great fortune into the bargain. Such a lovely, serious creature, in a fine state of high dissatisfaction with the world, and every thing in it. Such a delightful surprise I had prepared for you. Sir, I have pledged my honour to the contract—the honour of the Glowries of Nightmare Abbey: and now, sir, what is to be done?"

"Indeed, sir, I cannot say. I claim, on this occasion, that liberty of action which is the co-natal prerogative of every rational being."

"Liberty of action, sir? there is no such thing as liberty of action. We are all slaves and puppets of a blind and unpathetic necessity."

"Very true, sir; but liberty of action, between individuals, consists in their being differently influenced, or modified, by the same universal necessity; so that the results are unconsentaneous,[1] and their respective necessitated volitions clash and fly off in a tangent."

---

[1] Not suited or agreeable; this passage is the only one cited for the word in the *OED*.

"Your logic is good, sir: but you are aware, too, that one individual may be a medium of adhibiting to another a mode or form of necessity, which may have more or less influence in the production of consentaneity; and, therefore, sir, if you do not comply with my wishes in this instance (you have had your own way in every thing else), I shall be under the necessity of disinheriting you,[2] though I shall do it with tears in my eyes." Having said these words, he vanished suddenly, in the dread of Scythrop's logic.

Mr. Glowry immediately sought Mrs. Hilary, and communicated to her his views of the case in point. Mrs. Hilary, as the phrase is, was as fond of Marionetta as if she had been her own child: but—there is always a *but* on these occasions—she could do nothing for her in the way of fortune, as she had two hopeful sons, who were finishing their education at Brazen-nose,[3] and who would not like to encounter any diminution of their prospects, when they should be brought out of the house of mental bondage—i.e. the university—to the land flowing with milk and honey—i.e. the west end of London.

Mrs. Hilary hinted to Marionetta, that propriety, and delicacy, and decorum, and dignity, &c. &c. &c.,[4] would require them to leave the Abbey immediately. Marionetta listened in silent submission, for she knew that her inheritance was passive obedience; but, when Scythrop, who had watched the opportunity of Mrs. Hilary's departure, entered, and, without speaking a word, threw himself at her feet in a paroxysm of grief, the young lady, in equal silence and sorrow, threw her arms round his neck and burst into tears. A very tender scene ensued, which the sympathetic susceptibilities of the soft-hearted reader can more accurately imagine than we can delineate. But when

---

[2] When Shelley eloped with Harriet Westbrook, his father withheld his allowance (Shelley's only source of income) for five months. Sir Timothy also contemplated a means of keeping Shelley from inheriting the family estate.

[3] I.e., Brasenose College, Oxford, named for a brass knocker shaped like a nose, which adorned the door of a building occupied by students in 1344.

[4] We are not masters of the whole vocabulary. See any novel by any literary lady. [P]

Marionetta hinted that she was to leave the Abbey immediately, Scythrop snatched from its repository his ancestor's skull, filled it with Madeira, and presenting himself before Mr. Glowry, threatened to drink off the contents if Mr. Glowry did not immediately promise that Marionetta should not be taken from the Abbey without her own consent. Mr. Glowry, who took the Madeira to be some deadly brewage, gave the required promise in dismal panic. Scythrop returned to Marionetta with a joyful heart, and drank the Madeira by the way.

Mr. Glowry, during his residence in London, had come to an agreement with his friend Mr. Toobad, that a match between Scythrop and Mr. Toobad's daughter would be a very desirable occurrence. She was finishing her education in a German convent, but Mr. Toobad described her as being fully impressed with the truth of his Ahrimanic[5] philosophy, and being altogether as gloomy and antithalian[6] a young lady as Mr. Glowry himself could desire for the future mistress of Nightmare Abbey. She had a great fortune in her own right, which was not, as we have seen, without its weight in inducing Mr. Glowry to set his heart upon her as his daughter-in-law that was to be; he was therefore very much disturbed by Scythrop's untoward attachment to Marionetta. He condoled on the occasion with Mr. Toobad; who said, that he had been too long accustomed to the intermeddling of the devil in all his affairs, to be astonished at this new trace of his cloven claw; but that he

[5] Ahrimanes, in the Persian mythology, is the evil power, the prince of the kingdom of darkness. He is the rival of Oromazes, the prince of the kingdom of light. These two powers have divided and equal dominion. Sometimes one of the two has a temporary supremacy.—According to Mr. Toobad, the present period would be the reign of Ahrimanes. Lord Byron seems to be of the same opinion, by the use he has made of Ahrimanes in "Manfred;" where the great Alastor, or Κακος Δαιμων, of Persia, is hailed king of the world by the Nemesis of Greece, in concert with three of the Scandinavian Valkyræ, under the name of the Destinies; the astrological spirits of the alchemists of the middle ages; an elemental witch, transplanted from Denmark to the Alps; and a chorus of Dr. Faustus's devils, who come in the last act for a soul. It is difficult to conceive where this heterogeneous mythological company could have originally met, except at a *table d'hôte,* like the six kings in "Candide." [P]

[6] Opposed to Thalia, the muse of comedy. This passage provides the earliest citation for "antithalian" in the *OED.*

hoped to outwit him yet, for he was sure there could be no comparison between his daughter and Marionetta in the mind of any one who had a proper perception of the fact, that, the world being a great theatre of evil, seriousness and solemnity are the characteristics of wisdom, and laughter and merriment make a human being no better than a baboon. Mr. Glowry comforted himself with this view of the subject, and urged Mr. Toobad to expedite his daughter's return from Germany. Mr. Toobad said he was in daily expectation of her arrival in London, and would set off immediately to meet her, that he might lose no time in bringing her to Nightmare Abbey. "Then," he added, "we shall see whether Thalia or Melpomene—whether the Allegra or the Penserosa[7]—will carry off the symbol of victory."—"There can be no doubt," said Mr. Glowry, "which way the scale will incline, or Scythrop is no true scion of the venerable stem of the Glowrys."

Chapter V

MARIONETTA felt secure of Scythrop's heart; and notwithstanding the difficulties that surrounded her, she could not debar herself from the pleasure of tormenting her lover, whom she kept in a perpetual fever. Sometimes she would meet him with the most unqualified affection; sometimes with the most chilling indifference; rousing him to anger by artificial coldness —softening him to love by eloquent tenderness—or inflaming him to jealousy by coquetting with the Honourable Mr. Listless, who seemed, under her magical influence, to burst into sudden life, like the bud of the evening primrose. Sometimes she would sit by the piano, and listen with becoming attention to Scy-

[7] Milton's "L'Allegro" and "Il Penseroso," poems describing respectively the vivacious and the melancholy temperaments. Melpomene is the classical muse of tragedy.

throp's pathetic remonstrances; but, in the most impassioned part of his oratory, she would convert all his ideas into a chaos, by striking up some Rondo Allegro, and saying, "Is it not pretty?" Scythrop would begin to storm; and she would answer him with,

> "Zitti, zitti, piano, piano,
> Non facciamo confusione,"[1]

or some similar *facezia*,[2] till he would start away from her, and enclose himself in his tower, in an agony of agitation, vowing to renounce her, and her whole sex, for ever; and returning to her presence at the summons of the billet, which she never failed to send with many expressions of penitence and promises of amendment. Scythrop's schemes for regenerating the world, and detecting his seven golden candlesticks, went on very slowly in this fever of his spirit.

Things proceeded in this train for several days; and Mr. Glowry began to be uneasy at receiving no intelligence from Mr. Toobad; when one evening the latter rushed into the library, where the family and the visitors were assembled, vociferating, "The devil is come among you, having great wrath!" He then drew Mr. Glowry aside into another apartment, and after remaining some time together, they re-entered the library with faces of great dismay, but did not condescend to explain to any one the cause of their discomfiture.

The next morning, early, Mr. Toobad departed. Mr. Glowry sighed and groaned all day, and said not a word to any one. Scythrop had quarrelled, as usual, with Marionetta, and was enclosed in his tower, in a fit of morbid sensibility. Marionetta was comforting herself at the piano, with singing the airs of *Nina pazza per amore*,[3] and the Honourable Mr. Listless was listening to the harmony, as he lay supine on the sofa, with a

---

[1] "Silence, silence, quiet, quiet,/Let us not create confusion." From an aria in Rossini's *The Barber of Seville* (1816).

[2] Jest, pleasantry.

[3] *Nino, o sia La Pazza per Amore* (*Nino, or the Fool for Love*), a comic opera by Paisiello (1789).

book in his hand into which he peeped at intervals. The Reverend Mr. Larynx approached the sofa, and proposed a game at billiards.

THE HONOURABLE MR. LISTLESS.

Billiards! Really I should be very happy; but, in my present exhausted state, the exertion is too much for me. I do not know when I have been equal to such an effort.

[*He rang the bell for his valet. Fatout entered.*]
Fatout! when did I play at billiards last?

FATOUT.

De fourteen December de last year, Monsieur.

[*Fatout bowed and retired.*]

THE HONOURABLE MR. LISTLESS.

So it was. Seven months ago. You see, Mr. Larynx; you see, sir. My nerves, Miss O'Carroll, my nerves are shattered. I have been advised to try Bath. Some of the faculty recommended Cheltenham.[4] I think of trying both, as the seasons don't clash. The season, you know, Mr. Larynx—the season, Miss O'Carroll—the season is every thing.

MARIONETTA.

And health is something. *N'est-ce pas,* Mr. Larynx?

THE REVEREND MR. LARYNX.

Most assuredly, Miss O'Carroll. For, however reasoners may dispute about the *summum bonum,* none of them will deny that a very good dinner is a very good thing: and what is a good dinner without a good appetite? and whence is a good appetite but from good health? Now, Cheltenham, Mr. Listless, is famous for good appetites.

THE HONOURABLE MR. LISTLESS.

The best piece of logic I ever heard, Mr. Larynx; the very best, I assure you. I have thought very seriously of Cheltenham: very seriously and profoundly. I thought of it—let me see— when did I think of it?

[*He rang again, and Fatout re-appeared.*]
Fatout! when did I think of going to Cheltenham, and did not go?

---

[4] Bath and Cheltenham are English health spas known for their mineral springs.

FATOUT.

De Juillet twenty-von, de last summer, Monsieur.

[*Fatout retired.*]

THE HONOURABLE MR. LISTLESS.

So it was. An invaluable fellow that, Mr. Larynx—invaluable, Miss O'Carroll.

MARIONETTA.

So I should judge, indeed. He seems to serve you as a walking memory, and to be a living chronicle, not of your actions only, but of your thoughts.

THE HONOURABLE MR. LISTLESS.

An excellent definition of the fellow, Miss O'Carroll,—excellent, upon my honour. Ha! ha! he! Heigho! Laughter is pleasant, but the exertion is too much for me.

A parcel was brought in for Mr. Listless; it had been sent express. Fatout was summoned to unpack it; and it proved to contain a new novel, and a new poem, both of which had long been anxiously expected by the whole host of fashionable readers; and the last number of a popular Review, of which the editor and his coadjutors were in high favour at court, and enjoyed ample pensions[5] for their services to church and state. As Fatout left the room, Mr. Flosky entered, and curiously inspected the literary arrivals.

MR. FLOSKY.

[*Turning over the leaves.*]

"Devilman, a novel."[6] Hm. Hatred—revenge—misanthropy —and quotations from the Bible. Hm. This is the morbid anatomy of black bile.—"Paul Jones, a poem."[7] Hm. I see how it is. Paul Jones, an amiable enthusiast—disappointed in his affections—turns pirate from ennui and magnanimity—cuts various masculine throats, wins various feminine hearts—is hanged at the yard-arm! The catastrophe is very awkward, and very unpoetical.—"The Downing Street Review." Hm. First article—

---

[5] *"Pension.* Pay given to a slave of state for treason to his country."—Johnson's *Dictionary.* [P] [*Slave of state* should be *state hireling.*]

[6] William Godwin, *Mandeville* (1817).

[7] John Paul Jones, American adventurer, privateer and naval hero in the Revolutionary War. Flosky's synopsis of the poem contains parallels to Byron's "The Corsair" (1814).

An Ode to the Red Book, by Roderick Sackbut, Esquire.[8] Hm. His own poem reviewed by himself. Hm-m-m.

> [*Mr. Flosky proceeded in silence to look over the other articles of the review; Marionetta inspected the novel, and Mr. Listless the poem.*]

THE REVEREND MR. LARYNX.

For a young man of fashion and family, Mr. Listless, you seem to be of a very studious turn.

THE HONOURABLE MR. LISTLESS.

Studious! You are pleased to be facetious, Mr. Larynx. I hope you do not suspect me of being studious. I have finished my education. But there are some fashionable books that one must read, because they are ingredients of the talk of the day; otherwise, I am no fonder of books than I dare say you yourself are, Mr. Larynx.

THE REVEREND MR. LARYNX.

Why, sir, I cannot say that I am indeed particularly fond of books; yet neither can I say that I never do read. A tale or a poem, now and then, to a circle of ladies over their work, is no very heterodox employment of the vocal energy. And I must say, for myself, that few men have a more Job-like endurance of the eternally recurring questions and answers that interweave themselves, on these occasions, with the crisis of an adventure, and heighten the distress of a tragedy.

THE HONOURABLE MR. LISTLESS.

And very often make the distress when the author has omitted it.

MARIONETTA.

I shall try your patience some rainy morning, Mr. Larynx; and Mr. Listless shall recommend us the very newest new book, that every body reads.

---

[8] Robert Southey, currently Poet Laureate. Traditionally, the Laureate was allowed by the government a free butt (cask) of sack (sherry) each year. Southey was a major contributor to the *Quarterly* ("Downing Street") *Review,* a Tory review espousing the government position. *The Red Book of Hergest* is a compilation of medieval Welsh literature; Southey possessed extensive knowledge of primitive peoples and literatures, and was for many years the *Quarterly Review*'s leading reviewer of books on these topics.

THE HONOURABLE MR. LISTLESS.

You shall receive it, Miss O'Carroll, with all the gloss of novelty; fresh as a ripe green-gage in all the downiness of its bloom. A mail-coach copy from Edinburgh, forwarded express from London.

MR. FLOSKY.

This rage for novelty is the bane of literature. Except my works and those of my particular friends, nothing is good that is not as old as Jeremy Taylor: and, *entre nous,* the best parts of my friends' books were either written or suggested by myself.[9]

THE HONOURABLE MR. LISTLESS.

Sir, I reverence you. But I must say, modern books are very consolatory and congenial to my feelings. There is, as it were, a delightful north-east wind, an intellectual blight breathing through them; a delicious misanthropy and discontent, that demonstrates the nullity of virtue and energy, and puts me in good humour with myself and my sofa.

MR. FLOSKY.

Very true, sir. Modern literature is a north-east wind—a blight of the human soul. I take credit to myself for having helped to make it so. The way to produce fine fruit is to blight the flower. You call this a paradox. Marry, so be it. Ponder thereon.

The conversation was interrupted by the re-appearance of Mr. Toobad, covered with mud. He just showed himself at the door, muttered "The devil is come among you!" and vanished. The road which connected Nightmare Abbey with the civilised world, was artificially raised above the level of the fens, and ran through them in a straight line as far as the eye could reach, with a ditch on each side, of which the water was rendered invisible by the aquatic vegetation that covered the surface. Into one of these ditches the sudden action of a shy horse, which took fright at a windmill, had precipitated the travelling chariot

---

[9] Coleridge's collaboration with Wordsworth in *Lyrical Ballads* and other works is well known. He also collaborated with Southey in *The Devil's Thoughts.* Jeremy Taylor (1613–1667) was an Anglican divine "rediscovered" by Coleridge and other Romantics.

of Mr. Toobad, who had been reduced to the necessity of scrambling in dismal plight through the window. One of the wheels was found to be broken; and Mr. Toobad, leaving the postilion to get the chariot as well as he could to Claydyke for the purposes of cleaning and repairing, had walked back to Nightmare Abbey, followed by his servant with the imperial, and repeating all the way his favourite quotation from the Revelations.

Chapter VI

MR. TOOBAD had found his daughter Celinda in London, and after the first joy of meeting was over, told her he had a husband ready for her. The young lady replied, very gravely, that she should take the liberty to choose for herself. Mr. Toobad said he saw the devil was determined to interfere with all his projects, but he was resolved on his own part, not to have on his conscience the crime of passive obedience and non-resistance to Lucifer, and therefore she should marry the person he had chosen for her. Miss Toobad replied, *très posément*,[1] she assuredly would not. "Celinda, Celinda," said Mr. Toobad, "you most assuredly shall."—"Have I not a fortune in my own right, sir?" said Celinda. "The more is the pity," said Mr. Toobad: "but I can find means, miss; I can find means. There are more ways than one of breaking in obstinate girls." They parted for the night with the expression of opposite resolutions, and in the morning the young lady's chamber was found empty, and what was become of her Mr. Toobad had no clue to conjecture. He continued to investigate town and country in search of her; visiting and revisiting Nightmare Abbey at intervals, to consult with his friend, Mr. Glowry. Mr. Glowry agreed with Mr. Toobad that this was a very flagrant instance of filial dis-

---

[1] With great emphasis.

obedience and rebellion; and Mr. Toobad declared, that when he discovered the fugitive, she should find that "the devil was come unto her, having great wrath."

In the evening, the whole party met, as usual, in the library. Marionetta sat at the harp; the Honourable Mr. Listless sat by her and turned over her music, though the exertion was almost too much for him. The Reverend Mr. Larynx relieved him occasionally in this delightful labour. Scythrop, tormented by the demon Jealousy, sat in the corner biting his lips and fingers. Marionetta looked at him every now and then with a smile of most provoking good humour, which he pretended not to see, and which only the more exasperated his troubled spirit. He took down a volume of Dante, and pretended to be deeply interested in the Purgatorio,[2] though he knew not a word he was reading, as Marionetta was well aware; who, tripping across the room, peeped into his book, and said to him, "I see you are in the middle of Purgatory."—"I am in the middle of hell," said Scythrop furiously. "Are you?" said she; "then come across the room, and I will sing you the finale of Don Giovanni."[3]

"Let me alone," said Scythrop. Marionetta looked at him with a deprecating smile, and said, "You unjust, cross creature, you."—"Let me alone," said Scythrop, but much less emphatically than at first, and by no means wishing to be taken at his word. Marionetta left him immediately, and returning to the harp, said, just loud enough for Scythrop to hear—"Did you ever read Dante, Mr. Listless? Scythrop is reading Dante, and is just now in Purgatory."—"And I," said the Honourable Mr. Listless, "am not reading Dante, and am just now in Paradise," bowing to Marionetta.

MARIONETTA.

You are very gallant, Mr. Listless; and I dare say you are very fond of reading Dante.

THE HONOURABLE MR. LISTLESS.

I don't know how it is, but Dante never came in my way till lately. I never had him in my collection, and if I had had him

---

[2] The three parts of the *Comedia* of Dante are respectively the *Inferno* (Hell), the *Purgatorio,* and the *Paradiso.*

[3] By Mozart (1787); at the climax of the opera the Don is consumed by the flames of hell.

I should not have read him. But I find he is growing fashionable, and I am afraid I must read him some wet morning.

MARIONETTA.

No, read him some evening, by all means. Were you ever in love, Mr. Listless?

THE HONOURABLE MR. LISTLESS.

I assure you, Miss O'Carroll, never—till I came to Nightmare Abbey. I dare say it is very pleasant; but it seems to give so much trouble that I fear the exertion would be too much for me.

MARIONETTA.

Shall I teach you a compendious method of courtship, that will give you no trouble whatever?

THE HONOURABLE MR. LISTLESS.

You will confer on me an inexpressible obligation. I am all impatience to learn it.

MARIONETTA.

Sit with your back to the lady and read Dante; only be sure to begin in the middle, and turn over three or four pages at once—backwards as well as forwards, and she will immediately perceive that you are desperately in love with her—desperately.

[*The Honourable Mr. Listless sitting between Scythrop and Marionetta, and fixing all his attention on the beautiful speaker, did not observe Scythrop, who was doing as she described.*]

THE HONOURABLE MR. LISTLESS.

You are pleased to be facetious, Miss O'Carroll. The lady would infallibly conclude that I was the greatest brute in town.

MARIONETTA.

Far from it. She would say, perhaps, some people have odd methods of showing their affection.

THE HONOURABLE MR. LISTLESS.

But I should think, with submission——

MR. FLOSKY.

[*Joining them from another part of the room.*]

Did I not hear Mr. Listless observe that Dante is becoming fashionable?

THE HONOURABLE MR. LISTLESS.

I did hazard a remark to that effect, Mr. Flosky, though I

speak on such subjects with a consciousness of my own nothingness, in the presence of so great a man as Mr. Flosky. I know
not what is the colour of Dante's devils, but as he is certainly
becoming fashionable I conclude they are blue; for the blue
devils, as it seems to me, Mr. Flosky, constitute the fundamental
feature of fashionable literature.

MR. FLOSKY.

The blue are, indeed, the staple commodity; but as they will
not always be commanded, the black, red, and grey may be
admitted as substitutes. Tea, late dinners, and the French Revolution, have played the devil, Mr. Listless, and brought the
devil into play.

MR. TOOBAD.

Having great wrath.

MR. FLOSKY.

[*starting up.*]

This is no play upon words, but the sober sadness of veritable
fact.

THE HONOURABLE MR. LISTLESS.

Tea, late dinners, and the French Revolution. I cannot exactly see the connection of ideas.

MR. FLOSKY.

I should be sorry if you could; I pity the man who can see
the connection of his own ideas. Still more do I pity him, the
connection of whose ideas any other person can see. Sir, the
great evil is, that there is too much commonplace light in our
moral and political literature; and light is a great enemy to
mystery, and mystery is a great friend to enthusiasm. Now the
enthusiasm for abstract truth is an exceedingly fine thing, as
long as the truth, which is the object of the enthusiasm, is so
completely abstract as to be altogether out of the reach of the
human faculties; and, in that sense, I have myself an enthusiasm for truth, but in no other, for the pleasure of metaphysical
investigation lies in the means, not in the end; and if the end
could be found, the pleasure of the means would cease. The
mind, to be kept in health, must be kept in exercise. The proper
exercise of the mind is elaborate reasoning. Analytical reasoning is a base and mechanical process, which takes to pieces and

examines, bit by bit, the rude material of knowledge, and extracts therefrom a few hard and obstinate things called facts, every thing in the shape of which I cordially hate. But synthetical reasoning, setting up as its goal some unattainable abstraction, like an imaginary quantity in algebra, and commencing its course with taking for granted some two assertions which cannot be proved, from the union of these two assumed truths produces a third assumption, and so on in infinite series, to the unspeakable benefit of the human intellect. The beauty of this process is, that at every step it strikes out into two branches, in a compound ratio of ramification; so that you are perfectly sure of losing your way, and keeping your mind in perfect health, by the perpetual exercise of an interminable quest; and for these reasons I have christened my eldest son Emanuel Kant Flosky.[4]

THE REVEREND MR. LARYNX.

Nothing can be more luminous.

THE HONOURABLE MR. LISTLESS.

And what has all that to do with Dante, and the blue devils?

MR. HILARY.

Not much, I should think, with Dante, but a great deal with the blue devils.

MR. FLOSKY.

It is very certain, and much to be rejoiced at, that our literature is hag-ridden. Tea has shattered our nerves; late dinners make us slaves of indigestion; the French Revolution has made us shrink from the name of philosophy, and has destroyed, in the more refined part of the community (of which number I am one), all enthusiasm for political liberty. That part of the *reading public* which shuns the solid food of reason for the light diet of fiction, requires a perpetual adhibition of *sauce piquante* to the palate of its depraved imagination. It lived upon ghosts, goblins, and skeletons (I and my friend Mr. Sackbut served up a few of the best), till even the devil himself, though magnified

[4] Kant (1724–1804) was a German metaphysician whose philosophy profoundly influenced Coleridge. Coleridge had named his sons Hartley and Berkeley, after the eighteenth-century English philosophers.

to the size of Mount Athos,[5] became too base, common, and popular,[6] for its surfeited appetite. The ghosts have therefore been laid, and the devil has been cast into outer darkness, and now the delight of our spirits is to dwell on all the vices and blackest passions of our nature, tricked out in a masquerade dress of heroism and disappointed benevolence; the whole secret of which lies in forming combinations that contradict all our experience, and affixing the purple shred of some particular virtue to that precise character, in which we should be most certain not to find it in the living world; and making this single virtue not only redeem all the real and manifest vices of the character, but make them actually pass for necessary adjuncts, and indispensable accompaniments and characteristics of the said virtue.

MR. TOOBAD.

That is, because the devil is come among us, and finds it for his interest to destroy all our perceptions of the distinctions of right and wrong.

MARIONETTA.

I do not precisely enter into your meaning, Mr. Flosky, and should be glad if you would make it a little more plain to me.

MR. FLOSKY.

One or two examples will do it, Miss O'Carroll. If I were to take all the mean and sordid qualities of a money-dealing Jew, and tack on to them, as with a nail, the quality of extreme benevolence, I should have a very decent hero for a modern novel; and should contribute my quota to the fashionable method of administering a mass of vice, under a thin and unnatural covering of virtue, like a spider wrapt in a bit of gold leaf, and administered as a wholesome pill. On the same principle, if a man knocks me down, and takes my purse and watch by main force, I turn him to account, and set him forth in a tragedy as a dashing young fellow, disinherited for his romantic generosity,

---

[5] A mountain at the extremity of the Athos peninsula in Macedonia, northeast Greece. It is also called the "holy mountain" because of its twenty Greek orthodox monasteries.

[6] *Henry V*, IV.i.

and full of a most amiable hatred of the world in general, and his own country in particular, and of a most enlightened and chivalrous affection for himself: then, with the addition of a wild girl to fall in love with him, and a series of adventures in which they break all the Ten Commandments in succession (always, you will observe, for some sublime motive, which must be carefully analysed in its progress), I have as amiable a pair of tragic characters as ever issued from that new region of the belles lettres, which I have called the Morbid Anatomy of Black Bile, and which is greatly to be admired and rejoiced at, as affording a fine scope for the exhibition of mental power.

MR. HILARY.

Which is about as well employed as the power of a hot-house would be in forcing up a nettle to the size of an elm. If we go on in this way, we shall have a new art of poetry, of which one of the first rules will be: To remember to forget that there are any such things as sunshine and music in the world.

THE HONOURABLE MR. LISTLESS.

It seems to be the case with us at present, or we should not have interrupted Miss O'Carroll's music with this exceedingly dry conversation.

MR. FLOSKY.

I should be most happy if Miss O'Carroll would remind us that there are yet both music and sunshine——

THE HONOURABLE MR. LISTLESS.

In the voice and the smile of beauty. May I entreat the favour of—

[*turning over the pages of music.*]

All were silent, and Marionetta sung:—

Why are thy looks so blank, grey friar?
  Why are thy looks so blue?
Thou seem'st more pale and lank, grey friar,
  Than thou wast used to do:—
  Say, what has made thee rue?

Thy form was plump, and a light did shine
  In thy round and ruby face,
Which showed an outward visible sign
  Of an inward spiritual grace:—[7]
  Say, what has changed thy case?

Yet will I tell thee true, grey friar,
  I very well can see,
That, if thy looks are blue, grey friar,
  'Tis all for love of me,—
  'Tis all for love of me.

But breathe not thy vows to me, grey friar,
  Oh, breathe them not, I pray;
For ill beseems in a reverend friar,
  The love of a mortal may;
  And I needs must say thee nay.

But, could'st thou think my heart to move
  With that pale and silent scowl?
Know, he who would win a maiden's love,
  Whether clad in cap or cowl,
  Must be more of a lark than an owl.

Scythrop immediately replaced Dante on the shelf, and joined the circle round the beautiful singer. Marionetta gave him a smile of approbation that fully restored his complacency, and they continued on the best possible terms during the remainder of the evening. The Honourable Mr. Listless turned over the leaves with double alacrity, saying, "You are severe upon invalids, Miss O'Carroll: to escape your satire, I must try to be sprightly, though the exertion is too much for me."

[7] From the Book of Common Prayer ("On the Sacraments"), the service book of the Anglican Communion.

Chapter VII

A NEW VISITOR arrived at the Abbey, in the person of Mr. Asterias,[1] the ichthyologist. This gentleman had passed his life in seeking the living wonders of the deep through the four quarters of the world; he had a cabinet of stuffed and dried fishes, of shells, seaweeds, corals, and madrepores, that was the admiration and envy of the Royal Society.[2] He had penetrated into the watery den of the Sepia Octopus, disturbed the conjugal happiness of that turtle-dove of the ocean, and come off victorious in a sanguinary conflict. He had been becalmed in the tropical seas, and had watched, in eager expectation, though unhappily always in vain, to see the colossal polypus rise from the water, and entwine its enormous arms round the masts and the rigging. He maintained the origin of all things from water, and insisted that the polypodes were the first of animated things, and that, from their round bodies and many-shooting arms, the Hindoos had taken their gods, the most ancient of deities. But the chief object of his ambition, the end and aim of his researches, was to discover a triton and a mermaid, the existence of which he most potently and implicitly believed, and was prepared to demonstrate, *à priori, à posteriori, à fortiori*,[3] synthetically and analytically, syllogistically and inductively, by arguments deduced both from acknowledged facts and plausible hypotheses. A report that a mermaid had been seen "sleeking her soft alluring locks"[4] on the sea-coast of Lincolnshire, had brought him in great haste from London, to pay a long-promised and often-postponed visit to his old acquaintance, Mr. Glowry.

Mr. Asterias was accompanied by his son, to whom he had

[1] Literally, a type of starfish (from ἀστεριας, starry).
[2] The oldest and most prestigious scientific society in England, founded in 1660.
[3] From cause to effect, from effect to cause, more conclusively.
[4] Milton, *Comus,* l. 882.

given the name of Aquarius—flattering himself that he would, in the process of time, become a constellation among the stars of ichthyological science. What charitable female had lent him the mould in which this son was cast, no one pretended to know; and, as he never dropped the most distant allusion to Aquarius's mother, some of the wags of London maintained that he had received the favours of a mermaid, and that the scientific perquisitions which kept him always prowling about the sea-shore, were directed by the less philosophical motive of regaining his lost love.

Mr. Asterias perlustrated[5] the sea-coast for several days, and reaped disappointment, but not despair. One night, shortly after his arrival, he was sitting in one of the windows of the library, looking towards the sea, when his attention was attracted by a figure which was moving near the edge of the surf, and which was dimly visible through the moonless summer night. Its motions were irregular, like those of a person in a state of indecision. It had extremely long hair, which floated in the wind. Whatever else it might be, it certainly was not a fisherman. It might be a lady; but it was neither Mrs. Hilary nor Miss O'Carroll, for they were both in the library. It might be one of the female servants; but it had too much grace, and too striking an air of habitual liberty, to render it probable. Besides, what should one of the female servants be doing there at this hour, moving to and fro, as it seemed, without any visible purpose? It could scarcely be a stranger; for Claydyke, the nearest village, was ten miles distant; and what female would come ten miles across the fens, for no purpose but to hover over the surf under the walls of Nightmare Abbey? Might it not be a mermaid? It was possibly a mermaid. It was probably a mermaid. It was very probably a mermaid. Nay, what else could it be but a mermaid? It certainly was a mermaid. Mr. Asterias stole out of the library on tiptoe, with his finger on his lips, having beckoned Aquarius to follow him.

The rest of the party was in great surprise at Mr. Asterias's movement, and some of them approached the window to see if

[5] Viewed or surveyed thoroughly.

the locality would tend to elucidate the mystery. Presently they saw him and Aquarius cautiously stealing along on the other side of the moat, but they saw nothing more; and Mr. Asterias returning, told them, with accents of great disappointment, that he had had a glimpse of a mermaid, but she had eluded him in the darkness, and was gone, he presumed, to sup with some enamoured triton, in a submarine grotto.

"But, seriously, Mr. Asterias," said the Honourable Mr. List-less, "do you positively believe there are such things as mermaids?"

MR. ASTERIAS.

Most assuredly; and tritons too.

THE HONOURABLE MR. LISTLESS.

What! things that are half human and half fish?

MR. ASTERIAS.

Precisely. They are the oran-outangs of the sea. But I am persuaded that there are also complete sea men, differing in no respect from us, but that they are stupid, and covered with scales; for, though our organisation seems to exclude us essentially from the class of amphibious animals, yet anatomists well know that the *foramen ovale* may remain open in an adult, and that respiration is, in that case, not necessary to life: and how can it be otherwise explained that the Indian divers, employed in the pearl fishery, pass whole hours under the water; and that the famous Swedish gardener of Troningholm lived a day and a half under the ice without being drowned? A nereid, or mermaid, was taken in the year 1403 in a Dutch lake, and was in every respect like a French woman, except that she did not speak.[6] Towards the end of the seventeenth century, an English ship, a hundred and fifty leagues from land, in the Greenland seas, discovered a flotilla of sixty or seventy little skiffs, in each of which was a triton, or sea man: at the approach of the English vessel the whole of them, seized with simultaneous fear, disappeared, skiffs and all, under the water, as if they had been a human variety of the nautilus. The illustrious Don

---

[6] For a modern retelling of the legend, see Norman Douglas, *Siren Land*, Ch. I.

Feijoo[7] has preserved an authentic and well-attested story of a young Spaniard, named Francis de la Vega, who, bathing with some of his friends in June, 1674, suddenly dived under the sea and rose no more. His friends thought him drowned; they were plebians and pious Catholics; but a philosopher might very legitimately have drawn the same conclusion.

THE REVEREND MR. LARYNX.

Nothing could be more logical.

MR. ASTERIAS.

Five years afterwards, some fishermen near Cadiz found in their nets a triton, or sea man; they spoke to him in several languages——

THE REVEREND MR. LARYNX.

They were very learned fishermen.

MR. HILARY.

They had the gift of tongues by especial favour of their brother fishermen, Saint Peter.

THE HONOURABLE MR. LISTLESS.

Is Saint Peter the tutelar saint of Cadiz?

> [*None of the company could answer this question, and*
> MR. ASTERIAS *proceeded.*]

They spoke to him in several languages, but he was as mute as a fish. They handed him over to some holy friars, who exorcised him; but the devil was mute too. After some days he pronounced the name Lierganes. A monk took him to that village. His mother and brothers recognised and embraced him; but he was as insensible to their caresses as any other fish would have been. He had some scales on his body, which dropped off by degrees; but his skin was as hard and rough as shagreen.[8] He stayed at home nine years, without recovering his speech or his reason: he then disappeared again; and one of his old acquaintance, some years after, saw him pop his head out of the water near the coast of the Asturias. These facts were cer-

---

[7] Don Benito Geronimo Feijoo y Montenegro (1675–1764), a Benedictine monk, called "the Spanish Voltaire" because of his skepticism.

[8] Rough, untanned leather.

tified by his brothers, and by Don Gaspardo de la Riba Aguero Knight of Saint James, who lived near Lierganes, and often had the pleasure of our triton's company to dinner.—Pliny mentions an embassy of the Olyssiponians to Tiberius, to give him intelligence of a triton which had been heard playing on its shell in a certain cave; with several other authenticated facts on the subject of tritons and nereids.[9]

THE HONOURABLE MR. LISTLESS.

You astonish me. I have been much on the sea-shore, in the season, but I do not think I ever saw a mermaid.

> [*He rang, and summoned Fatout, who made his appearance half-seas-over.*]

Fatout! did I ever see a mermaid?

FATOUT.

Mermaid! mer-r-m-m-aid! Ah! merry maid! Oui, monsieur! Yes, sir, very many. I vish dere vas von or two here in de kitchen—ma foi! Dey be all as melancholic as so many tombstone.

THE HONOURABLE MR. LISTLESS.

I mean, Fatout, an odd kind of human fish.

FATOUT.

De odd fish! Ah, oui! I understand de phrase: ve have seen nothing else since ve left town—ma foi!

THE HONOURABLE MR. LISTLESS.

You seem to have a cup too much, sir.

FATOUT.

Non, monsieur: de cup too little. De fen be very unwholesome, and I drink-a-de ponch vid Raven de butler, to keep out de bad air.

THE HONOURABLE MR. LISTLESS.

Fatout! I insist on your being sober.

FATOUT.

Oui, monsieur; I vil be as sober as de révérendissime père Jean.[10] I should be ver glad of de merry maid; but de butler be

---

[9] Pliny, Book IX, Ch. 4.
[10] Frère Jean des Entommeures, the prodigious monk in Rabelais, Book I, Ch. 27.

de odd fish, and he swim in de bowl de ponch. Ah! ah! I do recollect de leetle-a song:—"About fair maids, and about fair maids, and about my merry maids all."

[*Fatout reeled out, singing.*]

THE HONOURABLE MR. LISTLESS.

I am overwhelmed: I never saw the rascal in such a condition before. But will you allow me, Mr. Asterias, to inquire into the *cui bono*[11] of all the pains and expense you have incurred to discover a mermaid? The *cui bono,* sir, is the question I always take the liberty to ask when I see any one taking much trouble for any object. I am myself a sort of Signor Pococurante,[12] and should like to know if there be any thing better or pleasanter, than the state of existing and doing nothing?

MR. ASTERIAS.

I have made many voyages, Mr. Listless, to remote and barren shores: I have travelled over desert and inhospitable lands: I have defied danger—I have endured fatigue—I have submitted to privation. In the midst of these I have experienced pleasures which I would not at any time have exchanged for that of existing and doing nothing. I have known many evils, but I have never known the worst of all, which, as it seems to me, are those which are comprehended in the inexhaustible varieties of *ennui:* spleen, chagrin, vapours, blue devils, time-killing, discontent, misanthropy, and all their interminable train of fretfulness, querulousness, suspicions, jealousies, and fears, which have alike infected society, and the literature of society; and which would make an arctic ocean of the human mind, if the more humane pursuits of philosophy and science did not keep alive the better feelings and more valuable energies of our nature.

THE HONOURABLE MR. LISTLESS.

You are pleased to be severe upon our fashionable belles lettres.

[11] "What good will it do?"

[12] Literally, "caring little"; an easygoing, happy-go-lucky fellow who wastes his concern over trifles.

MR. ASTERIAS.

Surely not without reason, when pirates, highwaymen, and other varieties of the extensive genus Marauder, are the only *beau idéal* of the active, as splenetic and railing misanthropy is of the speculative energy. A gloomy brow and a tragical voice seem to have been of late the characteristics of fashionable manners: and a morbid, withering, deadly, antisocial sirocco,[13] loaded with moral and political despair, breathes through all the groves and valleys of the modern Parnassus;[14] while science moves on in the calm dignity of its course, affording to youth delights equally pure and vivid—to maturity, calm and grateful occupation—to old age, the most pleasing recollections and inexhaustible materials of agreeable and salutary reflection; and, while its votary enjoys the disinterested pleasure of enlarging the intellect and increasing the comforts of society, he is himself independent of the caprices of human intercourse and the accidents of human fortune. Nature is his great and inexhaustible treasure. His days are always too short for his enjoyment: *ennui* is a stranger to his door. At peace with the world and with his own mind, he suffices to himself, makes all around him happy, and the close of his pleasing and beneficial existence is the evening of a beautiful day.[15]

THE HONOURABLE MR. LISTLESS.

Really I should like very well to lead such a life myself, but the exertion would be too much for me. Besides, I have been at college. I contrive to get through my day by sinking the morning in bed, and killing the evening in company; dressing and dining in the intermediate space, and stopping the chinks and crevices of the few vacant moments that remain with a little easy reading. And that amiable discontent and antisociality which you reprobate in our present drawing-room-table literature, I find, I do assure you, a very fine mental tonic, which

---

[13] A hot, blighting wind.

[14] Mountain in Greece, supposedly the home of Apollo and the muses.

[15] See Denys Montfort: *Histoire Naturelle des Mollusques; Vues Générales,* pp. 37, 38. [P]

reconciles me to my favourite pursuit of doing nothing, by showing me that nobody is worth doing any thing for.

MARIONETTA.

But is there not in such compositions a kind of unconscious self-detection, which seems to carry their own antidote with them? For surely no one who cordially and truly either hates or despises the world will publish a volume every three months to say so.[16]

MR. FLOSKY.

There is a secret in all this, which I will elucidate with a dusky remark. According to Berkeley, the *esse* of things is *percipi*. They exist as they are perceived. But, leaving for the present, as far as relates to the material world, the materialists, hyloists,[17] and antihyloists, to settle this point among them, which is indeed

> A subtle question, raised among
> Those out o' their wits, and those i' the wrong:[18]

for only we transcendentalists are in the right: we may very safely assert that the *esse* of happiness is *percipi*. It exists as it is perceived. "It is the mind that maketh well or ill." The elements of pleasure and pain are every where. The degree of happiness that any circumstances or objects can confer on us depends on the mental disposition with which we approach them. If you consider what is meant by the common phrases, a happy disposition and a discontented temper, you will perceive that the truth for which I am contending is universally admitted.

[*Mr. Flosky suddenly stopped: he found himself unintentionally trespassing within the limits of common sense.*]

---

[16] Perhaps Peacock is alluding to Byron, who between February 1816 and June 1817 had published five works, including the gloomy and misanthropic third canto of *Childe Harold's Pilgrimage* and *Manfred*.

[17] One who affirms that matter is God; Peacock's is the first known use of this word.

[18] Butler, *Hudibras*, Part I, Canto II, ll. 703–704.

MR. HILARY.

It is very true; a happy disposition finds materials of enjoyment every where. In the city, or the country—in society, or in solitude—in the theatre, or the forest—in the hum of the multitude, or in the silence of the mountains, are alike materials of reflection and elements of pleasure. It is one mode of pleasure to listen to the music of "Don Giovanni," in a theatre glittering with light, and crowded with elegance and beauty: it is another to glide at sunset over the bosom of a lonely lake, where no sound disturbs the silence but the motion of the boat through the waters. A happy disposition derives pleasure from both, a discontented temper from neither, but is always busy in detecting deficiencies, and feeding dissatisfaction with comparisons. The one gathers all the flowers, the other all the nettles, in its path. The one has the faculty of enjoying every thing, the other of enjoying nothing. The one realises all the pleasure of the present good; the other converts it into pain, by pining after something better, which is only better because it is not present, and which, if it were present, would not be enjoyed. These morbid spirits are in life what professed critics are in literature; they see nothing but faults, because they are predetermined to shut their eyes to beauties. The critic does his utmost to blight genius in its infancy; that which rises in spite of him he will not see; and then he complains of the decline of literature. In like manner, these cankers of society complain of human nature and society, when they have wilfully debarred themselves from all the good they contain, and done their utmost to blight their own happiness and that of all around them. Misanthropy is sometimes the product of disappointed benevolence; but it is more frequently the offspring of overweening and mortified vanity, quarrelling with the world for not being better treated than it deserves.

SCYTHROP.

[to Marionetta]

These remarks are rather uncharitable. There is great good in human nature, but it is at present ill-conditioned. Ardent spirits cannot but be dissatisfied with things as they are; and, according to their views of the probabilities of amelioration, they will rush into the extremes of either hope or despair—of which the first is enthusiasm, and the second misanthropy; but their sources in this case are the same, as the Severn and the Wye run in different directions, and both rise in Plinlimmon.

MARIONETTA.

"And there is salmon in both;"[19] for the resemblance is about as close as that between Macedon and Monmouth.

Chapter VIII

MARIONETTA observed the next day a remarkable perturbation in Scythrop, for which she could not imagine any probable cause. She was willing to believe at first that it had some transient and trifling source, and would pass off in a day or two; but, contrary to this expectation, it daily increased. She was well aware that Scythrop had a strong tendency to the love of mystery, for its own sake; that is to say, he would employ mystery to serve a purpose, but would first choose his purpose by its capability of mystery. He seemed now to have more mystery on his hands than the laws of the system allowed, and to wear his coat of darkness with an air of great discomfort. All her little playful arts lost by degrees much of their power either to irritate or to soothe; and the first perception of her diminished influence produced in her an immediate depression of spirits, and a consequent sadness of demeanour, that rendered her very interesting to Mr. Glowry; who, duly considering the improbability of accomplishing his wishes with respect to Miss Toobad (which improbability naturally increased in the diurnal ratio of that young lady's absence), began to reconcile himself by degrees to the idea of Marionetta being his daughter.

Marionetta made many ineffectual attempts to extract from Scythrop the secret of his mystery; and, in despair of drawing

[19] From *Henry V*, IV.vii, as is the following allusion.

it from himself, began to form hopes that she might find a clue
to it from Mr. Flosky, who was Scythrop's dearest friend, and
was more frequently than any other person admitted to his
solitary tower. Mr. Flosky, however, had ceased to be visible in
a morning. He was engaged in the composition of a dismal ballad; and, Marionetta's uneasiness overcoming her scruples of
decorum, she determined to seek him in the apartment which
he had chosen for his study. She tapped at the door, and at the
sound "Come in," entered the apartment. It was noon, and the
sun was shining in full splendour, much to the annoyance of
Mr. Flosky, who had obviated the inconvenience by closing the
shutters, and drawing the window-curtains. He was sitting at
his table by the light of a solitary candle, with a pen in one
hand, and a muffineer in the other, with which he occasionally
sprinkled salt on the wick, to make it burn blue. He sate with
"his eye in a fine frenzy rolling,"[1] and turned his inspired gaze
on Marionetta as if she had been the ghastly ladie of a magical
vision; then placed his hand before his eyes, with an appearance of manifest pain—shook his head—withdrew his hand—
rubbed his eyes, like a waking man—and said, in a tone of
ruefulness most jeremitaylorically pathetic, "To what am I to
attribute this very unexpected pleasure, my dear Miss O'Carroll?"

MARIONETTA.

I must apologise for intruding on you, Mr. Flosky; but the
interest which I—you—take in my cousin Scythrop——

MR. FLOSKY.

Pardon me, Miss O'Carroll; I do not take any interest in any
person or thing on the face of the earth; which sentiment, if
you analyze it, you will find to be the quintessence of the most
refined philanthropy.

MARIONETTA.

I will take it for granted that it is so, Mr. Flosky; I am not
conversant with metaphysical subtleties, but——

MR. FLOSKY.

Subtleties! my dear Miss O'Carroll. I am sorry to find you

[1] *A Midsummer Night's Dream,* V.i.

participating in the vulgar error of the *reading public,* to whom an unusual collocation of words, involving a juxtaposition of antiperistatical ideas, immediately suggests the notion of hyper-oxysophistical paradoxology.

MARIONETTA.

Indeed, Mr. Flosky, it suggests no such notion to me. I have sought you for the purpose of obtaining information.

MR. FLOSKY.

[*shaking his head*]

No one ever sought me for such a purpose before.

MARIONETTA.

I think, Mr. Flosky—that is, I believe—that is, I fancy—that is, I imagine——

MR. FLOSKY.

The τουτεστι, the *id est,* the *cioè,* the *c'est à dire,* the *that is,* my dear Miss O'Carroll, is not applicable in this case—if you will permit me to take the liberty of saying so. Think is not synonymous with believe—for belief, in many most important particulars, results from the total absence, the absolute negation of thought, and is thereby the sane and orthodox condition of mind; and thought and belief are both essentially different from fancy, and fancy, again, is distinct from imagination. This distinction between fancy and imagination is one of the most abstruse and important points of metaphysics. I have written seven hundred pages of promise to elucidate it, which promise I shall keep as faithfully as the bank will its promise to pay.[2]

MARIONETTA.

I assure you, Mr. Flosky, I care no more about metaphysics than I do about the bank; and, if you will condescend to talk to a simple girl in intelligible terms——

---

[2] Coleridge's distinction between the fancy and the imagination is both one of the most important, and one of the most debated, of all his critical theories. Chapter Thirteen of the *Biographia Literaria,* which begins as a discussion of the imagination, breaks off with the insertion by Coleridge of a fictitious "letter from a friend" imploring him to publish his remarks on the imagination separately, because they will run to several hundred pages. This Coleridge says he will do; but, as with other of his projected and announced major works, this one was never written. Peacock's mistrust of paper money (at that time issued by banks, not the government) appears throughout his works.

MR. FLOSKY.

Say not condescend! Know you not that you talk to the most humble of men, to one who has buckled on the armour of sanctity, and clothed himself with humility as with a garment?

MARIONETTA.

My cousin Scythrop has of late had an air of mystery about him, which gives me great uneasiness.

MR. FLOSKY.

That is strange: nothing is so becoming to a man as an air of mystery. Mystery is the very key-stone of all that is beautiful in poetry, all that is sacred in faith, and all that is recondite in transcendental psychology. I am writing a ballad which is all mystery; it is "such stuff as dreams are made of,"[3] and is, indeed, stuff made of a dream; for, last night I fell asleep as usual over my book, and had a vision of pure reason. I composed five hundred lines in my sleep;[4] so that, having had a dream of a ballad, I am now officiating as my own Peter Quince, and making a ballad of my dream, and it shall be called Bottom's Dream, because it has no bottom.[5]

MARIONETTA.

I see, Mr. Flosky, you think my intrusion unreasonable, and are inclined to punish it, by talking nonsense to me.

[*Mr. Flosky gave a start at the word nonsense, which almost overturned the table.*]

I assure you, I would not have intruded if I had not been very much interested in the question I wish to ask you.—

[*Mr. Flosky listened in sullen dignity.*]

—My cousin Scythrop seems to have some secret preying on his mind.—

[*Mr. Flosky was silent.*]

—He seems very unhappy—Mr. Flosky.—Perhaps you are acquainted with the cause.—

[*Mr. Flosky was still silent.*]

—I only wish to know—Mr. Flosky—if it is any thing—that

[3] *The Tempest,* IV.i. The line, frequently misquoted, ends with *on,* not *of.*

[4] Coleridge claimed that all of "Kubla Khan" had come to him in a dream.

[5] *A Midsummer Night's Dream,* IV.i.

could be remedied by any thing—that any one—of whom I
know any thing—could do.

MR. FLOSKY.

[*after a pause*]

There are various ways of getting at secrets. The most approved methods, as recommended both theoretically and prac-
tically in philosophical novels, are eavesdropping at key-holes,
picking the locks of chests and desks, peeping into letters, steam-
ing wafers,[6] and insinuating hot wire under sealing wax; none
of which methods I hold it lawful to practise.

MARIONETTA.

Surely, Mr. Flosky, you cannot suspect me of wishing to
adopt or encourage such base and contemptible arts.

MR. FLOSKY.

Yet are they recommended, and with well-strung reasons, by
writers of gravity and note, as simple and easy methods of
studying character, and gratifying that laudable curiosity which
aims at the knowledge of man.

MARIONETTA.

I am as ignorant of this morality which you do not approve,
as of the metaphysics which you do: I should be glad to know
by your means, what is the matter with my cousin; I do not like
to see him unhappy, and I suppose there is some reason for it.

MR. FLOSKY.

Now I should rather suppose there is no reason for it: it is
the fashion to be unhappy. To have a reason for being so would
be exceedingly common-place: to be so without any is the
province of genius: the art of being miserable for misery's sake,
has been brought to great perfection in our days; and the
ancient Odyssey, which held forth a shining example of the
endurance of real misfortune, will give place to a modern one,
setting out a more instructive picture of querulous impatience
under imaginary evils.

MARIONETTA.

Will you oblige me, Mr. Flosky, by giving me a plain answer
to a plain question?

6 Colored adhesive discs used for sealing letters.

MR. FLOSKY.

It is impossible, my dear Miss O'Carroll. I never gave a plain answer to a question in my life.

MARIONETTA.

Do you, or do you not, know what is the matter with my cousin?

MR. FLOSKY.

To say that I do not know, would be to say that I am ignorant of something; and God forbid, that a transcendental metaphysician, who has pure anticipated cognitions of every thing, and carries the whole science of geometry in his head without ever having looked into Euclid, should fall into so empirical an error as to declare himself ignorant of any thing: to say that I do know, would be to pretend to positive and circumstantial knowledge touching present matter of fact, which, when you consider the nature of evidence, and the various lights in which the same thing may be seen——

MARIONETTA.

I see, Mr. Flosky, that either you have no information, or are determined not to impart it; and I beg your pardon for having given you this unnecessary trouble.

MR. FLOSKY.

My dear Miss O'Carroll, it would have given me great pleasure to have said any thing that would have given you pleasure; but if any person living could make report of having obtained any information on any subject from Ferdinando Flosky, my transcendental reputation would be ruined for ever.

Chapter IX

SCYTHROP grew every day more reserved, mysterious, and *distrait;* and gradually lengthened the duration of his diurnal seclusions in his tower. Marionetta thought she perceived in all this very manifest symptoms of a warm love cooling.

It was seldom that she found herself alone with him in the morning, and, on these occasions, if she was silent in the hope of his speaking first, not a syllable would he utter; if she spoke to him indirectly, he assented monosyllabically; if she questioned him, his answers were brief, constrained, and evasive. Still, though her spirits were depressed, her playfulness had not so totally forsaken her, but that it illuminated at intervals the gloom of Nightmare Abbey; and if, on any occasion, she observed in Scythrop tokens of unextinguished or returning passion, her love of tormenting her lover immediately got the better both of her grief and her sympathy, though not of her curiosity, which Scythrop seemed determined not to satisfy. This playfulness, however, was in a great measure artificial, and usually vanished with the irritable Strephon,[1] to whose annoyance it had been exerted. The Genius Loci, the *tutela*[2] of Nightmare Abbey, the spirit of black melancholy, began to set his seal on her pallescent countenance. Scythrop perceived the change, found his tender sympathies awakened, and did his utmost to comfort the afflicted damsel, assuring her that his seeming inattention had only proceeded from his being involved in a profound meditation on a very hopeful scheme for the regeneration of human society. Marionetta called him ungrateful, cruel, coldhearted, and accompanied her reproaches with many sobs and tears: poor Scythrop growing every moment more soft and submissive—till, at length, he threw himself at her feet, and declared that no competition of beauty, however dazzling, genius, however transcendent, talents, however cultivated, or philosophy, however enlightened, should ever make him renounce his divine Marionetta.

"Competition!" thought Marionetta, and suddenly, with an air of the most freezing indifference, she said, "You are perfectly at liberty, sir, to do as you please; I beg you will follow your own plans, without any reference to me."

Scythrop was confounded. What was become of all her pas-

---

[1] Stock name for a languishing rustic lover; from Sidney's *Arcadia* (1590).

[2] Respectively, the "pervading spirit of the place," and the "guardian spirit."

sion and her tears? Still kneeling, he kissed her hand with rueful timidity, and said, in most pathetic accents, "Do you not love me, Marionetta?"

"No," said Marionetta, with a look of cold composure: "No." Scythrop still looked up incredulously. "No, I tell you."

"Oh! very well, madam," said Scythrop, rising, "if that is the case, there are those in the world——"

"To be sure there are, sir;—and do you suppose I do not see through your designs, you ungenerous monster?"

"My designs? Marionetta!"

"Yes, your designs, Scythrop. You have come here to cast me off, and artfully contrive that it should appear to be my doing, and not yours, thinking to quiet your tender conscience with this pitiful stratagem. But do not suppose that you are of so much consequence to me: do not suppose it: you are of no consequence to me at all—none at all: therefore, leave me: I renounce you: leave me; why do you not leave me?"

Scythrop endeavoured to remonstrate, but without success. She reiterated her injunctions to him to leave her, till, in the simplicity of his spirit, he was preparing to comply. When he had nearly reached the door, Marionetta said, "Farewell." Scythrop looked back. "Farewell, Scythrop," she repeated, "you will never see me again."

"Never see you again, Marionetta?"

"I shall go from hence to-morrow, perhaps to-day; and before we meet again, one of us will be married, and we might as well be dead, you know, Scythrop."

The sudden change of her voice in the last few words, and the burst of tears that accompanied them, acted like electricity on the tender-hearted youth; and, in another instant, a complete reconciliation was accomplished without the intervention of words.

There are, indeed, some learned casuists,[3] who maintain that love has no language, and that all the misunderstandings and dissensions of lovers arise from the fatal habit of employing

[3] Those who pronounce judgment upon matters of conscience, duty, or conduct; used here in its (usual) deprecatory sense.

words on a subject to which words are inapplicable; that love, beginning with looks, that is to say, with the physiognomical expression of congenial mental dispositions, tends through a regular gradation of signs and symbols of affection, to that consummation which is most devoutly to be wished;[4] and that it neither is necessary that there should be, nor probable that there would be, a single word spoken from first to last between two sympathetic spirits, were it not that the arbitrary institutions of society have raised, at every step of this very simple process, so many complicated impediments and barriers in the shape of settlements and ceremonies, parents and guardians, lawyers, Jew-brokers, and parsons, that many an adventurous knight (who, in order to obtain the conquest of the Hesperian fruit,[5] is obliged to fight his way through all these monsters,) is either repulsed at the onset, or vanquished before the achievement of his enterprise: and such a quantity of unnatural talking is rendered inevitably necessary through all the stages of the progression, that the tender and volatile spirit of love often takes flight on the pinions of some of the επεα πτεροεντα, or *winged words,*[6] which are pressed into his service in despite of himself.

At this conjuncture, Mr. Glowry entered, and sitting down near them, said, "I see how it is; and, as we are all sure to be miserable do what we may, there is no need of taking pains to make one another more so; therefore, with God's blessing and mine, there"—joining their hands as he spoke.

Scythrop was not exactly prepared for this decisive step; but he could only stammer out, "Really, sir, you are too good;" and Mr. Glowry departed to bring Mr. Hilary to ratify the act.

Now, whatever truth there may be in the theory of love and language, of which we have so recently spoken, certain it is, that during Mr. Glowry's absence, which lasted half an hour, not a single word was said by either Scythrop or Marionetta.

---

[4] *Hamlet,* III.i.

[5] Golden apples, a wedding gift to Hera and Zeus, guarded by a fearsome dragon. Hercules obtained them as one of his labors.

[6] An epithet frequently used by Homer to describe the long, dignified speeches of his characters. Peacock's use of the mock heroic here is consistent with his serio-comic attitude toward Scythrop and exemplifies how Peacock uses erudition for satiric purposes.

Doubtless, thought Scythrop, this is one of my golden candle-sticks. "I have constructed," said he, "in this tower, an entrance to a small suite of unknown apartments in the main building, which I defy any creature living to detect. If you would like to remain there a day or two, till I can find you a more suitable concealment, you may rely on the honour of a transcendental eleutherarch."

"I rely on myself," said the lady. "I act as I please, go where I please, and let the world say what it will. I am rich enough to set it at defiance. It is the tyrant of the poor and the feeble, but the slave of those who are above the reach of its injury."

Scythrop ventured to inquire the name of his fair *protégée.* "What is a name?" said the lady: "any name will serve the purpose of distinction. Call me Stella.[4] I see by your looks," she added, "that you think all this very strange. When you know me better, your surprise will cease. I submit not to be an accomplice in my sex's slavery. I am, like yourself, a lover of freedom, and I carry my theory into practice. *They alone are subject to blind authority who have no reliance on their own strength.*"[5]

Stella took possession of the recondite apartments. Scythrop intended to find her another asylum; but from day to day he postponed his intention, and by degrees forgot it. The young lady reminded him of it from day to day, till she also forgot it. Scythrop was anxious to learn her history; but she would add nothing to what she had already communicated, that she was shunning an atrocious persecution. Scythrop thought of Lord C. and the Alien Act, and said, "As you will not tell your name, I suppose it is in the green bag." Stella, not understanding what he meant, was silent; and Scythrop, translating silence into acquiescence, concluded that he was sheltering an *illuminée*

[4] Probably an allusion to Goethe's *Stella* (1775). Fernando, the hero of this play, vacillates between two women, the passionate Stella and his more reserved wife Cäcilie—a close parallel to the situations of both Scythrop and Shelley. In the play, Cäcilie, in a burst of self-sacrifice, decides that Fernando should have Stella and remains in the household as his "friend," in much the same capacity as Shelley had invited his wife Harriet to join himself and Mary Godwin.

[5] Mary Wollstonecraft (Mary Shelley's mother), *A Vindication of the Rights of Women,* Ch. V, section 4.

whom Lord S. suspected of an intention to take the Tower, and set fire to the Bank: exploits, at least, as likely to be accomplished by the hands and eyes of a young beauty, as by a drunken cobbler and doctor, armed with a pamphlet and an old stocking.[6]

Stella, in her conversations with Scythrop, displayed a highly cultivated and energetic mind, full of impassioned schemes of liberty, and impatience of masculine usurpation. She had a lively sense of all the oppressions that are done under the sun;[7] and the vivid pictures which her imagination presented to her of the numberless scenes of injustice and misery which are being acted at every moment in every part of the inhabited world, gave an habitual seriousness to her physiognomy, that made it seem as if a smile had never once hovered on her lips. She was intimately conversant with the German language and literature; and Scythrop listened with delight to her repetitions of her favourite passages from Schiller and Göethe, and to her encomiums on the sublime Spartacus Weishaupt, the immortal founder of the sect of the Illuminati.[8] Scythrop found that his soul had a greater capacity of love than the image of Marionetta had filled. The form of Stella took possession of every vacant corner of the cavity, and by degrees displaced that of Marionetta from many of the outworks of the citadel; though the latter still held possession of the *keep*.[9] He judged, from his new friend calling herself Stella, that, if it were not her real name, she was an admirer of the principles of the German play from which she had taken it, and took an opportunity of leading

[6] Lords C. and S. are Castlereagh (Foreign Secretary) and Sidworth (Home Secretary). Both were identified with repressive government policies in the period of unrest following Waterloo. The Alien Act (1816) provided for the deportation of suspect aliens. The green bag symbolizes the Attorney General's (i.e., prosecutor's) brief case. *Illuminée:* agitator; see note 8. The cobbler and doctor were one Carter, a cobbler, and Watson, a surgeon, agitators who were arrested in 1816 for leading a riotous mob which at one point seemed bent on attacking the Tower of London.

[7] Ecclesiastes 4:1.

[8] A secret society founded in Ingoldstadt in 1776 by Adam "Spartacus" Weishaupt. The order favored republican free thought and sought to replace Christianity with a religion of reason.

[9] The strongest, innermost structure in a medieval castle.

the conversation to that subject; but to his great surprise, the lady spoke very ardently of the singleness and exclusiveness of love, and declared that the reign of affection was one and indivisible; that it might be transferred, but could not be participated. "If I ever love," said she, "I shall do so without limit or restriction. I shall hold all difficulties light, all sacrifices cheap, all obstacles gossamer. But for love so total, I shall claim a return as absolute. I will have no rival: whether more or less favoured will be of little moment. I will be neither first nor second—I will be alone. The heart which I shall possess I will possess entirely, or entirely renounce."

Scythrop did not dare to mention the name of Marionetta; he trembled lest some unlucky accident should reveal it to Stella, though he scarcely knew what result to wish or anticipate, and lived in the double fever of a perpetual dilemma. He could not dissemble to himself that he was in love, at the same time, with two damsels of minds and habits as remote as the antipodes. The scale of predilection always inclined to the fair one who happened to be present; but the absent was never effectually outweighed, though the degrees of exaltation and depression varied according to accidental variations in the outward and visible signs of the inward and spiritual graces of his respective charmers. Passing and repassing several times a day from the company of the one to that of the other, he was like a shuttle-cock between two battle-dores, changing its direction as rapidly as the oscillations of a pendulum, receiving many a hard knock on the cork of a sensitive heart, and flying from point to point on the feathers of a super-sublimated head. This was an awful state of things. He had now as much mystery about him as any romantic transcendentalist or transcendental romancer could desire. He had his esoterical and his exoterical love. He could not endure the thought of losing either of them, but he trembled when he imagined the possibility that some fatal discovery might deprive him of both. The old proverb concerning two strings to a bow gave him some gleams of comfort; but that concerning two stools occurred to him more frequently, and covered his forehead with a cold perspiration.[10] With Stella, he

[10] *Two springs:* i.e., one can use the second if the first one breaks.

could indulge freely in all his romantic and philosophical visions. He could build castles in the air, and she would pile towers and turrets on the imaginary edifices. With Marionetta it was otherwise: she knew nothing of the world and society beyond the sphere of her own experience. Her life was all music and sunshine, and she wondered what any one could see to complain of in such a pleasant state of things. She loved Scythrop, she hardly knew why; indeed she was not always sure that she loved him at all: she felt her fondness increase or diminish in an inverse ratio to his. When she had manœuvred him into a fever of passionate love, she often felt and always assumed indifference: if she found that her coldness was contagious, and that Scythrop either was, or pretended to be, as indifferent as herself, she would become doubly kind, and raise him again to that elevation from which she had previously thrown him down. Thus, when his love was flowing, hers was ebbing: when his was ebbing, hers was flowing. Now and then there were moments of level tide, when reciprocal affection seemed to promise imperturbable harmony; but Scythrop could scarcely resign his spirit to the pleasing illusion, before the pinnace of the lover's affections was caught in some eddy of the lady's caprice, and he was whirled away from the shore of his hopes, without rudder or compass, into an ocean of mists and storms. It resulted, from this system of conduct, that all that passed between Scythrop and Marionetta consisted in making and unmaking love. He had no opportunity to take measure of her understanding by conversations on general subjects, and on his favourite designs; and, being left in this respect to the exercise of indefinite conjecture, he took it for granted, as most lovers would do in similar circumstances, that she had great natural talents, which she wasted at present on trifles: but coquetry would end with marriage, and leave room for philosophy to exert its influence on her mind. Stella had no coquetry, no disguise: she was an enthusiast in subjects of general interest; and her conduct to Scythrop was always uniform, or rather showed a regular progression of partiality which seemed fast ripening into love.

Two stools: i.e., he who tries to sit on two stools at the same time falls to the ground.

Chapter XI

SCYTHROP, attending one day the summons to dinner, found in the drawing-room his friend Mr. Cypress the poet,[1] whom he had known at college, and who was a great favourite of Mr. Glowry. Mr. Cypress said, he was on the point of leaving England, but could not think of doing so without a farewell-look at Nightmare Abbey and his respected friends, the moody Mr. Glowry and the mysterious Mr. Scythrop, the sublime Mr. Flosky and the pathetic Mr. Listless; to all of whom, and the morbid hospitality of the melancholy dwelling in which they were then assembled, he assured them he should always look back with as much affection as his lacerated spirit could feel for any thing. The sympathetic condolence of their respective replies was cut short by Raven's announcement of "dinner on table."

The conversation that took place when the wine was in circulation, and the ladies were withdrawn, we shall report with our usual scrupulous fidelity.

MR. GLOWRY.

You are leaving England, Mr. Cypress. There is a delightful melancholy in saying farewell to an old acquaintance, when the chances are twenty to one against ever meeting again. A smiling bumper to a sad parting, and let us all be unhappy together.

MR. CYPRESS.

[filling a bumper]

This is the only social habit that the disappointed spirit never unlearns.

THE REVEREND MR. LARYNX.

[filling]

It is the only piece of academical learning that the finished educatee retains.

---

[1] Lord Byron. The cypress tree is a symbol of mourning and of gloom generally.

MR. FLOSKY.

[*filling*]

It is the only objective fact which the sceptic can realise.

SCYTHROP.

[*filling*]

It is the only styptic for a bleeding heart.

THE HONOURARLE MR. LISTLESS.

[*filling*]

It is the only trouble that is very well worth taking.

MR. ASTERIAS.

[*filling*]

It is the only key of conversational truth.

MR. TOOBAD.

[*filling*]

It is the only antidote to the great wrath of the devil.

MR. HILARY.

[*filling*]

It is the only symbol of perfect life. The inscription "HIC NON BIBITUR" will suit nothing but a tombstone.[2]

MR. GLOWRY.

You will see many fine old ruins, Mr. Cypress; crumbling pillars, and mossy walls—many a one-legged Venus and headless Minerva—many a Neptune buried in sand—many a Jupiter turned topsy-turvy—many a perforated Bacchus doing duty as a water-pipe—many reminiscences of the ancient world, which I hope was better worth living in than the modern; though, for myself, I care not a straw more for one than the other, and would not go twenty miles to see any thing that either could show.

MR. CYPRESS.

It is something to seek, Mr. Glowry. The mind is restless, and must persist in seeking, though to find is to be disappointed. Do you feel no aspirations towards the countries of Socrates and Cicero? No wish to wander among the venerable remains of the greatness that has passed for ever?

---

[2] "No drinkers here"; Gargantua's genealogy was found in a tomb inscribed *Hic Bibitur*. See Rabelais, Book I, Ch. 1.

MR. GLOWRY.

Not a grain.

SCYTHROP.

It is, indeed, much the same as if a lover should dig up the buried form of his mistress, and gaze upon relics which are any thing but herself, to wander among a few mouldy ruins, that are only imperfect indexes to lost volumes of glory, and meet at every step the more melancholy ruins of human nature—a degenerate race of stupid and shrivelled slaves, grovelling in the lowest depths of servility and superstition.[3]

THE HONOURARLE MR. LISTLESS.

It is the fashion to go abroad. I have thought of it myself, but am hardly equal to the exertion. To be sure, a little eccentricity and originality are allowable in some cases; and the most eccentric and original of all characters is an Englishman who stays at home.

SCYTHROP.

I should have no pleasure in visiting countries that are past all hope of regeneration. There is great hope of our own; and it seems to me that an Englishman, who, either by his station in society, or by his genius, or (as in your instance, Mr. Cypress,) by both, has the power of essentially serving his country in its arduous struggle with its domestic enemies, yet forsakes his country, which is still so rich in hope, to dwell in others which are only fertile in the ruins of memory, does what none of those ancients, whose fragmentary memorials you venerate, would have done in similar circumstances.

MR. CYPRESS.

Sir, I have quarrelled with my wife; and a man who has quarrelled with his wife is absolved from all duty to his country.[4] I have written an ode to tell the people as much, and they may take it as they list.

SCYTHROP.

Do you suppose, if Brutus had quarrelled with his wife, he

---

[3] Shelley, writing to Peacock from Milan, 20 April 1818: "The men are hardly men, they look a tribe of stupid & shrivelled slaves . . . ."

[4] As a result of the notoriety and scandal surrounding his separation from his wife, Byron had left England in 1816, never to return.

would have given it as a reason to Cassius for having nothing to do with his enterprise? Or would Cassius have been satisfied with such an excuse?

MR. FLOSKY.

Brutus was a senator; so is our dear friend:[5] but the cases are different. Brutus had some hope of political good: Mr. Cypress has none. How should he, after what we have seen in France?[6]

SCYTHROP.

A Frenchman is born in harness, ready saddled, bitted, and bridled, for any tyrant to ride. He will fawn under his rider one moment, and throw him and kick him to death the next; but another adventurer springs on his back, and by dint of whip and spur on he goes as before. We may, without much vanity, hope better of ourselves.

MR. CYPRESS.

I have no hope for myself or for others. Our life is a false nature; it is not in the harmony of things; it is an all-blasting upas,[7] whose root is earth, and whose leaves are the skies which rain their poison-dews upon mankind. We wither from our youth; we gasp with unslaked thirst for unattainable good; lured from the first to the last by phantoms—love, fame, ambition, avarice—all idle, and all ill—one meteor of many names, that vanishes in the smoke of death.[8]

MR. FLOSKY.

A most delightful speech, Mr. Cypress. A most amiable and instructive philosophy. You have only to impress its truth on the minds of all living men, and life will then, indeed, be the desert and the solitude; and I must do you, myself, and our mutual friends, the justice to observe, that let society only give fair play at one and the same time, as I flatter myself it is inclined to do, to your system of morals, and my system of

---

[5] As a peer, Byron was automatically a member of the House of Lords.

[6] The bright promise of the French Revolution was followed by the Reign of Terror and then by the rise of Napoleon, considered by many of Peacock's countrymen a ruthless tyrant.

[7] The upas is a legendary tree, supposedly grown in Java, so poisonous as to destroy all animal and vegetable life in a fifteen-mile area.

[8] *Childe Harold,* canto 4. cxxiv, cxxvi. [P]

metaphysics, and Scythrop's system of politics, and Mr. Listless's system of manners, and Mr. Toobad's system of religion, and the result will be as fine a mental chaos as even the immortal Kant himself could ever have hoped to see; in the prospect of which I rejoice.

MR. HILARY.

"Certainly, ancient, it is not a thing to rejoice at:"[9] I am one of those who cannot see the good that is to result from all this mystifying and blue-devilling of society. The contrast it presents to the cheerful and solid wisdom of antiquity is too forcible not to strike any one who has the least knowledge of classical literature. To represent vice and misery as the necessary accompaniments of genius, is as mischievous as it is false, and the feeling is as unclassical as the language in which it is usually expressed.

MR. TOOBAD.

It is our calamity. The devil has come among us, and has begun by taking possession of all the cleverest fellows. Yet, forsooth, this is the enlightened age. Marry, how? Did our ancestors go peeping about with dark lanterns, and do we walk at our ease in broad sunshine? Where is the manifestation of our light? By what symptoms do you recognise it? What are its signs, its tokens, its symptoms, its symbols, its categories, its conditions? What is it, and why? How, where, when is it to be seen, felt, and understood? What do we see by it which our ancestors saw not, and which at the same time is worth seeing? We see a hundred men hanged, where they saw one. We see five hundred transported,[10] where they saw one. We see five thousand in the workhouse, where they saw one. We see scores of Bible Societies,[11] where they saw none. We see paper, where

[9] *Henry V*, III.vi.

[10] For many years those convicted of serious crimes had been sent (transported) to overseas penal colonies; both Georgia and Australia were originally settled in this manner.

[11] Such as the British and Foreign Bible Society, whose primary aim was the distribution of free Bibles at home and abroad. Founded in 1804 by the Methodists and Anglican Evangelicals, it was frowned upon by the High (Tory) Churchmen because it helped promulgate the views of the fundamentalist dissenting sects. By 1814 every county in England had its branch of the Society.

they saw gold. We see men in stays, where they saw men in armour. We see painted faces, where they saw healthy ones. We see children perishing in manufactories, where they saw them flourishing in the fields. We see prisons, where they saw castles. We see masters, where they saw representatives. In short they saw true men, where we see false knaves. They saw Milton, and we see Mr. Sackbut.

MR. FLOSKY.

The false knave, sir, is my honest friend; therefore, I beseech you, let him be countenanced. God forbid but a knave should have some countenance at his friend's request.[12]

MR. TOOBAD.

"Good men and true" was their common term, like the καλος κάγαθος[13] of the Athenians. It is so long since men have been either good or true, that it is to be questioned which is most obsolete, the fact or the phraseology.

MR. CYPRESS.

There is no worth nor beauty but in the mind's idea. Love sows the wind and reaps the whirlwind.[14] Confusion, thrice confounded, is the portion of him who rests even for an instant on that most brittle of reeds—the affection of a human being. The sum of our social destiny is to inflict or to endure.[15]

MR. HILARY.

Rather to bear and forbear, Mr. Cypress—a maxim which you perhaps despise. Ideal beauty is not the mind's creation: it is real beauty, refined and purified in the mind's alembic,[16] from the alloy which always more or less accompanies it in our mixed and imperfect nature. But still the gold exists in a very ample degree. To expect too much is a disease in the expectant, for which human nature is not responsible; and, in the common name of humanity, I protest against these false and mischievous ravings. To rail against humanity for not being abstract perfection, and against human love for not realising all the

---

12 *Henry IV, Part II,* V.i.
13 "Fair and good."
14 *Childe Harold,* canto 4. cxxiii. [P]
15 *Ibid.* canto 3. lxxi. [P]
16 An apparatus formerly used in distilling.

splendid visions of the poets of chivalry, is to rail at the summer for not being all sunshine, and at the rose for not being always in bloom.

MR. CYPRESS.

Human love! Love is not an inhabitant of the earth. We worship him as the Athenians did their unknown God: but broken hearts are the martyrs of his faith, and the eye shall never see the form which phantasy paints, and which passion pursues through paths of delusive beauty, among flowers whose odours are agonies, and trees whose gums are poison.[17]

MR. HILARY.

You talk like a Rosicrusian, who will love nothing but a sylph, who does not believe in the existence of a sylph, and who yet quarrels with the whole universe for not containing a sylph.[18]

MR. CYPRESS.

The mind is diseased of its own beauty, and fevers into false creation. The forms which the sculptor's soul has seized exist only in himself.[19]

MR. FLOSKY.

Permit me to discept. They are the mediums of common forms combined and arranged into a common standard. The ideal beauty of the Helen of Zeuxis was the combined medium of the real beauty of the virgins of Crotona.[20]

MR. HILARY.

But to make ideal beauty the shadow in the water, and, like the dog in the fable, to throw away the substance in catching at the shadow, is scarcely the characteristic of wisdom, whatever it may be of genius. To reconcile man as he is to the world as it

---

[17] *Childe Harold,* canto 4. cxxi, cxxxvi. [P]

[18] Rosicrucians were adherents of a metaphysical and occultist philosophy commonly considered mystical to the point of absurdity. Sylphs are spirits supposed to inhabit the air; see Pope's *Rape of the Lock.*

[19] *Childe Harold,* canto 4. cxxii. [P]

[20] Zeuxis (fl. ca. 400 B.C.) was one of the most famous of ancient Greek painters; his "Helen" is considered his masterpiece. Crotona was a powerful city at the toe of the Italian boot, the home of Pythagoras (fl. 530 B.C.), whose school of philosophy was so successful that the citizens became known for their decorous morality.

is, to preserve and improve all that is good, and destroy or alleviate all that is evil, in physical and moral nature—have been the hope and aim of the greatest teachers and ornaments of our species. I will say, too, that the highest wisdom and the highest genius have been invariably accompanied with cheerfulness. We have sufficient proofs on record that Shakspeare and Socrates were the most festive of companions. But now the little wisdom and genius we have seem to be entering into a conspiracy against cheerfulness.

MR. TOOBAD.

How can we be cheerful with the devil among us?

THE HONOURARLE MR. LISTLESS.

How can we be cheerful when our nerves are shattered?

MR. FLOSKY.

How can we be cheerful when we are surrounded by a *reading public,* that is growing too wise for its betters?

SCYTHROP.

How can we be cheerful when our great general designs are crossed every moment by our little particular passions?

MR. CYPRESS.

How can we be cheerful in the midst of disappointment and despair?

MR. GLOWRY.

Let us all be unhappy together.

MR. HILARY.

Let us sing a catch.

MR. GLOWRY.

No: a nice tragical ballad. The Norfolk Tragedy to the tune of the Hundredth Psalm.[21]

MR. HILARY.

I say a catch.

MR. GLOWRY.

I say no. A song from Mr. Cypress.

---

[21] "The Children in the Wood," a gloomy ballad written ca. 1595. *Hundredth Psalm:* "Old Hundredth" ("All People Who on Earth Do Dwell"), a hymn tune dating from 1551, used for the doxology in Protestant churches.

ALL.

A song from Mr. Cypress.

MR. CYPRESS.

[*sung*—]

There is a fever of the spirit,
    The brand of Cain's unresting doom,
Which in the lone dark souls that bear it
    Glows like the lamp in Tullia's tomb:
Unlike that lamp, its subtle fire
    Burns, blasts, consumes its cell, the heart,
Till, one by one, hope, joy, desire,
    Like dreams of shadowy smoke depart.

When hope, love, life itself, are only
    Dust—spectral memories—dead and cold—
The unfed fire burns bright and lonely,
    Like that undying lamp of old:
And by that drear illumination,
    Till time its clay-built home has rent,
Thought broods on feeling's desolation—
    The soul is its own monument.

MR. GLOWRY.

Admirable. Let us all be unhappy together.

MR. HILARY.

Now, I say again, a catch.

THE REVEREND MR. LARYNX.

I am for you.

MR. HILARY.

"Seamen three."

THE REVEREND MR. LARYNX.

Agreed. I'll be Harry Gill, with the voice of three.[22] Begin.

[22] Wordsworth, "Goody Blake and Harry Gill," l. 20.

MR. HILARY AND THE REVEREND MR. LARYNX.

> Seamen three! What men be ye?
> Gotham's three wise men we be.[23]
> Whither in your bowl so free?
> To rake the moon from out the sea.
> The bowl goes trim. The moon doth shine.
> And our ballast is old wine;
> And your ballast is old wine.
>
> Who art thou, so fast adrift?
> I am he they call Old Care.
> Here on board we will thee lift.
> No: I may not enter there.
> Wherefore so? 'Tis Jove's decree,
> In a bowl Care may not be;
> In a bowl Care may not be.
>
> Fear ye not the waves that roll?
> No: in charmed bowl we swim.
> What the charm that floats the bowl?
> Water may not pass the brim.
> The bowl goes trim. The moon doth shine.
> And our ballast is old wine;
> And your ballast is old wine.

This catch was so well executed by the spirit and science of
Mr. Hilary, and the deep tri-une[24] voice of the reverend gentleman, that the whole party, in spite of themselves, caught the
contagion, and joined in chorus at the conclusion, each raising
a bumper to his lips:

> The bowl goes trim: the moon doth shine:
> And our ballast is old wine.

[23] Perhaps an allusion to a tale found in the *Hundred Merry Tales*
(1526). The foolishness of the people of Gotham, England, was proverbial.
[24] Three in one; often used in reference to the Godhead.

Mr. Cypress, having his ballast on board, stepped, the same evening, into his bowl, or travelling chariot, and departed to rake seas and rivers, lakes and canals, for the moon of ideal beauty.

Chapter XII

IT WAS the custom of the Honourable Mr. Listless, on adjourning from the bottle to the ladies, to retire for a few moments to make a second toilette, that he might present himself in becoming taste. Fatout, attending as usual, appeared with a countenance of great dismay, and informed his master that he had just ascertained that the abbey was haunted. Mrs. Hilary's *gentlewoman,* for whom Fatout had lately conceived a *tendresse,* had been, as she expressed it, "fritted out of her seventeen senses" the preceding night, as she was retiring to her bedchamber, by a ghastly figure which she had met stalking along one of the galleries, wrapped in a white shroud, with a bloody turban on its head. She had fainted away with fear; and, when she recovered, she found herself in the dark, and the figure was gone. *"Sacre—cochon—bleu!"*[1] exclaimed Fatout, giving very deliberate emphasis to every portion of his terrible oath—"I vould not meet de *revenant,* de ghost—*non*—not for all de *bowl-de-ponch* in de vorld."

"Fatout," said the Honourable Mr. Listless, "did I ever see a ghost?"

"Jamais, monsieur, never."

"Then I hope I never shall, for, in the present shattered state of my nerves, I am afraid it would be too much for me. There—loosen the lace of my stays a little, for really this plebeian practice of eating—Not too loose—consider my shape."

[1] "Confound the beastly thing!"

That will do. And I desire that you bring me no more stories of ghosts; for, though I do not believe in such things, yet, when one is awake in the night, one is apt, if one thinks of them, to have fancies that give one a kind of a chill, particularly if one opens one's eyes suddenly on one's dressing gown, hanging in the moonlight, between the bed and the window."

The Honourable Mr. Listless, though he had prohibited Fatout from bringing him any more stories of ghosts, could not help thinking of that which Fatout had already brought; and, as it was uppermost in his mind, when he descended to the tea and coffee cups, and the rest of the company in the library, he almost involuntarily asked Mr. Flosky, whom he looked up to as a most oraculous personage, whether any story of any ghost that had ever appeared to any one, was entitled to any degree of belief?

MR. FLOSKY.

By far the greater number, to a very great degree.

THE HONOURARLE MR. LISTLESS.

Really, that is very alarming!

MR. FLOSKY.

Sunt geminæ somni portæ.[2] There are two gates through which ghosts find their way to the upper air: fraud and self-delusion. In the latter case, a ghost is a *deceptio visûs,* an ocular spectrum, an idea with the force of a sensation. I have seen many ghosts myself. I dare say there are few in this company who have not seen a ghost.

THE HONOURARLE MR. LISTLESS.

I am happy to say, I never have, for one.

THE REVEREND MR. LARYNX.

We have such high authority for ghosts, that it is rank scepticism to disbelieve them. Job saw a ghost, which came for the express purpose of asking a question, and did not wait for an answer.[3]

THE HONOURABLE MR. LISTLESS.

Because Job was too frightened to give one.

[2] "There are twin gates of sleep." Virgil, *Aeneid,* VI.893.
[3] Peacock may be referring to the dream of Eliphaz in Job 4:15–21.

THE REVEREND MR. LARYNX.

Spectres appeared to the Egyptians during the darkness with which Moses covered Egypt. The witch of Endor raised the ghost of Samuel. Moses and Elias appeared on Mount Tabor. An evil spirit was sent into the army of Sennacherib, and exterminated it in a single night.[4]

MR. TOOBAD.

Saying, The devil is come among you, having great wrath.

MR. FLOSKY.

Saint Macarius interrogated a skull, which was found in the desert, and made it relate, in presence of several witnesses, what was going forward in hell. Saint Martin of Tours, being jealous of a pretended martyr, who was the rival saint of his neighbourhood, called up his ghost, and made him confess that he was damned. Saint Germain, being on his travels, turned out of an inn a large party of ghosts, who had every night taken possession of the *table d'hôte,* and consumed a copious supper.[5]

MR. HILARY.

Jolly ghosts, and no doubt all friars. A similar party took possession of the cellar of M. Swebach, the painter, in Paris, drank his wine, and threw the empty bottles at his head.[6]

THE REVEREND MR. LARYNX.

An atrocious act.

MR. FLOSKY.

Pausanias relates, that the neighing of horses and the tumult of combatants were heard every night on the field of Marathon: that those who went purposely to hear these sounds suffered severely for their curiosity; but those who heard them by accident passed with impunity.[7]

[4] See respectively, Wisdom of Solomon 17:1–18:4; I Samuel 28:11–20; Mark 9:4 and Luke 9:30; II Kings 19:35 and Isaiah 37:36.

[5] Respectively St. Macarius of Alexandria (died ca. 394), Egyptian ascetic, monk, and priest; St. Martin of Tours (316–397), monk, Bishop of Tours, and patron saint of France; St. Germain (ca. 378–448), Bishop of Auxerre, whose travels on Papal business took him to England in 429 and 447.

[6] Probably Jacques Francois Joseph Swebach de Fontaine (1769–1823), known for his paintings of military scenes.

[7] *Pausanias,* I.32.¶4.

THE REVEREND MR. LARYNX.

I once saw a ghost myself, in my study, which is the last place where any one but a ghost would look for me. I had not been into it for three months, and was going to consult Tillotson,[8] when, on opening the door, I saw a venerable figure in a flannel dressing gown, sitting in my armchair, and reading my Jeremy Taylor. It vanished in a moment, and so did I; and what it was or what it wanted I have never been able to ascertain.

MR. FLOSKY.

It was an idea with the force of a sensation. It is seldom that ghosts appeal to two senses at once; but, when I was in Devonshire, the following story was well attested to me. A young woman, whose lover was at sea, returning one evening over some solitary fields, saw her lover sitting on a stile over which she was to pass. Her first emotions were surprise and joy, but there was a paleness and seriousness in his face that made them give place to alarm. She advanced towards him, and he said to her, in a solemn voice, "The eye that hath seen me shall see me no more. Thine eye is upon me, but I am not." And with these words he vanished; and on that very day and hour, as it afterwards appeared, he had perished by shipwreck.

The whole party now drew round in a circle, and each related some ghostly anecdote, heedless of the flight of time, till, in a pause of the conversation, they heard the hollow tongue of midnight sounding twelve.[9]

MR. HILARY.

All these anecdotes admit of solution on psychological principles. It is more easy for a soldier, a philosopher, or even a saint, to be frightened at his own shadow, than for a dead man to come out of his grave. Medical writers cite a thousand singular examples of the force of imagination. Persons of feeble, nervous, melancholy temperament, exhausted by fever, by labour, or by spare diet, will readily conjure up, in the magic ring of their own phantasy, spectres, gorgons, chimæras, and

---

[8] John Tillotson (1630–1694), whose sermons were often used as models.

[9] *A Midsummer Night's Dream,* V.i.

all the objects of their hatred and their love. We are most of us like Don Quixote, to whom a windmill was a giant, and Dulcinea a magnificent princess:[10] all more or less the dupes of our own imagination, though we do not all go so far as to see ghosts, or to fancy ourselves pipkins[11] and teapots.

MR. FLOSKY.

I can safely say I have seen too many ghosts myself to believe in their external existence.[12] I have seen all kinds of ghosts: black spirits and white, red spirits and grey. Some in the shapes of venerable old men, who have met me in my rambles at noon; some of beautiful young women, who have peeped through my curtains at midnight.

THE HONOURABLE MR. LISTLESS.

And have proved, I doubt not, "palpable to feeling as to sight."[13]

MR. FLOSKY.

By no means, sir. You reflect upon my purity. Myself and my friends, particularly my friend Mr. Sackbut, are famous for our purity. No, sir, genuine untangible ghosts. I live in a world of ghosts. I see a ghost at this moment.

Mr. Flosky fixed his eyes on a door at the farther end of the library. The company looked in the same direction. The door silently opened, and a ghastly figure, shrouded in white drapery, with the semblance of a bloody turban on its head, entered and stalked slowly up the apartment. Mr. Flosky, familiar as he was with ghosts, was not prepared for this apparition, and made the best of his way out at the opposite door. Mrs. Hilary and Marionetta followed, screaming. The Honourable Mr. Listless, by two turns of his body, rolled first off the sofa and then under it. The Reverend Mr. Larynx leaped up and

---

[10] In Cervantes's *Don Quixote,* a satire on chivalry, the delightfully mad Don imagines a country wench of his acquaintance to be a great lady whom he refers to as Dulcinea. His famous combat with the windmills occurs in Part I, Ch. 8.

[11] Small cooking pots.

[12] Supposedly said by Coleridge in reply to a question at one of his Shakespeare lectures. See C. R. Leslie, *Autobiographical Recollections,* 1860, Vol. I.

[13] A misquotation of *Macbeth,* II.i.

fled with so much precipitation, that he overturned the table
on the foot of Mr. Glowry. Mr. Glowry roared with pain in
the ear of Mr. Toobad. Mr. Toobad's alarm so bewildered his
senses, that, missing the door, he threw up one of the windows,
jumped out in his panic, and plunged over head and ears in the
moat. Mr. Asterias and his son, who were on the watch for their
mermaid, were attracted by the splashing, threw a net over
him, and dragged him to land.

Scythrop and Mr. Hilary meanwhile had hastened to his assistance, and, on arriving at the edge of the moat, followed by
several servants with ropes and torches, found Mr. Asterias and
Aquarius busy in endeavouring to extricate Mr. Toobad
from the net, who was entangled in the meshes, and floundering
with rage. Scythrop was lost in amazement; but Mr. Hilary saw,
at one view, all the circumstances of the adventure, and burst
into an immoderate fit of laughter; on recovering from which,
he said to Mr. Asterias, "You have caught an odd fish, indeed."
Mr. Toobad was highly exasperated at this unseasonable pleasantry; but Mr. Hilary softened his anger, by producing a knife,
and cutting the Gordian knot[14] of his reticular envelopement.
"You see," said Mr. Toobad, "you see, gentlemen, in my unfortunate person proof upon proof of the present dominion of
the devil in the affairs of this world; and I have no doubt but
that the apparition of this night was Apollyon[15] himself in disguise, sent for the express purpose of terrifying me into this
complication of misadventures. The devil is come among you,
having great wrath, because he knoweth that he hath but a
short time."

---

[14] A knot tied by King Gordius of Phrygia which supposedly
could by untied only by the man destined to rule Asia; Alexander the
Great cut through the knot with his sword.

[15] Greek name for the angel of hell (Revelations 9:11).

Chapter XIII

Mr. Glowry was much surprised, on occasionally visiting Scythrop's tower, to find the door always locked, and to be kept sometimes waiting many minutes for admission: during which he invariably heard a heavy rolling sound like that of a ponderous mangle, or of a waggon on a weighing-bridge, or of theatrical thunder.

He took little notice of this for some time: at length his curiosity was excited, and, one day, instead of knocking at the door, as usual, the instant he reached it, he applied his ear to the key-hole, and like Bottom, in the Midsummer Night's Dream, "spied a voice,"[1] which he guessed to be of the feminine gender, and knew to be not Scythrop's, whose deeper tones he distinguished at intervals. Having attempted in vain to catch a syllable of the discourse, he knocked violently at the door, and roared for immediate admission. The voices ceased, the accustomed rolling sound was heard, the door opened, and Scythrop was discovered alone. Mr. Glowry looked round to every corner of the apartment, and then said, "Where is the lady?"

"The lady, sir?" said Scythrop.

"Yes, sir, the lady."

"Sir, I do not understand you."

"You don't, sir?"

"No, indeed, sir. There is no lady here."

"But, sir, this is not the only apartment in the tower, and I make no doubt there is a lady up stairs."

"You are welcome to search, sir."

"Yes, and while I am searching, she will slip out from some lurking place, and make her escape."

"You may lock this door, sir, and take the key with you."

"But there is the terrace door: she has escaped by the terrace."

---

[1] *A Midsummer Night's Dream,* V.i.

"The terrace, sir, has no other outlet, and the walls are too high for a lady to jump down."

"Well, sir, give me the key."

Mr. Glowry took the key, searched every nook of the tower, and returned.

"You are a fox, Scythrop; you are an exceedingly cunning fox, with that demure visage of yours. What was that lumbering sound I heard before you opened the door?"

"Sound, sir?"

"Yes, sir, sound."

"My dear sir, I am not aware of any sound, except my great table, which I moved on rising to let you in."

"The table!—let me see that. No, sir; not a tenth part heavy enough, not a tenth part."

"But, sir, you do not consider the laws of acoustics: a whisper becomes a peal of thunder in the focus of reverberation. Allow me to explain this:[2] sounds striking on concave surfaces are reflected from them, and, after reflection, converge to points which are the foci of these surfaces. It follows, therefore, that the ear may be so placed in one, as that it shall hear a sound better than when situated nearer to the point of the first impulse: again, in the case of two concave surfaces placed opposite to each other——"

"Nonsense, sir. Don't tell me of foci. Pray, sir, will concave surfaces produce two voices when nobody speaks? I heard two voices, and one was feminine; feminine, sir: what say you to that?"

"Oh, sir, I perceive your mistake: I am writing a tragedy, and was acting over a scene to myself. To convince you, I will give you a specimen; but you must first understand the plot. It is a tragedy on the German model. The Great Mogul is in exile, and has taken lodgings at Kensington, with his only daughter, the Princess Rantrorina, who takes in needlework, and keeps a day school. *The princess is discovered hemming a set of shirts for the parson of the parish: they are to be marked with a large R. Enter to her the Great Mogul. A pause, during*

---

2 Shelley had been much interested in science from his boyhood.

which they look at each other expressively. The princess changes colour several times. The Mogul takes snuff in great agitation. Several grains are heard to fall on the stage. His heart is seen to beat through his upper benjamin.[3]—THE MOGUL (*with a mournful look at his left shoe*). "My shoestring is broken."—THE PRINCESS (*after an interval of melancholy reflection*). "I know it."—THE MOGUL. "My second shoe-string! The first broke when I lost my empire: the second has broken to-day. When will my poor heart break?"—THE PRINCESS. "Shoe-strings, hearts, and empires! Mysterious sympathy!"

"Nonsense, sir," interrupted Mr. Glowry. "That is not at all like the voice I heard."

"But, sir," said Scythrop, "a key-hole may be so constructed as to act like an acoustic tube, and an acoustic tube, sir, will modify sound in a very remarkable manner. Consider the construction of the ear, and the nature and causes of sound. The external part of the ear is a cartilaginous funnel."

"It wo'n't do, Scythrop. There is a girl concealed in this tower, and find her I will. There are such things as sliding panels and secret closets."—He sounded round the room with his cane, but detected no hollowness.—"I have heard, sir," he continued, "that during my absence, two years ago, you had a dumb carpenter closeted with you day after day. I did not dream that you were laying contrivances for carrying on secret intrigues. Young men will have their way: I had my way when I was a young man: but, sir, when your cousin Marionetta——"

Scythrop now saw that the affair was growing serious. To have clapped his hand upon his father's mouth, to have entreated him to be silent, would, in the first place, not have made him so; and, in the second, would have shown a dread of being overheard by somebody. His only resource, therefore, was to try to drown Mr. Glowry's voice; and, having no other subject, he continued his description of the ear, raising his voice continually as Mr. Glowry raised his.

---

[3] An overcoat, so called after a tailor of that name; Peacock's use of the term is the earliest cited in the *OED*.

"When your cousin Marionetta," said Mr. Glowry, "whom you profess to love—whom you profess to love, sir—"

"The internal canal of the ear," said Scythrop, "is partly bony and partly cartilaginous. This internal canal is—"

"Is actually in the house, sir; and, when you are so shortly to be—as I expect—"

"Closed at the further end by the *membrana tympani*—"

"Joined together in holy matrimony—"

"Under which is carried a branch of the fifth pair of nerves—"

"I say, sir, when you are so shortly to be married to your cousin Marionetta—"

"The *cavitas tympani*—"

A loud noise was heard behind the bookcase, which, to the astonishment of Mr. Glowry, opened in the middle, and the massy compartments, with all their weight of books, receding from each other in the manner of a theatrical scene, with a heavy rolling sound (which Mr. Glowry immediately recognised to be the same which had excited his curiosity,) disclosed an interior apartment, in the entrance of which stood the beautiful Stella, who, stepping forward, exclaimed, "Married! Is he going to be married? The profligate!"

"Really, madam," said Mr. Glowry, "I do not know what he is going to do, or what I am going to do, or what any one is going to do; for all this is incomprehensible."

"I can explain it all," said Scythrop, "in a most satisfactory manner, if you will but have the goodness to leave us alone."

"Pray, sir, to which act of the tragedy of the Great Mogul does this incident belong?"

"I entreat you, my dear sir, leave us alone."

Stella threw herself into a chair, and burst into a tempest of tears. Scythrop sat down by her, and took her hand. She snatched her hand away, and turned her back upon him. He rose, sat down on the other side, and took her other hand. She snatched it away, and turned from him again. Scythrop continued entreating Mr. Glowry to leave them alone; but the old gentleman was obstinate, and would not go.

"I suppose, after all," said Mr. Glowry maliciously, "it is

only a phænomenon in acoustics, and this young lady is a reflection of sound from concave surfaces."

Some one tapped at the door: Mr. Glowry opened it, and Mr. Hilary entered. He had been seeking Mr. Glowry, and had traced him to Scythrop's tower. He stood a few moments in silent surprise, and then addressed himself to Mr. Glowry for an explanation.

"The explanation," said Mr. Glowry, "is very satisfactory. The Great Mogul has taken lodgings at Kensington, and the external part of the ear is a cartilaginous funnel."

"Mr. Glowry, that is no explanation."

"Mr. Hilary, it is all I know about the matter."

"Sir, this pleasantry is very unseasonable. I perceive that my niece is sported with in a most unjustifiable manner, and I shall see if she will be more successful in obtaining an intelligible answer." And he departed in search of Marionetta.

Scythrop was now in a hopeless predicament. Mr. Hilary made a hue and cry in the abbey, and summoned his wife and Marionetta to Scythrop's apartment. The ladies, not knowing what was the matter, hastened in great consternation. Mr. Toobad saw them sweeping along the corridor, and judging from their manner that the devil had manifested his wrath in some new shape, followed from pure curiosity.

Scythrop meanwhile vainly endeavoured to get rid of Mr. Glowry and to pacify Stella. The latter attempted to escape from the tower, declaring she would leave the abbey immediately, and he should never see her or hear of her more. Scythrop held her hand and detained her by force, till Mr. Hilary reappeared with Mrs. Hilary and Marionetta. Marionetta, seeing Scythrop grasping the hand of a strange beauty, fainted away in the arms of her aunt. Scythrop flew to her assistance; and Stella with redoubled anger sprang towards the door, but was intercepted in her intended flight by being caught in the arms of Mr. Toobad, who exclaimed—"Celinda!"

"Papa!" said the young lady disconsolately.

"The devil is come among you," said Mr. Toobad, "how came my daughter here?"

"Your daughter!" exclaimed Mr. Glowry.

"Your daughter!" exclaimed Scythrop, and Mr. and Mrs. Hilary.

"Yes," said Mr. Toobad, "my daughter Celinda."

Marionetta opened her eyes and fixed them on Celinda; Celinda in return fixed hers on Marionetta. They were at remote points of the apartment. Scythrop was equidistant from both of them, central and motionless, like Mahomet's coffin.[4]

"Mr. Glowry," said Mr. Toobad, "can you tell by what means my daughter came here?"

"I know no more," said Mr. Glowry, "than the Great Mogul."

"Mr. Scythrop," said Mr. Toobad, "how came my daughter here?"

"I did not know, sir, that the lady was your daughter."

"But how came she here?"

"By spontaneous locomotion," said Scythrop, sullenly.

"Celinda," said Mr. Toobad, "what does all this mean?"

"I really do not know, sir."

"This is most unaccountable. When I told you in London that I had chosen a husband for you, you thought proper to run away from him; and now, to all appearance, you have run away to him."

"How, sir! was that your choice?"

"Precisely; and if he is yours too we shall be both of a mind, for the first time in our lives."

"He is not my choice, sir. This lady has a prior claim: I renounce him."

"And I renounce him," said Marionetta.

Scythrop knew not what to do. He could not attempt to conciliate the one without irreparably offending the other; and he was so fond of both, that the idea of depriving himself for ever of the society of either was intolerable to him: he therefore retreated into his strong hold, mystery; maintained an impenetrable silence; and contented himself with stealing occasionally a deprecating glance at each of the objects of his idolatry. Mr.

---

[4] According to legend, the coffin of Mohammed hangs suspended in mid-air in his tomb.

Toobad and Mr. Hilary, in the mean time, were each insisting
on an explanation from Mr. Glowry, who they thought had
been playing a double game on this occasion. Mr. Glowry was
vainly endeavouring to persuade them of his innocence in the
whole transaction. Mrs. Hilary was endeavouring to mediate
between her husband and brother. The Honourable Mr. Listless, the Reverend Mr. Larynx, Mr. Flosky, Mr. Asterias, and
Aquarius, were attracted by the tumult to the scene of action,
and were appealed to severally and conjointly by the respective
disputants. Multitudinous questions, and answers *en masse,*
composed a *charivari,*[5] to which the genius of Rossini alone
could have given a suitable accompaniment, and which was
only terminated by Mrs. Hilary and Mr. Toobad retreating
with the captive damsels. The whole party followed, with the
exception of Scythrop, who threw himself into his arm-chair,
crossed his left foot over his right knee, placed the hollow of
his left hand on the interior ancle of his left leg, rested his right
elbow on the elbow of the chair, placed the ball of his right
thumb against his right temple, curved the forefinger along
the upper part of his forehead, rested the point of the middle
finger on the bridge of his nose, and the points of the two
others on the lower part of the palm, fixed his eyes intently on
the veins in the back of his left hand, and sat in this position
like the immoveable Theseus,[6] who, as is well known to many
who have not been at college, and to some few who have, *sedet,
æternumque sedebit.*[7] We hope the admirers of the *minutiæ* in
poetry and romance will appreciate this accurate description of
a pensive attitude.

[5] A confused, discordant medley of sounds.
[6] Theseus was chained to a rock as punishment for his attempt
to carry off Proserpina.
[7] Sits, and will sit forever. [P] [Virgil, *Aeneid,* VI.617.]

Chapter XIV

SCYTHROP was still in this position when Raven entered to announce that dinner was on table.

"I cannot come," said Scythrop.

Raven sighed. "Something is the matter," said Raven: "but man is born to trouble."

"Leave me," said Scythrop: "go, and croak elsewhere."

"Thus it is," said Raven. "Five-and-twenty years have I lived in Nightmare Abbey, and now all the reward of my affection is —Go, and croak elsewhere. I have danced you on my knee, and fed you with marrow."[1]

"Good Raven," said Scythrop, "I entreat you to leave me."

"Shall I bring your dinner here?" said Raven. "A boiled fowl and a glass of Madeira are prescribed by the faculty in cases of low spirits. But you had better join the party: it is very much reduced already."

"Reduced! how?"

"The Honourable Mr. Listless is gone. He declared that, what with family quarrels in the morning, and ghosts at night, he could get neither sleep nor peace; and that the agitation was too much for his nerves: though Mr. Glowry assured him that the ghost was only poor Crow walking in his sleep, and that the shroud and bloody turban were a sheet and a red nightcap."

"Well, sir?"

"The Reverend Mr. Larynx has been called off on duty, to marry or bury (I don't know which) some unfortunate person or persons, at Claydyke: but man is born to trouble!"

"Is that all?"

"No. Mr. Toobad is gone too, and a strange lady with him."

"Gone!"

"Gone. And Mr. and Mrs. Hilary, and Miss O'Carroll: they

---

[1] A generic term for rich, nutritious food.

are all gone. There is nobody left but Mr. Asterias and his son, and they are going to-night."

"Then I have lost them both."

"Won't you come to dinner?"

"No."

"Shall I bring your dinner here?"

"Yes."

"What will you have?"

"A pint of port and a pistol."[2]

"A pistol!"

"And a pint of port. I will make my exit like Werter. Go. Stay. Did Miss O'Carroll say any thing?"

"No."

"Did Miss Toobad say any thing?"

"The strange lady? No."

"Did either of them cry?"

"No."

"What did they do?"

"Nothing."

"What did Mr. Toobad say?"

"He said, fifty times over, the devil was come among us."

"And they are gone?"

"Yes; and the dinner is getting cold. There is a time for every thing under the sun.[3] You may as well dine first, and be miserable afterwards."

"True, Raven. There is something in that. I will take your advice: therefore, bring me——"

"The port and the pistol?"

"No; the boiled fowl and Madeira."

Scythrop had dined, and was sipping his Madeira alone, immersed in melancholy musing, when Mr. Glowry entered, followed by Raven, who, having placed an additional glass and set a chair for Mr. Glowry, withdrew. Mr. Glowry sat down opposite Scythrop. After a pause, during which each filled and drank in silence, Mr. Glowry said, "So, sir, you have played

---

[2] See *The Sorrows of Werter,* Letter 93. [P]

[3] Ecclesiastes 3:1.

your cards well. I proposed Miss Toobad to you: you refused her. Mr. Toobad proposed you to her: she refused you. You fell in love with Marionetta, and were going to poison yourself, because, from pure fatherly regard to your temporal interests, I withheld my consent. When, at length, I offered you my consent, you told me I was too precipitate. And, after all, I find you and Miss Toobad living together in the same tower, and behaving in every respect like two plighted lovers. Now, sir, if there be any rational solution of all this absurdity, I shall be very much obliged to you for a small glimmering of information."

"The solution, sir, is of little moment; but I will leave it in writing for your satisfaction. The crisis of my fate is come: the world is a stage, and my direction is *exit*."

"Do not talk so, sir;—do not talk so, Scythrop. What would you have?"

"I would have my love."

"And pray, sir, who is your love?"

"Celinda—Marionetta—either—both."

"Both! That may do very well in a German tragedy; and the Great Mogul might have found it very feasible in his lodgings at Kensington; but it will not do in Lincolnshire. Will you have Miss Toobad?"

"Yes."

"And renounce Marionetta?"

"No."

"But you must renounce one."

"I cannot."

"And you cannot have both. What is to be done?"

"I must shoot myself."

"Don't talk so, Scythrop. Be rational, my dear Scythrop. Consider, and make a cool, calm choice, and I will exert myself in your behalf."

"Why should I choose, sir? Both have renounced *me:* I have no hope of either."

"Tell me which you will have, and I will plead your cause irresistibly."

"Well, sir,—I will have—no, sir, I cannot renounce either.

I cannot choose either. I am doomed to be the victim of eternal disappointments; and I have no resource but a pistol."

"Scythrop—Scythrop;—if one of them should come to you —what then?"

"That, sir, might alter the case: but that cannot be."

"It can be, Scythrop; it will be: I promise you it will be. Have but a little patience—but a week's patience; and it shall be."

"A week, sir, is an age: but, to oblige you, as a last act of filial duty, I will live another week. It is now Thursday evening, twenty-five minutes past seven. At this hour and minute, on Thursday next, love and fate shall smile on me, or I will drink my last pint of port in this world."

Mr. Glowry ordered his travelling chariot, and departed from the abbey.

Chapter XV

THE DAY after Mr. Glowry's departure was one of incessant rain, and Scythrop repented of the promise he had given. The next day was one of bright sunshine: he sat on the terrace, read a tragedy of Sophocles, and was not sorry, when Raven announced dinner, to find himself alive. On the third evening, the wind blew, and the rain beat, and the owl flapped against his windows; and he put a new flint in his pistol. On the fourth day, the sun shone again; and he locked the pistol up in a drawer, where he left it undisturbed, till the morning of the eventful Thursday, when he ascended the turret with a telescope, and spied anxiously along the road that crossed the fens from Claydyke: but nothing appeared on it. He watched in this manner from ten A.M. till Raven summoned him to dinner at five; when he stationed Crow at the telescope, and descended to his own funeral-feast. He left open the communications be-

tween the tower and turret, and called aloud at intervals to
Crow,—"Crow, Crow, is any thing coming?" Crow answered,
"The wind blows, and the windmills turn, but I see nothing
coming;" and, at every answer, Scythrop found the necessity
of raising his spirits with a bumper. After dinner, he gave Raven
his watch to set by the abbey clock. Raven brought it, Scythrop
placed it on the table, and Raven departed. Scythrop called
again to Crow; and Crow, who had fallen asleep, answered
mechanically, "I see nothing coming." Scythrop laid his pistol
between his watch and his bottle. The hour-hand passed the
VII.—the minute-hand moved on;—it was within three minutes
of the appointed time. Scythrop called again to Crow: Crow
answered as before. Scythrop rang the bell: Raven appeared.

"Raven," said Scythrop, "the clock is too fast."

"No, indeed," said Raven, who knew nothing of Scythrop's
intentions; "if any thing, it is too slow."

"Villain!" said Scythrop, pointing the pistol at him; "it is
too fast."

"Yes—yes—too fast, I meant," said Raven, in manifest fear.

"How much too fast?" said Scythrop.

"As much as you please," said Raven.

"How much, I say?" said Scythrop, pointing the pistol again.

"An hour, a full hour, sir," said the terrified butler.

"Put back my watch," said Scythrop.

Raven, with trembling hand, was putting back the watch,
when the rattle of wheels was heard in the court; and Scythrop,
springing down the stairs by three steps together, was at the
door in sufficient time to have handed either of the young ladies
from the carriage, if she had happened to be in it; but Mr.
Glowry was alone.

"I rejoice to see you," said Mr. Glowry; "I was fearful of
being too late, for I waited till the last moment in the hope of
accomplishing my promise; but all my endeavors have been
vain, as these letters will show."

Scythrop impatiently broke the seals. The contents were
these:—

"Almost a stranger in England, I fled from parental tyranny, and the dread of an arbitrary marriage, to the protection of a stranger and a philosopher, whom I expected to find something better than, or at least something different from, the rest of his worthless species. Could I, after what has occurred, have expected nothing more from you than the common-place impertinence of sending your father to treat with me, and with mine, for me? I should be a little moved in your favour, if I could believe you capable of carrying into effect the resolutions which your father says you have taken, in the event of my proving inflexible; though I doubt not you will execute them, as far as relates to the pint of wine, twice over, at least. I wish you much happiness with Miss O'Carroll. I shall always cherish a grateful recollection of Nightmare Abbey, for having been the means of introducing me to a true transcendentalist; and, though he is a little older than myself, which is all one in Germany, I shall very soon have the pleasure of subscribing myself

"CELINDA FLOSKY."

"I hope, my dear cousin, that you will not be angry with me, but that you will always think of me as a sincere friend, who will always feel interested in your welfare; I am sure you love Miss Toobad much better than me, and I wish you much happiness with her. Mr. Listless assures me that people do not kill themselves for love now-a-days, though it is still the fashion to talk about it. I shall, in a very short time, change my name and situation, and shall always be happy to see you in Berkeley Square,[1] when, to the unalterable designation of your affectionate cousin, I shall subjoin the signature of

"MARIONETTA LISTLESS."

Scythrop tore both the letters to atoms, and railed in good set terms against the fickleness of women.

"Calm yourself, my dear Scythrop," said Mr. Glowry; "there are yet maidens in England.

"Very true, sir," said Scythrop.

[1] A fashionable section of London.

"And the next time," said Mr. Glowry, "have but one string to your bow."

"Very good advice, sir," said Scythrop.

"And, besides," said Mr. Glowry, "the fatal time is past, for it is now almost eight."

"Then that villain, Raven," said Scythrop, "deceived me when he said that the clock was too fast; but, as you observe very justly, the time has gone by, and I have just reflected that these repeated crosses in love qualify me to take a very advanced degree in misanthropy; and there is, therefore, good hope that I may make a figure in the world. But I shall ring for the rascal Raven, and admonish him."

Raven appeared. Scythrop looked at him very fiercely two or three minutes; and Raven, still remembering the pistol, stood quaking in mute apprehension, till Scythrop, pointing significantly towards the dining-room, said, "Bring some Madeira."

THE END

THE

MISFORTUNES

OF

ELPHIN.

BY THE AUTHOR OF HEADLONG HALL.

Unlooked-for good betides us still,
And unanticipated ill:
Blind Fortune rules the hours that roll:
Then fill with good old wine the bowl.

LONDON:

PUBLISHED BY THOMAS HOOKHAM,
OLD BOND STREET.

1829.

THE

MISFORTUNES OF ELPHIN.

Quod non exspectes ex transverso fit,
Et suprà nos Fortuna negotia curat:
Quare da nobis vina Falerna, puer.

PETRONIUS ARBITER.[1]

---

[1] *Satiricon,* ¶55. Peacock's translation is on the title page.

Contents

Index to the Poetry

THE MISFORTUNES OF ELPHIN

Chapter I

THE PROSPERITY OF GWAELOD

Regardless of the sweeping whirlwind's sway,
That, hush'd in grim repose, expects his evening prey.
                                                    GRAY.[1]

IN THE BEGINNING of the sixth century, when Uther Pendragon held the nominal sovereignty of Britain over a number
of petty kings, Gwythno Garanhir was king of Caredigion. The
most valuable portion of his dominions was the Great Plain of
Gwaelod, an extensive tract of level land, stretching along that
part of the sea-coast which now belongs to the counties of
Merioneth and Cardigan. This district was populous and highly
cultivated. It contained sixteen fortified towns, superior to all
the towns and cities of the Cymry,[2] excepting Caer Lleon upon
Usk;[3] and, like Caer Lleon, they bore in their architecture, their
language, and their manners, vestiges of past intercourse with
the Roman lords of the world. It contained also one of the three
privileged ports of the isle of Britain, which was called the Port
of Gwythno. This port, we may believe if we please, had not
been unknown to the Phœnicians and Carthaginians, when they
visited the island for metal, accommodating the inhabitants, in

---

[1] "The Bard," II.2.75–76.
[2] Fellow countrymen.
[3] The "Camelot" of Arthurian legend; located in what is now
Monmouthshire, i.e. extreme southeast Wales at the mouth of the
Severn River.

99

return, with luxuries which they would not otherwise have dreamed of, and which they could very well have done without; of course, in arranging the exchange of what they denominated equivalents, imposing on their simplicity, and taking advantage of their ignorance, according to the approved practice of civilized nations; which they called imparting the blessings of Phœnician and Carthaginian light.

An embankment of massy stone protected this lowland country from the sea, which was said, in traditions older than the embankment, to have, in occasional spring-tides, paid short but unwelcome visits to the interior inhabitants, and to have, by slow aggressions, encroached considerably on the land. To prevent the repetition of the first of these inconveniences, and to check the progress of the second, the people of Gwaelod had built the stony rampart, which had withstood the shock of the waves for centuries, when Gwythno began his reign.

Gwythno, like other kings, found the business of governing too light a matter to fill up the vacancy of either his time or his head, and took to the more solid pursuits of harping and singing; not forgetting feasting, in which he was glorious; nor hunting, wherein he was mighty. His several pursuits composed a very harmonious triad. The chace conduced to the good cheer of the feast, and to the good appetite which consumed it; the feast inspired the song; and the song gladdened the feast, and celebrated the chace.

Gwythno and his subjects went on together very happily. They had little to do with him but to pay him revenue, and he had little to do with them but to receive it. Now and then they were called on to fight for the protection of his sacred person, and for the privilege of paying revenue to him rather than to any of the kings in his vicinity, a privilege of which they were particularly tenacious. His lands being far more fertile, and his people, consequently, far more numerous, than those of the rocky dwellers on his borders, he was always victorious in the defensive warfare to which he restricted his military achievements; and, after the invaders of his dominions had received two or three inflictions of signal chastisement, they limited their aggressions to coming quietly in the night, and vanishing, before

morning, with cattle: an heroic operation, in which the pre-
eminent glory of Scotland renders the similar exploits of other
nations not worth recording.

Gwythno was not fond of the sea: a moonstruck bard had
warned him to beware of the oppression of Gwenhidwy;[4] and
he thought he could best do so by keeping as far as possible
out of her way. He had a palace built of choice slate stone on
the rocky banks of the Mawddach, just above the point where
it quitted its native mountains, and entered the plain of
Gwaelod. Here, among green woods and sparkling waters, he
lived in festal munificence, and expended his revenue in en-
couraging agriculture, by consuming a large quantity of produce.

Watchtowers were erected along the embankment, and
watchmen were appointed to guard against the first approaches
of damage or decay. The whole of these towers, and their
companies of guards, were subordinate to a central castle,
which commanded the sea-port already mentioned, and wherein
dwelt Prince Seithenyn ap[5] Seithyn Saidi, who held the office
of Arglwyd Gorwarcheidwad yr Argae Breninawl, which
signifies, in English, Lord High Commissioner of Royal Embankment; and he executed it as a personage so denominated
might be expected to do: he drank the profits, and left the
embankment to his deputies, who left it to their assistants, who
left it to itself.

The condition of the head, in a composite as in a simple
body, affects the entire organization to the extremity of the tail,
excepting that, as the tail in the figurative body usually receives
the largest share in the distribution of punishment, and the
smallest in the distribution of reward, it has the stronger stimu-
lus to ward off evil, and the smaller supply of means to indulge
in diversion; and it sometimes happens that one of the least
regarded of the component parts of the said tail will, from a
pure sense of duty, or an inveterate love of business, or an
oppressive sense of ennui, or a development of the organ of

[4] *Gwen-hudiw,* "the white alluring one:" the name of a mermaid.
Used figuratively for the elemental power of the sea. [P]
[5] "Son of."

order, or some other equally cogent reason, cheerfully undergo
all the care and labour, of which the honour and profit will
redound to higher quarters.

Such a component portion of the Gwaelod High Commission of Royal Embankment was Teithrin ap Tathral, who had
the charge of a watchtower where the embankment terminated
at the point of Mochres, in the high land of Ardudwy. Teithrin
kept his portion of the embankment in exemplary condition,
and paced with daily care the limits of his charge; but one day,
by some accident, he strayed beyond them, and observed
symptoms of neglect that filled him with dismay. This circumstance induced him to proceed till his wanderings brought him
round to the embankment's southern termination in the high
land of Caredigion. He met with abundant hospitality at the
towers of his colleagues, and at the castle of Seithenyn: he was
supposed to be walking for his amusement; he was asked no
questions, and he carefully abstained from asking any. He
examined and observed in silence; and, when he had completed
his observations, he hastened to the palace of Gwythno.

Preparations were making for a high festival, and Gwythno
was composing an ode. Teithrin knew better than to interrupt
him in his *awen*.[6]

Gwythno had a son named Elphin, who is celebrated in
history as the most expert of fishers. Teithrin, finding the king
impracticable, went in search of the young prince.

Elphin had been all the morning fishing in the Mawddach,
in a spot where the river, having quitted the mountains and not
yet entered the plain, ran in alternate streams and pools sparkling through a pastoral valley. Elphin sat under an ancient
ash, enjoying the calm brightness of an autumnal noon, and the
melody and beauty of the flying stream, on which the shifting
sunbeams fell chequering through the leaves. The monotonous
music of the river, and the profound stillness of the air, had
contributed to the deep abstraction of a meditation into which
Elphin had fallen. He was startled into attention by a sudden
rush of the wind through the trees, and during the brief interval

[6] The rapturous and abstracted state of poetical inspiration. [P]

of transition from the state of reverie to that of perfect consciousness, he heard, or seemed to hear, in the gust that hurried by him, the repetition of the words, "Beware of the oppression of Gwenhidwy." The gust was momentary: the leaves ceased to rustle, and the deep silence of nature returned.

The prophecy, which had long haunted the memory and imagination of his father, had been often repeated to Elphin, and had sometimes occupied his thoughts, but it had formed no part of his recent meditation, and he could not persuade himself that the words had not been actually spoken near him. He emerged from the shade of the trees that fringed the river, and looked round him from the rocky bank.

At this moment Teithrin ap Tathral discovered and approached him.

Elphin knew him not, and inquired his name. He answered, "Teithrin ap Tathral."

"And what seek you here?" said Elphin.

"I seek," answered Teithrin, "the Prince of Gwaelod, Elphin ap Gwythno Garanhir."

"You spoke," said Elphin, "as you approached." Teithrin answered in the negative.

"Assuredly you did," said Elphin. "You repeated the words, 'Beware of the oppression of Gwenhidwy.' "

Teithrin denied having spoken the words; but their mysterious impression made Elphin listen readily to his information and advice; and the result of their conference was a determination, on the part of the Prince, to accompany Teithrin ap Tathral on a visit of remonstrance to the Lord High Commissioner.

They crossed the centre of the enclosed country to the privileged port of Gwythno, near which stood the castle of Seithenyn. They walked towards the castle along a portion of the embankment, and Teithrin pointed out to the Prince its dilapidated condition. The sea shone with the glory of the setting sun; the air was calm; and the white surf, tinged with the crimson of sunset, broke lightly on the sands below. Elphin turned his eyes from the dazzling splendour of ocean to the green meadows of the Plain of Gwaelod; the trees, that in the distance thickened into woods; the wreaths of smoke rising from among them,

marking the solitary cottages, or the populous towns; the massy
barrier of mountains beyond, with the forest rising from their
base; the precipices frowning over the forest; and the clouds
resting on their summits, reddened with the reflection of the
west. Elphin gazed earnestly on the peopled plain, reposing in
the calm of evening between the mountains and the sea, and
thought, with deep feelings of secret pain, how much of life and
human happiness was intrusted to the ruinous mound on which
he stood.

Chapter II

THE DRUNKENNESS OF SEITHENYN

*The three immortal drunkards of the isle of
Britain: Ceraint of Essyllwg; Gwrtheyrn Gwrthenau;
and Seithenyn ap Seithyn Saidi.*
TRIADS OF THE ISLE OF BRITAIN.

THE SUN had sunk beneath the waves when they reached
the castle of Seithenyn. The sound of the harp and the song
saluted them as they approached it. As they entered the great
hall, which was already blazing with torchlight, they found his
highness, and his highness's household, convincing themselves
and each other with wine and wassail, of the excellence of their
system of virtual superintendence; and the following jovial
chorus broke on the ears of the visitors:

The Circling of the Mead Horns.[1]

Fill the blue horn, the blue buffalo horn:
Natural is mead in the buffalo horn:
As the cuckoo in spring, as the lark in the morn,
So natural is mead in the buffalo horn.

[1] From a poem in John Parry's *A Selection of Welsh Melodies*

As the cup of the flower to the bee when he sips,
Is the full cup of mead to the true Briton's lips:
From the flower-cups of summer, on field and on
tree,
Our mead cups are filled by the vintager bee.

Seithenyn[2] ap Seithyn, the generous, the bold,
Drinks the wine of the stranger from vessels of gold;[3]
But we from the horn, the blue silver-rimmed horn,
Drink the ale and the mead in our fields that were
born.

The ale-froth is white, and the mead sparkles bright;
They both smile apart, and with smiles they unite:[4]
The mead from the flower, and the ale from the corn,
Smile, sparkle, and sing in the buffalo horn.

The horn, the blue horn, cannot stand on its tip;
Its path is right on from the hand to the lip:
Though the bowl and the wine-cup our tables adorn,
More natural the draught from the buffalo horn.

But Seithenyn ap Seithyn, the generous, the bold,
Drinks the bright-flowing wine from the far-gleaming
gold:
The wine, in the bowl by his lip that is worn,
Shall be glorious as mead in the buffalo horn.

The horns circle fast, but their fountains will last,
As the stream passes ever, and never is past:
Exhausted so quickly, replenished so soon,
They wax and they wane like the horns of the moon.

(1809?), reprinted in the *Cambro-Briton*, III (January 1822), 185.
Except for "The War-Song of Dinas Vawr" (Chap. XI), which Peacock
himself composed, the poems scattered through the novel are translations
or adaptations of authentic ancient Welsh poems.

[2] The accent is on the second syllable: Seithényn. [P]

[3] Gwin. . . .o eur. . . .ANEURIN. [P] [A great legendary Welsh
poet (fl. 600?) and friend of Taliesin.]

[4] The mixture of ale and mead made *bradawd,* a favourite drink
of the Ancient Britons. [P]

> Fill high the blue horn, the blue buffalo horn;
> Fill high the long silver-rimmed buffalo horn:
> While the roof of the hall by our chorus is torn,
> Fill, fill to the brim, the deep silver-rimmed horn.

Elphin and Teithrin stood some time on the floor of the hall before they attracted the attention of Seithenyn, who, during the chorus, was tossing and flourishing his golden goblet. The chorus had scarcely ended when he noticed them, and immediately roared aloud, "You are welcome all four."

Elphin answered, "We thank you: we are but two."

"Two or four," said Seithenyn, "all is one. You are welcome all. When a stranger enters, the custom in other places is to begin by washing his feet. My custom is, to begin by washing his throat. Seithenyn ap Seithyn Saidi bids you welcome."

Elphin, taking the wine-cup, answered, "Elphin ap Gwythno Garanhir thanks you."

Seithenyn started up. He endeavoured to straighten himself into perpendicularity, and to stand steadily on his legs. He accomplished half his object by stiffening all his joints but those of his ancles, and from these the rest of his body vibrated upwards with the inflexibility of a bar. After thus oscillating for a time, like an inverted pendulum, finding that the attention requisite to preserve his rigidity absorbed all he could collect of his dissipated energies, and that he required a portion of them for the management of his voice, which he felt a dizzy desire to wield with peculiar steadiness in the presence of the son of the king, he suddenly relaxed the muscles that perform the operation of sitting, and dropped into his chair like a plummet. He then, with a gracious gesticulation, invited Prince Elphin to take his seat on his right hand, and proceeded to compose himself into a dignified attitude, throwing his body back into the left corner of his chair, resting his left elbow on its arm and his left cheekbone on the middle of the back of his left hand, placing his left foot on a footstool, and stretching out his right leg as straight and as far as his position allowed. He had thus his right hand at liberty, for the ornament of his eloquence and the conduct of his liquor.

Elphin seated himself at the right hand of Seithenyn. Teithrin remained at the end of the hall: on which Seithenyn exclaimed, "Come on, man, come on. What, if you be not the son of a king, you are the guest of Seithenyn ap Seithyn Saidi. The most honourable place to the most honourable guest, and the next most honourable place to the next most honourable guest; the least honourable guest above the most honourable inmate; and, where there are but two guests, be the most honourable who he may, the least honourable of the two is next in honour to the most honourable of the two, because they are no more but two; and, where there are only two, there can be nothing between. Therefore sit, and drink. GWIN O EUR: wine from gold."

Elphin motioned Teithrin to approach, and sit next to him.

Prince Seithenyn, whose liquor was "his eating and his drinking solely,"[5] seemed to measure the gastronomy of his guests by his own; but his groom of the pantry thought the strangers might be disposed to eat, and placed before them a choice of provision, on which Teithrin ap Tathral did vigorous execution.

"I pray your excuses," said Seithenyn, "my stomach is weak, and I am subject to dizziness in the head, and my memory is not so good as it was, and my faculties of attention are somewhat impaired, and I would dilate more upon the topic, whereby you should hold me excused, but I am troubled with a feverishness and parching of the mouth, that very much injures my speech, and impedes my saying all I would say, and will say before I have done, in token of my loyalty and fealty to your highness and your highness's house. I must just moisten my lips, and I will then proceed with my observations. Cupbearer, fill."

"Prince Seithenyn," said Elphin, "I have visited you on a subject of deep moment. Reports have been brought to me, that the embankment, which has been so long intrusted to your care, is in a state of dangerous decay."

"Decay," said Seithenyn, "is one thing, and danger is another.[6] Every thing that is old must decay. That the embank-

---

[5] Beaumont and Fletcher, *The Scornful Lady,* IV.ii.
[6] According to a friend who was in close contact with Peacock while the novel was being written, what follows parodies the essence of several speeches against parliamentary reform delivered by George

ment is old, I am free to confess; that it is somewhat rotten in parts, I will not altogether deny; that it is any the worse for that, I do most sturdily gainsay. It does its business well: it works well: it keeps out the water from the land, and it lets in the wine upon the High Commission of Embankment. Cupbearer, fill. Our ancestors were wiser than we: they built it in their wisdom; and, if we should be so rash as to try to mend it, we should only mar it."

"The stonework," said Teithrin, "is sapped and mined: the piles are rotten, broken, and dislocated: the floodgates and sluices are leaky and creaky."

"That is the beauty of it," said Seithenyn. "Some parts of it are rotten, and some parts of it are sound."

"It is well," said Elphin, "that some parts are sound: it were better that all were so."

"So I have heard some people say before," said Seithenyn; "perverse people, blind to venerable antiquity: that very unamiable sort of people, who are in the habit of indulging their reason. But I say, the parts that are rotten give elasticity to those that are sound: they give them elasticity, elasticity, elasticity. If it were all sound, it would break by its own obstinate stiffness: the soundness is checked by the rottenness, and the stiffness is balanced by the elasticity. There is nothing so dangerous as innovation. See the waves in the equinoctial storms, dashing and clashing, roaring and pouring, spattering and battering, rattling and battling against it. I would not be so presumptuous as to say, I could build any thing that would stand against them half an hour; and here this immortal old work, which God forbid the finger of modern mason should bring into jeopardy, this immortal work has stood for centuries, and will stand for centuries more, if we let it alone. It is well: it works well: let well alone. Cupbearer, fill. It was half rotten when I was born, and that is a conclusive reason why it should be three parts rotten when I die."

Canning (1770–1827), Tory politician and outspoken defender of the status quo at a time when the need for parliamentary reform was increasingly obvious.

The whole body of the High Commission roared approbation.

"And after all," said Seithenyn, "the worst that could happen would be the overflow of a springtide, for that was the worst that happened before the embankment was thought of; and, if the high water should come in, as it did before, the low water would go out again, as it did before. We should be no deeper in it than our ancestors were, and we could mend as easily as they could make."

"The level of the sea," said Teithrin, "is materially altered."

"The level of the sea!" exclaimed Seithenyn. "Who ever heard of such a thing as altering the level of the sea? Alter the level of that bowl of wine before you, in which, as I sit here, I see a very ugly reflection of your very goodlooking face. Alter the level of that: drink up the reflection: let me see the face without the reflection, and leave the sea to level itself."

"Not to level the embankment," said Teithrin.

"Good, very good," said Seithenyn. "I love a smart saying, though it hits at me. But, whether yours is a smart saying or no, I do not very clearly see; and, whether it hits at me or no, I do not very sensibly feel. But all is one. Cupbearer, fill."

"I think," pursued Seithenyn, looking as intently as he could at Teithrin ap Tathral, "I have seen something very like you before. There was a fellow here the other day very like you: he stayed here some time: he would not talk: he did nothing but drink: he used to drink till he could not stand, and then he went walking about the embankment. I suppose he thought it wanted mending; but he did not say any thing. If he had, I should have told him to embank his own throat, to keep the liquor out of that. That would have posed him: he could not have answered that: he would not have had a word to say for himself after that."

"He must have been a miraculous person," said Teithrin, "to walk when he could not stand."

"All is one for that," said Seithenyn. "Cupbearer, fill."

"Prince Seithenyn," said Elphin, "if I were not aware that wine speaks in the silence of reason, I should be astonished at your strange vindication of your neglect of duty, which I take shame to myself for not having sooner known and remedied. The wise bard has well observed, 'Nothing is done without the eye of the king.' "

"I am very sorry," said Seithenyn, "that you see things in a wrong light: but we will not quarrel for three reasons: first, because you are the son of the king, and may do and say what you please, without any one having a right to be displeased: second, because I never quarrel with a guest, even if he grows riotous in his cups: third, because there is nothing to quarrel about; and perhaps that is the best reason of the three; or rather the first is the best, because you are the son of the king; and the third is the second, that is, the second best, because there is nothing to quarrel about; and the second is nothing to the purpose, because, though guests will grow riotous in their cups, in spite of my good orderly example, God forbid I should say, that is the case with you. And I completely agree in the truth of your remark, that reason speaks in the silence of wine."

Seithenyn accompanied his speech with a vehement swinging of his right hand: in so doing, at this point, he dropped his cup: a sudden impulse of rash volition, to pick it dexterously up before he resumed his discourse, ruined all his devices for maintaining dignity; in stooping forward from his chair, he lost his balance, and fell prostrate on the floor.

The whole body of the High Commission arose in simultaneous confusion, each zealous to be the foremost in uplifting his fallen chief. In the vehemence of their uprise, they hurled the benches backward and the tables forward; the crash of cups and bowls accompanied their overthrow; and rivulets of liquor ran gurgling through the hall. The household wished to redeem the credit of their leader in the eyes of the Prince; but the only service they could render him was to participate his discomfiture; for Seithenyn, as he was first in dignity, was also, as was fitting, hardest in skull; and that which had impaired his equilibrium had utterly destroyed theirs. Some fell, in the first impulse, with the tables and benches; others were tripped up by the rolling bowls; and the remainder fell at different points of progression, by jostling against each other, or stumbling over those who had fallen before them.

Chapter III

THE OPPRESSION OF GWENHIDWY

Nid meddw y dyn a allo
Cwnu ei hun a rhodio,
Ac yved rhagor ddiawd:
Nid yw hyny yn veddwdawd.

Not drunk is he, who from the floor
Can rise alone, and still drink more;
But drunk is he, who prostrate lies,
Without the power to drink or rise.

A SIDE DOOR, at the upper end of the hall, to the left of Seithenyn's chair, opened, and a beautiful young girl entered the hall, with her domestic bard, and her attendant maidens.

It was Angharad, the daughter of Seithenyn. The tumult had drawn her from the solitude of her chamber, apprehensive that some evil might befall her father in that incapability of self-protection to which he made a point of bringing himself by set of sun. She gracefully saluted Prince Elphin, and directed the cupbearers, (who were bound, by their office, to remain half sober till the rest of the company were finished off, after which they indemnified themselves at leisure,) she directed the cupbearers to lift up Prince Seithenyn, and bear him from the hall. The cupbearers reeled off with their lord, who had already fallen asleep, and who now began to play them a pleasant march with his nose, to inspirit their progression.

Elphin gazed with delight on the beautiful apparition, whose gentle and serious loveliness contrasted so strikingly with the broken trophies and fallen heroes of revelry that lay scattered at her feet.

"Stranger," she said, "this seems an unfitting place for you: let me conduct you where you will be more agreeably lodged."

"Still less should I deem it fitting for you, fair maiden," said Elphin.

111

She answered, "The pleasure of her father is the duty of Angharad."

Elphin was desirous to protract the conversation, and this very desire took from him the power of speaking to the purpose. He paused for a moment to collect his ideas, and Angharad stood still, in apparent expectation that he would show symptoms of following, in compliance with her invitation.

In this interval of silence, he heard the loud dashing of the sea, and the blustering of the wind through the apertures of the walls.

This supplied him with what has been, since Britain was Britain, the alpha and omega of British conversation. He said, "It seems a stormy night."

She answered, "We are used to storms: we are far from the mountains, between the lowlands and the sea, and the winds blow round us from all quarters."

There was another pause of deep silence. The noise of the sea was louder, and the gusts pealed like thunder through the apertures. Amidst the fallen and sleeping revellers, the confused and littered hall, the low and wavering torches, Angharad, lovely always, shone with single and surpassing loveliness. The gust died away in murmurs, and swelled again into thunder, and died away in murmurs again; and, as it died away, mixed with the murmurs of ocean, a voice, that seemed one of the many voices of the wind, pronounced the ominous words, "Beware of the oppression of Gwenhidwy."

They looked at each other, as if questioning whether all had heard alike.

"Did you not hear a voice?" said Angharad, after a pause.

"The same," said Elphin, "which has once before seemed to say to me, 'Beware of the oppression of Gwenhidwy.' "

Teithrin hurried forth on the rampart: Angharad turned pale, and leaned against a pillar of the hall. Elphin was amazed and awed, absorbed as his feelings were in her. The sleepers on the floor made an uneasy movement, and uttered an inarticulate cry.

Teithrin returned. "What saw you?" said Elphin.

Teithrin answered, "A tempest is coming from the west. The moon has waned three days, and is half hidden in clouds, just visible above the mountains: the bank of clouds is black in the west; the scud is flying before them; and the white waves are rolling to the shore."

"This is the highest of the springtides," said Angharad, "and they are very terrible in the storms from the west, when the spray flies over the embankment, and the breakers shake the tower which has its foot in the surf."

"Whence was the voice," said Elphin, "which we heard erewhile? Was it the cry of a sleeper in his drink, or an error of the fancy, or a warning voice from the elements?"

"It was surely nothing earthly," said Angharad, "nor was it an error of the fancy, for we all heard the words, 'Beware of the oppression of Gwenhidwy.' Often and often, in the storms of the springtides, have I feared to see her roll her power over the fields of Gwaelod."

"Pray heaven she do not tonight," said Teithrin.

"Can there be such a danger?" said Elphin.

"I think," said Teithrin, "of the decay I have seen, and I fear the voice I have heard."

A long pause of deep silence ensued, during which they heard the intermitting peals of the wind, and the increasing sound of the rising sea, swelling progressively into wilder and more menacing tumult, till, with one terrific impulse, the whole violence of the equinoctial tempest seemed to burst upon the shore. It was one of those tempests which occur once in several centuries, and which, by their extensive devastations, are chronicled to eternity; for a storm that signalizes its course with extraordinary destruction, becomes as worthy of celebration as a hero for the same reason. The old bard seemed to be of this opinion; for the turmoil which appalled Elphin, and terrified Angharad, fell upon his ears as the sound of inspiration: the *awen* came upon him; and, seizing his harp, he mingled his voice and his music with the uproar of the elements:

The Song of the Four Winds.[1]

Wind from the north: the young spring day
Is pleasant on the sunny mead;
The merry harps at evening play;
The dance gay youths and maidens lead:
The thrush makes chorus from the thorn:
The mighty drinker fills his horn.

Wind from the east: the shore is still;
The mountain-clouds fly tow'rds the sea;
The ice is on the winter-rill;
The great hall fire is blazing free:
The prince's circling feast is spread:
Drink fills with fumes the brainless head.

Wind from the south: in summer shade
'Tis sweet to hear the loud harp ring;
Sweet is the step of comely maid,
Who to the bard a cup doth bring:
The black crow flies where carrion lies:
Where pignuts lurk, the swine will work.

Wind from the west: the autumnal deep
Rolls on the shore its billowy pride:
He, who the rampart's watch must keep,
Will mark with awe the rising tide:
The high springtide, that bursts its mound,
May roll o'er miles of level ground.

Wind from the west: the mighty wave
Of ocean bounds o'er rock and sand;
The foaming surges roar and rave

---

[1] This poem is a specimen of a numerous class of ancient Welsh poems, in which each stanza begins with a repetition of the predominant idea, and terminates with a proverb, more or less applicable to the subject. In some poems, the sequence of the main images is regular and connected, and the proverbial terminations strictly appropriate: in others, the sequency of the main images is loose and incoherent, and the proverbial termination has little or nothing to do with the subject of the stanza. The basis of the poem in the text is in the *Englynion* of Llwyarch Hên. [P]

Against the bulwarks of the land:
When waves are rough, and winds are high,
Good is the land that's high and dry.

Wind from the west: the storm-clouds rise;
The breakers rave; the whirlblasts roar;
The mingled rage of seas and skies
Bursts on the low and lonely shore:
When safety's far, and danger nigh,
Swift feet the readiest aid supply.

Wind from the west—

His song was cut short by a tremendous crash. The tower, which had its foot in the sea, had long been sapped by the waves; the storm had prematurely perfected the operation, and the tower fell into the surf, carrying with it a portion of the wall of the main building, and revealing, through the chasm, the white raging of the breakers beneath the blackness of the midnight storm. The wind rushed into the hall, extinguishing the torches within the line of its course, tossing the grey locks and loose mantle of the bard, and the light white drapery and long black tresses of Angharad. With the crash of the falling tower, and the simultaneous shriek of the women, the sleepers started from the floor, staring with drunken amazement; and, shortly after, reeling like an Indian from the wine-rolling Hydaspes,[2] in staggered Seithenyn ap Seithyn.

Seithenyn leaned against a pillar, and stared at the sea through the rifted wall, with wild and vacant surprise. He perceived that there was an innovation, and he felt that he was injured: how, or by whom, he did not quite so clearly discern. He looked at Elphin and Teithrin, at his daughter, and at the members of his household, with a long and dismal aspect of

[2] In the fourteenth and fifteenth books of the Dionysiaca of Nonnus, Bacchus changes the river Astacis into wine; and the multitudinous army of water-drinking Indians, proceeding to quench their thirst in the stream, become franticly drunk, and fall an easy prey to the Bacchic invaders. In the thirty-fifth book, the experiment is repeated on the Hydaspes. *"Ainsi conquesta Bacchus l'Inde,"* as Rabelais has it. [P] ["Thus Bacchus conquered India."]

blank and mute interrogation, modified by the struggling consciousness of puzzled self-importance, which seemed to require from his chiefship some word of command in this incomprehensible emergency. But the longer he looked, the less clearly he saw; and the longer he pondered, the less he understood. He felt the rush of the wind; he saw the white foam of the sea; his ears were dizzy with their mingled roar. He remained at length motionless, leaning against the pillar, and gazing on the breakers with fixed and glaring vacancy.

"The sleepers of Gwaelod," said Elphin, "they who sleep in peace and security, trusting to the vigilance of Seithenyn, what will become of them?"

"Warn them with the beacon fire," said Teithrin, "if there be fuel on the summit of the landward tower."

"That of course has been neglected too," said Elphin.

"Not so," said Angharad, "that has been my charge."

Teithrin seized a torch, and ascended the eastern tower, and, in a few minutes, the party in the hall beheld the breakers reddening with the reflected fire, and deeper and yet deeper crimson tinging the whirling foam, and sheeting the massy darkness of the bursting waves.

Seithenyn turned his eyes on Elphin. His recollection of him was extremely faint, and the longer he looked on him he remembered him the less. He was conscious of the presence of strangers, and of the occurrence of some signal mischief, and associated the two circumstances in his dizzy perceptions with a confused but close connexion. He said at length, looking sternly at Elphin, "I do not know what right the wind has to blow upon me here; nor what business the sea has to show itself here; nor what business you have here: but one thing is very evident, that either my castle or the sea is on fire; and I shall be glad to know who has done it, for terrible shall be the vengeance of Seithenyn ap Seithyn. Show me the enemy," he pursued, drawing his sword furiously, and flourishing it over his head, "Show me the enemy; show me the enemy."

An unusual tumult mingled with the roar of the waves; a sound, the same in kind, but greater in degree, with that produced by the loose stones of the beach, which are rolled to and fro by the surf.

Teithrin rushed into the hall, exclaiming, "All is over! the mound is broken; and the springtide is rolling through the breach."

Another portion of the castle wall fell into the mining waves, and, by the dim and thickly-clouded moonlight, and the red blaze of the beacon fire, they beheld a torrent pouring in from the sea upon the plain, and rushing immediately beneath the castle walls, which, as well as the points of the embankment that formed the sides of the breach, continued to crumble away into the waters.

"Who has done this?" vociferated Seithenyn, "Show me the enemy."

"There is no enemy but the sea," said Elphin, "to which you, in your drunken madness, have abondoned the land. Think, if you can think, of what is passing in the plain. The storm drowns the cries of your victims; but the curses of the perishing are upon you."

"Show me the enemy," vociferated Seithenyn, flourishing his sword more furiously.

Angharad looked deprecatingly at Elphin, who abstained from further reply.

"There is no enemy but the sea," said Teithrin, "against which your sword avails not."

"Who dares to say so?" said Seithenyn. "Who dares to say that there is an enemy on earth against whom the sword of Seithenyn ap Seithyn is unavailing? Thus, thus I prove the falsehood."

And, springing suddenly forward, he leaped into the torrent, flourishing his sword as he descended.

"Oh, my unhappy father!" sobbed Angharad, veiling her face with her arm on the shoulder of one of her female attendants, whom Elphin dexterously put aside, and substituted himself as the supporter of the desolate beauty.

"We must quit the castle," said Teithrin, "or we shall be buried in its ruins. We have but one path of safety, along the summit of the embankment, if there be not another breach between us and the high land, and if we can keep our footing in this hurricane. But there is no alternative. The walls are melting away like snow."

The bard, who was now recovered from his *awen*, and beginning to be perfectly alive to his own personal safety, conscious at the same time that the first duty of his privileged order was to animate the less-gifted multitude by examples of right conduct in trying emergencies, was the first to profit by Teithrin's admonition, and to make the best of his way through the door that opened to the embankment, on which he had no sooner set his foot than he was blown down by the wind, his harp-strings ringing as he fell. He was indebted to the impediment of his harp, for not being rolled down the mound into the waters which were rising within.

Teithrin picked him up, and admonished him to abandon his harp to its fate, and fortify his steps with a spear. The bard murmured objections: and even the reflection that he could more easily get another harp than another life, did not reconcile him to parting with his beloved companion. He got over the difficulty by slinging his harp, cumbrous as it was, to his left side, and taking a spear in his right hand.

Angharad, recovering from the first shock of Seithenyn's catastrophe, became awake to the imminent danger. The spirit of the Cymric female, vigilant and energetic in peril, disposed her and her attendant maidens to use their best exertions for their own preservation. Following the advice and example of Elphin and Teithrin, they armed themselves with spears, which they took down from the walls.

Teithrin led the way, striking the point of his spear firmly into the earth, and leaning from it on the wind: Angharad followed in the same manner: Elphin followed Angharad, looking as earnestly to her safety as was compatible with moderate care of his own: the attendant maidens followed Elphin; and the bard, whom the result of his first experiment had rendered unambitious of the van, followed the female train. Behind them went the cupbearers, whom the accident of sobriety had qualified to march; and behind them reeled and roared those of the bacchanal rout who were able and willing to move; those more especially who had wives or daughters to support their tottering steps. Some were incapable of locomotion, and others, in the heroic madness of liquor, sat down to await their destiny, as they finished the half-drained vessels.

The bard, who had somewhat of a picturesque eye, could not help sparing a little leisure from the care of his body, to observe the effects before him: the volumed blackness of the storm; the white bursting of the breakers in the faint and scarcely-perceptible moonlight; the rushing and rising of the waters within the mound; the long floating hair and waving drapery of the young women; the red light of the beacon fire falling on them from behind; the surf rolling up the side of the embankment, and breaking almost at their feet; the spray flying above their heads; and the resolution with which they impinged the stony ground with their spears, and bore themselves up against the wind.

Thus they began their march. They had not proceeded far, when the tide began to recede, the wind to abate somewhat of its violence, and the moon to look on them at intervals through the rifted clouds, disclosing the desolation of the inundated plain, silvering the tumultuous surf, gleaming on the distant mountains, and revealing a lengthened prospect of their solitary path, that lay in its irregular line like a ribbon on the deep.

Chapter IV

THE LAMENTATIONS OF GWYTHNO

Οὐ παύσομαι τὰς Χάριτας
Μούσαις συγκαταμιγνύς,
Ἡδίσταν συζυγίαν.

EURIPIDES.[1]

Not, though grief my age defaces,
Will I cease, in concert dear,
Blending still the gentle graces
With the muses more severe.

[1] *Heracles*, ll. 674–676.

KING GWYTHNO had feasted joyously, and had sung his new ode to a chosen party of his admiring subjects, amidst their, of course, enthusiastic applause. He heard the storm raging without, as he laid himself down to rest: he thought it a very hard case for those who were out in it, especially on the sea; congratulated himself on his own much more comfortable condition; and went to sleep with a pious reflection on the goodness of Providence to himself.

He was roused from a pleasant dream by a confused and tumultuous dissonance, that mingled with the roar of the tempest. Rising with much reluctance, and looking forth from his window, he beheld in the moonlight a half-naked multitude, larger than his palace thrice multiplied could have contained, pressing round the gates, and clamouring for admission and shelter; while beyond them his eye fell on the phænomenon of stormy waters, rolling in the place of the fertile fields from which he derived his revenue.

Gwythno, though a king and his own laureate, was not without sympathy for the people who had the honour and happiness of victualling his royal house, and he issued forth on his balcony full of perplexities and alarms, stunned by the sudden sense of the half-understood calamity, and his head still dizzy from the effects of abruptly-broken sleep, and the vapours of the overnight's glorious festival.

Gwythno was altogether a reasonably good sort of person, and a poet of some note. His people were somewhat proud of him on the latter score, and very fond of him on the former; for even the tenth part of those homely virtues, that decorate the memories of "husbands kind and fathers dear" in every churchyard, are matters of plebeian admiration in the persons of royalty; and every tangible point in every such virtue so located, becomes a convenient peg for the suspension of love and loyalty. While, therefore, they were unanimous in consigning the soul of Seithenyn to a place that no well-bred divine will name to a polite congregation, they overflowed, in the abundance of their own griefs, with a portion of sympathy for Gwythno, and saluted him, as he issued forth on his balcony, with a hearty *Duw cadw y Brenin*, or God save the King, which he returned with a benevolent wave of the hand; but they followed it up by an intense vociferation for food and lodging, which he received with a pitiful shake of the head.

Meanwhile the morning dawned: the green spots, that peered with the ebbing tide above the waste of waters, only served to indicate the irremediableness of the general desolation.

Gwythno proceeded to hold a conference with his people, as deliberately as the stormy state of the weather and their minds, and the confusion of his own, would permit. The result of the conference was, that they should use their best exertions to catch some stray beeves, which had escaped the inundation, and were lowing about the rocks in search of new pastures. This measure was carried into immediate effect: the victims were killed and roasted, carved, distributed, and eaten, in a very Homeric fashion, and washed down with a large portion of the contents of the royal cellars; after which, having more leisure to dwell on their losses, the fugitives of Gwaelod proceeded to make loud lamentation, all collectively for home and for country, and severally for wife or husband, parent or child, whom the flood had made its victims.

In the midst of these lamentations arrived Elphin and Angharad, with her bard and attendant maidens, and Teithrin ap Tathral. Gwythno, after a consultation, despatched Teithrin and Angharad's domestic bard on an embassy to the court of Uther Pendragon, and to such of the smaller kings as lay in the way, to solicit such relief as their several majesties might be able and willing to afford to a king in distress. It is said, that the bard, finding a royal bardship vacant in a more prosperous court, made the most of himself in the market, and stayed where he was better fed and lodged than he could expect to be in Caredigion; but that Teithrin returned, with many valuable gifts, and most especially one from Merlin, being a hamper, which multiplied an hundredfold by morning whatever was put into it overnight, so that, for a ham and a flask put by in the evening, an hundred hams and an hundred flasks were taken out in the morning. It is at least certain that such a hamper is enumerated among the thirteen wonders of Merlin's art, and, in the authentic catalogue thereof, is called the Hamper of Gwythno.

Be this as it may, Gwythno, though shorn of the beams of his revenue, kept possession of his palace. Elphin married Angharad, and built a salmon-weir on the Mawddach, the produce of which, with that of a series of beehives, of which his princess and her maidens made mead, constituted for some time the principal wealth and subsistence of the royal family of Caredigion.

King Gwythno, while his son was delving or fishing, and his daughter spinning or making mead, sat all day on the rocks, with his harp between his knees, watching the rolling of ocean over the locality of his past dominion, and pouring forth his soul in pathetic song on the change of his own condition, and the mutability of human things. Two of his songs of lamentation have been preserved by tradition: they are the only relics of his muse which time has spared.

Gwyddnau Ei Cant,

PAN DDOAI Y MOR DROS CANTREV Y GWAELAWD.

A Song of Gwythno Garanhir,

ON THE INUNDATION OF THE SEA OVER THE
PLAIN OF GWAELOD.

Stand forth, Seithenyn: winds are high:
Look down beneath the lowering sky;
Look from the rock: what meets thy sight?
Nought but the breakers rolling white.

Stand forth, Seithenyn: winds are still:
Look from the rock and healthy hill
For Gwythno's realm: what meets thy view?
Nought but the ocean's desert blue.

Curst be the treacherous mound, that gave
A passage to the mining wave:
Curst be the cup, with mead-froth crowned,
That charmed from thought the trusted mound.

A tumult, and a cry to heaven!
The white surf breaks; the mound is riven:
Through the wide rift the ocean-spring
Bursts with tumultuous ravaging.

The western ocean's stormy might
Is curling o'er the rampart's height:
Destruction strikes with want and scorn
Presumption, from abundance born.

The tumult of the western deep
Is on the winds, affrighting sleep:
It thunders at my chamber-door;
It bids me wake, to sleep no more.

The tumult of the midnight sea
Swells inland, wildly, fearfully:
The mountain-caves respond its shocks
Among the unaccustomed rocks.

The tumult of the vext sea-coast
Rolls inland like an armed host:
It leaves, for flocks and fertile land,
But foaming waves and treacherous sand.

The wild sea rolls where long have been
Glad homes of men, and pastures green:
To arrogance and wealth succeed
Wide ruin and avenging need.

Seithenyn, come: I call in vain:
The high of birth and weak of brain
Sleeps under ocean's lonely roar
Between the rampart and the shore.

The eternal waste of waters, spread
Above his unrespected head,
The blue expanse, with foam besprent,
Is his too glorious monument.

Another Song of Gwythno.

I love the green and tranquil shore;
I hate the ocean's dizzy roar,
Whose devastating spray has flown
High o'er the monarch's barrier-stone.

Sad was the feast, which he who spread
Is numbered with the inglorious dead;
The feast within the torch-lit hall,
While stormy breakers mined the wall.

To him repentance came too late:
In cups the chatterer met his fate:
Sudden and sad the doom that burst
On him and me, but mine the worst.

I love the shore, and hate the deep:
The wave has robbed my nights of sleep:
The heart of man is cheered by wine;
But now the wine-cup cheers not mine.

The feast, which bounteous hands dispense,
Makes glad the soul, and charms the sense:
But in the circling feast I know
The coming of my deadliest foe.

Blest be the rock, whose foot supplied
A step to them that fled the tide;
The rock of bards, on whose rude steep
I bless the shore, and hate the deep.

"The sigh of Gwythno Garanhir when the breakers ploughed up his land"[2] is the substance of a proverbial distich, which may still be heard on the coast of Merioneth and Cardigan, to express the sense of an overwhelming calamity. The curious investigator may still land on a portion of the ancient stony rampart; which stretches, off the point of Mochres, far out into

---

[2] Ochenaid Gwyddnau Garanhir
    Pan droes y don dros ei dir. [P]

Cardigan Bay, nine miles of the summit being left dry, in calm weather, by the low water of the springtides; and which is now called Sarn Badrig, or St. Patrick's Causeway.

Thus the kingdom of Caredigion fell into ruin: its people were destroyed, or turned out of house and home; and its royal family were brought to a condition in which they found it difficult to get loaves to their fishes. We, who live in more enlightened times, amidst the "gigantic strides of intellect,"[3] when offices of public trust are so conscientiously and zealously discharged, and so vigilantly checked and superintended, may wonder at the wicked negligence of Seithenyn; at the sophisms with which, in his liquor, he vindicated his system, and pronounced the eulogium of his old dilapidations, and at the blind confidence of Gwythno and his people in this virtual guardian of their lives and property: happy that our own public guardians are too virtuous to act or talk like Seithenyn, and that we ourselves are too wise not to perceive, and too free not to prevent it, if they should be so disposed.

Chapter V

THE PRIZE OF THE WEIR

> *Weave a circle round him thrice,*
> *And close your eyes with holy dread;*
> *For he on honey-dew hath fed,*
> *And drank the milk of paradise.*
>
> COLERIDGE.[1]

PRINCE ELPHIN constructed his salmon-weir on the Mawddach at the point where the fresh water met the top of the

[3] See *Crochet Castle*, Chap. II.
[1] "Kubla Khan," ll. 51–54.

springtides. He built near it a dwelling for himself and Angharad, for which the old king Gwythno gradually deserted his palace. An amphitheatre of rocky mountains enclosed a pastoral valley. The meadows gave pasture to a few cows; and the flowers of the mountain-heath yielded store of honey to the bees of many hives, which were tended by Angharad and her handmaids. Elphin had also some sheep, which wandered on the mountains. The worst was, they often wandered out of reach; but, when he could not find his sheep, he brought down a wild goat, the venison of Gwyneth. The woods and turbaries supplied unlimited fuel. The straggling cultivators, who had escaped from the desolation of Gwaelod, and settled themselves above the level of the sea, on a few spots propitious to the plough, still acknowledged their royalty, and paid them tribute in corn. But their principal wealth was fish. Elphin was the first Briton who caught fish on a large scale, and salted them for other purposes than home consumption.

The weir was thus constructed: a range of piles crossed the river from shore to shore, slanting upwards from both shores, and meeting at an angle in the middle of the river. A little down the stream a second range of piles crossed the river in the same manner, having towards the middle several wide intervals with light wicker gates, which, meeting at an angle, were held together by the current, but were so constructed as to yield easily to a very light pressure from below. These gates gave all fish of a certain magnitude admission to a chamber, from which they could neither advance nor retreat, and from which, standing on a narrow bridge attached to the lower piles, Elphin bailed them up at leisure. The smaller fish passed freely up and down the river through the interstices of the piles. This weir was put together in the early summer, and taken to pieces and laid by in the autumn.

Prince Elphin, one fine July night, was sleepless and troubled in spirit. His fishery had been beyond all precedent unproductive, and the obstacle which this circumstance opposed to his arrangements for victualling his little garrison kept him for the better half of the night vigilant in unprofitable cogitation. Soon after the turn of midnight, when dreams are true, he was startled from an incipient doze by a sudden cry of Angharad, who had been favoured with a vision of a miraculous draught of fish. Elphin, as a drowning man catches at a straw, caught at the shadowy promise of Angharad's dream, and at once, beneath the clear light of the just-waning moon, he sallied forth with his princess to examine his weir.

The weir was built across the stream of the river, just above the flow of the ordinary tides; but the springtide had opened the wicker gates, and had floated up a coracle[2] between a pair of them, which closing, as the tide turned, on the coracle's nose, retained it within the chamber of the weir, at the same time that it kept the gates sufficiently open to permit the escape of any fish that might have entered the chamber. The great prize, which undoubtedly might have been there when Angharad dreamed of it, was gone to a fish.

Elphin, little pleased, stepped on the narrow bridge, and opened the gates with a pole that terminated piscatorially in a hook. The coracle began dropping down the stream. Elphin arrested its course, and guided it to land.

In the coracle lay a sleeping child, clothed in splendid apparel. Angharad took it in her arms. The child opened its eyes, and stretched its little arms towards her with a smile; and she uttered, in delight and wonder at its surpassing beauty, the exclamation of "Taliesin!" "Radiant brow!"

Elphin, nevertheless, looked very dismal on finding no food, and an additional mouth; so dismal, that his physiognomy on that occasion passed into a proverb: "As rueful as Elphin when he found Taliesin."[3]

In after years, Taliesin, being on the safe side of prophecy, and writing after the event, addressed a poem to Elphin, in the character of the foundling of the coracle, in which he supposes himself, at the moment of his discovery, to have addressed Elphin as follows:

---

[2] A small boat of basketwork, sheathed with leather. [P]
[3] Mor drist ac Elffin pan gavod Taliesin. [P]

Dyhuddiant Elffin.

The Consolation of Elphin.

Lament not, Elphin: do not measure
By one brief hour thy loss or gain:
Thy weir tonight has borne a treasure,
Will more than pay thee years of pain.
St. Cynllo's aid will not be vain:
Smooth thy bent brow, and cease to mourn:
Thy weir will never bear again
Such wealth as it tonight has borne.

The stormy seas, the silent rivers,
The torrents down the steeps that spring,
Alike of weal or woe are givers,
As pleases heaven's immortal king.
Though frail I seem, rich gifts I bring,
Which in Time's fulness shall appear,
Greater than if the stream should fling
Three hundred salmon in thy weir.

Cast off this fruitless sorrow, loading
With heaviness the unmanly mind:
Despond not; mourn not; evil boding
Creates the ill it fears to find.
When fates are dark, and most unkind
Are they who most should do thee right,
Then wilt thou know thine eyes were blind
To thy good fortune of tonight.

Though, small and feeble, from my coracle
To thee my helpless hands I spread,
Yet in me breathes a holy oracle
To bid thee lift thy drooping head.
When hostile steps around thee tread,
A spell of power my voice shall wield,
That, more than arms with slaughter red,
Shall be thy refuge and thy shield.

Two years after this event, Angharad presented Elphin with

a daughter, whom they named Melanghel. The fishery prospered; and the progress of cultivation and population among the more fertile parts of the mountain districts brought in a little revenue to the old king.

Chapter VI

THE EDUCATION OF TALIESIN

> *The three objects of intellect: the true, the beautiful, and the beneficial.*
> *The three foundations of wisdom: youth, to acquire learning; memory, to retain learning; and genius, to illustrate learning.*
> TRIADS OF WISDOM.[1]

> *The three primary requisites of poetical genius: an eye, that can see nature; a heart, that can feel nature; and a resolution, that dares follow nature.*
> TRIADS OF POETRY.[2]

As TALIESIN grew up, Gwythno instructed him in all the knowledge of the age, which was of course not much, in comparison with ours. The science of political economy was sleeping in the womb of time. The advantage of growing rich by getting into debt and paying interest was altogether unknown: the safe and economical currency, which is produced by a man writing his name on a bit of paper, for which other men give him their property, and which he is always ready to exchange for another bit of paper, of an equally safe and economical manufacture, being also equally ready to render his own person, at a moment's notice, as impalpable as the metal which he promises to pay, is a stretch of wisdom to which the people of

[1] *Cambro-Briton,* II (March 1821), 293.
[2] *Cambro-Briton,* I (Nov. 1820), 100.

those days had nothing to compare. They had no steam-engines, with fires as eternal as those of the nether world, wherein the squalid many, from infancy to age, might be turned into component portions of machinery for the benefit of the purple-faced few. They could neither poison the air with gas nor the waters with its dregs: in short, they made their money of metal, and breathed pure air, and drank pure water, like unscientific barbarians.

Of moral science they had little; but morals, without science, they had about the same as we have. They had a number of fine precepts, partly from their religion, partly from their bards, which they remembered in their liquor, and forgot in their business.

Political science they had none. The blessings of virtual representation[3] were not even dreamed of; so that, when any of their barbarous metallic currency got into their pockets or coffers, it had a chance to remain there, subjecting them to the inconvenience of unemployed capital. Still they went to work politically much as we do. The powerful took all they could get from their subjects and neighbours; and called something or other sacred and glorious, when they wanted the people to fight for them. They repressed disaffection by force, when it showed itself in an overt act; but they encouraged freedom of speech, when it was, like Hamlet's reading, "words, words, words."

There was no liberty of the press, because there was no press; but there was liberty of speech to the bards, whose persons were inviolable, and the general motto of their order was Y GWIR YN ERBYN Y BYD: the Truth against the World. If many of them, instead of acting up to this splendid profession, chose to advance their personal fortunes by appealing to the selfishness, the passions, and the prejudices, of kings, factions, and the rabble, our free press gentry may afford them a little charity out of the excess of their own virtue.

---

[3] A phrase used by opponents of Parliamentary reform to soft-pedal unfair electoral districting; because Parliament really represents all England, the argument went, even those cities which had no seats at all were "virtually" represented in the persons of all members of Parliament.

In physical science, they supplied the place of knowledge by converting conjectures into dogmas; an art which is not yet lost. They held that the earth was the centre of the universe; that an immense ocean surrounded the earth; that the sky was a vast frame resting on the ocean; that the circle of their contact was a mystery of infinite mist; with a great deal more of cosmogony and astronomy, equally correct and profound, which answered the same purpose as our more correct and profound astronomy answers now, that of elevating the mind, as the eidouranion[4] lecturers have it, to sublime contemplations.

Medicine was cultivated by the Druids, and it was just as much a science with them as with us; but they had not the wit or the means to make it a flourishing trade; the principal means to that end being women with nothing to do, articles which especially belong to a high state of civilization.

The laws lay in a small compass: every bard had those of his own community by heart. The king, or chief, was the judge; the plantiff and defendant told their own story; and the cause was disposed of in one hearing. We may well boast of the progress of light, when we turn from this picture to the statutes at large, and the Court of Chancery;[5] and we may indulge in a pathetic reflection on our sweet-faced myriads of "learned friends,"[6] who would be under the unpleasant necessity of suspending themselves by the neck, if this barbaric "practice of the courts" were suddenly revived.

The religion of the time was Christianity grafted on Druidism.[7] The Christian faith had been very early preached in Britain. Some of the Welsh historians are of opinion that it was first preached by some of the apostles: most probably by St. John. They think the evidence inconclusive with respect to St.

[4] A device for representing the motions of the heavenly bodies.
[5] Civil court infamous for dragging cases out for many years.
[6] Lord Brougham; see *Crochet Castle,* Chaps. II, XVII, XVIII.
[7] An ancient form of religious worship in Wales, Ireland, and Gaul about which almost nothing is known, although at one time human sacrifice evidently was practiced. Romanticized tales of weird mystic rites at such places as Stonehenge, accepted in Peacock's day, are the products of eighteenth-century scholarship long since discredited.

Paul. But, at any rate, the faith had made considerable progress among the Britons at the period of the arrival of Hengist;[8] for many goodly churches, and, what was still better, richly-endowed abbeys, were flourishing in many places. The British clergy were, however, very contumacious towards the see of Rome, and would only acknowledge the spiritual authority of the archbishopric of Caer Lleon, which was, during many centuries, the primacy of Britain. St. Augustin,[9] when he came over, at a period not long subsequent to that of the present authentic history, to preach Christianity to the Saxons, who had for the most part held fast to their Odinism,[10] had also the secondary purpose of making them instruments for teaching the British clergy submission to Rome: as a means to which end, the newly-converted Saxons set upon the monastery of Bangor Iscoed, and put its twelve hundred monks to the sword. This was the first overt act in which the Saxons set forth their new sense of a religion of peace. It is alleged, indeed, that these twelve hundred monks supported themselves by the labour of their own hands. If they did so, it was, no doubt, a gross heresy; but whether it deserved the castigation it received from St. Augustin's proselytes, may be a question in polemics.

As the people did not read the Bible, and had no religious tracts, their religion, it may be assumed, was not very pure. The rabble of Britons must have seen little more than the superficial facts, that the lands, revenues, privileges, and so forth, which once belonged to Druids and so forth, now belonged to abbots, bishops, and so forth, who, like their extruded precursors, walked occasionally in a row, chanting unintelligible words, and never speaking in common language but to exhort the people to fight; having indeed, better notions than their predecessors of building, apparel, and cookery; and a better

---

[8] King of the Jutes, who arrived in Britain ca. 449 A.D., marking the start of the Anglo-Saxon migration. See Chap. XII, note 12.

[9] First Archbishop of Canterbury (d. 604), sent by Pope Gregory I to convert the Saxons.

[10] Odin was the chief god of the Norse pantheon, whose worship was brought to Britain with the Saxon influx.

knowledge of the means of obtaining good wine, and of the final purpose for which it was made.

They were observant of all matters of outward form, and tradition even places among them personages who were worthy to have founded a society for the suppression of vice.[11] It is recorded, in the Triads, that "Gwrgi Garwlwyd killed a male and female of the Cymry daily, and devoured them; and, on the Saturday, he killed two of each, that he might not kill on the Sunday." This can only be a type of some sanctimonious hero, who made a cloak of piety for oppressing the poor.

But, even among the Britons, in many of the least populous and most mountainous districts, Druidism was still struggling with Christianity. The lamb had driven the wolf from the rich pastures of the vallies to the high places of the wilderness, where the rites and mysteries of the old religion flourished in secrecy, and where a stray proselyte of the new light was occasionally caught and roasted for the glory of Andraste.

Taliesin, worshipping Nature in her wildest solitudes, often strayed away for days from the dwelling of Elphin, and penetrated the recesses of Eryri,[12] where one especial spot on the banks of Lake Ceirionydd became the favourite haunt of his youth. In these lonely recesses, he became familiar with Druids, who initiated him in their mysteries, which, like all other mysteries, consisted of a quantity of allegorical mummery, pretending to be symbolical of the immortality of the soul, and of its progress through various stages of being; interspersed with a little, too literal, ducking and singeing of the aspirant, by way of trying his mettle, just enough to put him in fear, but not in risk, of his life.

That Taliesin was thoroughly initiated in these mysteries is evident from several of his poems, which have neither head nor tail, and which, having no sense in any other point of view,

[11] Founded in 1802, the Society for the Suppression of Vice was an outgrowth of the Methodist movement of the late eighteenth century. One of its main objects was the prohibition of all work and amusement on Sunday.

[12] Snowdon. [P]

must necessarily, as a learned mythologist has demonstrated, be assigned to the class of theology, in which an occult sense can be found or made for them, according to the views of the expounder. One of them, a shade less obscure than its companions, unquestionably adumbrates the Druidical doctrine of transmigration. According to this poem, Taliesin had been with the cherubim at the fall of Lucifer, in Paradise at the fall of man, and with Alexander at the fall of Babylon; in the ark with Noah, and in the milky-way with Tetragrammaton;[13] and in many other equally marvellous or memorable conditions: showing that, though the names and histories of the new religion were adopted, its doctrines had still to be learned; and, indeed, in all cases of this description, names are changed more readily than doctrines, and doctrines more readily than ceremonies.

When any of the Romans or Saxons, who invaded the island, fell into the hands of the Britons, before the introduction of Christianity, they were handed over to the Druids, who sacrificed them, with pious ceremonies, to their goddess Andraste. These human sacrifices have done much injury to the Druidical character, amongst us, who never practise them in the same way. They lacked, it must be confessed, some of our light, and also some of our prisons. They lacked some of our light, to enable them to perceive that the act of coming, in great multitudes, with fire and sword, to the remote dwellings of peaceable men, with the premeditated design of cutting their throats, ravishing their wives and daughters, killing their children, and appropriating their worldly goods, belongs, not to the department of murder and robbery, but to that of legitimate war, of which all the practitioners are gentlemen, and entitled to be treated like gentlemen. They lacked some of our prisons, in which our philanthropy has provided accommodation for so large a portion of our own people, wherein, if they had left their prisoners alive, they could have kept them from returning to their countrymen, and being at their old tricks again immediately. They would also, perhaps, have found some difficulty in feeding

[13] The four letters YHWH, referring to the Hebrew word Yahweh (or Jehova), symbolized the name of God.

them, from the lack of the county rates,[14] by which the most
sensible and amiable part of our nation, the country squires,
contrive to coop up, and feed, at the public charge, all who
meddle with the wild animals of which they have given themselves the monopoly. But as the Druids could neither lock up
their captives, nor trust them at large, the darkness of their
intellect could suggest no alternative to the process they
adopted, of putting them out of the way, which they did with
all the sanctions of religion and law. If one of these old Druids
could have slept, like the seven sleepers of Ephesus,[15] and
awaked, in the nineteenth century, some fine morning near
Newgate, the exhibition of some half-dozen funipendulous
forgers[16] might have shocked the tender bowels of his humanity, as much as one of his wicker baskets of captives in the
flames shocked those of Cæsar;[17] and it would, perhaps, have
been difficult to convince him that paper credit was not an idol,
and one of a more sanguinary character than his Andraste.
The Druids had their view of these matters, and we have ours;
and it does not comport with the steam-engine speed of our
march of mind[18] to look at more than one side of a question.

The people lived in darkness and vassalage. They were lost
in the grossness of beef and ale. They had no pamphleteering
societies to demonstrate that reading and writing are better than
meat and drink;[19] and they were utterly destitute of the blessings of those "schools for all," the house of correction, and the

[14] Taxes for the upkeep of charitable and penal institutions were
levied by county, rather than by civic or national, government.

[15] A legendary group of Christians who, fleeing from religious
persecution in 250 A.D., took refuge in a cave and fell asleep for 187
years.

[16] Newgate Prison was long associated with hangings ("funipendulous" = "hanging by a cord"). Until well into the nineteenth century
many lesser felonies were capital offenses, and the bodies of executed
criminals were sometimes displayed as object lessons.

[17] See Caesar, *Gallic Wars*, Bk. VI, ¶16.

[18] See *Crochet Castle*, Chaps. II, XVII, XVIII.

[19] An allusion to the Society for the Diffusion of Useful Knowledge; Brougham, its founder, favored education for the masses ("schools
for all"). The Society published cheap self-educatory pamphlets, several
written by Brougham, on subjects ranging from hydraulics to history.
See *Crotchet Castle*, Chap. II.

treadmill, wherein the autochthonal justice of our agrestic ka-
kistrocracy[20] now castigates the heinous sins which were then
committed with impunity, of treading on old footpaths, picking
up dead wood, and moving on the face of the earth within
sound of the whirr of a partridge.

The learning of the time was confined to the bards. It consisted in a somewhat complicated art of versification; in a great
number of pithy apophthegms, many of which have been
handed down to posterity under the title of the Wisdom of
Catog; in an interminable accumulation of Triads, in which
form they bound up all their knowledge, physical, traditional,
and mythological; and in a mighty condensation of mysticism,
being the still-cherished relics of the Druidical rites and doctrines.

The Druids were the sacred class of the bardic order. Before
the change of religion, it was by far the most numerous class;
for the very simple reason, that there was most to be got by it:
all ages and nations having been sufficiently enlightened to
make the trade of priest more profitable than that of poet.
During this period, therefore, it was the only class that much
attracted the notice of foreigners. After the change of religion,
the denomination was retained as that of the second class of
the order. The Bardd Braint, or Bard of Presidency, was of the
ruling order, and wore a robe of sky-blue. The Derwydd, or
Druid, wore a robe of white. The Ovydd, or Ovate, was of the
class of initiation, and wore a robe of green. The Awenyddion,
or disciples, the candidates for admission into the Bardic order,
wore a variegated dress of the three colours, and were passed
through a very severe moral and intellectual probation.

Gwythno was a Bardd Braint, or Bard of Presidency, and
as such he had full power in his own person, without the intervention of a Bardic Congress, to make his Awenydd or dis-

---

[20] I.e., "the home-grown justice of our rural government-by-the-
worst-citizens" (the first and last words were coined by Peacock). The
House of Commons was controlled by the country gentry who were also
justices of the peace and thus enforced at home the laws they passed in
London. They made trespass and poaching subject to severe penalties at
a time when the rural poor were increasingly hard-pressed economically.
See also Chap. XV, note 11 below, and *Crotchet Castle*, Chap. I, note 14.

ciple, Taliesin, an Ovydd or Ovate, which he did accordingly.
Angharad, under the old king's instructions, prepared the green
robe of the young aspirant's investiture. He afterwards acquired
the white robe amongst the Druids of Eryri.

In all Bardic learning, Gwythno was profound. All that he
knew he taught to Taliesin. The youth drew in the draughts of
inspiration among the mountain forests and the mountain
streams, and grew up under the roof of Elphin, in the perfection of genius and beauty.

Chapter VII

THE HUNTINGS OF MAELGON

> Αιεὶ τὸ μὲν ζῆ, τὸ δὲ μεθίσταται κακὸν,
> Τὸ δ' ἐκπέφηνεν ἀυτίκ' ἐξ ἀρχῆς νέον.
>
> EURIPIDES.

> *One ill is ever clinging;*
> *One treads upon its heels;*
> *A third, in distance springing,*
> *Its fearful front reveals.*

GWYTHNO SLEPT, not with his fathers,[1] for they were under the sea, but as near to them as was found convenient,
within the sound of the breakers that rolled over their ancient
dwellings. Elphin was now king of Caredigion, and was lord
of a large but thinly-peopled tract of rock, mountain, forest,
and bog. He held his sovereignty, however, not, as Gwythno
had done during the days of the glory of Gwaelod, by that most
indisputable sort of right which consists in might, but by the
more precarious tenure of the absence of inclination in any of
his brother kings to take away any thing he had.

[1] Cf. I Kings 2:10.

Uther Pendragon, like Gwythno, went the way of all flesh, and Arthur reigned in Caer Lleon, as king of the kings of Britain. Maelgon Gwyneth was then king of that part of North Wales which bordered on the kingdom of Caredigion.

Maelgon was a mighty hunter, and roused the echoes of the mountains with horn and with hound. He went forth to the chace as to war, provisioned for days and weeks, supported by bard and butler, and all the apparel of princely festivity. He pitched his tents in the forest of Snowdon, by the shore of lake or torrent; and, after hunting all the day, he feasted half the night. The light of his torches gleamed on the foam of the cataracts, and the sound of harp and song was mingled with their midnight roar.

When not thus employed, he was either feasting in his Castle of Diganwy, on the Conwy, or fighting with any of the neighbouring kings, who had any thing which he wanted, and which he thought himself strong enough to take from them.

Once, towards the close of autumn, he carried the tumult of the chace into the recesses of Meirion. The consonance, or dissonance, of men and dogs, outpealed the noise of the torrents among the rocks and woods of the Mawddach. Elphin and Teithrin were gone after the sheep or goats in the mountains; Taliesin was absent on the borders of his favourite lake; Angharad and Melanghel were alone. The careful mother, alarmed at the unusual din, and knowing, by rumour, of what materials the Nimrods[2] of Britain were made, fled, with her daughter and handmaids, to the refuge of a deeply-secluded cavern, which they had long before noted as a safe retreat from peril. As they ascended the hills that led to the cavern, they looked back, at intervals, through the openings of the woods, to the growing tumult on the opposite side of the valley. The wild goats were first seen, flying in all directions, taking prodigious leaps from crag to crag, now and then facing about, and rearing themselves on their hind legs, as if in act to butt, and immediately thinking better of it, and springing away on all

---

[2] A Babylonian famed as a hunter, builder of cities, and founder of kingdoms. See Genesis 10:9.

fours among the trees. Next, the more rare spectacle of a noble stag presented itself on the summit of a projecting rock, pausing a moment to snuff the air, then bounding down the most practicable slope to the valley. Next, on the summit which the stag had just deserted, appeared a solitary huntsman, sitting on a prancing horse, and waking a hundred echoes with the blast of his horn. Next rushed into view the main body of the royal company, and the two-legged and four-legged avalanche came thundering down on the track of the flying prey: not without imminent hazard of broken necks; though the mountain-bred horses, which possessed by nature almost the surefootedness of mules, had finished their education under the first professors of the age.

The stag swam the river, and stood at bay before the dwelling of Elphin, where he was in due time despatched by the conjoint valour of dog and man. The royal train burst into the solitary dwelling, where, finding nothing worthy of much note, excepting a large store of salt salmon and mead, they proceeded to broil and tap, and made fearful havoc among the family's winter provision. Elphin and Teithrin, returning to their expected dinner, stood aghast on the threshold of their plundered sanctuary. Maelgon condescended to ask them who they were; and, learning Elphin's name and quality, felt himself bound to return his involuntary hospitality by inviting him to Diganwy. So strong was his sense of justice on this head, that, on Elphin's declining the invitation, which Maelgon ascribed to modesty, he desired two of his grooms to take him up and carry him off.

So Elphin was impressed into royal favour, and was feasted munificently in the castle of Diganwy. Teithrin brought home the ladies from the cavern, and, during the absence of Elphin, looked after the sheep and goats, and did his master's business as well as his own.

One evening, when the royal "nowle" was "tottie of the must,"[3] while the bards of Maelgon were singing the praises of their master, and of all and every thing that belonged to

[3] The royal "head" was "dizzy from new wine." Spenser, *The Faerie Queene,* Bk. VII, Canto VII, St. 39.

him, as the most eximious and transcendent persons and things of the superficial garniture of the earth, Maelgon said to Elphin, "My bards say that I am the best and bravest of kings, that my queen is the most beautiful and chaste of women, and that they themselves, by virtue of belonging to me, are the best and wisest of bards. Now what say you, on these heads?"

This was a perplexing question to Elphin, who, nevertheless, answered: "That you are the best and bravest of kings I do not in the least doubt; yet I cannot think that any woman surpasses my own wife in beauty and chastity; or that any bard equals my bard in genius and wisdom."

"Hear you him, Rhûn?" said Maelgon.

"I hear," said Rhûn, "and mark."

Rhûn was the son of Maelgon, and a worthy heir-apparent of his illustrious sire. Rhûn set out the next morning on an embassy very similar to Tarquin's,[4] accompanied by only one attendant. They lost their way and each other, among the forests of Meirion. The attendant, after riding about some time in great trepidation, thought he heard the sound of a harp, mixed with the roar of the torrents, and following its indications, came at length within sight of an oak-fringed precipice, on the summit of which stood Taliesin, playing and singing to the winds and waters. The attendant could not approach him without dismounting; therefore, tying his horse to a branch, he ascended the rock, and, addressing the young bard, inquired his way to the dwelling of Elphin. Taliesin, in return, inquired his business there; and, partly by examination, partly by divination, ascertained his master's name, and the purport of his visit.

Taliesin deposited his harp in a dry cavern of the rock, and undertook to be the stranger's guide. The attendant remounted his horse, and Taliesin preceded him on foot. But the way by which he led him grew more and more rugged, till the stranger called out, "Whither lead you, my friend? My horse can no longer keep his footing." "There is no other way," said Taliesin. "But give him to my management, and do you follow on foot." The attendant consented. Taliesin mounted the horse, and pres-

---

[4] I.e., to rape Lucrece.

ently struck into a more practicable track; and immediately giving the horse the reins, he disappeared among the woods, leaving the unfortunate equerry to follow as he might, with no better guide than the uncertain recollection of the sound of his horse's heels.

Taliesin reached home before the arrival of Rhûn, and warned Angharad of the mischief that was designed her.

Rhûn, arriving at his destination, found only a handmaid dressed as Angharad, and another officiating as her attendant. The fictitious princess gave him a supper, and every thing else he asked for; and, at parting in the morning, a lock of her hair, and a ring, which Angharad had placed on her finger.

After riding a short distance on his return, Rhûn met his unlucky attendant, torn, tired, and half-starved, and cursing some villain who had stolen his horse. Rhûn was too happy in his own success to have a grain of sympathy for his miserable follower, whom he left to find his horse and his way, or either, or neither, as he might, and returned alone to Diganwy.

Maelgon exultingly laid before Elphin the proofs of his wife's infidelity. Elphin examined the lock of hair, and listened to the narration of Rhûn. He divined at once the trick that had been put upon the prince; but he contented himself with saying, "I do not believe that Rhûn has received the favours of Angharad; and I still think that no wife in Britain, not even the queen of Maelgon Gwyneth, is more chaste or more beautiful than mine."

Hereupon Maelgon waxed wroth. Elphin, in a point which much concerned him, held a belief of his own, different from that which his superiors in worldly power required him to hold. Therefore Maelgon acted as the possessors of worldly power usually act in similar cases: he locked Elphin up within four stone walls, with an intimation that he should keep him there till he pronounced a more orthodox opinion on the question in dispute.

Chapter VIII

THE LOVE OF MELANGHEL

Ἀλλὰ τεαῖς παλάμῃσι μαχήμονα θύρσον ἀείρων,
Αἰθέρσσ ἄξια ῥέξου· ἐπεὶ Διὸς ἄμβροτος αὐλὴ
Οὗ σε πόνων ἀπάνευθε δεδέξεται· οὐδέ σοι Ὧραι
Μήπω ἀεθλεύσαντι πύλας πετάσωσιν Ὀλύμπου.

Grasp the bold thyrsus; seek the field's array;
And do things worthy of ethereal day:
Not without toil to earthborn man befalls
To tread the floors of Jove's immortal halls:
Never to him, who not by deeds has striven,
Will the bright Hours roll back the gates of heaven.

IRIS TO BACCHUS, *in the* 13th *Book of the*
DIONYSIACA OF NONNUS.

THE HOUSEHOLD of Elphin was sufficiently improsperous during the absence of its chief. The havoc which Maelgon's visitation had made in their winter provision, it required the utmost exertions of their collective energies to repair. Even the young princess Melanghel sallied forth, in the garb of a huntress, to strike the deer or the wild goat among the wintry forests, on the summits of the bleak crags, or in the vallies of the flooded streams.

Taliesin, on these occasions, laid aside his harp, and the robe of his order, and accompanied the princess with his hunting spear, and more succinctly apparelled.

Their retinue, it may be supposed, was neither very numerous nor royal, nor their dogs very thoroughbred. It sometimes happened that the deer went one way, the dogs another; the attendants, losing sight of both, went a third, leaving Taliesin, who never lost sight of Melanghel, alone with her among the hills.

One day, the ardour of the chace having carried them far beyond their ordinary bounds, they stood alone together on Craig Aderyn, the Rock of Birds, which overlooks the river Dysyni. This rock takes its name from the flocks of birds which have made it their dwelling, and which make the air resonant with their multitudinous notes. Around, before, and above them, rose mountain beyond mountain, soaring above the leafless forests, to lose their heads in mist; beneath them lay the silent river; and along the opening of its narrow valley, they looked to the not-distant sea.

"Prince Llywarch," said Taliesin, "is a bard and a warrior: he is the son of an illustrious line. Taliesin is neither prince nor warrior: he is the unknown child of the waters."

"Why think you of Llywarch?" said Melanghel, to whom the name of the prince was known only from Taliesin, who knew it only from fame.

"Because," said Taliesin, "there is that in my soul which tells me that I shall have no rival among the bards of Britain: but, if its princes and warriors seek the love of Melanghel, I shall know that I am but a bard, and not as Llywarch."

"You would be Prince Taliesin," said Melanghel, smiling, "to make me your princess. Am I not a princess already? and such an one as is not on earth, for the land of my inheritance is under the sea, under those very waves that now roll within our view; and, in truth, you are as well qualified for a prince as I am for a princess, and have about as valuable a dominion in the mists and the clouds as I have under the waters."

Her eyes sparkled with affectionate playfulness, while her long black hair floated loosely in the breeze that pressed the folds of her drapery against the matchless symmetry of her form.

"Oh, maid!" said Taliesin, "what shall I do to win your love?"

"Restore me my father," said Melanghel, with a seriousness as winning as her playfulness had been fascinating.

"That will I do," said Taliesin, "for his own sake. What shall I do for yours?"

"Nothing more," said Melanghel, and she held out her hand to the youthful bard. Taliesin seized it with rapture, and pressed it to his lips; then, still grasping her hand, and throwing his left arm round her, he pressed his lips to hers.

Melanghel started from him, blushing, and looked at him a moment with something like severity; but he blushed as much as she did, and seemed even more alarmed at her displeasure than she was at his momentary audacity. She reassured him with a smile; and, pointing her spear in the direction of her distant home, she bounded before him down the rock.

This was the kiss of Taliesin to the daughter of Elphin, which is celebrated in an inedited triad, as one of "the Three Chaste Kisses of the island of Britain."

Chapter IX

THE SONGS OF DIGANWY

> *Three things that will always swallow, and never*
> *be satisfied: the sea; a burial ground; and a king.*
> TRIADS OF WISDOM.[1]

THE HALL of Maelgon Gwyneth was ringing with music and revelry, when Taliesin stood on the floor, with his harp, in the midst of the assembly, and, without introduction or preface, struck a few chords, that, as if by magic, suspended all other sounds, and fixed the attention of all in silent expectation. He then sang as follows:

Canu y Medd.

The Mead Song
of Taliesin.

The King of kings upholds the heaven,
And parts from earth the billowy sea:
By Him all earthly joys are given;
He loves the just, and guards the free.
Round the wide hall, for thine and thee,
With purest draughts the mead-horns foam,
Maelgon of Gwyneth! Can it be
That here a prince bewails his home?

---

[1] *Cambro-Briton,* I (April 1820), 284.

The bee tastes not the sparkling draught
Which mortals from his toils obtain;
That sends, in festal circles quaffed,
Sweet tumult through the heart and brain.
The timid, while the horn they drain,
Grow bold; the happy more rejoice;
The mourner ceases to complain;
The gifted bard exalts his voice.

To royal Elphin life I owe,
Nurture and name, the harp, and mead:
Full, pure, and sparkling be their flow,
The horns to Maelgon's lips decreed:
For him may horn to horn succeed,
Till, glowing with their generous fire,
He bid the captive chief be freed,
Whom at his hands my songs require.

Elphin has given me store of mead,
Mead, ale, and wine, and fish, and corn;[2]
A happy home; a splendid steed,
Which stately trappings well adorn.
Tomorrow be the auspicious morn
That home the expected chief shall lead;
So may King Maelgon drain the horn
In thrice three million feasts of mead.

"I give you," said Maelgon, "all the rights of hospitality, and as many horns as you please of the mead you so well and justly extol. If you be Elphin's bard, it must be confessed he spoke truth with respect to you, for you are a much better bard than any of mine, as they are all free to confess: I give them that liberty."

The bards availed themselves of the royal indulgence, and confessed their own inferiority to Taliesin, as the king had commanded them to do. Whether they were all as well convinced of it as they professed to be, may be left to the decision of that very large class of literary gentlemen who are in the

---

2 Wheat.

habit of favouring the reading public with their undisguised opinions.

"But," said Maelgon, "your hero of Caredigion indulged himself in a very unjustifiable bravado with respect to his queen; for he said she was as beautiful and as chaste as mine. Now Rhûn has proved the contrary, with small trouble, and brought away trophies of his triumph; yet still Elphin persists in his first assertion, wherein he grossly disparages the queen of Gwyneth; and for this I hold him in bondage, and will do, till he make recantation."

"That he will never do," said Taliesin. "Your son received only the favours of a handmaid, who was willing, by stratagem, to preserve her lady from violence. The real Angharad was concealed in a cavern."

Taliesin explained the adventure of Rhûn, and pronounced an eulogium on Angharad, which put the king and prince into a towering passion.

Rhûn secretly determined to set forth on a second quest; and Maelgon swore by his mead-horn he would keep Elphin till doomsday. Taliesin struck his harp again, and, in a tone of deep but subdued feeling, he poured forth the

Song of the Wind.[3]

The winds that wander far and free,
Bring whispers from the shores they sweep;
Voices of feast and revelry;
Murmurs of forests and the deep;
Low sounds of torrents from the steep
Descending on the flooded vale;
And tumults from the leaguered keep,
Where foes the dizzy rampart scale.

[3] This poem has little or nothing of Taliesin's *Canu y Gwynt,* with the exception of the title. That poem is apparently a fragment; and, as it now stands, is an incoherent and scarcely-intelligible rhapsody. It contains no distinct or explicit idea, except the proposition that it is an unsafe booty to carry off fat kine, which may be easily conceded in a case where nimbleness of heel, both in man and beast, must have been of great importance. The idea from which, if from any thing in the existing portion of the poem, it takes its name, that the whispers of the wind bring rumours of war from Deheubarth, is rather implied than expressed. [P]

The whispers of the wandering wind
Are borne to gifted ears alone;
For them it ranges unconfined,
And speaks in accents of its own.
It tells me of Deheubarth's throne;
The spider weaves not in its shield:[4]
Already from its towers is blown
The blast that bids the spoiler yield.

Ill with his prey the fox may wend,
When the young lion quits his lair:
Sharp sword, strong shield, stout arm, should tend
On spirits that unjustly dare.
To me the wandering breezes bear
The war-blast from Caer Lleon's brow;
The avenging storm is brooding there
To which Diganwy's towers shall bow.

"If the wind talks to you," said Maelgon, "I may say, with the proverb, you talk to the wind; for I am not to be sung, or cajoled, or vapoured,[5] or bullied out of my prisoner. And as to your war-blasts from Caer Lleon, which I construe into a threat that you will stir up King Arthur against me, I can tell you for your satisfaction, and to spare you the trouble of going so far, that he has enough to do with seeking his wife, who has

---

[4] The spider weaving in suspended armour, is an old emblem of peace and inaction. Thus Bacchylides, in his fragment on Peace:

Ἐν δὲ σιδαροδέτοις πόρπαξιν
Αἰθᾶν ἀραχνᾶν ἔργα πέλονται.

Euripedes, in a fragment of *Erechtheus:*

Κείσθω δόρυ μοι μίτον αμφιπλέκειν
Ἀράχναις.

And Nonnus, whom no poetical image escaped: (*Dionysiaca,* L. xxxviii.)

Οὐ φόνος, οὐ τότε δῆρις' ἔχειτο δὲ τηλόθι χάρμης
Βακχιὰς ἑξαέτηρος ἀραχνιόωσα βοείη.

And Beaumont and Fletcher, in the *Wife for a Month:*

"Would'st thou live so long, till thy sword hung by,
And lazy spiders filled the hilt with cobwebs?"

A Persian poet says, describing ruins:

"The spider spreads the veil in the palace of the Caesars."

And among the most felicitous uses of this emblem, must never be forgotten Hogarth's cobweb over the lid of the charity-box. [P]

[5] Frightened by big talk.

been carried off by some unknown marauder, and with fighting the Saxons, to have much leisure or inclination to quarrel with a true Briton, who is one of his best friends, and his heir presumptive; for, though he is a man of great prowess, and moreover, saving his reverence and your presence, a cuckold, he has not yet favoured his kingdom with an heir apparent. And I request you to understand, that when I extolled you above my bards, I did so only in respect of your verse and voice, melody and execution, figure and action, in short, of your manner; for your matter is naught; and I must do my own bards the justice to say, that, however much they may fall short of you in the requisites aforesaid, they know much better than you do, what is fitting for bards to sing, and kings to hear."

The bards, thus encouraged, recovered from the first shock of Maelgon's ready admission of Taliesin's manifest superiority, and struck up a sort of consecutive chorus, in a series of pennillion, or stanzas, in praise of Maelgon and his heirship presumptive, giving him credit for all the virtues of which the reputation was then in fashion; and, amongst the rest, they very loftily celebrated his justice and magnanimity.

Taliesin could not reconcile his notions of these qualities with Maelgon's treatment of Elphin. He changed his measure and his melody, and pronounced, in impassioned numbers, the poem which a learned Welsh historian calls "The Indignation of the Bards," though, as the indignation was Taliesin's, and not theirs, he seems to have made a small mistake in regard to the preposition.

The Indignation of Taliesin
with the
Bards of Maelgon Gwyneth.

False bards the sacred fire pervert,
Whose songs are won without desert;
Who falsehoods weave in specious lays,
To gild the base with virtue's praise.

From court to court, from tower to tower,
In warrior's tent, in lady's bower,
For gold, for wine, for food, for fire,
They tune their throats at all men's hire.

Their harps reecho wide and far
With sensual love, and bloody war,
And drunkenness, and flattering lies:
Truth's light may shine for other eyes.

In palaces they still are found,
At feasts, promoting senseless sound:
He is their demigod at least,
Whose only virtue is his feast.

They love to talk; they hate to think;
All day they sing; all night they drink:
No useful toils their hands employ;
In boisterous throngs is all their joy.

The bird will fly, the fish will swim,
The bee the honied flowers will skim;
Its food by toil each creature brings,
Except false bards and worthless kings.

Learning and wisdom claim to find
Homage and succour from mankind;
But learning's right, and wisdom's due,
Are falsely claimed by slaves like you.

True bards know truth, and truth will show;
Ye know it not, nor care to know:
Your king's weak mind false judgment warps;
Rebuke his wrong, or break your harps.

I know the mountain and the plain;
I know where right and justice reign;
I from the tower will Elphin free;
Your king shall learn his doom from me.

A spectre of the marsh shall rise,
With yellow teeth, and hair, and eyes,
From whom your king in vain aloof
Shall crouch beneath the sacred roof.

He through the half-closed door shall spy
The Yellow Spectre sweeping by;
To whom the punishment belongs
Of Maelgon's crimes and Elphin's wrongs.

By the name of the Yellow Spectre, Taliesin designated a pestilence, which afterwards carried off great multitudes of the people, and, amongst them, Maelgon Gwyneth, then sovereign of Britain, who had taken refuge from it in a church.

Maelgon paid little attention to Taliesin's prophecy, but he was much incensed by the general tenor of his song.

"If it were not," said Maelgon, "that I do not choose to add to the number of the crimes of which you so readily accuse me, that of disregarding the inviolability of your bardship, I would send you to keep company with your trout-catching king, and you might amuse his salmon-salting majesty with telling him as much truth as he is disposed to listen to; which, to judge by his reception of Rhûn's story of his wife, I take to be exceedingly little. For the present, you are welcome to depart; and, if you are going to Caer Lleon, you may present my respects to King Arthur, and tell him, I hope he will beat the Saxons, and find his wife; but I hope, also, that the cutting me off with an heir apparent will not be the consequence of his finding her, or (which, by the by, is more likely,) of his having lost her."

Taliesin took his departure from the hall of Diganwy, leaving the bards biting their lips at his rebuke, and Maelgon roaring with laughter at his own very excellent jest.

Chapter X

THE DISAPPOINTMENT OF RHÛN

Παρθένε, πῶς μετάμειψας ἐρευθαλέην σέο μορφήν;
Εἰαρινὴν δ'ἀκτῖνα τίς ἔσβεσε σεῖο προσώπου;
Οὐκέτι σῶν μελέων ἀμαρύσσεται ἄργυφος αἴγλη·
Οὐκέτι δ', ὡς τὸ πρόσθε, τεαὶ γελόωσιν ὀπωπαί·

Sweet maid, what grief has changed thy roseate grace,
And quenched the vernal sunshine of thy face?
No more thy light form sparkles as it flies,
Nor laughter flashes from thy radiant eyes.

VENUS TO PASITHEA, *in the 33d Book of the*
DIONYSIACA OF NONNUS.

TALIESIN RETURNED to the dwelling of Elphin, auguring that, in consequence of his information, Rhûn would pay it another visit. In this anticipation he was not mistaken, for Rhûn very soon appeared, with a numerous retinue, determined, apparently, to carry his point by force of arms. He found, however, no inmate in the dwelling but Taliesin and Teithrin ap Tathral.

Rhûn stormed, entreated, promised, and menaced, without success. He perlustrated the vicinity, and found various caverns, but not the one he sought. He passed many days in the search, and, finally, departed; but, at a short distance, he dismissed all his retinue, except his bard of all work, or laureate expectant, and, accompanied by this worthy, returned to the banks of the Mawddach, where they resolved themselves into an ambuscade. It was not long before they saw Taliesin issue from the dwelling, and begin ascending the hill. They followed him, at a cautious distance; first up a steep ascent of the forest-covered rocks; then along a small space of densely-wooded tableland, to the edge of a dingle;[1] and, again, by a slight descent, to the bed of a mountain stream, in a spot where the torrent flung itself, in a series of cataracts, down the rift of a precipitous rock, that towered high above their heads. About half way up the rock, near the base of one of these cataracts, was a projecting ledge, or natural platform of rock, behind which was seen the summit of the opening of a cave. Taliesin paused, and looked around him, as if to ascertain that he was unobserved; and then, standing on a projection of the rock below, he mingled, in spontaneous song, the full power of his voice with the roar of the waters.

[1] A narrow, wooded valley.

TALIESIN.

Maid of the rock! though loud the flood,
My voice will pierce thy cell:
No foe is in the mountain wood;
No danger in the dell:
The torrents bound along the glade;
Their path is free and bright;
Be thou as they, oh mountain maid!
In liberty and light.

Melanghel appeared on the rocky platform, and answered
the song of her lover:

MELANGHEL.

The cataracts thunder down the steep;
The woods all lonely wave:
Within my heart the voice sinks deep
That calls me from my cave.
The voice is dear, the song is sweet,
And true the words must be:
Well pleased I quit the dark retreat,
To wend away with thee.

TALIESIN.

Not yet; not yet: let nightdews fall,
And stars be bright above,
Ere to her long deserted hall
I guide my gentle love.
When torchlight flashes on the roof,
No foe will near thee stray:
Even now his parting courser's hoof
Rings from the rocky way.

MELANGHEL.

Yet climb the path, and comfort speak,
To cheer the lonely cave,
Where woods are bare, and rocks are bleak,
And wintry torrents rave.
A dearer home my memory knows,
A home I still deplore;
Where firelight glows, while winds and snows
Assail the guardian door.

Taliesin vanished a moment from the sight of Rhûn, and almost immediately reappeared by the side of Melanghel, who had now been joined by her mother. In a few minutes he returned, and Angharad and Melanghel withdrew.

Rhûn watched him from the dingle, and then proceeded to investigate the path by which he had gained the platform. After some search he discovered it, ascended to the platform, and rushed into the cavern.

They here found a blazing fire, a half-finished dinner, materials of spinning and embroidering, and other signs of female inhabitancy; but they found not the inhabitants. They searched the cavern to its depth, which was not inconsiderable; much marvelling how the ladies had vanished. While thus engaged, they heard a rushing sound, and a crash on the rocks, as of some ponderous body. The mystery of this noise was very soon explained to them, in a manner that gave an unusual length to their faces, and threw a deep tinge of blue into their rosy complexions. A ponderous stone, which had been suspended like a portcullis at the mouth of the cavern, had been dropped by some unseen agency, and made them as close prisoners as Elphin.

They were not long kept in suspense as to how this matter had been managed. The hoarse voice of Teithrin ap Tathral sounded in their ears from without, "Foxes! you have been seen through, and you are fairly trapped. Eat and drink. You shall want nothing but to get out; which you must want some time; for it is sworn that no hand but Elphin's shall raise the stone of your captivity."

"Let me out," vociferated Rhûn, "and on the word of a prince—" but, before he could finish the sentence, the retreating steps of Teithrin were lost in the roar of the torrent.

Chapter XI

THE HEROES OF DINAS VAWR

L'ombra sua torna ch'era dipartita.
DANTE.[1]

While there is life there is hope.
English Proverb.

PRINCE RHÛN being safe in schistous bastile, Taliesin commenced his journey to the court of King Arthur. On his way to Caer Lleon, he was received with all hospitality, entertained with all admiration, and dismissed with all honour, at the castles of several petty kings, and, amongst the rest, at the castle of Dinas Vawr, on the Towy, which was then garrisoned by King Melvas, who had marched with a great force out of his own kingdom, on the eastern shores of the Severn, to levy contributions in the country to the westward, where, as the pleasure of his company had been altogether unlooked for, he had got possession of a good portion of moveable property. The castle of Dinas Vawr presenting itself to him as a convenient hold, he had taken it by storm; and having cut the throats of the former occupants, thrown their bodies into the Towy, and caused a mass to be sung for the good of their souls, he was now sitting over his bowl, with the comfort of a good conscience, enjoying the fruits of the skill and courage with which he had planned and accomplished his scheme of ways and means for the year.

The hall of Melvas was full of magnanimous heroes, who were celebrating their own exploits in sundry chorusses, especially in that which follows, which is here put upon record as being the quintessence of all the war-songs that ever were written, and the sum and substance of all the appetencies, tendencies, and consequences of military glory:

1 "The soul that went from us returns." *Inferno,* IV, 81.

154

The War-Song of Dinas Vawr.

The mountain sheep are sweeter,
But the valley sheep are fatter;
We therefore deemed it meeter
To carry off the latter.
We made an expedition;
We met a host, and quelled it;
We forced a strong position,
And killed the men who held it.

On Dyfed's[2] richest valley,
Where herds of kine were brousing,
We made a mighty sally,
To furnish our carousing.
Fierce warriors rushed to meet us;
We met them, and o'erthrew them:
They struggled hard to beat us;
But we conquered them, and slew them.

As we drove our prize at leisure,
The king marched forth to catch us:
His rage surpassed all measure,
But his people could not match us.
He fled to his hall-pillars;
And, ere our force we led off,
Some sacked his house and cellars,
While others cut his head off.

We there, in strife bewild'ring,
Spilt blood enough to swim in:
We orphaned many children,
And widowed many women.
The eagles and the ravens
We glutted with our foemen;
The heroes and the cravens,
The spearmen and the bowmen.

---

[2] An area in southwest Wales (now Pembrokeshire).

We brought away from battle,
And much their land bemoaned them,
Two thousand head of cattle,
And the head of him who owned them:
Ednyfed, king of Dyfed,
His head was borne before us;
His wine and beasts supplied our feasts,
And his overthrow, our chorus.

As the doughty followers of Melvas, having sung themselves hoarse with their own praises, subsided one by one into drunken sleep, Taliesin, sitting near the great central fire, and throwing around a scrutinizing glance on all the objects in the hall, noticed a portly and somewhat elderly personage, of an aspect that would have been venerable, if it had been less rubicund and Bacchic, who continued plying his potations with undiminished energy, while the heroes of the festival dropped round him, like the leaves of autumn. This figure excited Taliesin's curiosity. The features struck him with a sense of resemblance to objects which had been somewhere familiar to him; but he perplexed himself in vain, with attempts at definite recollections. At length, when these two were almost the sole survivors of the evening, the stranger approached him with a golden goblet, which he had just replenished with the choicest wine of the vaults of Dinas Vawr, and pronounced the oracular monosyllable, "Drink!" to which he subjoined emphatically "GWIN O EUR: Wine from gold. That is my taste. Ale is well; mead is better; wine is best. Horn is well; silver is better; gold is best."

Taliesin, who had been very abstemious during the evening, took the golden goblet, and drank to please the inviter; in the hope that he would become communicative, and satisfy the curiosity his appearance had raised.

The stranger sat down near him, evidently in that amiable state of semi-intoxication which inflates the head, warms the heart, lifts up the veil of the inward man, and sets the tongue flying, or rather tripping, in the double sense of nimbleness and titubancy.

The stranger repeated, taking a copious draught, "My taste is wine from gold."

"I have heard those words," said Taliesin, "GWIN O EUR, repeated as having been the favourite saying of a person whose memory is fondly cherished by one as dear to me as a mother, though his name, with all others, is the by-word of all that is disreputable."

"I cannot believe," said the stranger, "that a man whose favourite saying was GWIN O EUR, could possibly be a disreputable person, or deserve any other than that honourable remembrance, which, you say, only one person is honest enough to entertain for him."

"His name," said Taliesin, "is too unhappily notorious throughout Britain, by the terrible catastrophe of which his GWIN O EUR was the cause."

"And what might that be?" said the stranger.

"The inundation of Gwaelod," said Taliesin.

"You speak then," said the stranger, taking an enormous potation, "of Seithenyn, Prince Seithenyn, Seithenyn ap Seithin Saidi, Arglwyd Gorwarcheidwad yr Argae Breninawl."

"I seldom hear his name," said Taliesin, "with any of those sounding additions; he is usually called Seithenyn the Drunkard."

The stranger goggled about his eyes in an attempt to fix them steadily on Taliesin, screwed up the corners of his mouth, stuck out his nether lip, pursed up his chin, thrust forward his right foot, and elevated his golden goblet in his right hand; then, in a tone which he intended to be strongly becoming of his impressive aspect and imposing attitude, he muttered, "Look at me."

Taliesin looked at him accordingly, with as much gravity as he could preserve.

After a silence, which he designed to be very dignified and solemn, the stranger spoke again: "I am the man."

"What man?" said Taliesin.

"The man," replied his entertainer, "of whom you have spoken so disparagingly; Seithenyn ap Seithyn Saidi."

"Seithenyn," said Taliesin, "has slept twenty years under the waters of the western sea, as King Gwythno's Lamentations have made known to all Britain."

"They have not made it known to me," said Seithenyn, "for the best of all reasons, that one can only know the truth; for, if that which we think we know is not truth, it is something which we do not know. A man cannot know his own death; for, while he knows any thing, he is alive; at least, I never heard of a dead man who knew any thing, or pretended to know any thing: if he had so pretended, I should have told him to his face he was no dead man."

"Your mode of reasoning," said Taliesin, "unquestionably corresponds with what I have heard of Seithenyn's: but how is it possible Seithenyn can be living?"

"Every thing that is, is possible, says Catog the Wise;" answered Seithenyn, with a look of great sapience. "I will give you proof that I am not a dead man; for, they say, dead men tell no tales: now I will tell you a tale, and a very interesting one it is. When I saw the sea sapping the tower, I jumped into the water, and just in the nick of time. It was well for me that I had been so provident as to empty so many barrels, and that somebody, I don't know who, but I suppose it was my daughter, had been so provident as to put the bungs into them, to keep them sweet; for the beauty of it was that, when there was so much water in the case, it kept them empty; and when I jumped into the sea, the sea was just making a great hole in the cellar, and they were floating out by dozens. I don't know how I managed it, but I got one arm over one, and the other arm over another: I nipped them pretty tight; and, though my legs were under water, the good liquor I had in me kept me warm. I could not help thinking, as I had nothing else to think of just then that touched me so nearly, that if I had left them full, and myself empty, as a sober man would have done, we should all three, that is, I and the two barrels, have gone to the bottom together, that is to say, separately; for we should never have come together, except at the bottom, perhaps; when no one of us could have done the other any good; whereas they have done me much good, and I have requited it; for, first, I did them the service of emptying them; and then they did me the service of floating me with the tide, whether the ebb, or the flood, or both, is more than I can tell, down to the coast of Dyfed, where I was picked up by fishermen; and such was my sense of gratitude, that, though I had always before detested an empty barrel, except as a trophy, I swore I would not budge from the water unless my two barrels went with me; so we were all marched inland together, and were taken into the service of King Ednyfed, where I stayed till his castle was sacked, and his head cut off, and his beeves marched away with, by the followers of King Melvas, of whom I killed two or three; but they were too many for us: therefore, to make the best of a bad bargain, I followed leisurely in the train of the beeves, and presented myself to King Melvas, with this golden goblet, saying GWIN O EUR. He was struck with my deportment, and made me his chief butler; and now my two barrels are the two pillars of his cellar, where I regularly fill them from affection, and as regularly empty them from gratitude, taking care to put the bungs in them, to keep them sweet."

"But all this while," said Taliesin, "did you never look back to the Plain of Gwaelod, to your old king, and, above all, to your daughter?"

"Why yes," said Seithenyn, "I did in a way! But as to the Plain of Gwaelod, that was gone, buried under the sea, along with many good barrels, which I had been improvident enough to leave full: then, as to the old king, though I had a great regard for him, I thought he might be less likely to feast me in his hall, than to set up my head on a spike over his gate: then, as to my daughter—"

Here he shook his head, and looked maudlin; and dashing two or three drops from his eyes, he put a great many into his mouth.

"Your daughter," said Taliesin, "is the wife of King Elphin, and has a daughter, who is now as beautiful as her mother was."

"Very likely," said Seithenyn, "and I should be very glad to see them all; but I am afraid King Elphin, as you call him, (what he is king of, you shall tell me at leisure,) would do me a mischief. At any rate, he would stint me in liquor. No! If they will visit me, here I am. Fish, and water, will not agree with me. I am growing old, and need cordial nutriment. King Melvas will never want for beeves and wine; nor, indeed, for any thing else that is good. I can tell you what," he added, in a very low voice, cocking his eye, and putting his finger on his lips, "he has got in this very castle the finest woman in Britain."

"That I doubt," said Taliesin.

"She is the greatest, at any rate," said Seithenyn, "and ought to be the finest."

"How the greatest?" said Taliesin.

Seithenyn looked round, to observe if there were any listener near, and fixed a very suspicious gaze on a rotund figure of a fallen hero, who lay coiled up like a maggot in a filbert, and snoring with an energy that, to the muddy apprehensions of Seithenyn, seemed to be counterfeit. He determined, by a gentle experiment, to ascertain if his suspicions were well founded; and proceeded, with what he thought great caution, to apply the point of his foot to the most bulging portion of the fat sleeper's circumference. But he greatly miscalculated his intended impetus, for he impinged his foot with a force that overbalanced himself, and hurled him headlong over his man, who instantly sprang on his legs, shouting "To arms!" Numbers started up at the cry; the hall rang with the din of arms, and with the vociferation of questions, which there were many to ask, and none to answer. Some stared about for the enemy; some rushed to the gates; others to the walls. Two or three, reeling in the tumult and the darkness, were jostled over the parapet, and went rolling down the precipitous slope of the castle hill, crashing through the bushes, and bellowing for some one to stop them, till their clamours were cut short by a plunge into the Towy, where the conjoint weight of their armour and their liquor carried them at once to the bottom. The rage which would have fallen on the enemy, if there had been one, was turned against the author of the false alarm; but, as none could point him out, the tumult subsided by degrees, through a descending scale of imprecations, into the last murmured malediction of him whom the intensity of his generous anger kept longest awake. By this time, the rotund hero had again coiled himself up into his ring; and Seithenyn was stretched in a

right line, as a tangent to the circle, in a state of utter inca-
pacity to elucidate the mystery of King Melvas's possession of
the finest woman in Britain.

Chapter XII

THE SPLENDOUR OF CAER LLEON

*The three principal cities of the isle of Britain: Caer
Llion upon Wysg in Cymru; Caer Llundain in Lloegr;
and Caer Evrawg in Deifr and Brynaich.*[1]
TRIADS OF THE ISLE OF BRITAIN.

THE SUNSET of a bright December day was glittering on
the waves of the Usk, and on the innumerable roofs, which,
being composed chiefly of the glazed tiles of the Romans, reflected the light almost as vividly as the river; when Taliesin
descended one of the hills that border the beautiful valley in
which then stood Caer Lleon, the metropolis of Britain, and in
which now stands, on a small portion of the selfsame space, a
little insignificant town, possessing nothing of its ancient glory
but the unaltered name of Caer Lleon.

The rapid Usk flowed then, as now, under the walls: the high
wooden bridge, with its slender piles, was then much the same
as it is at this day: it seems to have been never regularly re-
built, but to have been repaired, from time to time, on the
original Roman model. The same green and fertile meadows,
the same gently-sloping wood-covered hills, that now meet the
eye of the tourist, then met the eye of Taliesin; except that the
woods on one side of the valley, were then only the skirts of
an extensive forest, which the nobility and beauty of Caer

[1] Caer Lleon upon Usk in Cambria: London in Loegria: and York
in Deïra and Bernicia. [P] [*Cambro-Briton,* II (1821), 387.]

Lleon made frequently reecho to the clamours of the chace.

The city, which had been so long the centre of the Roman supremacy, which was now the seat of the most illustrious sovereign that had yet held the sceptre of Britain, could not be approached by the youthful bard, whose genius was destined to eclipse that of all his countrymen, without feelings and reflections of deep interest. The sentimental tourist, (who, perching himself on an old wall, works himself up into a soliloquy of philosophical pathos, on the vicissitudes of empire and the mutability of all sublunary things, interrupted only by an occasional peep at his watch, to ensure his not over-staying the minute at which his fowl, comfortably roasting at the nearest inn, has been promised to be ready,) has, no doubt, many fine thoughts well worth recording in a dapper volume; but Taliesin had an interest in the objects before him too deep to have a thought to spare, even for his dinner. The monuments of Roman magnificence, and of Roman domination, still existing in comparative freshness; the arduous struggle, in which his countrymen were then engaged with the Saxons, and which, notwithstanding the actual triumphs of Arthur, Taliesin's prophetic spirit told him would end in their being dispossessed of all the land of Britain, except the wild region of Wales, (a result which political sagacity might have apprehended from their disunion, but which, as he told it to his countrymen in that memorable prophecy which every child of the Cymry knows, has established for him, among them, the fame of a prophet;) the importance of himself and his benefactors of the objects of his visit to the city, on the result of which depended the liberation of Elphin, and the success of his love for Melanghel; the degree in which these objects might be promoted by the construction he had put on Seithenyn's imperfect communication respecting the lady in Dinas Vawr; furnished, altogether, more materials for absorbing thought, than the most zealous peregrinator, even if he be at once poet, antiquary, and philosopher, is likely to have at once in his mind, on the top of the finest old wall on the face of the earth.

Taliesin passed, in deep musing, through the gates of Caer Lleon; but his attention was speedily drawn to the objects around him. From the wild solitudes in which he had passed his earlier years, the transition to the castles and cities he had already visited, furnished much food to curiosity: but the ideas of them sunk into comparative nothingness before the magnificence of Caer Lleon.

He did not stop in the gateway to consider the knotty question, which has since puzzled so many antiquaries, whether the name of Caer Lleon signifies the City of Streams, the City of Legions, or the City of King Lleon? He saw a river filled with ships, flowing through fine meadows, bordered by hills and forests; walls of brick, as well as of stone; a castle, of impregnable strength; stately houses, of the most admirable architecture; palaces, with gilded roofs; Roman temples, and Christian churches; a theatre, and an amphitheatre. The public and private buildings of the departed Romans were in excellent preservation; though the buildings, and especially the temples, were no longer appropriated to their original purposes. The king's butler, Bedwyr, had taken possession of the Temple of Diana, as a cool place of deposit for wine: he had recently effected a stowage of vast quantities therein, and had made a most luminous arrangement of the several kinds; under the judicious and experienced superintendence of Dyvrig, the Ex-Archbishop of Caer Lleon; who had just then nothing else to do, having recently resigned his see in favour of King Arthur's uncle, David, who is, to this day, illustrious as the St. David in whose honour the Welshmen annually adorn their hats with a leek.[2] This David was a very respectable character in his way: he was a man of great sanctity and simplicity; and, in order to eschew the vanities of the world, which were continually present to him in Caer Lleon, he removed the metropolitan see, from Caer Lleon, to the rocky, barren, woodless, streamless, meadowless, tempest-beaten point of Mynyw, which was afterwards called St. David's. He was the mirror and pattern of a godly

[2] There is no historical evidence that St. David, patron saint of Wales, was Archbishop of Caer Lleon or related to Arthur. After a victory over the Saxons, he is said to have ordered each Welsh soldier to put a leek in his hat, as a sign of distinction; the leek has become a symbol of Welsh nationalism.

life; teaching by example, as by precept; admirable in words, and excellent in deeds; tall in stature, handsome in aspect, noble in deportment, affable in address, eloquent and learned, a model to his followers, the life of the poor, the protector of widows, and the father of orphans. This makes altogether a very respectable saint; and it cannot be said, that the honourable leek is unworthily consecrated. A long series of his Catholic successors maintained, in great magnificence, a cathedral, a college, and a palace; keeping them all in repair, and feeding the poor into the bargain, from the archiepiscopal, or, when the primacy of Caer Lleon had merged in that of Canterbury, from the episcopal, revenues: but these things were reformed altogether by one of the first Protestant bishops, who, having a lady that longed for the gay world, and wanting more than all the revenues for himself and his family, first raised the wind by selling off the lead from the roof of his palace, and then obtained permission to remove from it, on the plea that it was not watertight. The immediate successors of this bishop, whose name was Barlow,[3] were in every way worthy of him; the palace and college have, consequently, fallen into incurable dilapidation, and the cathedral has fallen partially into ruins, and, most impartially, into neglect and defacement.

To return to Taliesin, in the streets of Caer Lleon. Plautus and Terence[4] were not heard in the theatre, nor to be heard of in its neighbourhood; but it was thought an excellent place for an Eisteddfod, or Bardic Congress, and was made the principal place of assembly of the Bards of the island of Britain. This is what Ross of Warwick means, when he says there was a noble university of students in Caer Lleon.[5]

The mild precepts of the new religion had banished the ferocious sports to which the Romans had dedicated the amphi-

[3] William Barlow (d. 1569?), an adroit ecclesiastic politician who altered his theological views whenever necessary to retain royal favor, was Bishop of St. David's from 1536–1549.

[4] Roman comic dramatists (second century B.C.).

[5] John Ross, or Rous (1411?–1491), whose erratic *Historia Regum Angliae* traces the history of the British crown to 1486. He was also interested in the history of the British universities.

theatre, and, as Taliesin passed, it was pouring forth an improved and humanized multitude, who had been enjoying the pure British pleasure of baiting a bear.

The hot baths and aqueducts, the stoves of "wonderful artifice," as Giraldus[6] has it, which diffused hot air through narrow spiracles, and many other wonders of the place, did not all present themselves to a first observation. The streets were thronged with people, especially of the fighting order, of whom a greater number flocked about Arthur, than he always found it convenient to pay. Horsemen, with hawks and hounds, were returning from the neighbouring forest, accompanied by beautiful huntresses, in scarlet and gold.

Taliesin, having perlustrated the city, proceeded to the palace of Arthur. At the gates he was challenged by a formidable guard, but passed by his bardic privilege. It was now very near Christmas, and when Taliesin entered the great hall, it was blazing with artificial light, and glowing with the heat of the Roman stoves.

Arthur had returned victorious from the great battle of Badon hill, in which he had slain with his own hand four hundred and forty Saxons; and was feasting as merrily as an honest man can be supposed to do while his wife is away. Kings, princes, and soldiers of fortune, bards and prelates, ladies superbly apparelled, and many of them surpassingly beautiful; and a most gallant array of handsome young cupbearers, marshalled and well drilled by the king's butler, Bedwyr, who was himself a petty king, were the chief components of the illustrious assembly.

Amongst the ladies were the beautiful Tegau Eurvron; Dywir the Golden-haired; Enid, the daughter of Yniwl; Garwen, the daughter of Henyn; Gwyl, the daughter of Enddaud; and Indeg, the daughter of Avarwy Hir, of Maelienydd. Of these, Tegau Eurvron, or Tegau of the Golden Bosom, was the wife of Caradoc, and one of the Three Chaste Wives of the island of

---

[6] Giraldus de Barri, or Cambrensis (1146?–1220?), Welsh churchman and historian. See *Crotchet Castle,* Chap. XIII, note 2.

Britain. She is the heroine, who, as the lady of Sir Cradock, is distinguished above all the ladies of Arthur's court, in the ballad of the Boy and the Mantle.[7]

Amongst the bards were Prince Llywarch, then in his youth, afterwards called Llywarch Hên, or Llywarch the Aged; Aneurin, the British Homer, who sang the fatal battle of Cattraëth,[8] which laid the foundation of the Saxon ascendancy, in heroic numbers, which the gods have preserved to us, and who was called the Monarch of the Bards, before the days of the glory of Taliesin; and Merddin Gwyllt, or Merlin the Wild, who was so deep in the secrets of nature, that he obtained the fame of a magician, to which he had at least as good a title as either Friar Bacon or Cornelius Agrippa.[9]

Amongst the petty kings, princes, and soldiers of fortune, were twenty-four marchawg, or cavaliers, who were the counsellors and champions of Arthur's court. This was the heroic band, illustrious, in the songs of chivalry, as the Knights of the Round Table. Their names and pedigrees would make a very instructive and entertaining chapter; and would include the interesting characters of Gwalchmai ap Gwyar the Courteous, the nephew of Arthur; Caradoc, "Colofn Cymry," the Pillar of Cambria, whose lady, as above noticed, was the mirror of chastity; and Trystan ap Tallwch, the lover of the beautiful Essyllt, the daughter, or, according to some, the wife, of his uncle March ap Meirchion; persons known to all the world, as Sir Gawain, Sir Cradock, and Sir Tristram.

On the right hand of King Arthur sate the beautiful Indeg, and on his left the lovely Garwen. Taliesin advanced, along the tesselated floor, towards the upper end of the hall, and, kneeling before King Arthur, said, "What boon will King Arthur grant to him who brings news of his queen?"

"Any boon," said Arthur, "that a king can give."

---

[7] See Bishop Thomas Percy's *Reliques of Ancient English Poetry,* Series III, Bk. I.

[8] Depicted in Aneurin's epic poem *Gododin;* the battle was probably fought in 603.

[9] Roger Bacon (1214?–1294) and Heinrich Cornelius Agrippa von Nettesheim (1486–1535), English and German scholars whose researches on chemistry and alchemy earned each a reputation as a sorcerer.

"Queen Gwenyvar," said Taliesin, "is the prisoner of King Melvas, in the castle of Dinas Vawr."

The mien and countenance of his informant satisfied the king that he knew what he was saying; therefore, without further parlance, he broke up the banquet, to make preparations for assailing Dinas Vawr.

But, before he began his march, King Melvas had shifted his quarters, and passed beyond the Severn to the isle of Avallon,[10] where the marshes and winter-floods assured him some months of tranquillity and impunity.

King Arthur was highly exasperated, on receiving the intelligence of Melvas's movement; but he had no remedy, and was reduced to the alternative of making the best of his Christmas with the ladies, princes, and bards who crowded his court.

The period of the winter solstice had been always a great festival with the northern nations, the commencement of the lengthening of the days being, indeed, of all points in the circle of the year, that in which the inhabitants of cold countries have most cause to rejoice. This great festival was anciently called Yule; whether derived from the Gothic *Iola*, to make merry; or from the Celtic *Hiaul*, the sun; or from the Danish and Swedish *Hiul*, signifying wheel or revolution, December being *Hiul-month*, or the month of return; or from the Cimbric word *Ol*, which has the important signification of ALE, is too knotty a controversy to be settled here: but Yule had been long a great festival, with both Celts and Saxons; and, with the change of religion, became the great festival of Christmas, retaining most of its ancient characteristics while England was Merry England; a phrase which must be a mirifical[11] puzzle to any one who looks for the first time on its present most lugubrious inhabitants.

The mistletoe of the oak was gathered by the Druids with great ceremonies, as a symbol of the season. The misletoe continued to be so gathered, and to be suspended in halls and

---

[10] Where, according to legend, Arthur was carried after his final battle to be healed of his wounds and to return in Britain's hour of greatest need.

[11] Causing wonder or astonishment.

kitchens, if not in temples, implying an unlimited privilege of kissing; which circumstance, probably, led a learned antiquary to opine that it was the forbidden fruit.

The Druids, at this festival, made, in a capacious cauldron, a mystical brewage of carefully-selected ingredients, full of occult virtues, which they kept from the profane, and which was typical of the new year and of the transmigration of the soul. The profane, in humble imitation, brewed a bowl of spiced ale, or wine, throwing therein roasted crabs; the hissing of which, as they plunged, piping hot, into the liquor, was heard with much unction at midwinter, as typical of the conjunct benignant influences of fire and strong drink. The Saxons called this the Wassail-bowl, and the brewage of it is reported to have been one of the charms with which Rowena fascinated Vortigern.[12]

King Arthur kept his Christmas so merrily, that the memory of it passed into a proverb:[13] "As merry as Christmas in Caer Lleon."

Caer Lleon was the merriest of places, and was commonly known by the name of Merry Caer Lleon; which the English ballad-makers, for the sake of the smoother sound, and confounding Cambria with Cumbria,[14] most ignorantly or audaciously turned into Merry Carlisle; thereby emboldening a northern antiquary to set about proving that King Arthur was a Scotchman; according to the old principles of harry and foray, which gave Scotchmen a right to whatever they could find on the English border; though the English never admitted their title to any thing there, excepting a halter in Carlisle.[15]

The chace, in the neighbouring forest; tilting in the amphitheatre; trials of skill in archery, in throwing the lance and

[12] Vortigern, a legendary fifth-century King of Britain, married Rowena, daughter of King Hengist of the Jutes, which tribe he had invited to Britain as an ally in a war against the Picts; but after the marriage the Jutes refused to leave.

[13] Mor llawen ag Ngdolig yn Nghaerlleon. [P]

[14] I.e., confusing the name for Wales with the name for Scotland.

[15] Located at the border between England and Scotland, Carlisle had been a fortress and scene of constant wars and border raids since the time of the Romans. As such, the city had been long associated with executions.

riding at the quintain,[16] and similar amusements of the morning, created good appetites for the evening feasts; in which Prince Cei, who is well known as Sir Kay, the seneschal, superintended the viands, as King Bedwyr did the liquor; having each a thousand men at command, for their provision, arrangement, and distribution; and music worthy of the banquet was provided and superintended by the king's chief harper, Geraint, of whom a contemporary poet observes, that when he died, the gates of heaven were thrown wide open, to welcome the ingress of so divine a musician.

Chapter XIII

THE GHOSTLINESS OF AVALLON

> *Poco più, poco meno, tutti al mondo vivono d'impostura: e chi è di buon gusto, dissimula quando occorre, gode quando può, crede quel che vuole, ride de' pazzi, e figura un mondo a suo gusto.*
>
> GOLDONI.[1]

"WHERE is the young bard," said King Arthur, after some nights of Christmas had passed by, "who brought me the news of my queen, and to whom I promised a boon, which he has not yet claimed?"

None could satisfy the king's curiosity. Taliesin had disappeared from Caer Lleon. He knew the power and influence of Maelgon Gwyneth; and he was aware that King Arthur, how-

---

[16] A target, often a post or a revolving figure, for tilting at with lances.

[1] "Everyone in the world lives by deception, some a little more, some a little less: and the refined man dissimulates when necessary, has a good time when he can, believes what he wants, laughs at fools, and pictures the world to his own taste."

ever favourably he might receive his petition, would not find leisure to compel the liberation of Elphin, till he had enforced from Melvas the surrender of his queen. It occurred to him that her restoration might be effected by peaceable means; and he knew that, if he could be in any degree instrumental to this result, it would greatly strengthen his claims on the king. He engaged a small fishing-vessel, which had just landed a cargo for the Christmas feasts of Caer Lleon, and set sail for the isle of Avallon. At that period, the springtides of the sea rolled round a cluster of islands, of which Avallon was one, over the extensive fens, which wiser generations have embanked and reclaimed.

The abbey of Avallon, afterwards called Glastonbury, was, even then, a comely and commodious pile, though not possessing any of that magnificence which the accumulated wealth of ages subsequently gave to it. A large and strongly fortified castle, almost adjoining the abbey, gave to the entire place the air of a strong hold of the church militant. King Melvas was one of the pillars of the orthodoxy of those days: he was called the Scourge of the Pelagians;[2] and extended the shield of his temporal might over the spiritual brotherhood of Avallon, who, in return, made it a point of conscience not to stint him in absolutions.

Some historians pretend that a comfortable nunnery was erected at a convenient distance from the abbey, that is to say, close to it; but this involves a nice question in monastic antiquity, which the curious may settle for themselves.

It was about midway between nones and vespers when Taliesin sounded, on the gate of the abbey, a notice of his wish for admission. A small trapdoor in the gate was cautiously opened, and a face, as round and as red as the setting sun in November, shone forth in the aperture.

The topographers who have perplexed themselves about the origin of the name of Ynys Avallon, "the island of apples," had not the advantage of this piece of meteoroscopy:[3] if they

[2] The British monk Pelagius and his followers denied the doctrine of original sin and were declared heretics in 418.
[3] Literally, observation of the stars.

could have looked on this archetype of a Norfolk beefin,[4] with the knowledge that it was only a sample of a numerous fraternity, they would at once have perceived the fitness of the appellation. The brethren of Avallon were the apples of the church. It was the oldest monastic establishment in Britain; and consequently, as of reason, the most plump, succulent, and rosy. It had, even in the sixth century, put forth the fruits of good living, in a manner that would have done honour to a more enlightened age. It went on steadily improving in this line till the days of its last abbot, Richard Whiting, who built the stupendous kitchen, which has withstood the ravages of time and the Reformation; and who, as appears by authentic documents, and, amongst others, by a letter signed with the honoured name of Russell, was found guilty, by a right worshipful jury, of being suspected of great riches, and of an inclination to keep them; and was accordingly sentenced to be hanged forthwith, along with his treasurer and subtreasurer, who were charged with aiding and abetting him in the safe custody of his cash and plate; at the same time that the Abbot of Peterborough was specially reprieved from the gallows, on the ground that he was the said Russell's particular friend.[5] This was a compendium of justice and mercy according to the new light of King Henry the Eighth. The abbot's kitchen is the most interesting and perfect portion of the existing ruins. These ruins were overgrown with the finest ivy in England, till it was, not long since, pulled down by some Vandal, whom the Society of Antiquaries[6] had sent down to make drawings of the walls, which he executed literally, by stripping them bare, that he might draw the walls, and nothing else. Its shade no longer waves over the musing moralist, who, with folded arms, and

[4] Ox for slaughter.

[5] Whiting (d. 1539), the last Abbot of Glastonbury, was executed for treason in the course of Henry VIII's break with the Roman church. That he was officially charged with embezzlement is highly uncertain. Sir John Russell (1486?–1555), first Earl of Bedford, was a special agent and confidant of Henry VIII who assisted at the execution of Whiting.

[6] The first of many historical societies established to study and preserve England's past; founded about 1572. The pulling down of the ivy saved the ruins of Glastonbury from ultimate decay.

his back against a wall, dreams of the days that are gone; or the sentimental cockney, who, seating himself with much gravity on a fallen column, produces a flute from his pocket, and strikes up "I'd be a butterfly."[7]

From the phænomenon of a blushing fruit that was put forth in the abbey gate of Avallon issued a deep, fat, gurgling voice, which demanded of Taliesin his name and business.

"I seek the abbot of Avallon," said Taliesin.

"He is confessing a penitent," said the ghostly brother, who was officiating in turn as porter.

"I can await his leisure," said Taliesin, "but I must see him."

"Are you alone?" said the brother.

"I am," said Taliesin.

The gate unclosed slowly, just wide enough to give him admittance. It was then again barred and barricadoed.

The ghostly brother, of whom Taliesin had now a full view, had a figure corresponding with his face, and wanted nothing but a pair of horns and a beard in ringlets, to look like an avatar of Bacchus. He maintained, however, great gravity of face, and decorum of gesture, as he said to Taliesin, "Hospitality is the rule of our house; but we are obliged to be cautious in these times, though we live under powerful protection. Those bloody Nimrods, the Saxons, are athirst for the blood of the righteous. Monsters that are born with tails."

Taliesin had not before heard of this feature of Saxon conformation, and expressed his astonishment accordingly.

"How?" said the monk. "Did not a rabble of them fasten goats' tails to the robe of the blessed preacher in Riw, and did he not, therefore, pray that their posterity might be born with tails?[8] And it is so. But let that pass. Have they not sacked monasteries, plundered churches, and put holy brethren to the sword? The blood of the saints calls for vengeance."

"And will have it," said Taliesin, "from the hand of Arthur."

The name of Arthur evidently discomposed the monk, who,

---

[7] A popular song, written by Thomas Haynes Bayly.

[8] Evidently an episode in the career of St. Augustine (see Chap. VI); according to one version of the legend, the tails were fish tails, thrown at him by the men of Dorset.

desiring Taliesin to follow him, led the way across the hall of the abbey, and along a short wide passage, at the end of which was a portly door.

The monk disappeared through this door, and, presently returning, said, "The abbot requires your name and quality."

"Taliesin, the bard of Elphin ap Gwythno Garanhir," was the reply.

The monk disappeared again, and, returning, after a longer pause than before, said, "You may enter."

The abbot was a plump and comely man, of middle age, having three roses in his complexion; one in full blossom on each cheek, and one in bud on the tip of his nose.

He was sitting at a small table, on which stood an enormous vase, and a golden goblet; and opposite to him sat the penitent of whom the round-faced brother had spoken, and in whom Taliesin recognised his acquaintance of Dinas Vawr, who called himself Seithenyn ap Seithyn.

The abbot and Seithenyn sat with their arms folded on the table, leaning forward towards each other, as if in momentous discussion.

The abbot said to Taliesin, "Sit;" and to his conductor, "Retire, and be silent."

"Will it not be better," said the monk, "that I cross my lips with the sign of secrecy?"

"It is permitted," said the abbot.

Seithenyn held forth the goblet to the monk, who swallowed the contents with much devotion. He then withdrew, and closed the door.

"I bid you most heartily welcome," said Seithenyn to Taliesin. "Drink off this, and I will tell you more. You are admitted to this special sitting at my special instance. I told the abbot I knew you well. Now I will tell you what I know. You have told King Arthur that King Melvas has possession of Queen Gwenyvar, and, in consequence, King Arthur is coming here, to sack and raze the castle and abbey, and cut every throat in the isle of Avallon. I have just brought the abbot this pleasant intelligence, and, as I knew it would take him down a cup or two, I have also brought what I call my little jug, to have the benefit of his judgment on a piece of rare wine which I have broached this morning: there is no better in Caer Lleon. And now we are holding council on the emergency. But I must say you abuse your bardic privilege, to enjoy people's hospitality, worm out their secrets, and carry the news to the enemy. It was partly to give you this candid opinion, that I have prevailed on the abbot to admit you to this special sitting. Therefore drink. GWIN O EUR: Wine from gold."

King Arthur is not a Saxon, at any rate," sighed the abbot, winding up his fainting spirits with a draught. "Think not, young stranger, that I am transgressing the laws of temperance: my blood runs so cold when I think of the bloodthirsty Saxons, that I take a little wine medicinally, in the hope of warming it; but it is a slow and tedious remedy."

"Take a little more," said Seithenyn. "That is the true quantity. Wine is my medicine; and my quantity is a little more. A little more."

"King Arthur," said Taliesin, "is not a Saxon; but he does not brook injuries lightly. It were better for your abbey that he came not here in arms. The aiders and abettors of Melvas, even though they be spiritual, may not carry off the matter without some share of his punishment, which is infallible."

"That is just what I have been thinking," said Seithenyn.

"God knows," said abbot, "we are not abettors of Melvas, though we need his temporal power to protect us from the Saxons."

"How can it be otherwise," said Taliesin, "than that these Saxon despoilers should be insolent and triumphant, while the princes of Britain are distracted with domestic broils: and for what?"

"Ay," said Seithenyn, "that is the point. For what? For a woman, or some such rubbish."

"Rubbish, most verily," said the abbot. "Women are the flesh which we renounce with the devil."

"Holy father," said Taliesin, "have you not spiritual influence with Melvas, to persuade him to surrender the queen without bloodshed, and, renewing his allegiance to Arthur, assist him in his most sacred war against the Saxon invaders?"

"A righteous work," said the abbot; "but Melvas is head-strong and difficult."

"Screw yourself up with another goblet," said Seithenyn; "you will find the difficulty smooth itself off wonderfully. Wine from gold has a sort of double light, that illuminates a dark path miraculously."

The abbot sighed deeply, but adopted Seithenyn's method of throwing light on the subject.

"The anger of King Arthur," said Taliesin, "is certain, and its consequences infallible. The anger of King Melvas is doubtful, and its consequences to you cannot be formidable."

"That is nearly true," said the abbot, beginning to look resolute, as the rosebud at his nose-tip deepened into damask.

"A little more," said Seithenyn, "and it will become quite true."

By degrees the proposition ripened into absolute truth. The abbot suddenly inflated his cheeks, started on his legs, and stalked bolt upright out of the apartment, and forthwith out of the abbey, followed by Seithenyn, tossing his goblet in the air, and catching it in his hand, as he went.

The round-faced brother made his appearance almost immediately. "The abbot," he said, "commends you to the hospitality of the brotherhood. They will presently assemble to supper. In the meanwhile, as I am thirsty, and content with whatever falls in my way, I will take a simple and single draught of what happens to be here."

His draught was a model of simplicity and singleness; for, having uplifted the ponderous vase, he held it to his lips, till he had drained it of the very copious remnant which the abrupt departure of the abbot had caused Seithenyn to leave in it.

Taliesin proceeded to enjoy the hospitality of the brethren, who set before him a very comfortable hot supper, at which he quickly perceived, that, however dexterous King Elphin might be at catching fish, the monks of Avallon were very far his masters in the three great arts of cooking it, serving it up, and washing it down; but he had not time to profit by their skill and experience in these matters, for he received a pressing invitation to the castle of Melvas, which he obeyed immediately.

Chapter XIV

THE RIGHT OF MIGHT

> *The three triumphs of the bards of the isle of Britain: the triumph of learning over ignorance; the triumph of reason over error; and the triumph of peace over violence.*
>
> TRIADS OF BARDISM.[1]

"FRIEND SEITHENYN," said the abbot, when, having passed the castle gates, and solicited an audience, he was proceeding to the presence of Melvas, "this task, to which I have accinged myself,[2] is arduous, and in some degree awful; being, in truth, no less than to persuade a king to surrender a possession, which he has inclination to keep for ever, and power to keep, at any rate, for an indefinite time."

"Not so very indefinite," said Seithenyn; "for with the first song of the cuckoo (whom I mention on this occasion as a party concerned,) King Arthur will batter his castle about his ears, and, in all likelihood, the abbey about yours."

The abbot sighed heavily.

"If your heart fail you," said Seithenyn, "another cup of wine will set all to rights."

"Nay, nay, friend Seithenyn," said the abbot, "that which I have already taken has just brought me to the point at which the heart is inspirited, and the wit sharpened, without any infraction of the wisdom and gravity which become my character, and best suit my present business."

Seithenyn, however, took an opportunity of making signs to some cupbearers, and, when they entered the apartment of Melvas, they were followed by vessels of wine and goblets of gold.

King Melvas was a man of middle age, with a somewhat

---

1 *Cambro-Briton,* II (1821), 291.
2 Undertaken.

round, large, regular-featured face, and an habitual smile of extreme self-satisfaction, which he could occasionally convert into a look of terrific ferocity, the more fearful for being rare. His manners were, for the most part, pleasant. He did much mischief, not for mischief's sake, nor yet for the sake of excitement, but for the sake of something tangible. He had a total and most complacent indifference to every thing but his own will and pleasure. He took what he wanted wherever he could find it, by the most direct process, and without any false pretence. He would have disdained the trick which the chroniclers ascribe to Hengist, of begging as much land as a bull's hide would surround, and then shaving it into threads, which surrounded a goodly space. If he wanted a piece of land, he encamped upon it, saying, "This is mine." If the former possessor could eject him, so; it was not his: if not, so; it remained his. Cattle, wine, furniture, another man's wife, whatever he took a fancy to, he pounced upon and appropriated. He was intolerant of resistance; and, as the shortest way of getting rid of it, and not from any bloodthirstiness of disposition, or, as the phrenologists have it, development of the organ of destructiveness, he always cut through the resisting body, longitudinally, horizontally, or diagonally, as he found most convenient. He was the arch-marauder of West Britain. The abbey of Avallon shared largely in the spoil, and they made up together a most harmonious church and state. He had some respect for King Arthur; wished him success against the Saxons; knew the superiority of his power to his own; but he had heard that Queen Gwenyvar was the most beautiful woman in Britain; was, therefore, satisfied of his own title to her, and, as she was hunting in the forest, while King Arthur was absent from Caer Lleon, he seized her, and carried her off.

"Be seated, holy father," said Melvas; "and you, also, Seithenyn, unless the abbot wishes you away."

But the abbot's heart misgave him, and he assented readily to Seithenyn's stay.

MELVAS.

Now, holy father, to your important matter of private conference.

SEITHENYN.

He is tongue-tied, and a cup too low.

THE ABBOT.

Set the goblet before me, and I will sip in moderation.

MELVAS.

Sip, or not sip, tell me your business.

THE ABBOT.

My business, of a truth, touches the lady your prisoner, King Arthur's queen.

MELVAS.

She is my queen, while I have her, and no prisoner. Drink, man, and be not afraid. Speak your mind: I will listen, and weigh your words.

THE ABBOT.

This queen—

SEITHENYN.

Obey the king: first drink, then speak.

THE ABBOT.

I drink to please the king.

MELVAS.

Proceed.

THE ABBOT.

This queen, Gwenyvar, is as beautiful as Helen, who caused the fatal war that expelled our forefathers from Troy: and I fear she will be a second Helen, and expel their posterity from Britain.[3] The infidel Saxons, to whom the cowardly and perfidious Vortigern[4] gave footing in Britain, have prospered even more by the disunion of her princes than either by his villany, or their own valour. And now there is no human hope against them but in the arms of Arthur. And how shall his arms prosper against the common enemy, if he be forced to turn them on the children of his own land for the recovery of his own wife?

---

[3] According to the British Chronicles, Brutus, the great grandson of Æneas, having killed his father, Silvius, to fulfil a prophecy, went to Greece, where he found the posterity of Helenus, the son of Priam; collected all of the Trojan race within the limits of Greece; and, after some adventures by land and sea, settled them in Britain, which was before uninhabited, "except by a few giants." [P]

[4] Vortigern had supposedly usurped the crown he wore.

MELVAS.

What do you mean by his own? That which he has, is his own: but that which I have, is mine. I have the wife in question, and some of the land. Therefore they are mine.

THE ABBOT.

Not so. The land is yours under fealty to him.

MELVAS.

As much fealty as I please, or he can force me, to give him.

THE ABBOT.

His wife, at least, is most lawfully his.

MELVAS.

The winner makes the law, and his law is always against the loser. I am so far the winner; and, by my own law, she is lawfully mine.

THE ABBOT.

There is a law above all human law, by which she is his.

MELVAS.

From that it is for you to absolve me; and I dispense my bounty according to your indulgence.

THE ABBOT.

There are limits we must not pass.

MELVAS.

You set up your landmark, and I set up mine. They are both moveable.

THE ABBOT.

The Church has not been niggardly in its indulgences to King Melvas.

MELVAS.

Nor King Melvas in his gifts to the Church.

THE ABBOT.

But, setting aside this consideration, I would treat it as a question of policy.

SEITHENYN.

Now you talk sense. Right without might is the lees of an old barrel, without a drop of the original liquor.

THE ABBOT.

I would appeal to. you, King Melvas, by your love to your common country, by your love of the name of Britain, by your hatred of the infidel Saxons, by your respect for the character of Arthur; will you let your passion for a woman, even though she be a second Helen, frustrate, or even impede, the great cause, of driving these spoilers from a land in which they have no right even to breathe?

MELVAS.

They have a right to do all they do, and to have all they have. If we can drive them out, they will then have no right here. Have not you and I a right to this good wine, which seems to trip very merrily over your ghostly palate? I got it by seizing a good ship, and throwing the crew overboard, just to remove them out of the way, because they were troublesome. They disputed my right, but I taught them better. I taught them a great moral lesson, though they had not much time to profit by it. If they had had the might to throw me overboard, I should not have troubled myself about their right, any more, or, at any rate, any longer, than they did about mine.

SEITHENYN.

The wine was lawful spoil of war.

THE ABBOT.

But if King Arthur brings his might to bear upon yours, I fear neither you nor I shall have a right to this wine, nor to any thing else that is here.

SEITHENYN.

Then make the most of it while you have it.

THE ABBOT.

Now, while you have some months of security before you, you may gain great glory by surrendering the lady; and, if you be so disposed, you may no doubt claim, from the gratitude of King Arthur, the fairest princess of his court to wife, and an ample dower withal.

MELVAS.

That offers something tangible.

SEITHENYN.

Another ray from the golden goblet will set it in a most luminous view.

THE ABBOT.

Though I should advise the not making it a condition, but

asking it, as a matter of friendship, after the first victory that you have helped him to gain over the Saxons.

MELVAS.

The worst of those Saxons is, that they offer nothing tangible, except hard knocks. They bring nothing with them. They come to take; and lately they have not taken much. But I will muse on your advice; and, as it seems, I may get more by following than rejecting it, I shall very probably take it, provided that you now attend me to the banquet in the hall.

SEITHENYN.

Now you talk of the hall and the banquet, I will just intimate that the finest of all youths, and the best of all bards, is a guest in the neighbouring abbey.

MELVAS.

If so, I have a clear right to him, as a guest for myself.

The abbot was not disposed to gainsay King Melvas's right. Taliesin was invited accordingly, and seated at the left hand of the king, the abbot being on the right. Taliesin summoned all the energies of his genius to turn the passions of Melvas into the channels of Anti-Saxonism, and succeeded so perfectly, that the king and his whole retinue of magnanimous heroes were inflamed with intense ardour to join the standard of Arthur; and Melvas vowed most solemnly to Taliesin, that another sun should not set, before Queen Gwenyvar should be under the most honourable guidance on her return to Caer Lleon.

Chapter XV

THE CIRCLE OF THE BARDS

> *The three dignities of poetry: the union of the true and the wonderful; the union of the beautiful and the wise; and the union of art and nature.*
>
> TRIADS OF POETRY.[1]

[1] *Cambro-Briton,* II (1821), 291.

AMONGST the Christmas amusements of Caer Lleon, a grand Bardic Congress was held in the Roman theatre, when the principal bards of Britain contended for the preeminence in the art of poetry, and in its appropriate moral and mystical knowledge. The meeting was held by daylight. King Arthur presided, being himself an irregular bard, and admitted, on this public ocasion, to all the efficient honours of a Bard of Presidency.

To preside in the Bardic Congress was long a peculiar privilege of the kings of Britain. It was exercised in the seventh century by King Cadwallader. King Arthur was assisted by twelve umpires, chosen by the bards, and confirmed by the king.

The Court, of course, occupied the stations of honour, and every other part of the theatre was crowded with a candid and liberal audience.

The bards sate in a circle on that part of the theatre corresponding with the portion which we call the stage.

Silence was proclaimed by the herald; and, after a grand symphony, which was led off in fine style by the king's harper, Geraint, Prince Cei came forward, and made a brief oration, to the effect that any of the profane, who should be irregular and tumultuous, would be forcibly removed from the theatre, to be dealt with at the discretion of the officer of the guard. Silence was then a second time proclaimed by the herald.

Each bard, as he stood forward, was subjected to a number of interrogatories, metrical and mystical, which need not be here reported. Many bards sang many songs. Amongst them, Prince Llywarch sang

Gorwynion Y Gauav.

The Brilliancies of Winter.

Last of flowers, in tufts around
Shines the gorse's golden bloom:
Milkwhite lichens clothe the ground
'Mid the flowerless heath and broom:
Bright are holly-berries, seen
Red, through leaves of glossy green.

Brightly, as on rocks they leap,
Shine the sea-waves, white with spray;
Brightly, in the dingles deep,
Gleams the river's foaming way;
Brightly through the distance show
Mountain-summits clothed in snow.

Brightly, where the torrents bound,
Shines the frozen colonnade,
Which the black rocks, dripping round,
And the flying spray have made:
Bright the icedrops on the ash
Leaning o'er the cataract's dash.

Bright the hearth, where feast and song
Crown the warrior's hour of peace,
While the snow-storm drives along,
Bidding war's worse tempest cease;
Bright the hearthflame, flashing clear
On the up-hung shield and spear.

Bright the torchlight of the hall
When the wintry night-winds blow;
Brightest when its splendours fall
On the mead-cup's sparkling flow:
While the maiden's smile of light
Makes the brightness trebly bright.

Close the portals; pile the hearth;
Strike the harp; the feast pursue;
Brim the horns: fire, music, mirth,
Mead and love, are winter's due.
Spring to purple conflict calls
Swords that shine on winter's walls.

Llywarch's song was applauded, as presenting a series of images with which all present were familiar, and which were all of them agreeable.

Merlin sang some verses of the poem, which is called

Avallenau Myrddin.

Merlin's Apple-Trees.

Fair the gift to Merlin given,
Apple-trees seven score and seven;
Equal all in age and size;
On a green hill-slope, that lies
Basking in the southern sun,
Where bright waters murmuring run.

Just beneath the pure stream flows;
High above the forest grows;
Not again on earth is found
Such a slope of orchard ground:
Song of birds, and hum of bees,
Ever haunt the apple-trees.

Lovely green their leaves in spring;
Lovely bright their blossoming:
Sweet the shelter and the shade
By their summer foliage made:
Sweet the fruit their ripe boughs hold,
Fruit delicious, tinged with gold.

Gloyad, nymph with tresses bright,
Teeth of pearl, and eyes of light,
Guards these gifts of Ceidio's son,
Gwendol, the lamented one,
Him, whose keen-edged sword no more
Flashes 'mid the battle's roar.

War has raged on vale and hill:
That fair grove was peaceful still.
There have chiefs and princes sought
Solitude and tranquil thought:
There have kings, from courts and throngs,
Turned to Merlin's wild-wood songs.

Now from echoing woods I hear
Hostile axes sounding near:
On the sunny slope reclined,
Feverish grief disturbs my mind,
Lest the wasting edge consume
My fair spot of fruit and bloom.

Lovely trees, that long alone
In the sylvan vale have grown,
Bare, your sacred plot around,
Grows the once wood-waving ground:
Fervent valour guards ye still;
Yet my soul presages ill.

Well I know, when years have flown,
Briars shall grow where ye have grown:
Them in turn shall power uproot;
Then again shall flowers and fruit
Flourish in the sunny breeze,
On my new-born apple-trees.

This song was heard with much pleasure, especially by those
of the audience who could see, in the imagery of the apple-
trees, a mystical type of the doctrines and fortunes of Druidism,
to which Merlin was suspected of being secretly attached, even
under the very nose of St. David.

Aneurin sang a portion of his poem on the Battle of Cattraeth; in which he shadowed out the glory of Vortimer, the
weakness of Vortigern, the fascinations of Rowena, the treach-
ery of Hengist, and the vengeance of Emrys.

The Massacre of the Britons.

Sad was the day for Britain's land,
A day of ruin to the free,
When Gorthyn[2] stretched a friendly hand
To the dark dwellers of the sea.[3]

[2] Gwrtheyrn: Vortigern. [P]
[3] Hengist and Horsa. [P]

But not in pride the Saxon trod,
Nor force nor fraud oppressed the brave,
Ere the grey stone and flowery sod
Closed o'er the blessed hero's grave.[4]

The twice-raised monarch[5] drank the charm,
The love-draught of the ocean-maid:[6]
Vain then the Briton's heart and arm,
Keen spear, strong shield, and burnished blade.

"Come to the feast of wine and mead,"
Spake the dark dweller of the sea:[7]
"There shall the hours in mirth proceed;
There neither sword nor shield shall be."

Hard by the sacred temple's site,
Soon as the shades of evening fall,
Resounds with song and glows with light
The ocean-dweller's rude-built hall.

The sacred ground, where chiefs of yore
The everlasting fire adored,
The solemn pledge of safety bore,
And breathed not of the treacherous sword.

The amber wreath his temples bound;
His vest concealed the murderous blade;
As man to man, the board around,
The guileful chief his host arrayed.

None but the noblest of the land,
The flower of Britain's chiefs, were there:
Unarmed, amid the Saxon band,
They sate, the fatal feast to share.

Three hundred chiefs, three score and three,
Went, where the festal torches burned
Before the dweller of the sea:
They went; and three alone returned.

[4] Gwrthevyr: Vortimer: who drove the Saxons out of Britain. [P]
[5] Vortigern: who was, on the death of his son Vortimer, restored
to the throne from which he had been deposed. [P]
[6] Ronwen: Rowena. [P]
[7] Hengist. [P]

'Till dawn the pale sweet mead they quaffed:
The ocean-chief unclosed his vest;
His hand was on his dagger's haft,
And daggers glared at every breast.

But him, at Eidiol's[8] breast who aimed,
The mighty Briton's arm laid low:
His eyes with righteous anger flamed;
He wrenched the dagger from the foe;

And through the throng he cleft his way,
And raised without his battle cry;
And hundreds hurried to the fray,
From towns, and vales, and mountains high.

But Briton's best blood dyed the floor
Within the treacherous Saxon's hall;
Of all, the golden chain who wore,
Two only answered Eidiol's call.

Then clashed the sword; then pierced the lance;
Then by the axe the shield was riven;
Then did the steed on Cattraeth prance,
And deep in blood his hoofs were driven.

Even as the flame consumes the wood,
So Eidiol rushed along the field;
As sinks the snow-bank in the flood,
So did the ocean-rovers yield.

The spoilers from the fane he drove;
He hurried to the rock-built tower,
Where the base king,[9] in mirth and love,
Sate with his Saxon paramour.[9]

The storm of arms was on the gate,
The blaze of torches in the hall,
So swift, that ere they feared their fate,
The flames had scaled their chamber wall.

---

[8] Eidiol or Emrys: Emrys Wledig: Ambrosius. [P]
[9] Vortigen and Rowena. [P]

They died: for them no Briton grieves;
No planted flower above them waves;
No hand removes the withered leaves
That strew their solitary graves.

And time the avenging day brought round
That saw the sea-chief vainly sue:
To make his false host bite the ground
Was all the hope our warrior knew.

And evermore the strife he led,
Disdaining peace, with princely might,
Till, on a spear, the spoiler's[10] head
Was reared on Caer-y-Cynan's height.

The Song of Aneurin touched deeply on the sympathies of
the audience, and was followed by a grand martial symphony,
in the midst of which Taliesin appeared in the Circle of Bards.
King Arthur welcomed him with great joy, and sweet smiles
were showered upon him from all the beauties of the court.

Taliesin answered the metrical and mystical questions to the
astonishment of the most proficient; and, advancing, in his turn,
to the front of the circle, he sang a portion of a poem which is
now called HANES TALIESIN, The History of Taliesin; but
which shall be here entitled

The Cauldron of Ceridwen.

The sage Ceridwen was the wife
Of Tegid Voël, of Pemble Mere:
Two children blest their wedded life,
Morvran and Creirwy, fair and dear:
Morvran, a son of peerless worth,
And Creirwy, loveliest nymph of earth:
But one more son Ceridwen bare,
As foul as they before were fair.

[10] Hengist. [P]

She strove to make Avagddu wise;
She knew he never could be fair:
And, studying magic mysteries,
She gathered plants of virtue rare:
She placed the gifted plants to steep
Within the magic cauldron deep,
Where they a year and day must boil,
'Till three drops crown the matron's toil.

Nine damsels raised the mystic flame;
Gwion the Little near it stood:
The while for simples roved the dame
Through tangled dell and pathless wood.
And, when the year and day had past,
The dame within the cauldron cast
The consummating chaplet wild,
While Gwion held the hideous child.

But from the cauldron rose a smoke
That filled with darkness all the air:
When through its folds the torchlight broke,
Nor Gwion, nor the boy, was there.
The fire was dead, the cauldron cold,
And in it lay, in sleep uprolled,
Fair as the morning-star, a child,
That woke, and stretched its arms, and smiled.

What chanced her labours to destroy,
She never knew; and sought in vain
If 'twere her own misshapen boy,
Or little Gwion, born again:
And, vext with doubt, the babe she rolled
In cloth of purple and of gold,
And in a coracle consigned
Its fortunes to the sea and wind.

The summer night was still and bright,
The summer moon was large and clear,
The frail bark, on the springtide's height,
Was floated into Elphin's weir.
The baby in his arms he raised:
His lovely spouse stood by, and gazed,
And, blessing it with gentle vow,
Cried "TALIESIN!" "Radiant brow!"

And I am he: and well I know
Ceridwen's power protects me still;
And hence o'er hill and vale I go,
And sing, unharmed, whate'er I will.
She has for me Time's veil withdrawn:
The images of things long gone,
The shadows of the coming days,
Are present to my visioned gaze.

And I have heard the words of power,
By Ceirion's solitary lake,
That bid, at midnight's thrilling hour,
Eryri's hundred echoes wake.
I to Diganwy's towers have sped,
And now Caer Lleon's halls I tread,
Demanding justice, now, as then,
From Maelgon, most unjust of men.

The audience shouted with delight at the song of Taliesin,
and King Arthur, as President of the Bardic Congress, conferred
on him, at once, the highest honours of the sitting.

Where Taliesin picked up the story which he told of himself,
why he told it, and what he meant by it, are questions not easily
answered. Certain it is, that he told this story to his contemporaries, and that none of them contradicted it. It may, therefore,
be presumed that they believed it; as any one who pleases is
most heartily welcome to do now.

Besides the single songs, there were songs in dialogue, approaching very nearly to the character of dramatic poetry; and
pennillion, or unconnected stanzas, sung in series by different

singers, the stanzas being complete in themselves, simple as Greek epigrams, and presenting in succession moral precepts, pictures of natural scenery, images of war or of festival, the lamentations of absence or captivity, and the complaints or triumphs of love. This pennillion-singing long survived among the Welsh peasantry almost every other vestige of bardic customs, and may still be heard among them on the few occasions on which rack-renting, tax-collecting, common-enclosing,[11] methodist-preaching, and similar developments of the light of the age, have left them either the means or inclination of making merry.

Chapter XVI

THE JUDGMENTS OF ARTHUR

> *Three things to which success cannot fail where they shall justly be: discretion, exertion, and hope.*
> TRIADS OF WISDOM.

KING ARTHUR had not long returned to his hall, when Queen Gwenyvar arrived, escorted by the Abbot of Avallon and Seithenyn ap Seithyn Saidi, who had brought his golden goblet, to gain a new harvest of glory from the cellars of Caer Lleon.

Seithenyn assured King Arthur, in the name of King Melvas, and on the word of a king, backed by that of his butler, which, truth being in wine, is good warranty even for a king, that the queen returned as pure as on the day King Melvas had carried her off.

---

[11] *Rack-renting:* charging unreasonably high rent; *common-enclosing:* the annexing of public lands into a private estate. Both practices were common among the country gentry in Peacock's time.

"None here will doubt that;" said Gwenvach, the wife of Modred. Gwenyvar was not pleased with the compliment, and, almost before she had saluted King Arthur, she turned suddenly round, and slapped Gwenvach on the face, with a force that brought more crimson into one cheek than blushing had ever done into both. This slap is recorded in the Bardic Triads as one of the Three Fatal Slaps of the Island of Britain. A terrible effect is ascribed to this small cause; for it is said to have been the basis of that enmity between Arthur and Modred, which terminated in the battle of Camlan, wherein all the flower of Britain perished on both sides: a catastrophe more calamitous than any that ever before or since happened in Christendom, not even excepting that of the battle of Roncesvalles;[1] for, in the battle of Camlan, the Britons exhausted their own strength, and could no longer resist the progress of the Saxon supremacy. This, however, was a later result, and comes not within the scope of the present veridicous narrative.

Gwenvach having flounced out of the hall, and the tumult occasioned by this little incident having subsided, Queen Gwenyvar took her ancient seat by the side of King Arthur, who proceeded to inquire into the circumstances of her restoration. The Abbot of Avallon began an oration, in praise of his own eloquence, and its miraculous effects on King Melvas; but he was interrupted by Seithenyn, who said, "The abbot's eloquence was good and well timed; but the chief merit belongs to this young bard, who prompted him with good counsel, and to me, who inspirited him with good liquor. If he had not opened his mouth pretty widely when I handed him this golden goblet, exclaiming GWIN O EUR, he would never have had the heart to open it to any other good purpose. But the most deserving person is this very promising youth, in whom I can see no fault, but that he has not the same keen perception as my friend the abbot has of the excellent relish of wine from gold. To be sure, he plied me very hard with strong drink in the hall of Dinas Vawr, and thereby wormed out of me the secret of Queen

---

[1] The battle in 778 at which the great legendary French hero Roland fell while fighting a delaying action against the Saracens.

Gwenyvar's captivity; and, afterwards, he pursued us to Avallon, where he persuaded me and the abbot, and the abbot persuaded King Melvas, that it would be better for all parties to restore the queen peaceably: and then he clenched the matter with the very best song I ever heard in my life. And, as my young friend has a boon to ask, I freely give him all my share of the merit, and the abbot's into the bargain."

"Allow me, friend GWIN O EUR," said the abbot, "to dispose of my own share of merit in my own way. But, such as it is, I freely give it to this youth, in whom, as you say, I can see no fault, but that his head is brimfull of Pagan knowledge."

Arthur paid great honour to Taliesin, and placed him on his left hand at the banquet. He then said to him, "I judge, from your song of this morning, that the boon you require from me concerns Maelgon Gwyneth. What is his transgression, and what is the justice you require?"

Taliesin narrated the adventures of Elphin in such a manner as gave Arthur an insight into his affection for Melanghel; and he supplicated King Arthur to command and enforce the liberation of Elphin from the Stone Tower of Diganwy.

Before King Arthur could signify his assent, Maelgon Gwyneth stalked into the hall, followed by a splendid retinue. He had been alarmed by the absence of Rhûn, had sought him in vain on the banks of the Mawddach, had endeavoured to get at the secret by pouncing upon Angharad and Melanghel, and had been baffled in his project by the vigilance of Teithrin ap Tathral. He had, therefore, as a last resort, followed Taliesin to Caer Lleon, conceiving that he might have had some share in the mysterious disappearance of Rhûn.

Arthur informed him that he was in possession of all the circumstances, and that Rhûn, who was in safe custody, would be liberated on the restoration of Elphin.

Maelgon boiled with rage and shame, but had no alternative but submission to the will of Arthur.

King Arthur commanded that all the parties should be brought before him. Caradoc was charged with the execution of this order, and, having received the necessary communications and powers from Maelgon and Taliesin, he went first to

Diganwy, where he liberated Elphin, and then proceeded to give effect to Teithrin's declaration, that "no hand but Elphin's should raise the stone of Rhûn's captivity." Rhûn, while his pleasant adventure had all the gloss of novelty upon it, and his old renown as a gay deceiver was consequently in such dim eclipse, was very unwilling to present himself before the ladies of Caer Lleon; but Caradoc was peremptory, and carried off the crest-fallen prince, together with his bard of all work, who was always willing to go to any court, with any character, or none.

Accordingly, after a moderate lapse of time, Caradoc reappeared in the hall of Arthur, with the liberated captives, accompanied by Angharad and Melanghel, and Teithrin ap Tathral.

King Arthur welcomed the new comers with a magnificent festival, at which all the beauties of his court were present, and, addressing himself to Elphin, said, "We are all debtors to this young bard: my queen and myself for her restoration to me; you for your liberation from the Stone Tower of Diganwy. Now, if there be, amongst all these ladies, one whom he would choose for his bride, and in whose eyes he may find favour, I will give the bride a dowry worthy of the noblest princess in Britain."

Taliesin, thus encouraged, took the hand of Melanghel, who did not attempt to withdraw it, but turned to her father a blushing face, in which he read her satisfaction and her wishes. Elphin immediately said, "I have nothing to give him but my daughter; but her I most cordially give him."

Taliesin said, "I owe to Elphin more than I can ever repay: life, honour, and happiness."

Arthur said, "You have not paid him ill; but you owe nothing to Maelgon and Rhûn, who are your debtors for a lesson of justice, which I hope they will profit by during the rest of their lives. Therefore Maelgon shall defray the charge of your wedding, which shall be the most splendid that has been seen in Caer Lleon."

Maelgon looked exceedingly grim, and wished himself well back in Diganwy.

There was a very pathetic meeting of recognition between

Seithenyn and his daughter; at the end of which he requested her husband's interest to obtain for him the vacant post of second butler to King Arthur. He obtained this honourable office; and was so zealous in the fulfilment of its duties, that, unless on actual service with a detachment of liquor, he never was a minute absent from the Temple of Diana.

At a subsequent Bardic Congress, Taliesin was unanimously elected Pen Beirdd, or Chief of the Bards of Britain. The kingdom of Caredigion flourished under the protection of Arthur, and, in the ripeness of time, passed into the hands of Avaon, the son of Taliesin and Melanghel.

THE END.

CROTCHET CASTLE.

BY THE

THE AUTHOR OF HEADLONG HALL.

Le monde est plein de fous, et qui n'en veut pas voir,
Doit se tenir tout seul, et casser son miroir.[1]

LONDON:

PUBLISHED BY T. HOOKHAM,

OLD BOND STREET.

1831.

CROTCHET CASTLE.

Should once the world resolve to abolish
All that's ridiculous and foolish,
It would have nothing left to do,
To apply in jest or earnest to.

BUTLER[2]

---

[1] Title page: "The world is full of fools, and whoever does not wish to see them should keep to himself and break his mirror." A misquotation of the Marquis de Sade.

[2] Samuel Butler, "The World," ll. 7–10.

Contents

CROTCHET CASTLE

Chapter I

THE VILLA

Captain Jamy. I wad full fain hear some question 'tween you tway.—Henry V.[1]

IN ONE of those beautiful vallies, through which the Thames (not yet polluted[2] by the tide, the scouring of cities, or even the minor defilement of the sandy streams of Surrey,) rolls a clear flood through flowery meadows, under the shade of old beech woods, and the smooth mossy greensward of the chalk hills (which pour into it their tributary rivulets, as pure and pellucid as the fountain of Bandusium, or the wells of Scamander, by which the wives and daughters of the Trojans washed their splendid garments in the days of peace, before the coming of the Greeks);[3] in one of those beautiful vallies, on a bold round-surfaced lawn, spotted with juniper, that opened itself in the bosom of an old wood, which rose with a steep, but not precipitous ascent, from the river to the summit of the hill, stood the castellated villa of a retired citizen. Ebenezer Mac Crotchet, Esquire, was the London-born offspring of a

---

[1] III.ii.

[2] For hundreds of years the Thames had been the repository for London's wastes. As the city became increasingly industrialized in the nineteenth century, the problem grew; but at the time of the writing of *Crotchet Castle,* there seem to have been no organized efforts to combat it.

[3] *fountain of Bandusium:* see Horace, *Odes,* III.13. *wells of Scamander:* described thus by Homer in *Iliad* XXII.147ff.; the "wells" were two springs, one hot and one cold, that formed the source of the Scamander River, near Troy.

worthy native of the "north countrie," who had walked up to
London on a commercial adventure, with all his surplus capital, not very neatly tied up in a not very clean handkerchief,
suspended over his shoulder from the end of a hooked stick,
extracted from the first hedge on his pilgrimage; and who, after
having worked himself a step or two up the ladder of life, had
won the virgin heart of the only daughter of a highly respectable
merchant of Duke's Place,[4] with whom he inherited the honest
fruits of a long series of ingenuous dealings.

Mr. Mac Crotchet had derived from his mother the instinct,
and from his father the rational principle, of enriching himself
at the expense of the rest of mankind, by all the recognised
modes of accumulation on the windy side of the law.[5] After
passing many years in the alley,[6] watching the turn of the
market, and playing many games almost as desperate as that
of the soldier of Lucullus,[7] the fear of losing what he had so
righteously gained predominated over the sacred thirst of
paper-money; his caution got the better of his instinct, or rather
transferred it from the department of acquisition to that of
conservation. His friend, Mr. Ramsbottom, the zodiacal mythologist,[8] told him that he had done well to withdraw from the
region of Uranus or Brahma, the maker, to that of Saturn or
Veeshnu, the preserver, before he fell under the eye of Jupiter
or Seva, the destroyer who might have struck him down at a
blow.[9]

It is said, that a Scotchman returning home, after some
years' residence in England, being asked what he thought of
the English, answered: "They hanna ower muckle sense, but

[4] A section of London, since 1650 the location of a large Jewish
community.

[5] *Twelfth Night,* III.iv.

[6] 'Change Alley, or the London Stock Exchange.

[7] Luculli miles, &c., Hor. *Ep.* II.2.26. "In Anna's wars, a soldier
poor and bold," &c.—Pope's *Imitation.* [P]

[8] J. F. Newton (1767–1837), Zoroastrian astrologer (cf. Aries, the
Ram, one of the signs of the zodiac), vegetarian, and all-around eccentric.
His views were set forth in *The Return to Nature* (1811).

[9] Brahma, Veeshnu, and Seva comprise the Trimurti (trinity) of
Hindu mythology; Uranus, Saturn, and Jupiter are their Roman counter-
parts.

they are an unco braw[10] people to live amang;" which would be a very good story, if it were not rendered apocryphal, by the incredible circumstance of the Scotchman going back.

Mr. Mac Crotchet's experience had given him a just title to make, in his own person, the last-quoted observation, but he would have known better than to go back, even if himself, and not his father, had been the first comer of his line from the north. He had married an English Christian, and, having none of the Scotch accent, was ungracious enough to be ashamed of his blood. He was desirous to obliterate alike the Hebrew and Caledonian vestiges in his name, and signed himself E. M. Crotchet, which by degrees induced the majority of his neighbours to think that his name was Edward Matthew. The more effectually to sink the Mac, he christened his villa Crotchet Castle, and determined to hand down to posterity the honours of Crotchet of Crotchet. He found it essential to his dignity to furnish himself with a coat of arms, which, after the proper ceremonies (payment being the principal), he obtained, videlicet: Crest, a crotchet rampant, in A sharp: Arms, three empty bladders, turgescent, to show how opinions are formed; three bags of gold, pendent, to show why they are maintained; three naked swords, tranchant, to show how they are administered; and three barbers' blocks, gaspant, to show how they are swallowed.[11]

Mr. Crotchet was left a widower, with two children; and, after the death of his wife, so strong was his sense of the blessed comfort she had been to him, that he determined never to give any other woman an opportunity of obliterating the happy recollection.

He was not without a plausible pretence for styling his villa a castle, for, in its immediate vicinity, and within his own enclosed domain, were the manifest traces, on the brow of the

---

[10] Remarkably fine.

[11] It was becoming common for aspiring members of the middle class to purchase dignity by the acquisition of a formal coat of arms, which could be obtained from the College of Arms by anyone who could afford the fee. "Rampant" (erect) and "pendent" (hanging) are genuine heraldic terms; the others are Peacock's coinages as he parodies a heraldic description.

hill, of a Roman station, or *castellum*, which was still called the castle by the country people. The primitive mounds and trenches, merely overgrown with greensward, with a few patches of juniper and box on the vallum, and a solitary ancient beech surmounting the place of the prætorium, presented nearly the same depths, heights, slopes, and forms, which the Roman soldiers had originally given them. From this *castellum* Mr. Crotchet christened his villa. With his rustic neighbours he was of course immediately and necessarily a squire: Squire Crotchet of the castle; and he seemed to himself to settle down as naturally into an English country gentleman, as if his parentage had been as innocent of both Scotland and Jerusalem, as his education was of Rome and Athens.[12]

But as, though you expel nature with a pitchfork, she will yet always come back;[13] he could not become, like a true-born English squire, part and parcel of the barley-giving earth; he could not find in game-bagging, poacher-shooting, trespasser-pounding, footpath-stopping, common-enclosing, rack-renting, and all the other liberal pursuits and pastimes which make a country gentleman an ornament to the world, and a blessing to the poor;[14] he could not find in these valuable and amiable occupations, and in a corresponding range of ideas, nearly commensurate with that of the great King Nebuchadnezzar, when he was turned out to grass;[15] he could not find in this great variety of useful action, and vast field of comprehensive thought, modes of filling up his time that accorded with his Caledonian instinct. The inborn love of disputation, which the excitements and engagements of a life of business had smothered, burst forth through the calmer surface of a rural life. He grew as fain

[12] Squire Crotchet had had no formal education (at this time, still largely comprised of classical studies).

[13] Naturam expellas furcâ, tamen usque recurret.—Hor. *Ep*. I.10.24. [P]

[14] An amalgam of the abuses of which many of the country gentry were guilty: many estates were overstocked with game, but hunting even by tenants was considered poaching and was severely punished; common grazing lands were annexed (enclosed) onto already large estates; landowners charged unconscionably high rents.

[15] Daniel 4:32–33.

as Captain Jamy, "to hear some airgument betwixt ony tway;" and being very hospitable in his establishment, and liberal in his invitations, a numerous detachment from the advanced guard of the "march of intellect,"[16] often marched down to Crotchet Castle.

When the fashionable season filled London with exhibitors of all descriptions, lectures and else,[17] Mr. Crotchet was in his glory; for, in addition to the perennial literati of the metropolis, he had the advantage of the visits of a number of hardy annuals, chiefly from the north, who, as the interval of their metropolitan flowering allowed, occasionally accompanied their London brethren in excursions to Crotchet Castle.

Amongst other things, he took very naturally to political economy,[18] read all the books on the subject which were put forth by his own countrymen, attended all lectures thereon, and boxed[19] the technology of the sublime science as expertly as an able seaman boxes the compass.

With this agreeable mania he had the satisfaction of biting his son, the hope of his name and race, who had borne off from Oxford the highest academical honours; and who, treading in his father's footsteps to honour and fortune, had, by means of a portion of the old gentleman's surplus capital, made himself a junior partner in the eminent loan-jobbing firm of Catchflat and Company.[20] Here, in the days of paper prosperity, he applied his science-illumined genius to the blowing of bubbles,[21] the bursting of which sent many a poor devil to the jail, the

[16] I.e., those who profess the most up-to-date, "progressive" ideas. The phrase, coined by Edmund Burke in 1795, is of course used ironically in the novel, as is its variant "the march of mind."

[17] Attending scientific exhibits and lectures was a highly popular middle-class pastime in the early nineteenth century. A number of literary figures also lectured frequently, including Coleridge and Hazlitt.

[18] An early name for what is now called economics. During the nineteenth century the term was often used in reference to Jeremy Bentham, David Ricardo, and their Utilitarian ("the greatest good for the greatest number") doctrines.

[19] Learned by heart.

[20] In British slang, a "flat" is a greenhorn or dupe. A loan-jobber serves as a middleman in the discounting of loans.

[21] Financial speculation.

workhouse, or the bottom of the river, but left young Crotchet rolling in riches.

These riches he had been on the point of doubling, by a marriage with the daughter of Mr. Touchandgo, the great banker, when, one foggy morning, Mr. Touchandgo and the contents of his till were suddenly reported absent; and as the fortune which the young gentleman had intended to marry was not forthcoming, this tender affair of the heart was nipped in the bud.

Miss Touchandgo did not meet the shock of separation quite so complacently as the young gentleman; for he lost only the lady, whereas she lost a fortune as well as a lover. Some jewels, which had glittered on her beautiful person as brilliantly as the bubble of her father's wealth had done in the eyes of his gudgeons, furnished her with a small portion of paper currency; and this, added to the contents of a fairy purse of gold, which she found in her shoe on the eventful morning when Mr. Touchandgo melted into thin air, enabled her to retreat into North Wales, where she took up her lodging in a farm-house in Merionethshire, and boarded very comfortably for a trifling payment, and the additional consideration of teaching English, French, and music to the little Ap-Llymry's. In the course of this occupation, she acquired sufficient knowledge of Welsh to converse with the country people.

She climbed the mountains, and descended the dingles,[22] with a foot which daily habit made by degrees almost as steady as a native's. She became the nymph of the scene; and if she sometimes pined in thought for her faithless Strephon,[23] her melancholy was any thing but green and yellow;[24] it was as genuine white and red as occupation, mountain air, thyme-fed mutton, thick cream, and fat bacon, could make it: to say nothing of an occasional glass of double X,[25] which Ap-

[22] Narrow wooded valleys.

[23] Conventional name for a shepherd-lover in pastoral poetry.

[24] *Twelfth Night,* II.iv. The "white and red" which follows probably echoes *Love's Labours Lost,* I.ii, where the phrase occurs in a discussion of melancholy, but it could also refer to *Twelfth Night,* I.v., a passage on Olivia's beauty, which would be relevant here. In any case, the passage demonstrates Peacock's complex and pervading allusiveness.

[25] Probably double x porter (beer), the x used popularly to indicate strength and purity.

Llymry,[26] who yielded to no man west of the Wrekin in brewage, never failed to press upon her at dinner and supper. He was also earnest, and sometimes successful, in the recommendation of his mead, and most pertinacious on winter nights in enforcing a trial of the virtues of his elder wine. The young lady's personal appearance, consequently, formed a very advantageous contrast to that of her quondam lover, whose physiognomy the intense anxieties of his bubble-blowing days, notwithstanding their triumphant result, had left blighted, sallowed, and crow's-footed, to a degree not far below that of the fallen spirit who, in the expressive language of German romance, is described as "scathed by the ineradicable traces of the thunderbolts of Heaven;" so that, contemplating their relative geological positions, the poor deserted damsel was flourishing on slate, while her rich and false young knight was pining on chalk.

Squire Crotchet had also one daughter, whom he had christened Lemma, and who, as likely to be endowed with a very ample fortune, was, of course, an object very tempting to many young soldiers of fortune, who were marching with the march of mind, in a good condition for taking castles, as far as not having a groat is a qualification for such exploits.[27] She was also a glittering bait to divers young squires expectant (whose fathers were too well acquainted with the occult signification of mortgage), and even to one or two sprigs of nobility, who thought that the lining of a civic purse would superinduce a very passable factitious nap upon a threadbare title. The young lady had received an expensive and complicated education; complete in all the elements of superficial display. She was thus eminently qualified to be the companion of any masculine luminary who had kept due pace with the "astounding progress" of intelligence. It must be confessed, that a man who has not kept due pace with it is not very easily found; this march being one of that "astounding" character in which it seems impossible that the rear can be behind the van. The young lady was also tolerably good-looking: north of Tweed, or in Palestine,

---

[26] Llymry. *Anglicé* flummery. [P]

[27] "Let him take castles who has ne'er a groat."—Pope, *ubi supra*. [P]

she would probably have been a beauty; but for the vallies of the Thames, she was perhaps a little too much to the taste of Solomon, and had a nose which rather too prominently suggested the idea of the tower of Lebanon, which looked towards Damascus.[28]

In a village in the vicinity of the castle was the vicarage of the Reverend Doctor Folliott, a gentleman endowed with a tolerable stock of learning, an interminable swallow, and an indefatigable pair of lungs. His pre-eminence in the latter faculty gave occasion to some etymologists[29] to ring changes on his name, and to decide that it was derived from Follis Optimus, softened through an Italian medium into Folle Ottimo, contracted poetically into Folleotto, and elided Anglicé into Folliott, signifying a first-rate pair of bellows. He claimed to be descended lineally from the illustrious Gilbert Folliott, the eminent theologian, who was a bishop of London in the twelfth century,[30] whose studies were interrupted in the dead of night by the devil; when a couple of epigrams passed between them; and the devil, of course, proved the smaller wit of the two.[31]

[28] Song of Solomon 7:4.

[29] Here Peacock satirizes contemporary interest in etymology, as it was popularized in such widely read books as Horne Tooke's *Diversions of Purley* (1778; reprinted 1829), a work Peacock himself knew.

[30] Not possessing his fictional descendant's "interminable swallow," Bishop Foliot (d. 1186?) was known for the austerity of his habits.

[31] The devil began: (he had caught the bishop musing on politics.)

> Oh Gilberte Folliott!
> Dum revolvis tot et tot,
> Deus tuus est Astarot.

> Oh Gilbert Folliott!
> While thus you muse and plot,
> Your god is Astarot.

The bishop answered:

> Tace, daemon: qui est deus
> Sabbaot, est ille meus.

> Peace, fiend; the power I own
> Is Sabbaoth's Lord alone.

This reverend gentleman, being both learned and jolly, became by degrees an indispensable ornament to the new squire's table. Mr. Crotchet himself was eminently jolly, though by no means eminently learned. In the latter respect he took after the great majority of the sons of his father's land; had a smattering of many things, and a knowledge of none; but possessed the true northern art of making the most of his intellectual harlequin's jacket, by keeping the best patches always bright and prominent.

Chapter II

THE MARCH OF MIND

> *Quoth Ralpho: nothing but the abuse*
> *Of human learning you produce.*—BUTLER.[1]

"GOD BLESS my soul, sir!" exclaimed the Reverend Doctor Folliott, bursting, one fine May morning, into the breakfast-room at Crochet Castle, "I am out of all patience with this march of mind. Here has my house been nearly burned down, by my cook taking it into her head to study hydrostatics, in a sixpenny tract, published by the Steam Intellect Society, and

It must be confessed, the devil was easily posed in the twelfth century. He was a sturdier disputant in the sixteenth.

> Did not the devil appear to Martin
> Luther in Germany for certain?

when "the heroic student," as Mr. Coleridge calls him, was forced to proceed to *"voies de fait."* The curious may see at this day, on the wall of Luther's study, the traces of the ink-bottle which he threw at the devil's head. [P] [*Astarot*: Venus. *"the heroic student"*: see *The Friend,* I,98. *"voies de fait"*: violence.]

[1] *Hudibras,* Part I, Canto iii, ll. 1337–1338.

written by a learned friend who is for doing all the world's business as well as his own, and is equally well qualified to handle every branch of human knowledge.[2] I have a great abomination of this learned friend; as author, lawyer, and politician, he is *triformis,* like Hecate: and in every one of his three forms he is *bifrons,* like Janus; the true Mr. Facing-both-ways of Vanity Fair.[3] My cook must read his rubbish in bed; and as might naturally be expected, she dropped suddenly fast asleep, overturned the candle, and set the curtains in a blaze. Luckily, the footman went into the room at the moment, in time to tear down the curtains and throw them into the chimney, and a pitcher of water on her nightcap extinguished her wick: she is a greasy subject, and would have burned like a short mould."[4]

The reverend gentleman exhaled his grievance without looking to the right or to the left; at length, turning on his pivot, he perceived that the room was full of company, consisting of young Crotchet and some visitors whom he had brought from London. The Reverend Doctor Folliott was introduced to Mr. Mac Quedy,[5] the economist; Mr. Skionar,[6] the transcendental

[2] The Society for the Diffusion of Useful Knowledge ("Steam Intellect Society") was founded in 1827 by Henry Peter (later Lord) Brougham, a prominent politician and journalist, to promote technological skills among the artisan class; it published its Library of Useful Knowledge in 6d pamphlets. Brougham, who had contributed a pamphlet on hydrostatics (water pressure) to the series, was dubbed "the Learned Friend" by George Canning because of his wide-ranging knowledge and interests.

[3] Hecate, a Greek goddess often represented as triple-formed, was associated with the underworld, night, and sorcery. Janus, the Roman god of doorways, was often pictured as having two faces (*bifrons*), looking ahead and behind—an allusion, as is the following reference to Bunyan's *Pilgrim's Progress,* to Brougham's practice of courting both the liberal and conservative political factions.

[4] A type of candle.

[5] Quasi Mac Q. E. D., son of a demonstration. [P] [John Ramsay MacCulloch (1789–1864), a well-known Scots political economist. Cf. *Quod Erat Demonstrandum,* "which was to be demonstrated."]

[6] ΣΚΙᾶς ΟΝΑΡ. *Umbriae somnium.* [P] [Coleridge. Each phrase means "a dream of a shadow" and epitomizes Peacock's estimate of transcendentalism.]

poet; Mr. Firedamp, the meteorologist;[7] and Lord Bossnowl, son of the Earl of Foolincourt, and member for the borough of Rogueingrain.

The divine took his seat at the breakfast-table, and began to compose his spirits by the gentle sedative of a large cup of tea, the demulcent of a well-buttered muffin, and the tonic of a small lobster.

THE REV. DR. FOLLIOTT.

You are a man of taste, Mr. Crotchet. A man of taste is seen at once in the array of his breakfast-table. It is the foot of Hercules, the far-shining face of the great work, according to Pindar's doctrine: ἀρχομένου ἔργου, πρόσωπον χρὴ θέμεν τηλαυγές.[8] The breakfast is the πρόσωπον of the great work of the day. Chocolate, coffee, tea, cream, eggs, ham, tongue, cold fowl,— all these are good, and bespeak good knowledge in him who sets them forth: but the touchstone is fish: anchovy is the first step, prawns and shrimps the second; and I laud him who reaches even to these: potted char and lampreys are the third, and a fine stretch of progression; but lobster is, indeed, matter for a May morning, and demands a rare combination of knowledge and virtue in him who sets it forth.

MR. MAC QUEDY.

Well, sir, and what say you to a fine fresh trout, hot and dry, in a napkin? or a herring out of the water into the frying pan, on the shore of Loch Fyne?

THE REV. DR. FOLLIOTT.

Sir, I say every nation has some eximious virtue; and your country is pre-eminent in the glory of fish for breakfast. We have much to learn from you in that line at any rate.

MR. MAC QUEDY.

And in many others, sir, I believe. Morals and metaphysics,

---

[7] Firedamp is a type of explosive and noxious marsh gas; as a "meteorologist," Mr. Firedamp is interested in the effects of the weather on water and especially the relationship between water and the spreading of disease.

[8] Far-shining be the face
    Of a great work begun.—Pind. *Ol.* vi. [P] [Ll. 4–5 of Pindar's sixth Olympian Ode.]

politics and political economy, the way to make the most of all
the modifications of smoke; steam, gas, and paper currency;
you have all these to learn from us; in short, all the arts and
sciences. We are the modern Athenians.

THE REV. DR. FOLLIOTT.

I, for one, sir, am content to learn nothing from you but the
art and science of fish for breakfast. Be content, sir, to rival the
Bœotians, whose redeeming virtue was in fish, touching which
point you may consult Aristophanes and his scholiast, in the
passage of Lysistrata, ἀλλ᾽ ἄφελε τὰς ἐγχελεις,[9] and leave the
name of Athenians to those who have a sense of the beautiful,
and a perception of metrical quantity.

MR. MAC QUEDY.

Then, sir, I presume you set no value on the right principles
of rent, profit, wages, and currency?

THE REV. DR. FOLLIOTT.

My principles, sir, in these things are, to take as much as I
can get, and to pay no more than I can help. These are every
man's principles, whether they be the right principles or no.
There, sir, is political economy in a nutshell.

MR. MAC QUEDY.

The principles, sir, which regulate production and consumption, are independent of the will of any individual as to giving
or taking, and do not lie in a nutshell by any means.

THE REV. DR. FOLLIOTT.

Sir, I will thank you for a leg of that capon.

LORD BOSSNOWL.

But, sir, by the by, how came your footman to be going into
your cook's room? It was very providential to be sure, but——

THE REV. DR. FOLLIOTT.

Sir, as good came of it, I shut my eyes, and asked no questions. I suppose he was going to study hydrostatics, and he
found himself under the necessity of practising hydraulics.

---

[9] Calonice wishes destruction to all Bœotians. Lysistrata answers,
"Except the eels." Lysistrata, 36. [P] [The ancient Boeotians were known
both for their crudity and for the excellent seafood (especially eels)
they provided Athens.]

MR. FIREDAMP.

Sir, you seem to make very light of science.

THE REV. DR. FOLLIOTT.

Yes, sir, such science as the learned friend deals in: every thing for every body, science for all, schools for all, rhetoric for all, law for all, physic for all, words for all, and sense for none. I say, sir, law for lawyers, and cookery for cooks: and I wish the learned friend, for all his life, a cook that will pass her time in studying his works; then every dinner he sits down to at home, he will sit on the stool of repentance.[10]

LORD BOSSNOWL.

Now really that would be too severe: my cook should read nothing but Ude.[11]

THE REV. DR. FOLLIOTT.

No, sir! let Ude and the learned friend singe fowls together; let both avaunt from my kitchen. Θύρας δ᾽ ἐπίθεσθε βεβήλοις.[12] Ude says an elegant supper may be given with sandwiches. *Horresco referens.* An elegant supper! *Dî meliora piis.* No Ude for me. Conviviality went out with punch and suppers. I cherish their memory. I sup when I can, but not upon sandwiches. To offer me a sandwich, when I am looking for a supper, is to add insult to injury. Let the learned friend, and the modern Athenians, sup upon sandwiches.

MR. MAC QUEDY.

Nay, sir; the modern Athenians know better than that. A literary supper in sweet Edinbroo' would cure you of the prejudice you seem to cherish against us.

THE REV. DR. FOLLIOTT.

Well, sir, well; there is cogency in a good supper; a good

[10] A low stool used in Scots churches on which a transgressor was made to sit during divine service and receive public rebuke from the minister at the sermon's end.

[11] Louis Eustache Ude, whose books on French cooking had gone through many editions, was chef to Louis XVI and head chef at Crockford's, one of London's most fashionable private clubs.

[12] "Shut the doors against the profane." *Orphica, passim.* [P] [Fragment 245. The two following exclamations are "I shudder to relate (it)" and "The gods are kinder to the devout." The latter quotes Virgil's *Georgics,* III.513.]

supper, in these degenerate days, bespeaks a good man; but much more is wanted to make up an Athenian. Athenians, indeed! where is your theatre? who among you has written a comedy? where is your attic salt? which of you can tell who was Jupiter's great grandfather? or what metres will successively remain, if you take off the three first syllables, one by one, from a pure antispastic acatalectic tetrameter? Now, sir, there are three questions for you; theatrical, mythological, and metrical; to every one of which an Athenian would give an answer that would lay me prostrate in my own nothingness.[13]

MR. MAC QUEDY.

Well, sir, as to your metre and your mythology, they may e'en wait a wee. For your comedy, there is the Gentle Shepherd of the divine Allan Ramsay.[14]

THE REV. DR. FOLLIOTT.

The Gentle Shepherd! It is just as much a comedy as the book of Job.

MR. MAC QUEDY.

Well, sir, if none of us have written a comedy, I cannot see that it is any such great matter, any more than I can conjecture what business a man can have at this time of day with Jupiter's great grandfather.

THE REV. DR. FOLLIOTT.

The great business is, sir, that you call yourselves Athenians, while you know nothing that the Athenians thought worth knowing, and dare not show your noses before the civilised world in the practice of any one art in which they were excellent. Modern Athens, sir! the assumption is a personal affront to every man who has a Sophocles in his library. I will thank you for an anchovy.

---

[13] Attic salt is a refined, delicate wit characteristic of the ancient Athenians (*sal* is Latin for both "salt" and "wit"). "Jupiter's great-grandfather," if such a title is appropriate, was Chaos. Dr. Folliott's altered antispastic acatalectic tetrameter would probably scan $--\cup/--\cup/--\cup/--\cup/$.

[14] Ramsay (1686–1758) was a Scots poet, wigmaker, and bookseller, whose poetry (including a pastoral drama, *The Gentle Shepherd*, 1725) contributed to the revival of Scots vernacular poetry.

MR. MAC QUEDY.

Metaphysics, sir; metaphysics. Logic and moral philosophy. There we are at home. The Athenians only sought the way, and we have found it; and to all this we have added political economy, the science of sciences.

THE REV. DR. FOLLIOTT.

A hyperbarbarous technology, that no Athenian ear could have borne. Premises assumed without evidence, or in spite of it; and conclusions drawn from them so logically, that they must necessarily be erroneous.

MR. SKIONAR.

I cannot agree with you, Mr. Mac Quedy, that you have found the true road of metaphysics, which the Athenians only sought. The Germans have found it, sir: the sublime Kant, and his disciples.[15]

MR. MAC QUEDY.

I have read the sublime Kant, sir, with an anxious desire to understand him; and I confess I have not succeeded.

THE REV. DR. FOLLIOTT.

He wants the two great requisites of head and tail.

MR. SKIONAR.

Transcendentalism is the philosophy of intuition, the development of universal convictions; truths which are inherent in the organisation of mind, which cannot be obliterated, though they may be obscured, by superstitious prejudice on the one hand, and by the Aristotelian logic on the other.

MR. MAC QUEDY.

Well, sir, I have no notion of logic obscuring a question.

MR. SKIONAR.

There is only one true logic, which is the transcendental; and this can prove only the one true philosophy, which is also the transcendental. The logic of your modern Athens can prove every thing equally; and that is, in my opinion, tantamount to proving nothing at all.

---

[15] Immanuel Kant (1724–1804), German transcendentalist philosopher, highly influential on English and American Romantic thought, especially that of Coleridge. His "disciples" include Friedrich Schelling (1775–1854) and G. W. F. Hegel (1770–1831).

MR. CROTCHET.

The sentimental against the rational, the intuitive against the inductive, the ornamental against the useful, the intense against the tranquil, the romantic against the classical; these are great and interesting controversies, which I should like, before I die, to see satisfactorily settled.

MR. FIREDAMP.

There is another great question, greater than all these, seeing that it is necessary to be alive in order to settle any question; and this is the question of water against human woe. Wherever there is water, there is *malaria,* and wherever there is *malaria,* there are the elements of death. The great object of a wise man should be to live on a gravelly hill, without so much as a duck-pond within ten miles of him, eschewing cisterns and water-butts, and taking care that there be no gravel-pits for lodging the rain. The sun sucks up infection from water, wherever it exists on the face of the earth.[16]

THE REV. DR. FOLLIOTT.

Well, sir, you have for you the authority of the ancient mystagogue, who said: Ἔστιν ὕδωρ ψυχῇ θάνατος.[17] For my part I care not a rush (or any other aquatic and inesculent vegetable) who or what sucks up either the water or the infection. I think the proximity of wine a matter of much more importance than the longinquity of water. You are here within a quarter of a mile of the Thames; but in the cellar of my friend, Mr. Crotchet, there is the talismanic antidote of a thousand dozen of old wine; a beautiful spectacle, I assure you, and a model of arrangement.

MR. FIREDAMP.

Sir, I feel the malignant influence of the river in every part of my system. Nothing but my great friendship for Mr. Crotchet would have brought me so nearly within the jaws of the lion.

THE REV. DR. FOLLIOTT.

After dinner, sir, after dinner, I will meet you on this ques-

---

16 Cf. "All the infections that the sun sucks up/From bogs, fens, flats" (*Tempest,* II.ii) and "Infect her beauty,/You fen-sucked fogs" (*King Lear,* II.iv).

17 Literally, which is sufficient for the present purpose, "Water is death to the soul." *Orphica: Fr.* XIX. [P]

tion. I shall then be armed for the strife. You may fight like Hercules against Achelous, but I shall flourish the Bacchic thyrsus, which changed rivers into wine: as Nonnus sweetly sings, Οἴνῳ κυματόεντι μέλας κελάρυζεν Ὑδάσπης.[18]

MR. CROTCHET, JUN.

I hope, Mr. Firedamp, you will let your friendship carry you a little closer into the jaws of the lion. I am fitting up a flotilla of pleasure boats, with spacious cabins, and a good cellar, to carry a choice philosophical party up the Thames and Severn, into the Ellesmere canal, where we shall be among the mountains of North Wales; which we may climb or not, as we think proper; but we will, at any rate, keep our floating hotel well provisioned, and we will try to settle all the questions over which a shadow of doubt yet hangs in the world of philosophy.

MR. FIREDAMP.

Out of my great friendship for you, I will certainly go; but I do not expect to survive the experiment.

THE REV. DR. FOLLIOTT.

Alter erit tum Tiphys, et altera quæ vehat Argo Delectos Heroas.[19] I will be of the party, though I must hire an officiating curate, and deprive poor Mrs. Folliott, for several weeks, of the pleasure of combing my wig.

LORD BOSSNOWL.

I hope, if I am to be of the party, our ship is not to be the ship of fools: He! He![20]

THE REV. DR. FOLLIOTT.

If you are one of the party, sir, it most assuredly will not: Ha! Ha!

LORD BOSSNOWL.

Pray sir, what do you mean by Ha! Ha!?

---

[18] Hydaspes gurgled, dark with billowy wine. *Dionysiaca,* XXV, 280. [P] [Achelous was a river god who, taking the form of a bull, was defeated by Hercules in a quarrel over the princess Deianera. The thyrsus was the wand of Bacchus (Dionysus), god of fertility and of wine.]

[19] "Another Typhys on the waves shall float
And chosen heroes freight his glorious boat."

Virgil. *Ecl.* IV. [P] [ll. 34–35]

[20] Sebastian Brant, *Ship of Fools* (1494), a satire on human nature first translated into English in 1509.

THE REV. DR. FOLLIOTT.

Precisely, sir, what you mean by He! He!

MR. MAC QUEDY.

You need not dispute about terms; they are two modes of expressing merriment, with or without reason; reason being in no way essential to mirth. No man should ask another why he laughs, or at what, seeing that he does not always know, and that, if he does, he is not a responsible agent. Laughter is an involuntary action of certain muscles, developed in the human species by the progress of civilisation. The savage never laughs.

THE REV. DR. FOLLIOTT.

No, sir, he has nothing to laugh at. Give him Modern Athens, the "learned friend," and the Steam Intellect Society. They will develope his muscles.

Chapter III

THE ROMAN CAMP

> *He loved her more then seven yere,*
> *Yet was he of her love never the nere;*
> *He was not ryche of golde and fe,*
> *A gentyll man forsoth was he.*
> *The Squyr of Low Degre.*[1]

THE REVEREND Doctor Folliott having promised to return to dinner, walked back to his vicarage, meditating whether he should pass the morning in writing his next sermon, or in angling for trout, and had nearly decided in favour of the latter proposition, repeating to himself, with great unction, the lines of Chaucer:—

[1] A metrical romance dating from the early fourteenth century, ll. 17–20.

And as for me, though that I can but lite,
On bokis for to read I me delite,
And to 'hem yeve I faithe and full credence,
And in mine herte have 'hem in reverence,
So hertily, that there is gamé none,
That fro my bokis makith me to gone,
But it be seldome, on the holie daie;
Save certainly whan that the month of Maie
Is comin, and I here the foulis sing,
And that the flouris ginnin for to spring,
Farewell my boke and my devocion:[2]

when his attention was attracted by a young gentleman who was sitting on a camp stool with a portfolio on his knee, taking a sketch of the Roman Camp, which, as has been already said, was within the enclosed domain of Mr. Crotchet. The young stranger, who had climbed over the fence, espying the portly divine, rose up, and hoped that he was not trespassing. "By no means, sir," said the divine; "all the arts and sciences are welcome here: music, painting, and poetry; hydrostatics, and political economy; meteorology, transcendentalism, and fish for breakfast."

THE STRANGER.

A pleasant association, sir, and a liberal and discriminating hospitality. This is an old British camp, I believe, sir?

THE REV. DR. FOLLIOTT.

Roman, sir; Roman: undeniably Roman. The vallum is past controversy. It was not a camp, sir, a *castrum*, but a *castellum*, a little camp, or watch-station, to which was attached, on the peak of the adjacent hill, a beacon for transmitting alarms. You will find such here and there, all along the range of chalk hills, which traverses the country from north-east to south-west, and along the base of which runs the ancient Ikenild road, whereof you may descry a portion in that long strait white line.

THE STRANGER.

I beg your pardon, sir: do I understand this place to be your property?

[2] *The Legend of Good Women* (F text), ll. 29–39.

THE REV. DR. FOLLIOTT.

It is not mine, sir: the more is the pity; yet is it so far well, that the owner is my good friend, and a highly respectable gentleman.

THE STRANGER.

Good and respectable, sir, I take it, mean rich?

THE REV. DR. FOLLIOTT.

That is their meaning, sir.

THE STRANGER.

I understand the owner to be a Mr. Crotchet. He has a handsome daughter, I am told.

THE REV. DR. FOLLIOTT.

He has, sir. Her eyes are like the fishpools of Heshbon, by the gate of Bethrabbim;[3] and she is to have a handsome fortune, to which divers disinterested gentlemen are paying their addresses. Perhaps you design to be one of them.

THE STRANGER.

No, sir; I beg pardon if my questions seem impertinent; I have no such design. There is a son, too, I believe, sir, a great and successful blower of bubbles.

THE REV. DR. FOLLIOTT.

A hero, sir, in his line. Never did angler in September hook more gudgeons.

THE STRANGER.

To say the truth, two very amiable young people, with whom I have some little acquaintance, Lord Bossnowl, and his sister, Lady Clarinda, are reported to be on the point of concluding a double marriage with Miss Crotchet and her brother, by way of putting a new varnish on old nobility. Lord Foolincourt, their father, is terribly poor for a lord who owns a borough.[4]

THE REV. DR. FOLLIOTT.

Well, sir, the Crotchets have plenty of money, and the old gentleman's weak point is a hankering after high blood. I saw your acquaintance Lord Bossnowl this morning; but I did not

3 Song of Solomon, 7:4.
4 I.e., controls, by wealth and political influence, the selection of a Member of Parliament from an electoral district. Peacock was writing during a period of great agitation for the elimination of such practices.

see his sister. She may be there, nevertheless, and doing fashionable justice to this fine May morning, by lying in bed till noon.

THE STRANGER.

Young Mr. Crotchet, sir, has been, like his father, the architect of his own fortune, has he not? An illustrious example of the reward of honesty and industry?

THE REV. DR. FOLLIOTT.

As to honesty, sir, he made his fortune in the city of London; and if that commodity be of any value there, you will find it in the price current. I believe it is below par, like the shares of young Crotchet's fifty companies. But his progress has not been exactly like his father's: it has been more rapid, and he started with more advantages. He began with a fine capital from his father. The old gentleman divided his fortune into three not exactly equal portions: one for himself, one for his daughter, and one for his son, which he handed over to him, saying, "Take it once for all, and make the most of it; if you lose it where I won it, not another stiver do you get from me during my life." But, sir, young Crotchet doubled, and trebled, and quadrupled it, and is, as you say, a striking example of the reward of industry; not that I think his labour has been so great as his luck.

THE STRANGER.

But, sir, is all this solid? is there no danger of reaction? no day of reckoning, to cut down in an hour prosperity that has grown up like a mushroom?

THE REV. DR. FOLLIOTT.

Nay, sir, I know not. I do not pry into these matters. I am, for my own part, very well satisfied with the young gentleman. Let those who are not so look to themselves. It is quite enough for me that he came down last night from London, and that he had the good sense to bring with him a basket of lobsters. Sir, I wish you a good morning.

The stranger, having returned the reverend gentleman's good morning, resumed his sketch, and was intently employed on it when Mr. Crotchet made his appearance, with Mr. Mac Quedy and Mr. Skionar, whom he was escorting round his grounds, according to his custom with new visitors; the principal pleasure of possessing an extensive domain being that of showing it to other people. Mr. Mac Quedy, according also to the laudable custom of his countrymen, had been appraising every thing that fell under his observation; but, on arriving at the Roman camp, of which the value was purely imaginary, he contented himself with exclaiming, "Eh! this is just a curiosity, and very pleasant to sit in on a summer day."

MR. SKIONAR.

And call up the days of old, when the Roman eagle spread its wings in the place of that beechen foliage. It gives a fine idea of duration, to think that that fine old tree must have sprung from the earth ages after this camp was formed.

MR. MAC QUEDY.

How old, think you, may the tree be?

MR. CROTCHET.

I have records which show it to be three hundred years old.

MR. MAC QUEDY.

That is a great age for a beech in good condition. But you see the camp is some fifteen hundred years, or so, older; and three times six being eighteen, I think you get a clearer idea of duration out of the simple arithmetic than out of your eagle and foliage.

MR. SKIONAR.

That is a very unpoetical, if not unphilosophical, mode of viewing antiquities. Your philosophy is too literal for our imperfect vision. We cannot look directly into the nature of things; we can only catch glimpses of the mighty shadow in the camera obscura of transcendental intelligence. These six and eighteen are only words to which we give conventional meanings. We can reason, but we cannot feel, by help of them. The tree and the eagle, contemplated in the ideality of space and time, become subjective realities, that rise up as landmarks in the mystery of the past.

MR. MAC QUEDY.

Well, sir, if you understand that, I wish you joy. But I must be excused for holding that my proposition, three times six are eighteen, is more intelligible than yours. A worthy friend of mine, who is a sort of amateur in philosophy, criticism, politics, and a wee bit of many things more, says, "Men never begin to study antiquities till they are saturated with civilisation."[5]

MR. SKIONAR.

What is civilisation?

MR. MAC QUEDY.

It is just respect for property: a state in which no man takes wrongfully what belongs to another, is a perfectly civilised state.

MR. SKIONAR.

Your friend's antiquaries must have lived in El Dorado,[6] to have an opportunity of being saturated with such a state.

MR. MAC QUEDY.

It is a question of degree. There is more respect for property here than in Angola.[7]

MR. SKIONAR.

That depends on the light in which things are viewed.

Mr. Crotchet was rubbing his hands, in hopes of a fine discussion, when they came round to the side of the camp where the picturesque gentleman was sketching. The stranger was rising up, when Mr. Crotchet begged him not to disturb himself, and presently walked away with his two guests.

Shortly after Miss Crotchet and Lady Clarinda, who had breakfasted by themselves, made their appearance at the same spot, hanging each on an arm of Lord Bossnowl, who very much preferred their company to that of the philosophers, though he would have preferred the company of the latter, or any company, to his own. He thought it very singular that so agreeable a person as he held himself to be to others, should be so exceedingly tiresome to himself: he did not attempt to investigate the cause of this phenomenon, but was contented with acting on his knowledge of the fact, and giving himself as little of his own private society as possible.

The stranger rose as they approached, and was immediately

---

[5] *Edinburgh Review,* somewhere. [P] [Probably written by Brougham.]

[6] Mythical city of gold and perfect happiness.

[7] The Portuguese colonial government in Angola was notorious for its rapacious exploitation of the native population.

recognised by the Bossnowls as an old acquaintance, and saluted with the exclamation of "Captain Fitzchrome!" The interchange of salutation between Lady Clarinda and the Captain was accompanied with an amiable confusion on both sides, in which the observant eyes of Miss Crotchet seemed to read the recollection of an affair of the heart.

Lord Bossnowl was either unconscious of any such affair, or indifferent to its existence. He introduced the Captain very cordially to Miss Crotchet, and the young lady invited him, as the friend of their guests, to partake of her father's hospitality; an offer which was readily accepted.

The Captain took his portfolio under his right arm, his camp stool in his right hand, offered his left arm to Lady Clarinda, and followed at a reasonable distance behind Miss Crotchet and Lord Bossnowl, contriving, in the most natural manner possible, to drop more and more into the rear.

LADY CLARINDA.

I am glad to see you can make yourself so happy with drawing old trees and mounds of grass.

CAPTAIN FITZCHROME.

Happy, Lady Clarinda! oh, no! How can I be happy when I see the idol of my heart about to be sacrificed on the shrine of Mammon?

LADY CLARINDA.

Do you know, though Mammon has a sort of ill name, I really think he is a very popular character; there must be at the bottom something amiable about him. He is certainly one of those pleasant creatures whom every body abuses, but without whom no evening party is endurable. I dare say, love in a cottage is very pleasant; but then it positively must be a cottage ornée:[8] but would not the same love be a great deal safer in a castle, even if Mammon furnished the fortification?

CAPTAIN FITZCHROME.

Oh, Lady Clarinda! there is a heartlessness in that language that chills me to the soul.

LADY CLARINDA.

Heartlessness! No: my heart is on my lips. I speak just what

8 Ornate.

I think. You used to like it, and say it was as delightful as it was rare.

CAPTAIN FITZCHROME.

True, but you did not then talk as you do now, of love in a castle.

LADY CLARINDA.

Well, but only consider: a dun is a horridly vulgar creature; it is a creation I cannot endure the thought of: and a cottage lets him in so easily. Now a castle keeps him at bay. You are a half-pay officer, and are at leisure to command the garrison: but where is the castle? and who is to furnish the commissariat?

CAPTAIN FITZCHROME.

Is it come to this, that you make a jest of my poverty? Yet is my poverty only comparative. Many decent families are maintained on smaller means.

LADY CLARINDA.

Decent families: aye, decent is the distinction from respectable. Respectable means rich, and decent means poor. I should die if I heard my family called decent. And then your decent family always lives in a snug little place: I hate a little place; I like large rooms and large looking-glasses, and large parties, and a fine large butler, with a tinge of smooth red in his face; an outward and visible sign[9] that the family he serves is respectable; if not noble, highly respectable.

CAPTAIN FITZCHROME.

I cannot believe that you say all this in earnest. No man is less disposed than I am to deny the importance of the substantial comforts of life. I once flattered myself that in our estimate of these things we were nearly of a mind.

LADY CLARINDA.

Do you know, I think an opera-box a very substantial comfort, and a carriage. You will tell me that many decent people walk arm in arm through the snow, and sit in clogs and bonnets in the pit at the English theatre. No doubt it is very pleasant to those who are used to it; but it is not to my taste.

[9] From the (Anglican) Book of Common Prayer ("On the Sacraments").

CAPTAIN FITZCHROME.

You always delighted in trying to provoke me; but I cannot believe that you have not a heart.

LADY CLARINDA.

You do not like to believe that I have a heart, you mean. You wish to think I have lost it, and you know to whom; and when I tell you that it is still safe in my own keeping, and that I do not mean to give it away, the unreasonable creature grows angry.

CAPTAIN FITZCHROME.

Angry! far from it: I am perfectly cool.

LADY CLARINDA.

Why you are pursing your brows, biting your lips, and lifting up your foot as if you would stamp it into the earth. I must say anger becomes you; you would make a charming Hotspur.[10] Your every-day-dining-out face is rather insipid: but I assure you my heart is in danger when you are in the heroics. It is so rare, too, in these days of smooth manners, to see any thing like natural expression in a man's face. There is one set form for every man's face in female society; a sort of serious comedy, walking gentleman's[11] face: but the moment the creature falls in love, he begins to give himself airs, and plays off all the varieties of his physiognomy, from the Master Slender to the Petruchio;[12] and then he is actually very amusing.

CAPTAIN FITZCHROME.

Well, Lady Clarinda, I will not be angry, amusing as it may be to you: I listen more in sorrow than in anger. I half believe you in earnest, and mourn as over a fallen angel.

LADY CLARINDA.

What, because I have made up my mind not to give away my heart when I can sell it? I will introduce you to my new acquaintance, Mr. Mac Quedy: he will talk to you by the hour about exchangeable value, and show you that no rational being will part with any thing, except to the highest bidder.

---

[10] Fiery rebel lord in Shakespeare's *Henry IV, Pt. I.*

[11] A very minor role in a play, usually assigned to beginners.

[12] Wooers of ladies in, respectively, *The Merry Wives of Windsor* and *The Taming of the Shrew,* the former weak and ridiculous, the latter forceful.

CAPTAIN FITZCHROME.

Now, I am sure you are not in earnest. You cannot adopt such sentiments in their naked deformity.

LADY CLARINDA.

Naked deformity: why Mac Quedy will prove to you that they are the cream of the most refined philosophy. You live a very pleasant life as a bachelor, roving about the country with your portfolio under your arm. I am not fit to be a poor man's wife. I cannot take any kind of trouble, or do any one thing that is of any use. Many decent families roast a bit of mutton on a string; but if I displease my father I shall not have as much as will buy the string, to say nothing of the meat; and the bare idea of such cookery gives me the horrors.

By this time they were near the castle, and met Miss Crotchet and her companion, who had turned back to meet them. Captain Fitzchrome was shortly after heartily welcomed by Mr. Crotchet, and the party separated to dress for dinner, the captain being by no means in an enviable state of mind, and full of misgivings as to the extent of belief that he was bound to accord to the words of the lady of his heart.

Chapter IV

THE PARTY

> *En quoi cognoissez-vous la folie anticque? En quoi cognoissez-vous la sagesse présente?*—RABELAIS.[1]

"IF I WERE sketching a bandit who had just shot his last pursuer, having outrun all the rest, that is the very face I would give him," soliloquised the captain, as he studied the features of his rival in the drawing-room, during the miserable half-hour

---

[1] "Pray, how came you to know that men were formerly fools? How did you find that they are now wise?" Prologue to Bk. V. Urquhart and Motteux translation.

before dinner, when dulness reigns predominant over the expectant company, especially when they are waiting for some one last comer, whom they all heartily curse in their hearts, and whom, nevertheless, or indeed therefore-the-more, they welcome as a sinner, more heartily than all the just persons who had been punctual to their engagement.[2] Some new visitors had arrived in the morning, and, as the company dropped in one by one, the captain anxiously watched the unclosing door for the form of his beloved; but she was the last to make her appearance, and on her entry gave him a malicious glance, which he construed into a telegraphic communication that she had stayed away to torment him. Young Crotchet escorted her with marked attention to the upper end of the drawing-room, where a great portion of the company was congregated around Miss Crotchet. These being the only ladies in the company, it was evident that old Mr. Crotchet would give his arm to Lady Clarinda, an arrangement with which the captain could not interfere. He therefore took his station near the door, studying his rival from a distance, and determined to take advantage of his present position, to secure the seat next to his charmer. He was meditating on the best mode of operation for securing this important post with due regard to *bienséance*,[3] when he was twitched by the button by Mr. Mac Quedy, who said to him: "Lady Clarinda tells me, sir, that you are anxious to talk with me on the subject of exchangeable value, from which I infer that you have studied political economy; and as a great deal depends on the definition of value, I shall be glad to set you right on that point."—"I am much obliged to you, sir," said the captain, and was about to express his utter disqualification for the proposed instruction, when Mr. Skionar walked up, and said: "Lady Clarinda informs me that you wish to talk over with me the question of subjective reality. I am delighted to fall in with a gentleman who duly appreciates the transcendental philosophy."—"Lady Clarinda is too good," said the captain; and was about to protest that he had never heard the word transcendental before, when the butler announced dinner. Mr.

[2] See Luke 15:7.
[3] Propriety.

Crotchet led the way with Lady Clarinda: Lord Bossnowl followed with Miss Crotchet: the economist and transcendentalist pinned in the captain, and held him, one by each arm, as he impatiently descended the stairs in the rear of several others of the company, whom they had forced him to let pass; but the moment he entered the dining-room he broke loose from them, and a the expense of a little *brusquerie*, secured his position.

"Well, captain," said Lady Clarinda, "I perceive you can still manœuvre."

"What could possess you," said the captain, "to send two unendurable and inconceivable bores, to intercept me with rubbish about which I neither know nor care any more than the man in the moon?"

"Perhaps," said Lady Clarinda, "I saw your design, and wished to put your generalship to the test. But do not contradict any thing I have said about you, and see if the learned will find you out."

"There is fine music, as Rabelais observes, in the *cliquetis d'assiettes*, a refreshing shade in the *ombre de salle à manger*, and an elegant fragrance in the *fumée de rôti*,"[4] said a voice at the captain's elbow. The captain turning round, recognised his clerical friend of the morning, who knew him again immediately, and said he was extremely glad to meet him there; more especially as Lady Clarinda had assured him that he was an enthusiastic lover of Greek poetry.

"Lady Clarinda," said the captain, "is a very pleasant young lady."

THE REV. DR. FOLLIOTT.

So she is, sir: and I understand she has all the wit of the family to herself, whatever that *totum* may be. But a glass of wine after soup is, as the French say, the *verre de santé*.[5] The current of opinion sets in favour of Hock: but I am for Madeira; I do not fancy Hock till I have laid a substratum of Madeira. Will you join me?

---

[4] Respectively, the "clatter of plates," "shade of the dining room," and "steam from a roast."
[5] Glass of health.

CAPTAIN FITZCHROME.

With pleasure.

THE REV. DR. FOLLIOTT.

Here is a very fine salmon before me: and May is the very
point nommé[6] to have salmon in perfection. There is a fine
turbot close by, and there is much to be said in his behalf; but
salmon in May is the king of fish.

MR. CROTCHET.

That salmon before you, doctor, was caught in the Thames
this morning.

THE REV. DR. FOLLIOTT.

Παπαπαῖ! Rarity of rarities! A Thames salmon caught this
morning. Now, Mr. Mac Quedy, even in fish your Modern
Athens must yield. *Cedite Graii.*[7]

MR. MAC QUEDY.

Eh! sir, on its own ground, your Thames salmon has two
virtues over all others: first, that it is fresh; and, second, that
it is rare; for I understand you do not take half a dozen in a
year.

THE REV. DR. FOLLIOTT.

In some years, sir, not one. Mud, filth, gas dregs, lock-weirs,
and the march of mind, developed in the form of poaching,
have ruined the fishery. But when we do catch a salmon, happy
the man to whom he falls.

MR. MAC QUEDY.

I confess, sir, this is excellent; but I cannot see why it should
be better than a Tweed salmon at Kelso.

THE REV. DR. FOLLIOTT.

Sir, I will take a glass of Hock with you.

MR. MAC QUEDY.

With all my heart, sir. There are several varieties of the
salmon genus: but the common salmon, the *salmo salar*, is
only one species, one and the same every where, just like the
human mind. Locality and education make all the difference.

---

6 Perfect time.
7 "Yield, you Greeks." Propertius, *Elegy* II.xxxiv.65, referring to
Virgil's *Aeneid*, which will surpass even the *Iliad*. Dr. Folliott is also
sniping at the "modern Athenians."

THE REV. DR. FOLLIOTT.

Education! Well, sir, I have no doubt schools for all are just as fit for the species *salmo salar* as for the genus *homo*. But you must allow, that the specimen before us has finished his education in a manner that does honour to his college. However, I doubt that the *salmo salar* is only one species, that is to say, precisely alike in all localities. I hold that every river has its own breed, with essential differences; in flavour especially. And as for the human mind, I deny that it is the same in all men. I hold that there is every variety of natural capacity from the idiot to Newton and Shakspeare; the mass of mankind, midway between these extremes, being blockheads of different degrees; education leaving them pretty nearly as it found them, with this single difference, that it gives a fixed direction to their stupidity, a sort of incurable wry neck to the thing they call their understanding. So one nose points always east, and another always west, and each is ready to swear that it points due north.

MR. CROTCHET.

If that be the point of truth, very few intellectual noses point due north.

MR. MAC QUEDY.

Only those that point to the Modern Athens.

THE REV. DR. FOLLIOTT.

Where all native noses point southward.

MR. MAC QUEDY.

Eh, sir, northward for wisdom, and southward for profit.

MR. CROTCHET, JUN.

Champagne, doctor?

THE REV. DR. FOLLIOTT.

Most willingly. But you will permit my drinking it while it sparkles. I hold it a heresy to let it deaden in my hand, while the glass of my *compotator* is being filled on the opposite side of the table. By the bye, captain, you remember a passage in Athenæus, where he cites Menander on the subject of fish-sauce: ὀψάριον ἐπὶ ἰχθύος.[8] *(The captain was aghast for an answer that*

---

[8] "Sauce for fish." *The Deipnosophists,* 385E.

would satisfy both his neighbours, when he was relieved by the divine continuing.) The science of fish sauce, Mr. Mac Quedy, is by no means brought to perfection; a fine field of discovery still lies open in that line.

MR. MAC QUEDY.

Nay, sir, beyond lobster sauce, I take it, ye cannot go.

THE REV. DR. FOLLIOTT.

In their line, I grant you, oyster and lobster sauce are the pillars of Hercules.[9] But I speak of the cruet sauces, where the quintessence of the sapid is condensed in a phial. I can taste in my mind's palate a combination, which, if I could give it reality, I would christen with the name of my college, and hand it down to posterity as a seat of learning indeed.

MR. MAC QUEDY.

Well, sir, I wish you success, but I cannot let slip the question we started just now. I say, cutting off idiots, who have no minds at all, all minds are by nature alike. Education (which begins from their birth) makes them what they are.

THE REV. DR. FOLLIOTT.

No, sir, it makes their tendencies, not their power. Cæsar would have been the first wrestler on the village common. Education might have made him a Nadir Shah; it might also have made him a Washington; it could not have made him a merry-andrew, for our newspapers to extol as a model of eloquence.[10]

MR. MAC QUEDY.

Now, sir, I think education would have made him just any thing, and fit for any station, from the throne to the stocks; saint or sinner, aristocrat or democrat, judge, counsel, or prisoner at the bar.

THE REV. DR. FOLLIOTT.

I will thank you for a slice of lamb, with lemon and pepper. Before I proceed with this discussion,—Vin de Grave, Mr. Skionar,—I must interpose one remark. There is a set of persons

[9] The Rock of Gibraltar and an opposing hill across the Strait, the farthest limit of ancient man's western exploration.

[10] *Nadir Shah:* Persian general who usurped the throne in 1736. A merry-andrew is a demagogue with pretensions to wit. Dr. Folliott is doubtless thinking of Brougham, a well-known speaker.

in your city, Mr. Mac Quedy, who concoct every three or four months a thing which they call a review: a sort of sugar-plum manufacturers to the Whig aristocracy.[11]

MR. MAC QUEDY.

I cannot tell, sir, exactly, what you mean by that; but I hope you will speak of those gentlemen with respect, seeing that I am one of them.

THE REV. DR. FOLLIOTT.

Sir, I must drown my inadvertence in a glass of Sauterne with you. There is a set of gentlemen in your city——

MR. MAC QUEDY.

Not in our city, exactly; neither are they a set. There is an editor, who forages for articles in all quarters, from John O'Groat's house to the Land's End.[12] It is not a board, or a society: it is a mere intellectual bazaar, where A., B., and C. bring their wares to market.

THE REV. DR. FOLLIOTT.

Well, sir, these gentlemen among them, the present company excepted, have practised as much dishonesty, as, in any other department than literature, would have brought the practitioner under the cognisance of the police. In politics, they have run with the hare and hunted with the hound. In criticism they have, knowingly and unblushingly, given false characters, both for good and for evil: sticking at no art of misrepresentation, to clear out of the field of literature all who stood in the way of the interests of their own clique. They have never allowed their own profound ignorance of any thing (Greek, for instance) to throw even an air of hesitation into their oracular decision on the matter. They set an example of profligate contempt for truth, of which the success was in proportion to the effrontery; and when their prosperity had filled the market with competitors, they cried out against their own reflected sin, as if they had never committed it, or were entitled to a monopoly of it. The latter, I rather think, was what they wanted.

[11] The *Edinburgh Review,* which promoted the Whig (liberal) point of view, MacCulloch (Mac Quedy) was a frequent contributor.
[12] I.e., from one end of Britain to the other.

MR. CROTCHET.

Hermitage, doctor?[13]

THE REV. DR. FOLLIOTT.

Nothing better, sir. The father who first chose the solitude of that vineyard, knew well how to cultivate his spirit in retirement. Now, Mr. Mac Quedy, Achilles was distinguished above all the Greeks for his inflexible love of truth: could education have made Achilles one of your reviewers?

MR. MAC QUEDY.

No doubt of it, even if your character of them were true to the letter.

THE REV. DR. FOLLIOTT.

And I say, sir—chicken and asparagus—Titan had made him of better clay.[14] I hold with Pindar: "All that is most excellent is so by nature." Τὸ δὲ φυᾷ κράτιστον ἅπαν.[15] Education can give purposes, but not powers; and whatever purposes had been given him, he would have gone straight forward to them; straight forward, Mr. Mac Quedy.

MR. MAC QUEDY.

No, sir, education makes the man, powers, purposes, and all.

THE REV. DR. FOLLIOTT.

There is the point, sir, on which we join issue.

Several others of the company now chimed in with their opinions, which gave the divine an opportunity to degustate one or two side dishes, and to take a glass of wine with each of the young ladies.

---

[13] A French wine named for a ruin, supposedly a hermit's cave, in the locale where it is produced.

[14] Juv. xiv.35. [P]

[15] *Ol*. ix.152. [P]

Chapter V

CHARACTERS

Ay imputé a honte plus que mediocre être vu spec-
tateur ocieux de tant vaillans, disertz, et chevalereux
personnaiges.—RABELAIS.[1]

LADY CLARINDA.

[*to the Captain*]

I DECLARE the creature has been listening to all this rig-
marole, instead of attending to me. Do you ever expect forgiveness? But now that they are all talking together, and you
cannot make out a word they say, nor they hear a word that
we say, I will describe the company to you. First, there is the
old gentleman on my left hand, at the head of the table, who is
now leaning the other way to talk to my brother. He is a good
tempered, half-informed person, very unreasonably fond of
reasoning, and of reasoning people; people that talk nonsense
logically: he is fond of disputation himself, when there are only
one or two, but seldom does more than listen in a large company
of *illuminés*. He made a great fortune in the city, and has the
comfort of a good conscience. He is very hospitable, and is
generous in dinners; though nothing would induce him to give
sixpence to the poor, because he holds that all misfortune is from
imprudence, that none but the rich ought to marry, and that all
ought to thrive by honest industry, as he did. He is ambitious
of founding a family, and of allying himself with nobility; and
is thus as willing as other grown children, to throw away thou-
sands for a gew-gaw, though he would not part with a penny
for charity. Next to him is my brother, whom you know as well
as I do. He has finished his education with credit, and as he

---

[1] "I held it not a little disgraceful to be only an idle spectator of
so many valorous, eloquent, and warlike persons." Prologue to Bk. III.
Urquhart and Motteux translation.

235

never ventures to oppose me in any thing, I have no doubt he is very sensible. He has good manners, is a model of dress, and is reckoned ornamental in all societies. Next to him is Miss Crotchet, my sister-in-law that is to be. You see she is rather pretty, and very genteel. She is tolerably accomplished, has her table always covered with new novels, thinks Mr. Mac Quedy an oracle, and is extremely desirous to be called "my lady." Next to her is Mr. Firedamp, a very absurd person, who thinks that water is the evil principle. Next to him is Mr. Eavesdrop, a man who, by dint of a certain something like smartness, has got into good society. He is a sort of bookseller's tool, and coins all his acquaintance in reminiscences and sketches of character. I am very shy of him, for fear he should print me.[2]

CAPTAIN FITZCHROME.

If he print you in your own likeness, which is that of an angel, you need not fear him. If he print you in any other, I will cut his throat. But proceed—

LADY CLARINDA.

Next to him is Mr. Henbane, the toxicologist, I think he calls himself.[3] He has passed half his life in studying poisons and antidotes. The first thing he did on his arrival here, was to kill the cat; and while Miss Crotchet was crying over her, he brought her to life again. I am more shy of him than the other.

CAPTAIN FITZCHROME.

They are two very dangerous fellows, and I shall take care to keep them both at a respectful distance. Let us hope that Eavesdrop will sketch off Henbane, and that Henbane will poison him for his trouble.

LADY CLARINDA.

Well, next to him sits Mr. Mac Quedy, the Modern Athenian, who lays down the law about every thing, and therefore may be taken to understand every thing. He turns all the affairs of this world into questions of buying and selling. He is the Spirit of

---

[2] Perhaps Leigh Hunt, poet and radical journalist. His *Lord Byron and Some of His Contemporaries* (1828) was considered by many (including Peacock) a gross violation of confidence and propriety.

[3] Henbane is a poisonous plant. The character reflects the great contemporary interest in toxicology.

the Frozen Ocean to every thing like romance and sentiment. He condenses their volume of steam into a drop of cold water in a moment. He has satisfied me that I am a commodity in the market, and that I ought to set myself at a high price. So you see he who would have me must bid for me.

CAPTAIN FITZCHROME.

I shall discuss that point with Mr. Mac Quedy.

LADY CLARINDA.

Not a word for your life. Our flirtation is our own secret. Let it remain so.

CAPTAIN FITZCHROME.

Flirtation, Clarinda! Is that all that the most ardent——

LADY CLARINDA.

Now, don't be rhapsodical here. Next to Mr. Mac Quedy is Mr. Skionar, a sort of poetical philosopher, a curious compound of the intense and the mystical. He abominates all the ideas of Mr. Mac Quedy, and settles every thing by sentiment and intuition.

CAPTAIN FITZCHROME.

Then, I say, he is the wiser man.

LADY CLARINDA.

They are two oddities; but a little of them is amusing, and I like to hear them dispute. So you see I am in training for a philosopher myself.

CAPTAIN FITZCHROME.

Any philosophy, for heaven's sake, but the pound-shilling-and-pence philosophy of Mr. Mac Quedy.

LADY CLARINDA.

Why, they say that even Mr. Skionar, though he is a great dreamer,[4] always dreams with his eyes open, or with one eye at any rate, which is an eye to his gain: but I believe that in this respect the poor man has got an ill name by keeping bad company. He has two dear friends, Mr. Wilful Wontsee, and Mr. Rumblesack Shantsee, poets of some note, who used to see visions of Utopia, and pure republics beyond the Western

----

[4] Coleridge claimed that "Kubla Khan" came to him in an opium dream.

deep: but finding that these El Dorados brought them no revenue, they turned their vision-seeing faculty into the more profitable channel of espying all sorts of virtues in the high and the mighty, who were able and willing to pay for the discovery.[5]

CAPTAIN FITZCHROME.

I do not fancy these virtue-spyers.

LADY CLARINDA.

Next to Mr. Skionar, sits Mr. Chainmail, a good-looking young gentleman, as you see, with very antiquated tastes. He is fond of old poetry, and is something of a poet himself. He is deep in monkish literature, and holds that the best state of society was that of the twelfth century, when nothing was going forward but fighting, feasting, and praying, which he says are the three great purposes for which man was made. He laments bitterly over the inventions of gunpowder, steam, and gas, which he says have ruined the world. He lives within two or three miles, and has a large hall, adorned with rusty pikes, shields, helmets, swords, and tattered banners, and furnished with yew-tree chairs, and two long, old, worm-eaten oak tables, where he dines with all his household, after the fashion of his favourite age. He wants us all to dine with him, and I believe we shall go.[6]

CAPTAIN FITZCHROME.

That will be something new at any rate.

LADY CLARINDA.

Next to him is Mr. Toogood, the co-operationist, who will

[5] Wordsworth and Robert Southey, both of whom had long had a reputation as apostates because of their abandonment of the ardent liberalism of their youth. Both had accepted government sinecures, Southey being Poet Laureate. "Rumblesack" alludes to the free butt of sack (wine) provided a Laureate by the government each year. At one time Southey and Coleridge had planned to form a quasi-communistic society in America.

[6] Chainmail epitomizes the growing interest in England's medieval past stimulated by Scott's works. Antiquarian studies had long been a favorite diversion of many cultured Englishmen, and numerous antiquarian organizations had been formed. One, the Young England Movement, even held a medieval tournament, replete with jousting, period costumes, and much pageantry.

have neither fighting nor praying; but wants to parcel out the world into squares like a chess-board, with a community on each, raising every thing for one another, with a great steam-engine to serve them in common for tailor and hosier, kitchen and cook.[7]

CAPTAIN FITZCHROME.

He is the strangest of the set, so far.

LADY CLARINDA.

This brings us to the bottom of the table, where sits my humble servant, Mr. Crotchet the younger. I ought not to describe him.

CAPTAIN FITZCHROME.

I entreat you do.

LADY CLARINDA.

Well, I really have very little to say in his favour.

CAPTAIN FITZCHROME.

I do not wish to hear any thing in his favour; and I rejoice to hear you say so, because——

LADY CLARINDA.

Do not flatter yourself. If I take him, it will be to please my father, and to have a town and country-house, and plenty of servants, and a carriage and an opera-box, and make some of my acquaintance who have married for love, or for rank, or for any thing but money, die for envy of my jewels. You do not think I would take him for himself. Why he is very smooth and spruce, as far as his dress goes; but as to his face, he looks as if he had tumbled headlong into a volcano, and been thrown up again among the cinders.

CAPTAIN FITZCHROME.

I cannot believe, that, speaking thus of him, you mean to take him at all.

LADY CLARINDA.

Oh! I am out of my teens. I have been very much in love;

[7] Robert Owen (1771–1858), industrialist turned social reformer, and pioneer of socialist thought in England. A pacifist and anti-religionist, he believed that the society of the future would be divided into small, self-contained, self-governing communities; his own model communities, established in the U.S.A. in 1824, were laid out in squares.

but now I am come to years of discretion, and must think, like other people, of settling myself advantageously. He was in love with a banker's daughter, and cast her off on her father's bankruptcy, and the poor girl has gone to hide herself in some wild place.

CAPTAIN FITZCHROME.

She must have a strange taste, if she pines for the loss of him.

LADY CLARINDA.

They say he was good-looking, till his bubble-schemes, as they call them, stamped him with the physiognomy of a desperate gambler. I suspect he has still a *penchant* towards his first flame. If he takes me, it will be for my rank and connection, and the second seat of the borough of Rogueingrain. So we shall meet on equal terms, and shall enjoy all the blessedness of expecting nothing from each other.

CAPTAIN FITZCHROME.

You can expect no security with such an adventurer.

LADY CLARINDA.

I shall have the security of a good settlement, and then if *andare al diavolo*[8] be his destiny, he may go, you know, by himself. He is almost always dreaming and *distrait*. It is very likely that some great reverse is in store for him: but that will not concern me, you perceive.

CAPTAIN FITZCHROME.

You torture me, Clarinda, with the bare possibility.

LADY CLARINDA.

Hush! Here is music to soothe your troubled spirit. Next to him, on this side, sits the dilettante composer, Mr. Trillo; they say his name was O'Trill, and he has taken the O from the beginning, and put it at the end. I do not know how this may be. He plays well on the violoncello, and better on the piano: sings agreeably; has a talent at verse-making, and improvises a song with some felicity. He is very agreeable company in the evening, with his instruments and music-books. He maintains that the sole end of all enlightened society is to get up a good opera, and laments that wealth, genius, and energy, are squan-

8 To go to the devil.

dered upon other pursuits, to the neglect of this one great matter.[9]

CAPTAIN FITZCHROME.

That is a very pleasant fancy at any rate.

LADY CLARINDA.

I assure you he has a great deal to say for it. Well, next to him again, is Dr. Morbific, who has been all over the world to prove that there is no such thing as contagion;[10] and has inoculated himself with plague, yellow fever, and every variety of pestilence, and is still alive to tell the story. I am very shy of him, too; for I look on him as a walking phial of wrath, corked full of all infections, and not to be touched without extreme hazard.

CAPTAIN FITZCHROME.

This is the strangest fellow of all.

LADY CLARINDA.

Next to him sits Mr. Philpot,[11] the geographer, who thinks of nothing but the heads and tails of rivers, and lays down the streams of Terra Incognita as accurately as if he had been there. He is a person of pleasant fancy, and makes a sort of fairy land of every country he touches, from the Frozen Ocean to the Deserts of Zahara.

CAPTAIN FITZCHROME.

How does he settle matters with Mr. Firedamp?

LADY CLARINDA.

You see Mr. Firedamp has got as far as possible out of his way. Next to him is Sir Simon Steeltrap, of Steeltrap Lodge, Member for Crouching-Curtown, Justice of Peace for the

[9] This description suggests that Tom Moore (1779–1852) may have been the model, although there is undoubtedly an element of self-parody in the character as well: Peacock was an opera buff, and, beginning about 1829, music critic for two London periodicals.

[10] From *morbificus,* disease. Perhaps suggested by the career of Charles Maclean (fl. 1788–1824), an outspoken anti-contagionist and foe of quarantine.

[11] ΦΙΛοΠΟΤαμος. *Fluviorum amans.* [P] ["Lover of rivers"; perhaps MacGregor Laird (1808–1861), shipbuilder, explorer, expert on African and Indian rivers, and a friend of Peacock. The trip down the Niger, proposed in Chapter VI by Philpot, was being planned by Laird during the time *Crotchet Castle* was written.]

county, and Lord of the United Manors of Spring-gun and Treadmill; a great preserver of game and public morals. By administering the laws which he assists in making, he disposes, at his pleasure, of the land and its live stock, including all the two-legged varieties, with and without feathers, in a circumference of several miles round Steeltrap Lodge. He has enclosed commons and woodlands; abolished cottage-gardens; taken the village cricket-ground into his own park, out of pure regard to the sanctity of Sunday; shut up footpaths and alehouses, (all but those which belong to his electioneering friend, Mr. Quassia, the brewer;)[12] put down fairs and fiddlers; committed many poachers; shot a few; convicted one third of the peasantry; suspected the rest; and passed nearly the whole of them through a wholesome course of prison discipline, which has finished their education at the expense of the county.

CAPTAIN FITZCHROME.

He is somewhat out of his element here: among such a diversity of opinions he will hear some he will not like.

LADY CLARINDA.

It was rather ill-judged in Mr. Crotchet to invite him to-day. But the art of assorting company is above these *parvenus*. They invite a certain number of persons without considering how they harmonise with each other. Between Sir Simon and you is the Reverend Doctor Folliott. He is said to be an excellent scholar, and is fonder of books than the majority of his cloth; he is very fond, also, of the good things of this world. He is of an admirable temper, and says rude things in a pleasant half-earnest manner, that nobody can take offence with. And next to him, again, is one Captain Fitzchrome, who is very much in love with a certain person that does not mean to have any thing to say to him, because she can better her fortune by taking somebody else.

CAPTAIN FITZCHROME.

And next to him, again, is the beautiful, the accomplished, the witty, the fascinating, the tormenting Lady Clarinda, who traduces herself to the said captain by assertions which it would drive him crazy to believe.

---

[12] Quassia is a medicinal product extracted from trees; its taste is quite bitter.

LADY CLARINDA.

Time will show, sir. And now we have gone the round of the table.

CAPTAIN FITZCHROME.

But I must say, though I know you had always a turn for sketching characters, you surprise me by your observation, and especially by your attention to opinions.

LADY CLARINDA.

Well, I will tell you a secret: I am writing a novel.

CAPTAIN FITZCHROME.

A novel!

LADY CLARINDA.

Yes, a novel. And I shall get a little finery by it: trinkets and fal-lals, which I cannot get from papa. You must know I have been reading several fashionable novels, the fashionable this, and the fashionable that; and I thought to myself, why I can do better than any of these myself. So I wrote a chapter or two, and sent them as a specimen to Mr. Puffall,[13] the bookseller, telling him they were to be a part of the fashionable something or other, and he offered me, I will not say how much, to finish it in three volumes, and let him pay all the newspapers for recommending it as the work of a lady of quality, who had made very free with the characters of her acquaintance.[14]

CAPTAIN FITZCHROME.

Surely you have not done so?

LADY CLARINDA.

Oh, no; I leave that to Mr. Eavesdrop. But Mr. Puffall made it a condition that I should let him say so.

CAPTAIN FITZCHROME.

A strange recommendation.

LADY CLARINDA.

Oh, nothing else will do. And it seems you may give yourself any character you like, and the newspapers will print it as if it came from themselves. I have commended you to three of our

---

[13] Cf. puffing, i.e. writing, or hiring someone to write, a laudatory review of your own book.

[14] This type of novel had become popular with the publication in 1816 of Lady Caroline Lamb's *Glenarvon,* which described (with little camouflage) her love affair with Byron.

friends here, as an economist, a transcendentalist, and a classical scholar; and if you wish to be renowned through the world for these, or any other accomplishments, the newspapers will confirm you in their possession for half-a-guinea a piece.

CAPTAIN FITZCHROME.

Truly, the praise of such gentry must be a feather in any one's cap.

LADY CLARINDA.

So you will see, some morning, that my novel is "the most popular production of the day." This is Mr. Puffall's favourite phrase. He makes the newspapers say it of every thing he publishes. But "the day," you know, is a very convenient phrase; it allows of three hundred and sixty-five "most popular productions" in a year. And in leap-year one more.

Chapter VI

THEORIES

> *But when they came to shape the model,*
> *Not one could fit the other's noddle.*—BUTLER.[1]

MEANWHILE, the last course, and the dessert, passed by. When the ladies had withdrawn, young Crotchet addressed the company.

MR. CROTCHET, JUN.

There is one point in which philosophers of all classes seem to be agreed; that they only want money to regenerate the world.

MR. MAC QUEDY.

No doubt of it. Nothing is so easy as to lay down the outlines of perfect society. There wants nothing but money to set it

[1] *Hudibras*, Pt. III. Canto 2, ll. 253–254.

going. I will explain myself clearly and fully by reading a paper. [*Producing a large scroll.*] "In the infancy of society—"

THE REV. DR. FOLLIOTT.

Pray, Mr. Mac Quedy, how is it that all gentlemen of your nation begin every thing they write with the "infancy of society?"

MR. MAC QUEDY.

Eh, sir, it is the simplest way to begin at the beginning. "In the infancy of society, when government was invented to save a percentage; say two and a half per cent.—"

THE REV. DR. FOLLIOTT.

I will not say any such thing.

MR. MAC QUEDY.

Well, say any percentage you please.

THE REV. DR. FOLLIOTT.

I will not say any percentage at all.

MR. MAC QUEDY.

"On the principle of the division of labour—"

THE REV. DR. FOLLIOTT.

Government was invented to spend a percentage.

MR. MAC QUEDY.

To save a percentage.

THE REV. DR. FOLLIOTT.

No, sir, to spend a percentage; and a good deal more than two and a half per cent. Two hundred and fifty per cent.; that is intelligible.

MR. MAC QUEDY.

"In the infancy of society"—

MR. TOOGOOD.

Never mind the infancy of society. The question is of society in its maturity. Here is what it should be. [*Producing a paper.*] I have laid it down in a diagram.[2]

MR. SKIONAR.

Before we proceed to the question of government, we must nicely discriminate the boundaries of sense, understanding, and reason. Sense is a receptivity—

---

[2] Owen liked to use charts, tables, and diagrams in his writings.

MR. CROTCHET, JUN.

We are proceeding too fast. Money being all that is wanted to regenerate society, I will put into the hands of this company a large sum for the purpose. Now let us see how to dispose of it.

MR. MAC QUEDY.

We will begin by taking a committee-room in London, where we will dine together once a week, to deliberate.

THE REV. DR. FOLLIOTT.

If the money is to go in deliberative dinners, you may set me down for a committee man and honorary caterer.

MR. MAC QUEDY.

Next, you must all learn political economy, which I will teach you, very compendiously, in lectures over the bottle.

THE REV. DR. FOLLIOTT.

I hate lectures over the bottle. But pray, sir, what is political economy?

MR. MAC QUEDY.

Political economy is to the state what domestic economy is to the family.

THE REV. DR. FOLLIOTT.

No such thing, sir. In the family there is a *paterfamilias*, who regulates the distribution, and takes care that there shall be no such thing in the household as one dying of hunger, while another dies of surfeit. In the state it is all hunger at one end, and all surfeit at the other.[3] Matchless claret, Mr. Crotchet.

MR. CROTCHET.

Vintage of fifteen, doctor.

MR. MAC QUEDY.

The family consumes, and so does the state.

THE REV. DR. FOLLIOTT.

Consumes, sir! Yes: but the mode, the proportions; there is the essential difference between the state and the family. Sir, I hate false analogies.

---

[3] In the first several decades of the nineteenth century the economic gap between the middle and upper classes on the one hand, and the laboring class on the other, was very wide, the poverty of the latter being extreme.

MR. MAC QUEDY.

Well, sir, the analogy is not essential. Distribution will come under its proper head.

THE REV. DR. FOLLIOTT.

Come where it will, the distribution of the state is in no respect analogous to the distribution of the family. The *paterfamilias*, sir: the *paterfamilias*.

MR. MAC QUEDY.

Well, sir, let that pass. The family consumes, and in order to consume, it must have supply.

THE REV. DR. FOLLIOTT.

Well, sir, Adam and Eve knew that, when they delved and span.[4]

MR. MAC QUEDY.

Very true, sir [*reproducing his scroll*]. "In the infancy of society—"

MR. TOOGOOD.

The reverend gentleman has hit the nail on the head. It is the distribution that must be looked to: it is the *paterfamilias* that is wanting in the state. Now here I have provided him. [*Reproducing his diagram.*]

MR. TRILLO.

Apply the money, sir, to building and endowing an opera house, where the ancient altar of Bacchus[5] may flourish, and justice may be done to sublime compositions. [*Producing a part of a manuscript opera.*]

MR. SKIONAR.

No, sir, build *sacella* for transcendental oracles to teach the world how to see through a glass darkly.[6] [*Producing a scroll.*]

MR. TRILLO.

See through an opera-glass brightly.

---

[4] "When Adam delved and Eve span/ Who was then a gentleman?" Attributed to John Ball in a speech during Wat Tyler's Rebellion, 1381; now proverbial.

[5] The drama began as hymns sung to Bacchus, Greek god of fertility and wine.

[6] I Corinthians 13:12. *Sacella* are small chapels.

THE REV. DR. FOLLIOTT.

See through a wine-glass, full of claret: then you see both darkly and brightly. But, gentlemen, if you are all in the humour for reading papers, I will read you the first half of my next Sunday's sermon. [*Producing a paper.*]

OMNES.

No sermon! No sermon!

THE REV. DR. FOLLIOTT.

Then I move that our respective papers be committed to our respective pockets.

MR. MAC QUEDY.

Political economy is divided into two great branches, production and consumption.

THE REV. DR. FOLLIOTT.

Yes, sir; there are two great classes of men; those who produce much and consume little; and those who consume much and produce nothing. The *fruges consumere nati*,[7] have the best of it. Eh, captain! you remember the characteristics of a great man according to Aristophanes: ὅστις γε πίνειν ὃιδε καὶ βίνειν μόνον.[8] Ha! ha! ha! Well, captain, even in these tight-laced days, the obscurity of a learned language allows a little pleasantry.

CAPTAIN FITZCHROME.

Very true, sir: the pleasantry and the obscurity go together: they are all one, as it were;—to me at any rate [*aside.*]

MR. MAC QUEDY.

Now, sir—

THE REV. DR. FOLLIOTT.

Pray, sir, let your science alone, or you will put me under the painful necessity of demolishing it bit by bit, as I have done your exordium.[9] I will undertake it any morning; but it is too hard exercise after dinner.

MR. MAC QUEDY.

Well, sir, in the meantime I hold my science established.

THE REV. DR. FOLLIOTT.

And I hold it demolished.

---

7 "Those born to consume the fruits." Horace, *Epistles,* I.ii.27.
8 "He is all for wine and women." *The Frogs,* l. 740.
9 Beginning of a formal discourse.

CHAPTER VI

MR. CROTCHET, JUN.

Pray, gentlemen, pocket your manuscripts; fill your glasses; and consider what we shall do with our money.

MR. MAC QUEDY.

Build lecture rooms and schools for all.

MR. TRILLO.

Revive the Athenian theatre: regenerate the lyrical drama.

MR. TOOGOOD.

Build a grand co-operative parallelogram, with a steam-engine in the middle for a maid of all work.

MR. FIREDAMP.

Drain the country, and get rid of *malaria*, by abolishing duck-ponds.

DR. MORBIFIC.

Found a philanthropic college of anti-contagionists, where all the members shall be inoculated with the virus of all known diseases. Try the experiment on a grand scale.

MR. CHAINMAIL.

Build a great dining-hall: endow it with beef and ale, and hang the hall round with arms to defend the provisions.

MR. HENBANE.

Found a toxicological institution for trying all poisons and antidotes. I myself have killed a frog twelve times, and brought him to life eleven; but the twelfth time he died. I have a phial of the drug which killed him in my pocket, and shall not rest till I have discovered its antidote.

THE REV. DR. FOLLIOTT.

I move that the last speaker be dispossessed of his phial, and that it be forthwith thrown into the Thames.

MR. HENBANE.

How, sir? my invaluable, and in the present state of human knowledge, infallible poison?

THE REV. DR. FOLLIOTT.

Let the frogs have all the advantage of it.

MR. CROTCHET.

Consider, doctor, the fish might participate. Think of the salmon.

THE REV. DR. FOLLIOTT.

Then let the owner's right-hand neighbour swallow it.

MR. EAVESDROP.

Me, sir! What have I done, sir, that I am to be poisoned, sir?

THE REV. DR. FOLLIOTT.

Sir, you have published a character of your facetious friend, the Reverend Doctor F., wherein you have sketched off me; me, sir, even to my nose and wig. What business have the public with my nose and wig?

MR. EAVESDROP.

Sir, it is all good humoured: all in *bonhommie:* all friendly and complimentary.

THE REV. DR. FOLLIOTT.

Sir, the bottle, *la Dive Bouteille*,[10] is a recondite oracle, which makes an Eleusinian temple of the circle in which it moves.[11] He who reveals its mysteries must die. Therefore, let the dose be administered. *Fiat experimentum in animâ vili.*[12]

MR. EAVESDROP.

Sir, you are very facetious at my expense.

THE REV. DR. FOLLIOTT.

Sir, you have been very unfacetious, very inficete at mine. You have dished me up, like a savory omelette, to gratify the appetite of the reading rabble for gossip. The next time, sir, I will respond with the *argumentum baculinum.*[13] Print that, sir; put it on record as a promise of the Reverend Doctor F., which shall be most faithfully kept, with an exemplary bamboo.

MR. EAVESDROP.

Your cloth protects you, sir.

THE REV. DR. FOLLIOTT.

My bamboo shall protect me, sir.

MR. CROTCHET.

Doctor, doctor, you are growing too polemical.

---

[10] "The divine bottle."

[11] Temple of Demeter, Greek goddess of grain, the site of secret rites called the Elusinian Mysteries.

[12] "Let the experiment be made on a worthless mind"; proverbial.

[13] Appeal to the rod, i.e. force.

THE REV. DR. FOLLIOTT.

Sir, my blood boils. What business have the public with my nose and wig?

MR. CROTCHET.

Doctor! Doctor!

MR. CROTCHET, JUN.

Pray, gentlemen, return to the point. How shall we employ our fund?

MR. PHILPOT.

Surely in no way so beneficially as in exploring rivers. Send a fleet of steamboats down the Niger, and another up the Nile. So shall you civilise Africa, and establish stocking factories in Abyssinia and Bambo.

THE REV. DR. FOLLIOTT.

With all submission, breeches and petticoats must precede stockings. Send out a crew of tailors. Try if the king of Bambo will invest inexpressibles.

MR. CROTCHET, JUN.

Gentlemen, it is not for partial, but for general benefit, that this fund is proposed: a grand and universally applicable scheme for the amelioration of the condition of man.

SEVERAL VOICES.

That is my scheme. I have not heard a scheme but my own that has a grain of common sense.

MR. TRILLO.

Gentlemen, you inspire me. Your last exclamation runs itself into a chorus, and sets itself to music. Allow me to lead, and to hope for your voices in harmony.

> After careful meditation,
> And profound deliberation,
> On the various pretty projects which have just been shown,
> Not a scheme in agitation,
> For the world's amelioration,
> Has a grain of common sense in it, except my own.

SEVERAL VOICES.

We are not disposed to join in any such chorus.

THE REV. DR. FOLLIOTT.

Well, of all these schemes, I am for Mr. Trillo's. Regenerate the Athenian theatre. My classical friend here, the captain, will vote with me.

CAPTAIN FITZCHROME.

I, sir? oh! of course, sir.

MR. MAC QUEDY.

Surely, captain, I rely on you to uphold political economy.

CAPTAIN FITZCHROME.

Me, sir? oh! to be sure, sir.

THE REV. DR. FOLLIOTT.

Pray, sir, will political economy uphold the Athenian theatre?

MR. MAC QUEDY.

Surely not. It would be a very unproductive investment.

THE REV. DR. FOLLIOTT.

Then the captain votes against you. What, sir, did not the Athenians, the wisest of nations, appropriate to their theatre their most sacred and intangible fund? Did not they give to melopœia, choregraphy, and the sundry forms of didascalics,[14] the precedence of all other matters, civil and military? Was it not their law, that even the proposal to divert this fund to any other purpose should be punished with death? But, sir, I further propose that the Athenian theatre being resuscitated, the admission shall be free to all who can expound the Greek choruses, constructively, mythologically, and metrically, and to none others. So shall all the world learn Greek: Greek, the Alpha and Omega of all knowledge. At him who sits not in the theatre, shall be pointed the finger of scorn: he shall be called in the highway of the city, "a fellow without Greek."

MR. TRILLO.

But the ladies, sir, the ladies.

THE REV. DR. FOLLIOTT.

Every man may take in a lady: and she who can construe and metricise a chorus, shall, if she so please, pass in by herself.

---

[14] Respectively, the arts of musical composition, dancing and teaching.

MR. TRILLO.

But, sir, you will shut me out of my own theatre. Let there at least be a double passport, Greek and Italian.

THE REV. DR. FOLLIOTT.

No, sir; I am inexorable. No Greek, no theatre.

MR. TRILLO.

Sir, I cannot consent to be shut out from my own theatre.

THE REV. DR. FOLLIOTT.

You see how it is, Squire Crotchet the younger; you can scarcely find two to agree on a scheme, and no two of those can agree on the details. Keep your money in your pocket. And so ends the fund for regenerating the world.

MR. MAC QUEDY.

Nay, by no means. We are all agreed on deliberative dinners.

THE REV. DR. FOLLIOTT.

Very true; we will dine and discuss. We will sing with Robin Hood, "If I drink water while this doth last;" and while it lasts we will have no adjournment, if not to the Athenian theatre.

MR. TRILLO.

Well, gentlemen, I hope this chorus at least will please you:

> If I drink water while this doth last,
> May I never again drink wine:
> For how can a man, in his life of a span,
> Do any thing better than dine?
> We'll dine and drink, and say if we think
> That any thing better can be;
> And when we have dined, wish all mankind
> May dine as well as we.
>
> And though a good wish will fill no dish,
> And brim no cup with sack,
> Yet thoughts will spring, as the glasses ring,
> To illume our studious track.
> On the brilliant dreams of our hopeful schemes
> The light of the flask shall shine;
> And we'll sit till day, but we'll find the way
> To drench the world with wine.

The schemes for the world's regeneration evaporated in a tumult of voices.

Chapter VII

THE SLEEPING VENUS

> Quoth he: In all my life till now,
> I ne'er saw so profane a show.—BUTLER.[1]

THE LIBRARY of Crotchet Castle was a large and well furnished apartment, opening on one side into an anteroom, on the other into a music-room. It had several tables stationed at convenient distances; one consecrated to the novelties of literature, another to the novelties of embellishment; others unoccupied, and at the disposal of the company. The walls were covered with a copious collection of ancient and modern books; the ancient having been selected and arranged by the Reverend Doctor Folliott. In the anteroom were card-tables; in the music-room were various instruments, all popular operas, and all fashionable music. In this suite of apartments, and not in the drawing-room, were the evenings of Crotchet Castle usually passed.

The young ladies were in the music-room; Miss Crotchet at the piano, Lady Clarinda, at the harp, playing and occasionally singing, at the suggestion of Mr. Trillo, portions of *Matilde di Shabran*.[2] Lord Bossnowl was turning over the leaves for Miss Crotchet; the captain was performing the same office for Lady Clarinda, but with so much more attention to the lady than the book, that he often made sad work with the harmony, by turning over two leaves together. On these occasions Miss Crotchet

---

[1] *Hudibras*, Pt. II, Canto II, ll. 665–666.
[2] Comic opera (1821) by Rossini.

paused, Lady Clarinda laughed, Mr. Trillo scolded, Lord Bossnowl yawned, the captain apologised, and the performance proceeded.

In the library, Mr. Mac Quedy was expounding political economy to the Reverend Doctor Folliott, who was *pro more* demolishing its doctrines *seriatim*.[3]

Mr. Chainmail was in hot dispute with Mr. Skionar, touching the physical and moral well-being of man. Mr. Skionar was enforcing his friend Mr. Shantsee's views of moral discipline; maintaining that the sole thing needful for man in this world, was loyal and pious education; the giving men good books to read, and enough of the hornbook to read them; with a judicious interspersion of the lessons of Old Restraint, which was his poetic name for the parish stocks.[4] Mr. Chainmail, on the other hand, stood up for the exclusive necessity of beef and ale, lodging and raiment, wife and children, courage to fight for them all, and armour wherewith to do so.

Mr. Henbane had got his face scratched, and his finger bitten, by the cat, in trying to catch her for a second experiment in killing and bringing to life; and Doctor Morbific was comforting him with a disquisition, to prove that there were only four animals having the power to communicate hydrophobia, of which the cat was one; and that it was not necessary that the animal should be in a rabid state, the nature of the wound being every thing, and the idea of contagion a delusion. Mr. Henbane was listening very lugubriously to this dissertation.

Mr. Philpot had seized on Mr. Firedamp, and pinned him down to a map of Africa, on which he was tracing imaginary courses of mighty inland rivers, terminating in lakes and marshes, where they were finally evaporated by the heat of the sun; and Mr. Firedamp's hair was standing on end at the bare imagination of the mass of *malaria* that must be engendered by the operation. Mr. Toogood had begun explaining his diagrams to Sir Simon Steeltrap; but Sir Simon grew testy, and told Mr. Toogood that the promulgators of such doctrines ought to be

---

[3] *Pro more:* by habit; *seriatim:* in series, methodically.

[4] See, for example, Southey's essay "On the Means of Improving the People" (1818).

consigned to the treadmill. The philanthropist walked off from
the country gentleman, and proceeded to hold forth to young
Crotchet, who stood silent, as one who listens, but in reality
without hearing a syllable. Mr. Crotchet senior, as the master
of the house, was left to entertain himself with his own meditations, till the Reverend Doctor Folliott tore himself from Mr.
Mac Quedy, and proceeded to expostulate with Mr. Crotchet
on a delicate topic.

There was an Italian painter, who obtained the name of *Il
Bragatore,* by the superinduction of inexpressibles on the naked
Apollos and Bacchuses of his betters.[5] The fame of this worthy
remained one and indivisible, till a set of heads, which had
been, by a too common mistake of nature's journeymen, stuck
upon magisterial shoulders, as the Corinthian capitals of "fair
round bellies with fat capon lined,"[6] but which nature herself
had intended for the noddles of porcelain mandarins, promul-
gated simultaneously from the east and the west of London, an
order that no plaster-of-Paris Venus should appear in the streets
without petticoats. Mr. Crotchet, on reading this order in the
evening paper, which, by the postman's early arrival, was always laid on his breakfast-table, determined to fill his house
with Venuses of all sizes and kinds. In pursuance of this resolution, came packages by water-carriage, containing an infinite
variety of Venuses. There were the Medicean Venus, and the
Bathing Venus; the Uranian Venus, and the Pandemian Venus;
the Crouching Venus, and the Sleeping Venus; the Venus rising
from the sea, the Venus with the apple of Paris, and the Venus
with the armour of Mars.[7]

The Reverend Doctor Folliott had been very much astonished at this unexpected display. Disposed, as he was, to hold,
that whatever had been in Greece, was right; he was more than

[5] Perhaps a corruption of *Il Bragghetone* ("the breeches-maker"),
a nickname of Daniele Ricciarelli da Volterra (1509–1566), a pupil of
Michelangelo, who was hired by Pope Paul IV to put draperies on some
of the nudes in Michelangelo's "Last Judgement."

[6] *As You Like It,* II.vii.

[7] Except for the Sleeping Venus, which if real was of more recent
vintage, these are reproductions of famous ancient Greek works and all,
of course, are unclothed.

doubtful of the propriety of throwing open the classical *adytum*[8] to the illiterate profane. Whether, in his interior mind, he was at all influenced, either by the consideration that it would be for the credit of his cloth, with some of his vice-suppressing neighbours, to be able to say that he had expostulated; or by curiosity, to try what sort of defence his city-bred friend, who knew the classics only by translations, and whose reason was always a little a-head of his knowledge, would make for his somewhat ostentatious display of liberality in matters of taste; is a question, on which the learned may differ: but, after having duly deliberated on two full-sized casts of the Uranian and Pandemian Venus, in niches on each side of the chimney, and on three alabaster figures, in glass cases, on the mantel-piece, he proceeded, peirastically,[9] to open his fire.

THE REV. DR. FOLLIOTT.

These little alabaster figures on the mantlepiece, Mr. Crotchet, and those large figures in the niches—may I take the liberty to ask you what they are intended to represent?

MR. CROTCHET.

Venus, sir; nothing more, sir; just Venus.

THE REV. DR. FOLLIOTT.

May I ask you, sir, why they are there?

MR. CROTCHET.

To be looked at, sir; just to be looked at: the reason for most things in a gentleman's house being in it at all; from the paper on the walls, and the drapery of the curtains, even to the books in the library, of which the most essential part is the appearance of the back.

THE REV. DR. FOLLIOTT.

Very true, sir. As great philosophers hold that the *esse* of things is *percipi*,[10] so a gentleman's furniture exists to be looked at. Nevertheless, sir, there are some things more fit to be looked at than others; for instance, there is nothing more fit to be looked at than the outside of a book. It is, as I may say, from repeated experience, a pure and unmixed pleasure to have a

---

[8] Innermost recess of a temple, accessible only to priests.
[9] Tentatively (coined by Peacock).
[10] Cf. Berkeley's *esse est percipi* ("to be is to be perceived").

goodly volume lying before you, and to know that you may open it if you please, and need not open it unless you please. It is a resource against *ennui,* if *ennui* should come upon you. To have the resource and not to feel the *ennui,* to enjoy your bottle in the present, and your book in the indefinite future, is a delightful condition of human existence. There is no place, in which a man can move or sit, in which the outside of a book can be otherwise than an innocent and becoming spectacle. Touching this matter, there cannot, I think, be two opinions. But with respect to your Venuses there can be, and indeed there are, two very distinct opinions. Now, sir, that little figure in the centre of the mantlepiece,—as a grave *paterfamilias,* Mr. Crotchet, with a fair nubile daughter, whose eyes are like the fishpools of Heshbon,[11]—I would ask you if you hold that figure to be altogether delicate?

MR. CROTCHET.

The Sleeping Venus, sir? Nothing can be more delicate than the entire contour of the figure, the flow of the hair on the shoulders and neck, the form of the feet and fingers. It is altogether a most delicate morsel.

THE REV. DR. FOLLIOTT.

Why, in that sense, perhaps, it is as delicate as whitebait[12] in July. But the attitude, sir, the attitude.

MR. CROTCHET.

Nothing can be more natural, sir.

THE REV. DR. FOLLIOTT.

That is the very thing, sir. It is too natural: too natural, sir: it lies for all the world like——I make no doubt, the pious cheesemonger, who recently broke its plaster fac-simile over the head of the itinerant vendor, was struck by a certain similitude to the position of his own sleeping beauty, and felt his noble wrath thereby justly aroused.[13]

MR. CROTCHET.

Very likely, sir. In my opinion, the cheesemonger was a fool, and the justice who sided with him was a greater.

---

[11] Song of Solomon 7:4.
[12] A type of fish.
[13] Perhaps an incident in the career of Joseph Livesey (1794–1884), a cheesemonger and agitator for various moral reforms.

THE REV. DR. FOLLIOTT.

Fool, sir, is a harsh term: call not thy brother a fool.

MR. CROTCHET.

Sir, neither the cheesemonger nor the justice is a brother of mine.

THE REV. DR. FOLLIOTT.

Sir, we are all brethren.

MR. CROTCHET.

Yes, sir, as the hangman is of the thief; the 'squire of the poacher; the judge of the libeller; the lawyer of his client; the statesman of his colleague; the bubble-blower of the bubble-buyer; the slave-driver of the negro: as these are brethren, so am I and the worthies in question.

THE REV. DR. FOLLIOTT.

To be sure, sir, in these instances, and in many others, the term brother must be taken in its utmost latitude of interpretation: we are all brothers, nevertheless. But to return to the point. Now these two large figures, one with drapery on the lower half of the body, and the other with no drapery at all; upon my word, sir, it matters not what godfathers and godmothers may have promised and vowed for the children of this world, touching the devil and other things to be renounced, if such figures as those are to be put before their eyes.

MR. CROTCHET.

Sir, the naked figure is the Pandemian Venus, and the half-draped figure is the Uranian Venus; and I say, sir, that figure realises the finest imaginings of Plato, and is the personification of the most refined and exalted feeling of which the human mind is susceptible; the love of pure, ideal, intellectual beauty.

THE REV. DR. FOLLIOTT.

I am aware, sir, that Plato, in his Symposium, discourseth very eloquently touching the Uranian and Pandemian Venus: but you must remember that, in our Universities, Plato is held to be little better than a misleader of youth; and they have shown their contempt for him, not only by never reading him (a mode of contempt in which they deal very largely), but even by never printing a complete edition of him; although they have printed many ancient books, which nobody suspects to have been ever read on the spot, except by a person attached to the press, who is therefore emphatically called "the reader."

MR. CROTCHET.

Well, sir?

THE REV. DR. FOLLIOTT.

Why, sir, to "the reader" aforesaid (supposing either of our Universities to have printed an edition of Plato), or to any one else who can be supposed to have read Plato, or indeed to be ever likely to do so, I would very willingly show these figures; because to such they would, I grant you, be the outward and visible signs of poetical and philosophical ideas: but, to the multitude, the gross carnal multitude, they are but two beautiful women, one half undressed, and the other quite so.

MR. CROTCHET.

Then, sir, let the multitude look upon them and learn modesty.

THE REV. DR. FOLLIOTT.

I must say that, if I wished my footman to learn modesty, I should not dream of sending him to school to a naked Venus.

MR. CROTCHET.

Sir, ancient sculpture is the true school of modesty. But where the Greeks had modesty, we have cant; where they had poetry, we have cant; where they had patriotism, we have cant; where they had any thing that exalts, delights, or adorns humanity, we have nothing but cant, cant, cant. And, sir, to show my contempt for cant in all its shapes, I have adorned my house with the Greek Venus, in all her shapes, and am ready to fight her battle against all the societies that ever were instituted for the suppression of truth and beauty.[14]

THE REV. DR. FOLLIOTT.

My dear sir, I am afraid you are growing warm. Pray be cool. Nothing contributes so much to good digestion as to be perfectly cool after dinner.

MR. CROTCHET.

Sir, the Lacedæmonian virgins wrestled naked with young

---

[14] The Society for the Suppression of Vice (founded 1802) may be meant here, although numerous other bluenose organizations flourished at this time.

men: and they grew up, as the wise Lycurgus[15] had foreseen, into the most modest of women, and the most exemplary of wives and mothers.

THE REV. DR. FOLLIOTT.

Very likely, sir; but the Athenian virgins did no such thing, and they grew up into wives who stayed at home,—stayed at home, sir; and looked after the husband's dinner,—his dinner, sir, you will please to observe.

MR. CROTCHET.

And what was the consequence of that, sir? that they were such very insipid persons that the husband would not go home to eat his dinner, but preferred the company of some Aspasia, or Lais.[16]

THE REV. DR. FOLLIOTT.

Two very different persons, sir, give me leave to remark.

MR. CROTCHET.

Very likely, sir; but both too good to be married in Athens.

THE REV. DR. FOLLIOTT.

Sir, Lais was a Corinthian.

MR. CROTCHET.

'Od's vengeance, sir, some Aspasia and any other Athenian name of the same sort of person you like——

THE REV. DR. FOLLIOTT.

I do not like the sort of person at all: the sort of person I like, as I have already implied, is a modest woman, who stays at home and looks after her husband's dinner.

MR. CROTCHET.

Well, sir, that was not the taste of the Athenians. They preferred the society of women who would not have made any scruple about sitting as models to Praxiteles; as you know, sir, very modest women in Italy did to Canova:[17] one of whom, an Italian countess, being asked by an English lady, "how she could bear it?" answered, "Very well; there was a good fire in the room."

---

[15] A legendary Spartan (Lacedaemonian) legislator and reformer.
[16] Famous Greek courtesans.
[17] Italian sculptor and painter (1757–1822); Praxiteles (fl. 420 B. C.) was one of the greatest sculptors of classical Greece.

THE REV. DR. FOLLIOTT.

Sir, the English lady should have asked how the Italian lady's husband could bear it. The phials of my wrath overflow if poor dear Mrs. Folliott——: sir, in return for your story, I will tell you a story of my ancestor, Gilbert Folliott. The devil haunted him, as he did Saint Francis, in the likeness of a beautiful damsel; but all he could get from the exemplary Gilbert was an admonition to wear a stomacher and longer petticoats.

MR. CROTCHET.

Sir, your story makes for my side of the question. It proves that the devil, in the likeness of a fair damsel, with short petticoats and no stomacher, was almost too much for Gilbert Folliott. The force of the spell was in the drapery.

THE REV. DR. FOLLIOTT.

Bless my soul, sir!

MR. CROTCHET.

Give me leave, sir. Diderot——

THE REV. DR. FOLLIOTT.

Who was he, sir?

MR. CROTCHET.

Who was he, sir? the sublime philosopher, the father of the encyclopædia, of all the encyclopædias that have ever been printed.

THE REV. DR. FOLLIOTT.

Bless me, sir, a terrible progeny! they belong to the tribe of *Incubi*.[18]

MR. CROTCHET.

The great philosopher, Diderot——

THE REV. DR. FOLLIOTT.

Sir, Diderot is not a man after my heart. Keep to the Greeks, if you please; albeit this Sleeping Venus is not an antique.

MR. CROTCHET.

Well, sir, the Greeks: why do we call the Elgin marbles[19] inestimable? Simply because they are true to nature. And why are they so superior in that point to all modern works, with all

[18] Demons which have sexual intercourse with women as they lie asleep.

[19] Sculptures taken from the Parthenon at Athens by Lord Elgin (1766–1841) and brought to England for display.

our greater knowledge of anatomy? Why, sir, but because the Greeks, having no cant, had better opportunities of studying models?

THE REV. DR. FOLLIOTT.

Sir, I deny our greater knowledge of anatomy. But I shall take the liberty to employ, on this occasion, the *argumentum ad hominem.*[20] Would you have allowed Miss Crotchet to sit for a model to Canova?

MR. CROTCHET.

Yes, sir.

"God bless my soul, sir!" exclaimed the Reverend Doctor Folliott, throwing himself back into a chair, and flinging up his heels, with the premeditated design of giving emphasis to his exclamation: but by miscalculating his *impetus,* he overbalanced his chair, and laid himself on the carpet in a right angle, of which his back was the base.

Chapter VIII

SCIENCE AND CHARITY

> *Chi sta nel mondo un par d'ore contento,*
> *Nè gli vien tolta, ovver contaminata,*
> *Quella sua pace in veruno momento,*
> *Può dir che Giove drittamente il guata.*
>
> FORTEGUERRI.[1]

THE REVEREND Doctor Folliott took his departure about ten o'clock, to walk home to his vicarage. There was no moon; but the night was bright and clear, and afforded him as much light as he needed. He paused a moment by the Roman camp,

[20] "Argument to the man," i.e. shifting from legitimate issues to the character or feelings of one's opponent.

[1] "He who lives content in the world a few hours and whose peace is not destroyed at a moment's notice, can say that Jove is looking directly at him." From the burlesque chivalric poem *Il Ricciardetto.*

to listen to the nightingale; repeated to himself a passage of Sophocles; proceeded through the park gate, and entered the narrow lane that led to the village. He walked on in a very pleasant mood of the state called *reverie;* in which fish and wine, Greek and political economy, the Sleeping Venus he had left behind and poor dear Mrs. Folliott, to whose fond arms he was returning, passed as in a *camera obscura* over the tablets of his imagination. Presently the image of Mr. Eavesdrop, with a printed sketch of the Reverend Doctor F., presented itself before him, and he began mechanically to flourish his bamboo. The movement was prompted by his good genius, for the uplifted bamboo received the blow of a ponderous cudgel, which was intended for his head. The reverend gentleman recoiled two or three paces, and saw before him a couple of ruffians, who were preparing to renew the attack, but whom, with two swings of his bamboo, he laid with cracked sconces on the earth, where he proceeded to deal with them like corn beneath the flail of the thresher. One of them drew a pistol, which went off in the very act of being struck aside by the bamboo, and lodged a bullet in the brain of the other. There was then only one enemy, who vainly struggled to rise, every effort being attended with a new and more signal prostration. The fellow roared for mercy. "Mercy, rascal!" cried the divine; "what mercy were you going to show me, villain? What! I warrant me, you thought it would be an easy matter, and no sin, to rob and murder a parson on his way home from dinner. You said to yourself, doubtless, 'We'll waylay the fat parson (you irreverent knave) as he waddles home (you disparaging ruffian), half-seas-over (you calumnious vagabond).' " And with every dyslogistic[2] term, which he supposed had been applied to himself, he inflicted a new bruise on his rolling and roaring antagonist. "Ah, rogue!" he proceeded; "you can roar now, marauder; you were silent enough when you devoted my brains to dispersion under your cudgel. But seeing that I cannot bind you, and that I intend you not to escape, and that it would be dangerous to let you rise, I will disable you in all your mem-

---

[2] Disparaging.

bers; I will contund you as Thestylis did strong-smelling herbs,[3] in the quality whereof you do most gravely partake, as my nose beareth testimony, ill weed that you are. I will beat you to a jelly, and I will then roll you into the ditch, to lie till the constable comes for you, thief."

"Hold! hold! reverend sir," exclaimed the penitent culprit, "I am disabled already in every finger, and in every joint. I will roll myself into the ditch, reverend sir."

"Stir not, rascal," returned the divine, "stir not so much as the quietest leaf above you, or my bamboo rebounds on your body like hail in a thunder storm. Confess speedily, villain; are you simple thief, or would you have manufactured me into a subject, for the benefit of science? Ay, miscreant caitiff, you would have made me a subject for science, would you? You are a schoolmaster abroad, are you?[4] You are marching with a detachment of the march of mind, are you? You are a member of the Steam Intellect Society, are you? You swear by the learned friend, do you?"

"Oh, no! reverend sir," answered the criminal, "I am innocent of all these offenses, whatever they are, reverend sir. The only friend I had in the world is lying dead beside me, reverend sir."

The reverend gentleman paused a moment, and leaned on his bamboo. The culprit, bruised as he was, sprang on his legs, and went off in double quick time. The doctor gave him chase, and had nearly brought him within arm's length, when the fellow turned at right angles, and sprang clean over a deep dry ditch. The divine, following with equal ardour, and less dexterity, went down over head and ears into a thicket of nettles. Emerging with much discomposure, he proceeded to the village, and roused the constable; but the constable found, on reaching

---

[3] Thestylis . . .
    . . . herbas contundit olentes.
                             Virg. *Ecl.* ii.10.11. [P]

[4] A phrase attributed to Brougham, referring to the spread of education among the masses. *a subject for science:* at this time so-called "resurrectionists" robbed graves and even committed murders to obtain corpses to sell to medical schools, which had difficulty obtaining cadavers because of public opposition to dissection.

the scene of action, that the dead man was gone, as well as his living accomplice.

"Oh, the monster!" exclaimed the Reverend Doctor Folliott, "he has made a subject for science of the only friend he had in the world." "Ay, my dear," he resumed, the next morning at breakfast, "if my old reading, and my early gymnastics (for as the great Hermann says, before I was demulced by the Muses, I was *ferocis ingenii puer, et ad arma quam ad literas paratior*[5]), had not imbued me indelibly with some of the holy rage of *Frère Jean des Entommeures*,[6] I should be, at this moment, lying on the table of some flinty-hearted anatomist,[7] who would have sliced and disjointed me as unscrupulously as I do these remnants of the capon and chine, wherewith you consoled yourself yesterday for my absence at dinner. Phew! I have a noble thirst upon me, which I will quench with floods of tea."

The reverend gentleman was interrupted by a messenger, who informed him that the Charity Commissioners requested his presence at the inn, where they were holding a sitting.[8]

"The Charity Commissioners!" exclaimed the reverend gentleman, "who on earth are they?"

The messenger could not inform him, and the reverend gentleman took his hat and stick, and proceeded to the inn.

On entering the best parlour, he saw three well-dressed and bulky gentlemen sitting at a table, and a fourth officiating as clerk, with an open book before him, and a pen in his hand. The churchwardens, who had been also summoned, were already in attendance.

The chief commissioner politely requested the Reverend Doctor Folliott to be seated; and after the usual meteorological

[5] "A boy of fierce disposition, more inclined to arms than to letters."—Hermann's *Dedication of Homer's Hymns to his Preceptor Ilgen*. [P]

[6] Rabelais, Bk. I, Ch. xxvii; a drunken monk who, singlehanded, routed an army which was despoiling the monastery vineyard.

[7] Robert Knox (1791–1862) was a respected anatomist who from 1827–1829 had purchased for dissection several corpses from two notorious murderers named Burke and Hare.

[8] The Inquiry Commissions had been established in 1818, largely at the instigation of Brougham, to investigate public charities.

preliminaries had been settled by a resolution, *nem. con.,*[9] that it was a fine day but very hot, the chief commissioner stated, that in virtue of the commission of Parliament, which they had the honour to hold, they were now to inquire into the state of the public charities of this village.

THE REV. DR. FOLLIOTT.

The state of the public charities, sir, is exceedingly simple. There are none. The charities here are all private, and so private, that I for one know nothing of them.

FIRST COMMISSIONER.

We have been informed, sir, that there is an annual rent charged on the land of Hautbois, for the endowment and repair of an almshouse.

THE REV. DR. FOLLIOTT.

Hautbois! Hautbois!

FIRST COMMISSIONER.

The manorial farm of Hautbois, now occupied by Farmer Seedling, is charged with the endowment and maintenance of an almshouse.

THE REV. DR. FOLLIOTT.

[to the Churchwarden]

How is this, Mr. Bluenose?

FIRST CHURCHWARDEN.

I really do not know, sir. What say you, Mr. Appletwig?

MR. APPLETWIG.

[parish-clerk and schoolmaster; an old man]

I do remember, gentlemen, to have been informed, that there did stand at the end of the village a ruined cottage, which had once been an almshouse, which was endowed and maintained, by an annual revenue of a mark and a half, or one pound sterling, charged some centuries ago on the farm of Hautbois; but the means, by the progress of time, having become inadequate to the end, the almshouse tumbled to pieces.

FIRST COMMISSIONER.

But this is a right which cannot be abrogated by desuetude, and the sum of one pound per annum is still chargeable for charitable purposes on the manorial farm of Hautbois.

[9] No one contradicting.

THE REV. DR. FOLLIOTT.

Very well, sir.

MR. APPLETWIG.

But sir, the one pound per annum is still received by the parish, but was long ago, by an unanimous vote in open vestry, given to the minister.

THE THREE COMMISSIONERS.

[*unâ voce*]

The minister!

FIRST COMMISSIONER.

This is an unjustifiable proceeding.

SECOND COMMISSIONER.

A misappropriation of a public fund.

THIRD COMMISSIONER.

A flagrant perversion of a charitable donation.

THE REV. DR. FOLLIOTT.

God bless my soul, gentlemen! I know nothing of this matter. How is this, Mr. Bluenose? Do I receive this one pound per annum?

FIRST CHURCHWARDEN.

Really, sir, I know no more about it than you do.

MR. APPLETWIG.

You certainly receive it, sir. It was voted to one of your predecessors. Farmer Seedling lumps it in with his tithes.

FIRST COMMISSIONER.

Lumps it in, sir! Lump in a charitable donation!

SECOND AND THIRD COMMISSIONER.

Oh-oh-oh-h-h!

FIRST COMMISSIONER.

Reverend sir, and gentlemen, officers of this parish, we are under the necessity of admonishing you that this is a most improper proceeding; and you are hereby duly admonished accordingly. Make a record, Mr. Milky.

MR. MILKY.

[*writing*]

The clergyman and churchwardens of the village of Hm-m-m-m gravely admonished. Hm-m-m-m.

THE REV. DR. FOLLIOTT.

Is that all, gentlemen?

THE COMMISSIONERS.

That is all, sir; and we wish you a good morning.

THE REV. DR. FOLLIOTT.

A very good morning to you, gentlemen.

"What in the name of all that is wonderful, Mr. Bluenose," said the Reverend Doctor Folliott, as he walked out of the inn, "what in the name of all that is wonderful, can those fellows mean? They have come here in a chaise and four, to make a fuss about a pound per annum, which, after all, they leave as it was. I wonder who pays them for their trouble, and how much."

MR. APPLETWIG.

The public pay for it, sir. It is a job of the learned friend whom you admire so much. It makes away with public money in salaries, and private money in lawsuits, and does no particle of good to any living soul.

THE REV. DR. FOLLIOTT.

Ay, ay, Mr. Appletwig; that is just the sort of public service to be looked for from the learned friend. Oh, the learned friend! the learned friend! He is the evil genius of every thing that falls in his way.

The reverend doctor walked off to Crotchet Castle, to narrate his misadventures, and exhale his budget of grievances on Mr. Mac Quedy, whom he considered a ringleader of the march of mind.

Chapter IX

THE VOYAGE

Οἱ μὲν ἔπειτ' ἀναβάντες ἐπέπλεον ὑγρὰ κέλευθα.
Mounting the bark, they cleft the watery ways.
HOMER.[1]

FOUR BEAUTIFUL cabined pinnaces, one for the ladies, one for the gentlemen, one for kitchen and servants, one for a dining-room and band of music, weighed anchor, on a fine July morning, from below Crotchet Castle, and were towed merrily, by strong trotting horses, against the stream of the Thames. They passed from the district of chalk, successively into the districts of clay, of sand-rock, of oolite, and so forth. Sometimes they dined in their floating dining-room, sometimes in tents, which they pitched on the dry smooth-shaven green of a newly mown meadow; sometimes they left their vessels to see sights in the vicinity; sometimes they passed a day or two in a comfortable inn.

At Oxford, they walked about to see the curiosities of architecture, painted windows, and undisturbed libraries. The Reverend Doctor Folliott laid a wager with Mr. Crotchet "that in all their perlustrations they would not find a man reading," and won it. "Ay, sir," said the reverend gentleman, "this is still a seat of learning, on the principle of—once a captain always a captain. We may well ask, in these great reservoirs of books whereof no man ever draws a sluice, *Quorsum pertinuit stipare Platona Menandro?*[2] What is done here for the classics? Reprinting German editions on better paper. A great boast, verily! What for mathematics? What for metaphysics? What for history? What for any thing worth knowing? This was a seat of

---

[1] *Iliad*, I.312.
[2] Wherefore is Plato on Menander piled?

Hor. *Sat*.ii.3.11. [P]

270

learning in the days of Friar Bacon. But the friar is gone, and his learning with him. Nothing of him is left but the immortal nose, which when his brazen head had tumbled to pieces, crying "Time's past," was the only palpable fragment among its minutely pulverised atoms, and which is still resplendent over the portals of its cognominal college. That nose, sir, is the only thing to which I shall take off my hat, in all this Babylon of buried literature.[3]

MR. CROTCHET.

But, doctor, it is something to have a great reservoir of learning, at which some may draw if they please.

THE REV. DR. FOLLIOTT.

But, here, good care is taken that nobody shall please. If even a small drop from the sacred fountain, πίδακος ἐξ ἱερῆς ὀλίγη λιβάς, as Callimachus has it,[4] were carried off by any one, it would be evidence of something to hope for. But the system of dissuasion from all good learning is brought here to a pitch of perfection that baffles the keenest aspirant. I run over to myself the names of the scholars of Germany, a glorious catalogue! but ask for those of Oxford—Where are they? The echoes of their courts, as vacant as their heads, will answer, Where are they? The tree shall be known by its fruit; and seeing that this great tree, with all its specious seeming, brings forth no fruit, I do denounce it as a barren fig.[5]

MR. MAC QUEDY.

I shall set you right on this point. We do nothing without motives. If learning get nothing but honour, and very little of that; and if the good things of this world, which ought to be the rewards of learning, become the mere gifts of self-interested patronage; you must not wonder if, in the finishing of

---

[3] In Robert Greene's *Friar Bacon and Friar Bungay* (ca. 1594), Roger Bacon (1214?–1294, a scholar, teacher at Oxford and inventor of eyeglasses) conjures up a brazen head which says "Time is," "Time was," and "Time is past" and thereupon breaks. A brass doorknocker, shaped like a nose, is said to have given Brasenose College, Oxford, its name.

[4] "A small trickle from the sacred spring." "Hymn to Apollo," no. II, line 112.

[5] See Matthew 12:33 and Luke 13:6–9 (the parable of the barren fig).

education, the science which takes precedence of all others, should be the science of currying favour.

THE REV. DR. FOLLIOTT.

Very true, sir. Education is well finished, for all worldly purposes, when the head is brought into the state whereinto I am accustomed to bring a marrow-bone, when it has been set before me on a toast, with a white napkin wrapped round it. Nothing trundles along the high road of preferment so trimly as a well-biased sconce, picked clean within, and polished without; *totus teres atque rotundus.*[6] The perfection of the finishing lies in the bias, which keeps it trundling in the given direction. There is good and sufficient reason for the fig being barren, but it is not therefore the less a barren fig.

At Godstow, they gathered hazel on the grave of Rosamond;[7] and, proceeding on their voyage, fell into a discussion on legendary histories.

LADY CLARINDA.

History is but a tiresome thing in itself; it becomes more agreeable the more romance is mixed up with it. The great enchanter has made me learn many things which I should never have dreamed of studying, if they had not come to me in the form of amusement.

THE REV. DR. FOLLIOTT.

What enchanter is that? There are two enchanters: he of the North, and he of the South.[8]

MR. TRILLO.

Rossini?

THE REV. DR. FOLLIOTT.

Ay, there is another enchanter. But I mean the great enchanter of Covent Garden: he who, for more than a quarter of a century, has produced two pantomimes a year, to the

---

[6] All smooth and round. [P] [Horace, *Satires,* II.vii.86.]

[7] Rosamond Clifford, mistress of King Henry II, who was supposedly poisoned (ca. 1176) by Queen Eleanor and buried in Godstow Abbey.

[8] The former is Sir Walter Scott, the latter probably Charles Farley (1771–1859), who produced pantomimes at Covent Garden from 1806–1834.

delight of children of all ages, including myself at all ages. That is the enchanter for me. I am for the pantomimes. All the northern enchanter's romances put together would not furnish materials for half the southern enchanter's pantomimes.

LADY CLARINDA.

Surely you do not class literature with pantomime?

THE REV. DR. FOLLIOTT.

In these cases I do. They are both one, with a slight difference. The one is the literature of pantomime, the other is the pantomime of literature. There is the same variety of character, the same diversity of story, the same copiousness of incident, the same research into costume, the same display of heraldry, falconry, minstrelsy, scenery, monkery, witchery, devilry, robbery, poachery, piracy, fishery, gipsy-astrology, demonology, architecture, fortification, castrametation, navigation; the same running base of love and battle. The main difference is, that the one set of amusing fictions is told in music and action; the other in all the worst dialects of the English language. As to any sentence worth remembering, any moral or political truth, any thing having a tendency, however remote, to make men wiser or better, to make them think, to make them even think of thinking; they are both precisely alike: *nuspiam, nequaquam, nullibi, nullimodis.*[9]

LADY CLARINDA.

Very amusing, however.

THE REV. DR. FOLLIOTT.

Very amusing, very amusing.

MR. CHAINMAIL.

My quarrel with the northern enchanter is, that he has grossly misrepresented the twelfth century.

THE REV. DR. FOLLIOTT.

He has misrepresented every thing, or he would not have been very amusing. Sober truth is but dull matter to the reading rabble. The angler, who puts not on his hook the bait that best pleases the fish, may sit all day on the bank without catching a gudgeon.[10]

---

[9] Never, by no means, nowhere, in no manner.
[10] Eloquentiae magister, nisi, tamquam piscator eam imposuerit

MR. MAC QUEDY.

But how do you mean that he has misrepresented the twelfth century? By exhibiting some of its knights and ladies in the colours of refinement and virtue, seeing that they were all no better than ruffians, and something else that shall be nameless?

MR. CHAINMAIL.

By no means. By depicting them as much worse than they were, not, as you suppose, much better.[11] No one would infer from his pictures that theirs was a much better state of society than this which we live in.

MR. MAC QUEDY.

No, nor was it. It was a period of brutality, ignorance, fanaticism, and tyranny; when the land was covered with castles, and every castle contained a gang of banditti, headed by a titled robber, who levied contributions with fire and sword; plundering, torturing, ravishing, burying his captives in loathsome dungeons, and broiling them on gridirons, to force from them the surrender of every particle of treasure which he suspected them of possessing; and fighting every now and then with the neighbouring lords, his conterminal[12] bandits, for the right of marauding on the boundaries. This was the twelfth century, as depicted by all contemporary historians and poets.

MR. CHAINMAIL.

No, sir. Weigh the evidence of specific facts; you will find more good than evil. Who was England's greatest hero; the mirror of chivalry, the pattern of honour, the fountain of generosity, the model to all succeeding ages of military glory? Richard the First. There is a king of the twelfth century. What was the first step of liberty? Magna Charta. That was the best thing ever done by lords. There are lords of the twelfth century. You must remember, too, that these lords were petty princes,

---

hamis escam, quam scierit appetituros esse pisciculos, sine spe praedae moratur in scopulo. Petronius Arbiter. [P] ["A master of oratory is like a fisherman; he must put on his hook the bait which he knows will tempt the fish, or he may sit waiting on his rock with no hope of a catch." *The Satyricon,* ¶ 3.]

[11] Scott's *The Fair Maid of Perth* (1828), which Peacock may have in mind here, portrayed the brutality of medieval life.

[12] Sharing a common border (coined by Peacock).

and made war on each other as legitimately as the heads of larger communities did or do. For their system of revenue, it was, to be sure, more rough and summary than that which has succeeded it, but it was certainly less searching and less productive. And as to the people, I content myself with these great points: that every man was armed, every man was a good archer, every man could and would fight effectively with sword or pike, or even with oaken cudgel: no man would live quietly without beef and ale; if he had them not, he fought till he either got them, or was put out of condition to want them. They were not, and could not be, subjected to that powerful pressure of all the other classes of society, combined by gunpowder, steam, and *fiscality*, which has brought them to that dismal degradation in which we see them now. And there are the people of the twelfth century.

MR. MAC QUEDY.

As to your king, the enchanter has done him ample justice, even in your own view.[13] As to your lords and their ladies, he has drawn them too favourably, given them too many of the false colours of chivalry, thrown too attractive a light on their abominable doings. As to the people, he keeps them so much in the back-ground, that he can hardly be said to have represented them at all, much less misrepresented them, which indeed he could scarcely do, seeing that, by your own showing, they were all thieves, ready to knock down any man for what they could not come by honestly.

MR. CHAINMAIL.

No, sir. They could come honestly by beef and ale, while they were left to their simple industry. When oppression interfered with them in that, then they stood on the defensive, and fought for what they were not permitted to come by quietly.

MR. MAC QUEDY.

If A, being aggrieved by B, knocks down C, do you call that standing on the defensive?

MR. CHAINMAIL.

That depends on who or what C is.

[13] Richard I appeared in *Ivanhoe* (1819) and *The Talisman* (1825).

THE REV. DR. FOLLIOTT.

Gentlemen, you will never settle this controversy, till you have first settled what is good for man in this world; the great question, *de finibus*, which has puzzled all philosophers. If the enchanter has represented the twelfth century too brightly for one, and too darkly for the other of you, I should say, as an impartial man, he has represented it fairly. My quarrel with him is, that his works contain nothing worth quoting; and a book that furnishes no quotations, is, *me judice*,[14] no book— it is a plaything. There is no question about the amusement— amusement of multitudes; but if he who amuses us most, is to be our enchanter κατ' ἐξοχὴν,[15] then my enchanter is the enchanter of Covent Garden.

Chapter X

THE VOYAGE, CONTINUED

> *Continuant nostre routte, navigasmes par trois jours sans rien descouvrir.*—RABELAIS.[1]

"THERE IS a beautiful structure," said Mr. Chainmail, as they glided by Lechlade church; "a subject for the pencil, Captain. It is a question worth asking, Mr. Mac Quedy, whether the religious spirit which reared these edifices, and connected with them everywhere an asylum for misfortune and a provision for poverty, was not better than the commercial spirit, which has turned all the business of modern life into schemes of profit, and processes of fraud and extortion. I do not see, in all your boasted improvements, any compensation for the religious

---

14 In my opinion.
15 *Par excellence.*
1 "Pursuing our voyage, we sailed three days, without discovering anything." Bk. V, Ch. I. Urquhart and Motteux translation.

charity of the twelfth century. I do not see any compensation for that kindly feeling which, within their own little communities, bound the several classes of society together, while full scope was left for the development of natural character, wherein individuals differed as conspicuously as in costume. Now, we all wear one conventional dress, one conventional face; we have no bond of union, but pecuniary interest; we talk any thing that comes uppermost, for talking's sake, and without expecting to be believed; we have no nature, no simplicity, no picturesqueness: every thing about us is as artificial and as complicated as our steam-machinery: our poetry is a kaleidoscope of false imagery, expressing no real feeling, portraying no real existence. I do not see any compensation for the poetry of the twelfth century."

MR. MAC QUEDY.

I wonder to hear you, Mr. Chainmail, talking of the religious charity of a set of lazy monks and beggarly friars, who were much more occupied with taking than giving; of whom, those who were in earnest did nothing but make themselves, and every body about them, miserable, with fastings, and penances, and other such trash; and those who were not, did nothing but guzzle and royster, and, having no wives of their own, took very unbecoming liberties with those of honester men. And as to your poetry of the twelfth century, it is not good for much.

MR. CHAINMAIL.

It has, at any rate, what ours wants, truth to nature, and simplicity of diction. The poetry, which was addressed to the people of the dark ages, pleased in proportion to the truth with which it depicted familiar images, and to their natural connection with the time and place to which they were assigned. In the poetry of our enlightened times, the characteristics of all seasons, soils, and climates, may be blended together, with much benefit to the author's fame as an original genius. The cowslip of a civic poet is always in blossom, his fern is always in full feather; he gathers the celandine, the primrose, the heath-flower, the jasmine, and the chrysanthemum, all on the same day, and from the same spot: his nightingale sings all the year round, his moon is always full, his cygnet is as white as his swan, his cedar is as tremulous as his aspen, and his poplar as embowering as his beech. Thus all nature marches with the march of mind; but, among barbarians, instead of mead and wine, and the best seat by the fire, the reward of such a genius would have been, to be summarily turned out of doors in the snow, to meditate on the difference between day and night, and between December and July. It is an age of liberality, indeed, when not to know an oak from a burdock is no disqualification for sylvan minstrelsy. I am for truth and simplicity.

THE REV. DR. FOLLIOTT.

Let him who loves them read Greek: Greek, Greek, Greek.

MR. MAC QUEDY.

If he can, sir.

THE REV. DR. FOLLIOTT.

Very true, sir; if he can. Here is the captain, who can. But I think he must have finished his education at some very rigid college, where a quotation, or any other overt act showing acquaintance with classical literature, was visited with a severe penalty. For my part, I make it my boast that I was not to be so subdued. I could not be abated of a single quotation by all the bumpers in which I was fined.[2]

In this manner they glided over the face of the waters, discussing every thing and settling nothing. Mr. Mac Quedy and the Reverend Doctor Folliott had many digladiations[3] on political economy: wherein, each in his own view, Doctor Folliott demolished Mr. Mac Quedy's science, and Mr. Mac Quedy demolished Doctor Folliott's objections.

We would print these dialogues if we thought any one would read them: but the world is not yet ripe for this *haute sagesse Pantagrueline*.[4] We must, therefore, content ourselves with an *échantillon*[5] of one of the Reverend Doctor's perorations.

---

[2] According to an Oxford tradition, a student who committed a *faux pas* had either to buy a round for his companions or chugalug several pints himself. Dr. Folliott doubtless chose the latter. That quoting classical literature was a transgression indicates the intellectual poverty of the universities of Peacock's time.

[3] Arguments.

[4] "Lofty Pantagrueline wisdom."

[5] Specimen. Dr. Folliott proceeds to summarize and then attack

"You have given the name of a science to what is yet an imperfect inquiry; and the upshot of your so-called science is this, that you increase the wealth of a nation by increasing in it the quantity of things which are produced by labour: no matter what they are, no matter how produced, no matter how distributed. The greater the quantity of labour that has gone to the production of the quantity of things in a community, the richer is the community. That is your doctrine. Now, I say, if this be so, riches are not the object for a community to aim at. I say, the nation is best off, in relation to other nations, which has the greatest quantity of the common necessaries of life distributed among the greatest number of persons; which has the greatest number of honest hearts and stout arms united in a common interest, willing to offend no one, but ready to fight in defence of their own community against all the rest of the world, because they have something in it worth fighting for. The moment you admit that one class of things, without any reference to what they respectively cost, is better worth having than another; that a smaller commercial value, with one mode of distribution, is better than a greater commercial value, with another mode of distribution; the whole of that curious fabric of postulates and dogmas, which you call the science of political economy, and which I call *politicæ œconomiæ inscientia*,[6] tumbles to pieces."

Mr. Toogood agreed with Mr. Chainmail against Mr. Mac Quedy, that the existing state of society was worse than that of the twelfth century; but he agreed with Mr. Mac Quedy against Mr. Chainmail, that it was in progress to something much better than either,—to which "something much better" Mr. Toogood and Mr. Mac Quedy attached two very different meanings.[7]

Mr. Chainmail fought with Doctor Folliott, the battle of the

the principles of Utilitarianism as outlined by David Ricardo (1772–1823), a leading economic theorist.

[6] "Ignorance of political economy."

[7] Both the Benthamites and the Owenites (Toogood) envisioned an ideal society governed in response to principles of economics; they agreed that the means of effecting this state should be peaceful ones, and that improvement was already taking place; but for the Owenites, the "something much better" meant doing away with private ownership altogether in favor of communal ownership.

romantic against the classical in poetry; and Mr. Skionar contended with Mr. Mac Quedy for intuition and synthesis, against analysis and induction in philosophy.

Mr. Philpot would lie along for hours, listening to the gurgling of the water round the prow, and would ocasionally edify the company with speculations on the great changes that would be effected in the world by the steam-navigation of rivers: sketching the course of a steam-boat up and down some mighty stream which civilisation had either never visited, or long since deserted; the Missouri and the Columbia, the Oroonoko and the Amazon, the Nile and the Niger, the Euphrates and the Tigris, the Oxus and the Indus, the Ganges and the Hoangho; under the overcanopying forests of the new, or by the long-silent ruins of the ancient, world; through the shapeless mounds of Babylon, or the gigantic temples of Thebes.

Mr. Trillo went on with the composition of his opera, and took the opinions of the young ladies on every step in its progress; occasionally regaling the company with specimens, and wondering at the blindness of Mr. Mac Quedy, who could not, or would not, see that an opera in perfection, being the union of all the beautiful arts,—music, painting, dancing, poetry,— exhibiting female beauty in its most attractive aspects, and in its most becoming costume,—was, according to the well-known precept, *Ingenuas didicisse, &c.*,[8] the most efficient instrument of civilisation, and ought to take precedence of all other pursuits in the minds of true philanthropists. The Reverend Doctor Folliott, on these occasions, never failed to say a word or two on Mr. Trillo's side, derived from the practice of the Athenians, and from the combination, in their theatre, of all the beautiful arts, in a degree of perfection unknown to the modern world.

Leaving Lechlade, they entered the canal that connects the Thames with the Severn; ascended by many locks; passed by a tunnel three miles long, through the bowels of Sapperton Hill; agreed unanimously that the greatest pleasure derivable from

---

[8] *Ingenuas didicisse fideliter artes/ Emollit mores, nec sinit esse feros* ("To have thoroughly learned the liberal arts refines the manners, and keeps them from savagery"). Ovid, *Epistolem ex Ponto*, Bk. II, Epistle 9, ll. 47–48.

visiting a cavern of any sort was that of getting out of it; descended by many locks again, through the valley of Stroud into the Severn; continued their navigation into the Ellesmere canal; moored their pinnaces in the Vale of Llangollen by the aqueduct of Pontycysyllty;[9] and determined to pass some days in inspecting the scenery, before commencing their homeward voyage.

The captain omitted no opportunity of pressing his suit on Lady Clarinda, but could never draw from her any reply but the same doctrines of worldly wisdom, delivered in a tone of *badinage*,[10] mixed with a certain kindness of manner that induced him to hope she was not in earnest.

But the morning after they had anchored under the hills of the Dee,—whether the lady had reflected more seriously than usual, or was somewhat less in good humour than usual, or the Captain was more pressing than usual,—she said to him, "It must not be, Captain Fitzchrome; 'the course of true love never did run smooth:'[11] my father must keep his borough, and I must have a town house and a country house, and an opera box, and a carriage. It is not well for either of us that we should flirt any longer: 'I must be cruel only to be kind.'[12] Be satisfied with the assurance that you alone, of all men, have ever broken my rest. To be sure, it was only for about three nights in all; but that is too much."

The captain had *le cœur navré*.[13] He took his portfolio under his arm, made up the little *valise* of a pedestrian, and, without saying a word to any one, wandered off at random among the mountains.

After the lapse of a day or two, the captain was missed, and every one marvelled what was become of him. Mr. Philpot thought he must have been exploring a river, and fallen in and got drowned in the process. Mr. Firedamp had no doubt he had been crossing a mountain bog, and had been suddenly deprived

---

[9] I.e. they have sailed from south-central to west-central England, and then westward to their destination in northeast Wales.
[10] Raillery.
[11] *A Midsummer Night's Dream*, I.i.
[12] *Hamlet*, III. iv.
[13] A broken heart.

of life by the exhalations of marsh miasmata. Mr. Henbane deemed it probable that he had been tempted in some wood by the large black brilliant berries of the *Atropa Belladonna,* or Deadly Nightshade; and lamented that he had not been by, to administer an infallible antidote. Mr. Eavesdrop hoped the particulars of his fate would be ascertained; and asked if any one present could help him to any authentic anecdotes of their departed friend. The Reverend Doctor Folliott proposed that an inquiry should be instituted as to whether the march of intellect had reached that neighbourhood; as, if so, the captain had probably been made a subject for science. Mr. Mac Quedy said it was no such great matter to ascertain the precise mode in which the surplus population was diminished by one. Mr. Toogood asseverated that there was no such thing as surplus population, and that the land, properly managed, would maintain twenty times its present inhabitants: and hereupon they fell into a disputation.

Lady Clarinda did not doubt that the captain had gone away designedly: she missed him more than she could have anticipated; and wished she had at least postponed her last piece of cruelty till the completion of their homeward voyage.

Chapter XI

CORRESPONDENCE

"Base is the slave that pays."—Ancient Pistol.[1]

The captain was neither drowned nor poisoned, neither miasmatised nor anatomised. But, before we proceed to account for him, we must look back to a young lady, of whom some little notice was taken in the first chapter; and who, though she has

[1] *Henry V,* II.i.

since been out of sight, has never with us been out of mind; Miss Susannah Touchandgo, the forsaken of the junior Crotchet, whom we left an inmate of a solitary farm, in one of the deep valleys under the cloudcapt summits of Meirion, comforting her wounded spirit with air and exercise, rustic cheer, music, painting, and poetry, and the prattle of the little Ap Llymrys.

One evening, after an interval of anxious expectation, the farmer, returning from market, brought for her two letters, of which the contents were these:—

> "DOTANDCARRYONETOWN,
> STATE OF APODIDRASKIANA:[2]
> *April* 1. 18 . .

"My dear Child,

"I am anxious to learn what are your present position, intention, and prospects. The fairies who dropped gold in your shoe, on the morning when I ceased to be a respectable man in London, will soon find a talismanic channel for transmitting you a stocking full of dollars, which will fit the shoe, as well as the foot of Cinderella fitted her slipper. I am happy to say, I am again become a respectable man. It was always my ambition to be a respectable man; and I am a very respectable man here, in this new township of a new state, where I have purchased five thousand acres of land, at two dollars an acre, hard cash, and established a very flourishing bank. The notes of Touchandgo and Company, soft cash, are now the exclusive currency of all this vicinity. This is the land in which all men flourish; but there are three classes of men who flourish especially,—Methodist preachers, slave-drivers, and paper-money manufacturers; and as one of the latter, I have just painted the word BANK on a fine slab of maple, which was green and growing when I arrived, and have discounted for the settlers, in my own currency, sundry bills, which are to be paid when the proceeds of the crop they have just sown shall return from New Orleans; so that my notes are the representatives of vegetation that is to be, and I am accordingly a capitalist of the first

[2] From a Greek word meaning "to run away."

magnitude. The people here know very well that I ran away from London, but the most of them have run away from some place or other; and they have a great respect for me, because they think I ran away with something worth taking, which few of them had the luck or the wit to do. This gives them confidence in my resources, at the same time that, as there is nothing portable in the settlement except my own notes, they have no fear that I shall run away with them. They know I am thoroughly conversant with the principles of banking; and as they have plenty of industry, no lack of sharpness, and abundance of land, they wanted nothing but capital to organise a flourishing settlement; and this capital I have manufactured to the extent required, at the expense of a small importation of pens, ink, and paper, and two or three inimitable copper plates. I have abundance here of all good things, a good conscience included; for I really cannot see that I have done any wrong. This was my position: I owed half a million of money; and I had a trifle in my pocket. It was clear that this trifle could never find its way to the right owner. The question was, whether I should keep it, and live like a gentleman; or hand it over to lawyers and commissioners of bankruptcy, and die like a dog on a dunghill. If I could have thought that the said lawyers, &c., had a better title to it than myself, I might have hesitated; but, as such title was not apparent to my satisfaction, I decided the question in my own favour; the right owners, as I have already said, being out of the question altogether. I have always taken scientific views of morals and politics, a habit from which I derive much comfort under existing circumstances.

"I hope you adhere to your music, though I cannot hope again to accompany your harp with my flute. My last *andante* movement was too *forte* for those whom it took by surprise. Let not your *allegro vivace* be damped by young Crotchet's desertion, which, though I have not heard it, I take for granted. He is, like myself, a scientific politician, and has an eye as keen as a needle, to his own interest. He has had good luck so far, and is gorgeous in the spoils of many gulls; but I think the Polar Basin and Walrus Company will be too much for him yet. There has been a splendid outlay on credit; and he is the only man, of the original parties concerned, of whom his majesty's sheriffs could give any account.

"I will not ask you to come here. There is no husband for you. The men smoke, drink, and fight, and break more of their own heads than of girls' hearts. Those among them who are musical sing nothing but psalms. They are excellent fellows in their way, but you would not like them.

"*Au reste,* here are no rents, no taxes, no poor-rates, no tithes, no church-establishment, no routs, no clubs, no rotten boroughs, no operas, no concerts, no theatres, no beggars, no thieves, no king, no lords, no ladies, and only one gentleman, videlicet, your loving father,

"*Timothy Touchandgo*[3]

"P.S.—I send you one of my notes; I can afford to part with it. If you are accused of receiving money from me, you may pay it over to my assignees. Robthetill continues to be my factotum; I say no more of him in this place: he will give you an account of himself."

"DOTANDCARRYONETOWN, &c.

"*Dear Miss,*

"Mr. Touchandgo will have told you of our arrival here, of our setting up a bank, and so forth. We came here in a tilted[4] waggon, which served us for parlour, kitchen, and all. We soon got up a log-house; and, unluckily, we as soon got it down again, for the first fire we made in it burned down house and all. However, our second experiment was more fortunate; and we are pretty well lodged in a house of three rooms on a floor; I should say the floor, for there is but one.

"This new state is free to hold slaves; all the new states have not this privilege: Mr. Touchandgo has bought some, and they

---

[3] Suggested by the career of Rowland Stevenson, a London banker, who had absconded on debts of £100,000 in 1828. At this time there was no national banking system in England as there is in the U.S. today. Each bank issued its own paper currency, which was as good as its issuer's solvency.

[4] A type of covered wagon, much smaller than a prairie schooner.

are building him a villa. Mr. Touchandgo is in a thriving way, but he is not happy here: he longs for parties and concerts, and a seat in congress. He thinks it very hard that he cannot buy one with his own coinage, as he used to do in England. Besides, he is afraid of the regulators,[5] who, if they do not like a man's character, wait upon him and flog him, doubling the dose at stated intervals, till he takes himself off. He does not like this system of administering justice: though I think he has nothing to fear from it. He has the character of having money, which is the best of all characters here, as at home. He lets his old English prejudices influence his opinions of his new neighbours; but I assure you they have many virtues. Though they do keep slaves, they are all ready to fight for their own liberty; and I should not like to be an enemy within reach of one of their rifles. When I say enemy, I include bailiff in the term. One was shot not long ago. There was a trial; the jury gave two dollars damages; the judge said they must find guilty or not guilty; but the counsel for the defendant (they would not call him prisoner), offered to fight the judge upon the point: and as this was said literally, not metaphorically, and the counsel was a stout fellow, the judge gave in. The two dollars damages were not paid after all; for the defendant challenged the foreman to box for double or quits, and the foreman was beaten. The folks in New York made a great outcry about it, but here it was considered all as it should be. So you see, Miss, justice, liberty, and every thing else of that kind, are different in different places, just as suits the convenience of those who have the sword in their own hands. Hoping to hear of your health and happiness, I remain,

> "Dear Miss, your dutiful servant,
> "*Roderick Robthetill*"

Miss Touchandgo replied as follows, to the first of these letters:—

"*My dear Father,*
  "I am sure you have the best of hearts, and I have no doubt

[5] Vigilantes.

you have acted with the best intentions. My lover, or I should rather say, my fortune's lover, has indeed forsaken me. I cannot say I did not feel it; indeed, I cried very much; and the altered looks of people who used to be so delighted to see me, really annoyed me so that I determined to change the scene altogether. I have come into Wales, and am boarding with a farmer and his wife. Their stock of English is very small, but I managed to agree with them; and they have four of the sweetest children I ever saw, to whom I teach all I know, and I manage to pick up some Welsh. I have puzzled out a little song, which I think very pretty; I have translated it into English, and I send it you, with the original air. You shall play it on your flute at eight o'clock every Saturday evening, and I will play and sing it at the same time, and I will fancy that I hear my dear papa accompanying me.

"The people in London said very unkind things of you: they hurt me very much at the time; but now I am out of their way, I do not seem to think their opinion of much consequence. I am sure, when I recollect, at leisure, every thing I have seen and heard among them, I cannot make out what they do that is so virtuous as to set them up for judges of morals. And I am sure they never speak the truth about any thing, and there is no sincerity in either their love or their friendship. An old Welsh bard here, who wears a waistcoat embroidered with leeks, and is called the Green Bard of Cadair Idris, says the Scotch would be the best people in the world if there was nobody but themselves to give them a character; and so, I think, would the Londoners. I hate the very thought of them, for I do believe they would have broken my heart if I had not got out of their way. Now I shall write you another letter very soon, and describe to you the country, and the people, and the children, and how I amuse myself, and every thing that I think you will like to hear about: and when I seal this letter, I shall drop a kiss on the cover.

> "Your loving daughter,
> "*Susannah Touchandgo*

"P.S.—Tell Mr. Robthetill I will write to him in a day or two. This is the little song I spoke of:—

'Beyond the sea, beyond the sea,
My heart is gone, far, far from me;
And ever on its track will flee
My thoughts, my dreams, beyond the sea.

Beyond the sea, beyond the sea,
The swallow wanders fast and free:
Oh, happy bird! were I like thee,
I, too, would fly beyond the sea.

Beyond the sea, beyond the sea,
Are kindly hearts and social glee:
But here for me they may not be;
My heart is gone beyond the sea.' "

Chapter XII

THE MOUNTAIN INN

Ὡς ἡδὺ τῷ μισοῦντι τοὺς φαύλους τρόπους
Ἐρημία.

*How sweet to minds that love not sordid ways
Is solitude!*—MENANDER.[1]

THE CAPTAIN wandered despondingly up and down hill for several days, passing many hours of each in sitting on rocks; making, almost mechanically, sketches of waterfalls, and mountain pools; taking care, nevertheless, to be always before nightfall in a comfortable inn, where, being a temperate man, he wiled away the evening with making a bottle of sherry into negus.[2] His rambles brought him at length into the interior of Merionethshire, the land of all that is beautiful in nature, and all that is lovely in woman.

[1] Fragment 466K.
[2] A type of wine punch.

Here, in a secluded village, he found a little inn, of small pretension and much comfort. He felt so satisfied with his quarters, and discovered every day so much variety in the scenes of the surrounding mountains, that his inclination to proceed farther diminished progressively.

It is one thing to follow the high road through a country, with every principally remarkable object carefully noted down in a book, taking, as therein directed, a guide, at particular points, to the more recondite sights: it is another to sit down on one chosen spot, especially when the choice is unpremeditated, and from thence, by a series of explorations, to come day by day on unanticipated scenes. The latter process has many advantages over the former; it is free from the disappointment which attends excited expectation, when imagination has outstripped reality, and from the accidents that mar the scheme of the tourist's single day, when the valleys may be drenched with rain, or the mountains shrouded with mist.

The captain was one morning preparing to sally forth on his usual exploration, when he heard a voice without, inquiring for a guide to the ruined castle. The voice seemed familiar to him, and going forth into the gateway, he recognised Mr. Chainmail. After greetings and inquiries for the absent, "You vanished very abruptly, captain," said Mr. Chainmail, "from our party on the canal."

CAPTAIN FITZCHROME.

To tell you the truth, I had a particular reason for trying the effect of absence from a part of that party.

MR. CHAINMAIL.

I surmised as much: at the same time, the unusual melancholy of an in general most vivacious young lady made me wonder at your having acted so precipitately. The lady's heart is yours, if there be truth in signs.

CAPTAIN FITZCHROME.

Hearts are not now what they were in the days of the old song, "Will love be controlled by advice?"[3]

[3] From John Gay's *Beggar's Opera* (1728).

MR. CHAINMAIL.

Very true; hearts, heads, and arms have all degenerated, most sadly. We can no more feel the high impassioned love of the ages, which some people have the impudence to call dark, than we can wield King Richard's battleaxe, bend Robin Hood's bow, or flourish the oaken graff of the Pinder of Wakefield.[4] Still we have our tastes and feelings, though they deserve not the name of passions; and some of us may pluck up spirit to try to carry a point, when we reflect that we have to contend with men no better than ourselves.

CAPTAIN FITZCHROME.

We do not now break lances for ladies.

MR. CHAINMAIL.

No, nor even bulrushes. We jingle purses for them, flourish paper-money banners, and tilt with scrolls of parchment.

CAPTAIN FITZCHROME.

In which sort of tilting I have been thrown from the saddle. I presume it was not love that led you from the flotilla.

MR. CHAINMAIL.

By no means. I was tempted by the sight of an old tower, not to leave this land of ruined castles, without having collected a few hints for the adornment of my baronial hall.

CAPTAIN FITZCHROME.

I understand you live *en famille* with your domestics. You will have more difficulty in finding a lady who would adopt your fashion of living, than one who would prefer you to a richer man.

MR. CHAINMAIL.

Very true. I have tried the experiment on several as guests; but once was enough for them: so, I suppose, I shall die a bachelor.

CAPTAIN FITZCHROME.

I see, like some others of my friends, you will give up any thing except your hobby.

[4] A character in the Robin Hood legends; see Robert Greene's play *George a Greene, the Pinner of Wakefield* (1595). A pinder or pinner was similar to a modern dog catcher; *graff* can mean either *staff* or *pencil*. Thus Peacock is probably making a complex pun on the poet Pindar, the office of pinder, the symbol of that office, and a poet's writing instrument.

MR. CHAINMAIL.

I will give up any thing but my baronial hall.

CAPTAIN FITZCHROME.

You will never find a wife for your purpose, unless in the daughter of some old-fashioned farmer.

MR. CHAINMAIL.

No, I thank you. I must have a lady of gentle blood; I shall not marry below my own condition: I am too much of a herald; I have too much of the twelfth century in me for that.

CAPTAIN FITZCHROME.

Why then your chance is not much better than mine. A well-born beauty would scarcely be better pleased with your baronial hall, than with my more humble offer of love in a cottage. She must have a town-house, and an opera-box, and roll about the streets in a carriage; especially if her father has a rotten borough, for the sake of which he sells his daughter, that he may continue to sell his country. But you were inquiring for a guide to the ruined castle in this vicinity; I know the way, and will conduct you.

The proposal pleased Mr. Chainmail, and they set forth on their expedition.

Chapter XIII

THE LAKE—THE RUIN

Or vieni, Amore, e quà meco t'assetta.
ORLANDO INNAMORATO.[1]

MR. CHAINMAIL.

WOULD IT not be a fine thing, captain,—you being picturesque, and I poetical; you being for the lights and shadows

[1] "Come, my love, and sit here with me"; from either the unfinished portion of the epic romance by Mateo Boiardo (1434–1494) or the recasting by Francesco Berni (1490–1526).

of the present, and I for those of the past,—if we were to go together over the ground which was travelled in the twelfth century by Giraldus de Barri,[2] when he accompanied Archbishop Baldwin to preach the crusade?

CAPTAIN FITZCHROME.

Nothing, in my present frame of mind, could be more agreeable to me.

MR. CHAINMAIL.

We would provide ourselves with his *Itinerarium;* compare what has been with what is; contemplate in their decay the castles and abbeys which he saw in their strength and splendour; and, while you were sketching their remains, I would dispassionately inquire what has been gained by the change.

CAPTAIN FITZCHROME.

Be it so.

But the scheme was no sooner arranged than the captain was summoned to London by a letter on business, which he did not expect to detain him long. Mr. Chainmail, who, like the captain, was fascinated with the inn and the scenery, determined to await his companion's return; and, having furnished him with a list of books, which he was to bring with him from London, took leave of him, and began to pass his days like the heroes of Ariosto, who

> ——tutto il giorno, al bel oprar intenti,
> Saliron balze, e traversar torrenti.[3]

One day Mr. Chainmail traced upwards the course of a mountain-stream, to a spot where a small waterfall threw itself over a slab of perpendicular rock, which seemed to bar his farther progress. On a nearer view, he discovered a flight of steps, roughly hewn in the rock, on one side of the fall. Ascending these steps, he entered a narrow winding pass, between high

---

2 DeBarri (1146?–1220?), Archdeacon of Brecon, was refused high church office because he was a Welshman; his history of the Crusade of 1190 gives prominence to Archbishop Baldwin (d.1190).

3 "All day, intent on fine deeds,
Ascended cliffs and crossed torrents."

(*Orlando Furioso*)

and naked rocks, that afforded only space for a rough footpath carved on one side, at some height above the torrent.

The pass opened on a lake, from which the stream issued, and which lay like a dark mirror, set in a gigantic frame of mountain precipices. Fragments of rock lay scattered on the edge of the lake, some half-buried in the water: Mr. Chainmail scrambled some way over these fragments, till the base of a rock, sinking abruptly in the water, effectually barred his progress. He sat down on a large smooth stone; the faint murmur of the stream he had quitted, the ocasional flapping of the wings of the heron, and at long intervals the solitary springing of a trout, were the only sounds that came to his ear. The sun shone brightly half-way down the opposite rocks, presenting, on their irregular faces, strong masses of light and shade. Suddenly he heard the dash of a paddle, and, turning his eyes, saw a solitary and beautiful girl gliding over the lake in a coracle;[4] she was proceeding from the vicinity of the point he had quitted towards the upper end of the lake. Her apparel was rustic, but there was in its style something more *recherché*,[5] in its arrangement something more of elegance and precision, than was common to the mountain peasant girl. It had more of the *contadina*[6] of the opera than of the genuine mountaineer; so at least thought Mr. Chainmail; but she passed so rapidly, and took him so much by surprise, that he had little opportunity for accurate observation. He saw her land, at the farther extremity, and disappear among the rocks: he rose from his seat, returned to the mouth of the pass, stepped from stone to stone across the stream, and attempted to pass round by the other side of the lake; but there again the abruptly sinking precipice closed his way.

Day after day he haunted the spot, but never saw again either the damsel or the coracle. At length, marvelling at himself for being so solicitous about the apparition of a peasant girl in a coracle, who could not, by any possibility, be any thing to him, he resumed his explorations in another direction.

[4] A small boat, similar in construction to a canoe.
[5] Exquisite.
[6] Italian peasant girl.

One day he wandered to the ruined castle, on the seashore, which was not very distant from his inn; and sitting on the rock, near the base of the ruin, was calling up the forms of past ages on the wall of an ivied tower, when on its summit appeared a female figure, whom he recognised in an instant for his nymph of the coracle. The folds of the blue gown pressed by the sea breeze against one of the most symmetrical of figures, the black feather of the black hat, and the ringleted hair beneath it fluttering in the wind; the apparent peril of her position, on the edge of the mouldering wall, from whose immediate base the rock went down perpendicularly to the sea, presented a singularly interesting combination to the eye of the young antiquary.

Mr. Chainmail had to pass half round the castle, on the land side, before he could reach the entrance: he coasted the dry and bramble-grown moat, crossed the unguarded bridge, passed the unportcullised arch of the gateway, entered the castle court, ascertained the tower, ascended the broken stairs, and stood on the ivied wall. But the nymph of the place was gone. He searched the ruins within and without, but he found not what he sought: he haunted the castle day after day, as he had done the lake, but the damsel appeared no more.

Chapter XIV

THE DINGLE

> *The stars of midnight shall be dear*
> *To her, and she shall lean her ear*
> *In many a secret place,*
> *Where rivulets dance their wayward round,*
> *And beauty, born of murmuring sound,*
> *Shall pass into her face.*—WORDSWORTH.[1]

MISS SUSANNAH TOUCHANDGO had read the four great poets of Italy,[2] and many of the best writers of France. About

---

[1] "Three Years She Grew in Sun and Shower," ll. 25–30.
[2] Dante, Petrarch, Tasso, and Ariosto.

the time of her father's downfall, accident threw into her way *Les Rêveries du Promeneur Solitaire;*[3] and from the impression which these made on her, she carried with her into retirement all the works of Rousseau. In the midst of that startling light which the conduct of old friends on a sudden reverse of fortune throws on a young and inexperienced mind, the doctrines of the philosopher of Geneva struck with double force upon her sympathies; she imbibed the sweet poison, as somebody calls it, of his writings, even to a love of truth; which, every wise man knows, ought to be left to those who can get any thing by it. The society of children, the beauties of nature, the solitude of the mountains, became her consolation, and, by degrees, her delight. The gay society from which she had been excluded remained on her memory only as a disagreeable dream. She imbibed her new monitor's ideas of simplicity of dress, assimilating her own with that of the peasant girls in the neighbourhood; the black hat, the blue gown, the black stockings, the shoes tied on the instep.

Pride was, perhaps, at the bottom of the change; she was willing to impose in some measure on herself, by marking a contemptuous indifference to the characteristics of the class of society from which she had fallen,

> "And with the food of pride sustained her soul
>   In solitude."[4]

It is true that she somewhat modified the forms of her rustic dress: to the black hat she added a black feather, to the blue gown she added a tippet, and a waistband fastened in front with a silver buckle; she wore her black stockings very smooth and tight on her ancles, and tied her shoes in tasteful bows, with the nicest possible ribbon. In this apparel, to which, in winter, she added a scarlet cloak, she made dreadful havoc among the rustic mountaineers, many of whom proposed to "keep company" with her in the Cambrian fashion, an honour which, to their great surprise, she always declined. Among

[3] *The Musings of a Solitary Walker* (pub. 1782) by Rousseau.
[4] Wordsworth, "Lines Left Upon a Seat in a Yew-Tree," ll. 23–24.

these, Harry Ap-Heather, whose father rented an extensive sheepwalk, and had a thousand she-lambs wandering in the mountains, was the most strenuous in his suit, and the most pathetic in his lamentations for her cruelty.

Miss Susannah often wandered among the mountains alone, even to some distance from the farm-house. Sometimes she descended into the bottom of the dingles, to the black rocky beds of the torrents, and dreamed away hours at the feet of the cataracts. One spot in particular, from which she had at first shrunk with terror, became by degrees her favourite haunt. A path turning and returning at acute angles, led down a steep wood-covered slope to the edge of a chasm, where a pool, or resting-place of a torrent, lay far below. A cataract fell in a single sheet into the pool; the pool boiled and bubbled at the base of the fall, but through the greater part of its extent lay calm, deep, and black, as if the cataract had plunged through it to an unimaginable depth without disturbing its eternal repose. At the opposite extremity of the pool, the rocks almost met at their summits, the trees of the opposite banks intermingled their leaves, and another cataract plunged from the pool into a chasm on which the sunbeams never gleamed. High above, on both sides, the steep woody slopes of the dingle soared into the sky; and from a fissure in the rock, on which the little path terminated, a single gnarled and twisted oak stretched itself over the pool, forming a fork with its boughs at a short distance from the rock. Miss Susannah often sat on the rock, with her feet resting on this tree: in time, she made her seat on the tree itself, with her feet hanging over the abyss; and at length she accustomed herself to lie along upon its trunk, with her side on the mossy boll of the fork, and an arm round one of the branches. From this position a portion of the sky and the woods was reflected in the pool, which, from its bank, was but a mass of darkness. The first time she reclined in this manner, her heart beat audibly; in time, she lay down as calmly as on the mountain heather: the perception of the sublime was probably heightened by an intermingled sense of danger; and perhaps that indifference to life, which early disappointment forces upon sensitive minds, was necessary to the first experiment. There was, in the novelty and strangeness of the position, an excitement which never wholly passed away, but which became gradually subordinate to the influence, at once tranquillising and elevating, of the mingled eternity of motion, sound, and solitude.

One sultry noon, she descended into this retreat with a mind more than usually disturbed by reflections on the past. She lay in her favourite position, sometimes gazing on the cataract; looking sometimes up the steep sylvan acclivities into the narrow space of the cloudless ether; sometimes down into the abyss of the pool, and the deep bright-blue reflections that opened another immensity below her. The distressing recollections of the morning, the world, and all its littlenesses, faded from her thoughts like a dream; but her wounded and wearied spirit drank in too deeply the tranquillising power of the place, and she dropped asleep upon the tree like a ship-boy on the mast.

At this moment Mr. Chainmail emerged into daylight, on a projection of the opposite rock, having struck down through the woods in search of unsophisticated scenery. The scene he discovered filled him with delight: he seated himself on the rock, and fell into one of his romantic reveries; when suddenly the semblance of a black hat and feather caught his eye among the foliage of the projecting oak. He started up, shifted his position, and got a glimpse of a blue gown. It was his lady of the lake, his enchantress of the ruined castle, divided from him by a barrier, which, at a few yards below, he could almost overleap, yet unapproachable but by a circuit perhaps of many hours. He watched with intense anxiety. To listen if she breathed was out of the question: the noses of a dean and chapter would have been soundless in the roar of the torrent. From her extreme stillness, she appeared to sleep: yet what creature, not desperate, would go wilfully to sleep in such a place? Was she asleep then? Nay, was she alive? She was as motionless as death. Had she been murdered, thrown from above, and caught in the tree? She lay too regularly and too composedly for such a supposition. She was asleep then, and in all probability her waking would be fatal. He shifted his position. Below the pool two beetle-browed[5] rocks nearly overarched the chasm, leaving just such a space at the summit as was within the possibility of a leap; the torrent roared below in a fearful gulf. He paused some time on the brink, measuring the practicability and the danger, and casting every now and then an anxious glance to his sleeping beauty. In one of these glances he saw a slight movement of the blue gown, and, in a moment after, the black hat and feather dropped into the pool. Reflection was lost for a moment, and, by a sudden impulse, he bounded over the chasm.

He stood above the projecting oak; the unknown beauty lay like the nymph of the scene; her long black hair, which the fall of her hat had disengaged from its fastenings, drooping through the boughs: he saw that the first thing to be done was to prevent her throwing her feet off the trunk, in the first movements of waking. He sat down on the rock, and placed his feet on the stem, securing her ancles between his own: one of her arms was round a branch of the fork, the other lay loosely on her side. The hand of this arm he endeavoured to reach, by leaning forward from his seat; he approximated, but could not touch it: after several tantalising efforts, he gave up the point in despair. He did not attempt to wake her, because he feared it might have bad consequences, and he resigned himself to expect the moment of her natural waking, determined not to stir from his post, if she should sleep till midnight.

In this period of forced inaction, he could contemplate at leisure the features and form of his charmer. She was not one of the slender beauties of romance; she was as plump as a partridge; her cheeks were two roses, not absolutely damask, yet verging thereupon; her lips twin-cherries, of equal size; her nose regular, and almost Grecian; her forehead high, and delicately fair; her eyebrows symmetrically arched; her eyelashes long, black, and silky, fitly corresponding with the beautiful tresses that hung among the leaves of the oak, like clusters of wandering grapes.[6] Her eyes were yet to be seen; but how

---

5 Cf. "the dreadful summit of the cliff/ That beetles o'er his base into the sea." *Hamlet,* I.iv.

6 Ἀλήμονα βότρυν εθείρας.—Nonnus. [P] ["hair like wandering clusters of grapes." *Dionysiaca,* I.528.]

could he doubt that their opening would be the rising of the sun, when all that surrounded their fringy portals was radiant as "the forehead of the morning sky?"[7]

Chapter XV

THE FARM

> Da ydyw'r gwaith, rhaid d'we'yd y gwir,
> Ar fryniau Sîr Meirionydd;
> Golwg oer o'r gwaela gawn
> Mae hi etto yn llawn llawenydd.[1]
>
> Though Meirion's rocks, and hills of heath
>   Repel the distant sight;
> Yet where, than those bleak hills beneath,
>   Is found more true delight?

AT LENGTH the young lady awoke. She was startled at the sudden sight of the stranger, and somewhat terrified at the first perception of her position. But she soon recovered her self-possession, and, extending her hand to the offered hand of Mr. Chainmail, she raised herself up on the tree, and stepped on the rocky bank.

Mr. Chainmail solicited permission to attend her to her home, which the young lady graciously conceded. They emerged from the woody dingle, traversed an open heath, wound along a mountain road by the shore of a lake, descended to the deep bed of another stream, crossed it by a series of stepping stones, ascended to some height on the opposite side, and followed upwards the line of the stream, till the banks opened into a

---

[7] Milton, "Lycidas," l. 171.
[1] *Penillon* ("Stanzas"), No. XXXIX, ll. 1–4, published in *The Cambro-Briton,* I(February 1820), 230. Presumably Peacock's own translation.

spacious amphitheatre, where stood, in its fields and meadows, the farm-house of Ap-Llymry.

During this walk, they had kept up a pretty animated conversation. The lady had lost her hat; and, as she turned towards Mr. Chainmail, in speaking to him, there was no envious projection of brim to intercept the beams of those radiant eyes he had been so anxious to see unclosed. There was in them a mixture of softness and brilliancy, the perfection of the beauty of female eyes, such as some men have passed through life without seeing, and such as no man ever saw, in any pair of eyes, but once; such as can never be seen and forgotten. Young Crotchet had seen it; he had not forgotten it; but he had trampled on its memory, as the renegade tramples on the emblems of a faith which his interest only, and not his heart or his reason, has rejected.

Her hair streamed over her shoulders; the loss of the black feather had left nothing but the rustic costume, the blue gown, the black stockings, and the ribbon-tied shoes. Her voice had that full soft volume of melody which gives to common speech the fascination of music. Mr. Chainmail could not reconcile the dress of the damsel with her conversation and manners. He threw out a remote question or two, with the hope of solving the riddle; but, receiving no reply, he became satisfied that she was not disposed to be communicative respecting herself, and, fearing to offend her, fell upon other topics. They talked of the scenes of the mountains, of the dingle, the ruined castle, the solitary lake. She told him that lake lay under the mountains behind her home, and the coracle and the pass at the extremity saved a long circuit to the nearest village, whither she sometimes went to inquire for letters.

Mr. Chainmail felt curious to know from whom these letters might be; and he again threw out two or three fishing questions, to which, as before, he obtained no answer.

The only living biped they met in their walk was the unfortunate Harry Ap-Heather, with whom they fell in by the stepping-stones, who, seeing the girl of his heart hanging on another man's arm, and concluding at once that they were "keeping company," fixed on her a mingled look of surprise, reproach, and tribulation; and, unable to control his feelings under the sudden shock, burst into a flood of tears, and blubbered till the rocks re-echoed.

They left him mingling his tears with the stream, and his lamentations with its murmurs. Mr. Chainmail inquired who that strange creature might be, and what was the matter with him. The young lady answered, that he was a very worthy young man, to whom she had been the innocent cause of much unhappiness.

"I pity him sincerely," said Mr. Chainmail; and, nevertheless, he could scarcely restrain his laughter at the exceedingly original figure which the unfortunate rustic lover had presented by the stepping-stones.

The children ran out to meet their dear Miss Susan, jumped all round her, and asked what was become of her hat. Ap-Llymry came out in great haste, and invited Mr. Chainmail to walk in and dine: Mr. Chainmail did not wait to be asked twice. In a few minutes the whole party, Miss Susan and Mr. Chainmail, Mr. and Mrs. Ap-Llymry, and progeny, were seated over a clean homespun tablecloth, ornamented with fowls and bacon, a pyramid of potatoes, another of cabbage, which Ap-Llymry said "was poiled with the pacon, and as coot as marrow," a bowl of milk for the children, and an immense brown jug of foaming ale, with which Ap-Llymry seemed to delight in filling the horn of his new guest.

Shall we describe the spacious apartment, which was at once kitchen, hall, and dining-room,—the large dark rafters, the pendent bacon and onions, the strong old oaken furniture, the bright and trimly arranged utensils? Shall we describe the cut of Ap-Llymry's coat, the colour and tie of his neckcloth, the number of buttons at his knees,—the structure of Mrs. Ap-Llymry's cap, having lappets over the ears, which were united under the chin, setting forth especially whether the bond of union were a pin or a ribbon? We shall leave this tempting field of interesting expatiation[2] to those whose brains are high-pressure steam engines for spinning prose by the furlong,[3] to

[2] "Opportunity to write at length" (rare); but literally, "to walk about," and thus probably an erudite pun with "field."

[3] An allusion to the "three-decker" novel, whose length was sometimes achieved by padding the narrative with nonfunctional descriptive details.

be trumpeted in paid-for paragraphs in the quack's corner of newspapers: modern literature having attained the honourable distinction of sharing with blacking and macassar oil, the space which used to be monopolized by razor-strops and the lottery, whereby that very enlightened community, the reading public, is tricked into the perusal of much exemplary nonsense; though the few who see through the trickery have no reason to complain, since as "good wine needs no bush,"[4] so, *ex vi oppositi*, these bushes of venal panegyric point out very clearly that the things they celebrate are not worth reading.

The party dined very comfortably in a corner most remote from the fire; and Mr. Chainmail very soon found his head swimming with two or three horns of ale, of a potency to which even he was unaccustomed. After dinner, Ap-Llymry made him finish a bottle of mead, which he willingly accepted, both as an excuse to remain, and as a drink of the dark ages, which he had no doubt was a genuine brewage, from uncorrupted tradition.

In the meantime, as soon as the cloth was removed, the children had brought out Miss Susannah's harp. She began, without affectation, to play and sing to the children, as was her custom of an afternoon, first in their own language, and their national melodies, then in English; but she was soon interrupted by a general call of little voices for "Ouf! di giorno." She complied with the request, and sang the ballad from Paër's Camilla: *Un dì carco il mulinaro*.[5] The children were very familiar with every

[4] *As You Like It,* Epilogue.
[5] In this ballad, the terrors of the Black Forest are narrated to an assemblage of domestics and peasants who, at the end of every stanza, dance in a circle around the narrator. The second stanza is as follows:

> Una notte in un stradotto
> Un incauto s'inoltrò;
> E uno strillo udì di botto
> Che l'orecchio gl'intronò:—
> Era l'ombra di sua nonna,
> Che pel naso lo pigliò.
>   Ouf! di giorno nè di sera,
> Non passiam la selva nera.—
>   (*Ballano in Giro.*) [P]

["One night an incautious person passed through a street and suddenly heard a deafening scream; it was his grandmother's ghost, which tweaked him by the nose. Ouf! let's not go through the Black Forest by day or by night. (They dance in a circle)"]

syllable of this ballad, which had been often fully explained to them. They danced in a circle with the burden of every verse, shouting out the chorus with good articulation and joyous energy; and at the end of the second stanza, where the traveller has his nose pinched by his grandmother's ghost, every nose in the party was nipped by a pair of little fingers. Mr. Chainmail, who was not prepared for the process, came in for a very energetic tweak, from a chubby girl that sprang suddenly on his knees for the purpose, and made the roof ring with her laughter.

So passed the time till evening, when Mr. Chainmail moved to depart. But it turned out on inquiry that he was some miles from his inn, that the way was intricate, and that he must not make any difficulty about accepting the farmer's hospitality till morning. The evening set in with rain: the fire was found agreeable; they drew around it. The young lady made tea; and afterwards, from time to time, at Mr. Chainmail's special request, delighted his ear with passages of ancient music. Then came a supper of lake trout, fried on the spot, and thrown, smoking hot, from the pan to the plate. Then came a brewage, which the farmer called his nightcap, of which he insisted on Mr. Chainmail's taking his full share. After which the gentleman remembered nothing, till he awoke, the next morning, to the pleasant consciousness that he was under the same roof with one of the most fascinating creatures under the canopy of heaven.

Chapter XVI

THE NEWSPAPER

Ποίας δ' ἀποσπασθεῖσα φύτλας
Ὀρέων κευθμῶνας ἔχει σκιοέντων;

Sprung from what line, adorns the maid
These valleys deep in mountain shade?—

PIND. *Pyth.* IX.[1]

MR. CHAINMAIL forgot the captain and the route of Giraldus de Barri. He became suddenly satisfied that the ruined castle in his present neighbourhood was the best possible specimen of its class, and that it was needless to carry his researches further.

He visited the farm daily: found himself always welcome; flattered himself that the young lady saw him with pleasure, and dragged a heavier chain at every new parting[2] from Miss Susan, as the children called his nymph of the mountains. What might be her second name, he had vainly endeavoured to discover. Mr. Chainmail was in love; but the determination he had long before formed and fixed in his mind, to marry only a lady of gentle blood, without a blot on her escutcheon, repressed the declarations of passion which were often rising to his lips. In the meantime, he left no means untried, to pluck out the heart of her mystery.[3]

The young lady soon divined his passion, and penetrated his prejudices. She began to look on him with favourable eyes; but she feared her name and parentage would present an insuperable barrier to his feudal pride.

Things were in this state when the captain returned, and unpacked his maps and books in the parlour of the inn.

[1] Ll. 59–60.
[2] Oliver Goldsmith, "The Traveller," l. 10.
[3] *Hamlet,* III.ii.

MR. CHAINMAIL.

Really, captain, I find so many objects of attraction in this neighbourhood, that I would gladly postpone our purpose.

CAPTAIN FITZCHROME.

Undoubtedly, this neighbourhood has many attractions; but there is something very inviting in the scheme you laid down.

MR. CHAINMAIL.

No doubt, there is something very tempting in the route of Giraldus de Barri. But there are better things in this vicinity even than that. To tell you the truth, captain, I have fallen in love.

CAPTAIN FITZCHROME.

What! while I have been away?

MR. CHAINMAIL.

Even so.

CAPTAIN FITZCHROME.

The plunge must have been very sudden, if you are already over head and ears.

MR. CHAINMAIL.

As deep as Llyn-y-dreiddiad-vrawd.

CAPTAIN FITZCHROME.

And what may that be?

MR. CHAINMAIL.

A pool not far off: a resting-place of a mountain stream, which is said to have no bottom. There is a tradition connected with it; and here is a ballad on it, at your service:—

Llyn-Y-Dreiddiad-Vrawd.
The Pool of the Diving Friar.

Gwenwynwyn withdrew from the feasts of his hall;
He slept very little, he prayed not at all;
He pondered, and wandered, and studied alone;
And sought, night and day, the philosopher's stone.

He found it at length, and he made its first proof
By turning to gold all the lead of his roof:
Then he bought some magnanimous heroes, all fire,
Who lived but to smite and be smitten for hire.

With these, on the plains like a torrent he broke;
He filled the whole country with flame and with
    smoke;
He killed all the swine, and he broached all the wine;
He drove off the sheep, and the beeves, and the kine;

He took castles and towns; he cut short limbs and
    lives;
He made orphans and widows of children and wives:
This course many years he triumphantly ran,
And did mischief enough to be called a great man.

When, at last, he had gained all for which he had
    striven,
He bethought him of buying a passport to heaven;
Good and great as he was, yet he did not well know
How soon, or which way, his great spirit might go.

He sought the grey friars, who, beside a wild stream,
Refected their frames on a primitive scheme;
The gravest and wisest Gwenwynwyn found out,
All lonely and ghostly, and angling for trout.

Below the white dash of a mighty cascade,
Where a pool of the stream a deep resting-place
    made,
And rock-rooted oaks stretched their branches on
    high,
The friar stood musing, and throwing his fly.

To him said Gwenwynwyn, "Hold, father, here's
    store,
For the good of the church, and the good of the
    poor;"
Then he gave him the stone; but, ere more he could
    speak,
Wrath came on the friar, so holy and meek:

He had stretched forth his hand to receive the red
gold,
And he thought himself mocked by Gwenwynwyn
the Bold;
And in scorn of the gift, and in rage at the giver,
He jerked it immediately into the river.

Gwenwynwyn, aghast, not a syllable spake;
The philosopher's stone made a duck and a drake:[4]
Two systems of circles a moment were seen,
And the stream smoothed them off, as they never
had been.

Gwenwynwyn regained, and uplifted, his voice:
"Oh friar, grey friar, full rash was thy choice;
The stone, the good stone, which away thou hast
thrown,
Was the stone of all stones, the philosopher's stone!"

The friar looked pale, when his error he knew;
The friar looked red, and the friar looked blue;
And heels over head, from the point of a rock,
He plunged, without stopping to pull off his frock.

He dived very deep, but he dived all in vain,
The prize he had slighted he found not again:
Many times did the friar his diving renew,
And deeper and deeper the river still grew.

Gwenwynwyn gazed long, of his senses in doubt,
To see the grey friar a diver so stout:
Then sadly and slowly his castle he sought,
And left the friar diving, like dabchick distraught.

Gwenwynwyn fell sick with alarm and despite,
Died, and went to the devil, the very same night:
The magnanimous heroes he held in his pay
Sacked his castle, and marched with the plunder
away.

---

[4] As in skimming a stone over the water.

No knell on the silence of midnight was rolled,
For the flight of the soul of Gwenwynwyn the Bold:
The brethren, unfeed, let the mighty ghost pass.
Without praying a prayer, or intoning a mass.

The friar haunted ever beside the dark stream;
The philosopher's stone was his thought and his
    dream:
And day after day, ever head under heels
He dived all the time he could spare from his meals.

He dived, and he dived, to the end of his days,
As the peasants oft witnessed with fear and amaze:
The mad friar's diving-place long was their theme,
And no plummet can fathom that pool of the stream.

And still, when light clouds on the midnight winds
    ride,
If by moonlight you stray on the lone river-side,
The ghost of the friar may be seen diving there,
With head in the water, and heels in the air.

CAPTAIN FITZCHROME.

Well, your ballad is very pleasant: you shall show me the scene, and I will sketch it; but just now I am more interested about your love. What heroine of the twelfth century has risen from the ruins of the old castle, and looked down on you from the ivied battlements?

MR. CHAINMAIL.

You are nearer the mark than you suppose. Even from those battlements a heroine of the twelfth century has looked down on me.

CAPTAIN FITZCHROME.

Oh! some vision of an ideal beauty. I suppose the whole will end in another tradition and a ballad.

MR. CHAINMAIL.

Genuine flesh and blood; as genuine as Lady Clarinda. I will tell you the story.

Mr. Chainmail narrated his adventures.

CAPTAIN FITZCHROME.

Then you seem to have found what you wished. Chance has thrown in your way what none of the gods would have ventured to promise you.[5]

MR. CHAINMAIL.

Yes, but I know nothing of her birth and parentage. She tells me nothing of herself, and I have no right to question her directly.

CAPTAIN FITZCHROME.

She appears to be expressly destined for the light of your baronial hall. Introduce me: in this case, two heads are better than one.

MR. CHAINMAIL.

No, I thank you. Leave me to manage my chance of a prize, and keep you to your own chance of a——

CAPTAIN FITZCHROME.

Blank. As you please. Well, I will pitch my tent here, till I have filled my portfolio, and shall be glad of as much of your company as you can spare from more attractive society.

Matters went on pretty smoothly for several days, when an unlucky newspaper threw all into confusion. Mr. Chainmail received newspapers by the post, which came in three times a week. One morning, over their half-finished breakfast, the captain had read half a newspaper very complacently, when suddenly he started up in a frenzy, hurled over the breakfast table, and, bouncing from the apartment, knocked down Harry Ap-Heather, who was coming in at the door to challenge his supposed rival to a boxing-match.

Harry sprang up, in a double rage, and intercepted Mr. Chainmail's pursuit of the captain, placing himself in the doorway, in a pugilistic attitude. Mr. Chainmail, not being disposed for this mode of combat, stepped back into the parlour, took the poker in his right hand, and displacing the loose bottom of a large elbow chair, threw it over his left arm, as a shield. Harry, not liking the aspect of the enemy in this imposing attitude, retreated with backward steps into the kitchen, and

[5] Virgil, *Aeneid,* IX.6–7.

tumbled over a cur, which immediately fastened on his rear.

Mr. Chainmail, half-laughing, half-vexed, anxious to over-take the captain, and curious to know what was the matter with him, pocketed the newspaper, and sallied forth, leaving Harry roaring for a doctor and a tailor, to repair the lacerations of his outward man.

Mr. Chainmail could find no trace of the captain. Indeed, he sought him but in one direction, which was that leading to the farm; where he arrived in due time, and found Miss Susan alone. He laid the newspaper on the table, as was his custom, and proceeded to converse with the young lady: a conversation of many pauses, as much of signs as of words. The young lady took up the paper, and turned it over and over, while she listened to Mr. Chainmail, whom she found every day more and more agreeable, when, suddenly, her eye glanced on some-thing which made her change colour, and dropping the paper on the ground, she rose from her seat, exclaiming, "Miserable must she be who trusts any of your faithless sex! Never, never, never, will I endure such misery twice." And she vanished up the stairs. Mr. Chainmail was petrified. At length, he cried aloud, "Cornelius Agrippa must have laid a spell on this ac-cursed newspaper;[6] and was turning it over, to look for the source of the mischief, when Mrs. Ap-Llymry made her ap-pearance.

MRS. AP-LLYMRY.

What have you done to poor dear Miss Susan? She is crying, ready to break her heart.

MR. CHAINMAIL.

So help me the memory of Richard Cœur-de-Lion, I have not the most distant notion of what is the matter!

MRS. AP-LLYMRY.

Oh, don't tell me, sir; you must have ill-used her. I know how it is. You have been keeping company with her, as if you wanted to marry her; and now, all at once, you have been trying

---

[6] Heinrich Cornelius Agrippa von Nettesheim (1486–1535), Ger-man writer whose works on occultism earned him a reputation as a sorcerer.

to make her your mistress. I have seen such tricks more than once, and you ought to be ashamed of yourself.

MR. CHAINMAIL.

My dear madam, you wrong me utterly. I have none but the kindest feelings and the most honourable purposes towards her. She has been disturbed by something she has seen in this rascally paper.

MRS. AP-LLYMRY.

Why, then, the best thing you can do is to go away, and come again to-morrow.

MR. CHAINMAIL.

Not I, indeed, madam. Out of this house I stir not, till I have seen the young lady, and obtained a full explanation.

MRS. AP-LLYMRY.

I will tell Miss Susan what you say. Perhaps she will come down.

Mr. Chainmail sate with as much patience as he could command, running over the paper, from column to column. At length, he lighted on an announcement of the approaching marriage of Lady Clarinda Bossnowl with Mr. Crotchet the younger. This explained the captain's discomposure, but the cause of Miss Susan's was still to be sought; he could not know that it was one and the same.

Presently the sound of the longed-for step was heard on the stairs; the young lady reappeared, and resumed her seat: her eyes showed that she had been weeping. The gentleman was now exceedingly puzzled how to begin, but the young lady relieved him by asking, with great simplicity, "What do you wish to have explained, sir?"

MR. CHAINMAIL.

I wish, if I may be permitted, to explain myself to you. Yet could I first wish to know what it was that disturbed you in this unlucky paper. Happy should I be if I could remove the cause of your inquietude!

MISS SUSANNAH.

The cause is already removed. I saw something that excited

painful recollections; nothing that I could now wish otherwise than as it is.

MR. CHAINMAIL.

Yet, may I ask why it is that I find one so accomplished living in this obscurity, and passing only by the name of Miss Susan?

MISS SUSANNAH.

The world and my name are not friends. I have left the world, and wish to remain for ever a stranger to all whom I once knew in it.

MR. CHAINMAIL.

You can have done nothing to dishonour your name.

MISS SUSANNAH.

No, sir. My father has done that of which the world disapproves, in matters of which I pretend not to judge. I have suffered for it as I will never suffer again. My name is my own secret; I have no other, and that is one not worth knowing. You see what I am, and all I am. I live according to the condition of my present fortune; and here, so living, I have found tranquillity.

MR. CHAINMAIL.

Yet, I entreat you, tell me your name.

MISS SUSANNAH.

Why, sir?

MR. CHAINMAIL.

Why, but to throw my hand, my heart, my fortune, at your feet, if——

MISS SUSANNAH.

If my name be worthy of them.

MR. CHAINMAIL.

Nay, nay, not so; if your hand and heart are free.

MISS SUSANNAH.

My hand and heart are free; but they must be sought from myself, and not from my name.

She fixed her eyes on him, with a mingled expression of mistrust, of kindness, and of fixed resolution, which the fargone *innamorato* found irresistible.

MR. CHAINMAIL.

Then from yourself alone I seek them.

MISS SUSANNAH.

Reflect. You have prejudices on the score of parentage. I have not conversed with you so often, without knowing what they are. Choose between them and me. I too have my own prejudices on the score of personal pride.

MR. CHAINMAIL.

I would choose you from all the world, were you even the daughter of the *exécuteur des hautes œuvres*,[7] as the heroine of a romantic story I once read turned out to be.

MISS SUSANNAH.

I am satisfied. You have now a right to know my history; and, if you repent, I absolve you from all obligations.

She told him her history; but he was out of the reach of repentance. "It is true," as at a subsequent period he said to the captain, "she is the daughter of a money-changer; one who, in the days of Richard the First, would have been plucked by the beard in the streets; but she is, according to modern notions, a lady of gentle blood. As to her father's running away, that is a minor consideration: I have always understood, from Mr. Mac Quedy, who is a great oracle in this way, that promises to pay ought not to be kept; the essence of a safe and economical currency being an interminable series of broken promises. There seems to be a difference among the learned as to the way in which the promises ought to be broken; but I am not deep enough in their casuistry to enter into such nice distinctions."

In a few days there was a wedding, a pathetic leave-taking of the farmer's family, a hundred kisses from the bride to the children, and promises twenty times reclaimed and renewed, to visit them in the ensuing year.

[7] Executioner. The tale referred to may be "The Headsman: a Tale of Doom," which had appeared anonymously in *Blackwood's Edinburgh Magazine* for February 1830.

Chapter XVII

THE INVITATION

> *A cup of wine, that's brisk and fine,*
> *And drink unto the leman mine.*
>
> Master Silence.[1]

This veridicous history began in May, and the occurrences already narrated have carried it on to the middle of autumn. Stepping over the interval to Christmas, we find ourselves in our first locality, among the chalk hills of the Thames; and we discover our old friend, Mr. Crotchet, in the act of accepting an invitation, for himself, and any friends who might be with him, to pass their Christmas-day at Chainmail Hall, after the fashion of the twelfth century. Mr. Crotchet had assembled about him, for his own Christmas-festivities, nearly the same party which was introduced to the reader in the spring. Three of that party were wanting. Dr. Morbific, by inoculating himself once too often with non-contagious matter, had explained himself out of the world. Mr. Henbane had also departed, on the wings of an infallible antidote. Mr. Eavesdrop, having printed in a magazine some of the after-dinner conversations of the castle, had had sentence of exclusion passed upon him, on the motion of the Reverend Doctor Folliott, as a flagitious violator of the confidences of private life.

Miss Crotchet had become Lady Bossnowl, but Lady Clarinda had not yet changed her name to Crotchet. She had, on one pretence and another, procrastinated the happy event, and the gentleman had not been very pressing; she had, however, accompanied her brother and sister-in-law, to pass Christmas at Crotchet Castle. With these, Mr. Mac Quedy, Mr. Philpot, Mr. Trillo, Mr. Skionar, Mr. Toogood, and Mr. Firedamp, were sit-

[1] *Henry IV*, V.iii.

ting at breakfast, when the Reverend Doctor Folliott entered and took his seat at the table.

THE REV. DR. FOLLIOTT.

Well, Mr. Mac Quedy, it is now some weeks since we have met: how goes on the march of mind?

MR. MAC QUEDY.

Nay, sir; I think you may see that with your own eyes.

THE REV. DR. FOLLIOTT.

Sir, I have seen it, much to my discomfiture. It has marched into my rick-yard and set my stacks on fire, with chemical materials, most scientifically compounded. It has marched up to the door of my vicarage, a hundred and fifty strong; ordered me to surrender half my tithes; consumed all the provisions I had provided for my audit feast, and drunk up my old October. It has marched in through my back-parlour shutters, and out again with my silver spoons, in the dead of the night.[2] The policeman, who was sent down to examine, says my house has been broken open on the most scientific principles. All this comes of education.

MR. MAC QUEDY.

I rather think it comes of poverty.

THE REV. DR. FOLLIOTT.

No, sir. Robbery perhaps comes of poverty, but scientific principles of robbery come of education. I suppose the learned friend has written a sixpenny treatise on mechanics, and the rascals who robbed me have been reading it.

MR. CROTCHET.

Your house would have been very safe, doctor, if they had had no better science than the learned friend's to work with.

THE REV. DR. FOLLIOTT.

Well, sir, that may be. Excellent potted char. The Lord deliver me from the learned friend.

---

[2] This and the next chapter refer to the agricultural riots of 1830, a protest by farm laborers against the low wages and unemployment caused by machinery. Much of the vandalism was directed against the beneficed clergy, perhaps as symbols of unearned privilege.

MR. CROTCHET.

Well, doctor, for your comfort, here is a declaration of the learned friend's that he will never take office.[3]

THE REV. DR. FOLLIOTT.

Then, sir, he will be in office next week. Peace be with him! Sugar and cream.

MR. CROTCHET.

But, doctor, are you for Chainmail Hall on Christmas-day?

THE REV. DR. FOLLIOTT.

That am I, for there will be an excellent dinner, though, peradventure, grotesquely served.

MR. CROTCHET.

I have not seen my neighbour since he left us on the canal.

THE REV. DR. FOLLIOTT.

He has married a wife, and brought her home.

LADY CLARINDA.

Indeed! If she suits him, she must be an oddity: it will be amusing to see them together.

LORD BOSSNOWL.

Very amusing. He! he!

MR. FIREDAMP.

Is there any water about Chainmail Hall?

THE REV. DR. FOLLIOTT.

An old moat.

MR. FIREDAMP.

I shall die of *malaria*.

MR. TRILLO.

Shall we have any music?

THE REV. DR. FOLLIOTT.

An old harper.

MR. TRILLO.

Those fellows are always horridly out of tune. What will he play?

THE REV. DR. FOLLIOTT.

Old songs and marches.

---

[3] On 16 November 1830 Brougham had been offered the attorney-generalship, which he declined.

MR. SKIONAR.

Amongst so many old things, I hope we shall find Old Philosophy.

THE REV. DR. FOLLIOTT.

An old woman.

MR. PHILPOT.

Perhaps an old map of the river in the twelfth century.

THE REV. DR. FOLLIOTT.

No doubt.

MR. MAC QUEDY.

How many more old things?

THE REV. DR. FOLLIOTT.

Old hospitality, old wine, old ale—all the images of old England; an old butler.

MR. TOOGOOD.

Shall we all be welcome?

THE REV. DR. FOLLIOTT.

Heartily; you will be slapped on the shoulder, and called old boy.

LORD BOSSNOWL.

I think we should all go in our old clothes. He! he!

THE REV. DR. FOLLIOTT.

You will sit on old chairs, round an old table, by the light of old lamps, suspended from pointed arches, which, Mr. Chainmail says, first came into use in the twelfth century; with old armour on the pillars, and old banners in the roof.

LADY CLARINDA.

And what curious piece of antiquity is the lady of the mansion?

THE REV. DR. FOLLIOTT.

No antiquity there; none.

LADY CLARINDA.

Who was she?

THE REV. DR. FOLLIOTT.

That I know not.

LADY CLARINDA.

Have you seen her?

THE REV. DR. FOLLIOTT.

I have.

LADY CLARINDA.

Is she pretty?

THE REV. DR. FOLLIOTT.

More—beautiful. A subject for the pen of Nonnus, or the pencil of Zeuxis.[4] Features of all loveliness, radiant with all virtue and intelligence. A face for Antigone. A form at once plump and symmetrical, that, if it be decorous to divine it by externals, would have been a model for the Venus of Cnidos. Never was any thing so goodly to look on, the present company expected, and poor dear Mrs. Folliott. She reads moral philosophy, Mr. Mac Quedy, which indeed she might as well let alone; she reads Italian poetry, Mr. Skionar; she sings Italian music, Mr. Trillo; but, with all this, she has the greatest of female virtues, for she superintends the household, and looks after her husband's dinner. I believe she was a mountaineer: παρθένος οὐρεσίφοιτος, ἐρήμαδι σύντροφος ὕλῃ,[5] as Nonnus sweetly sings.

---

[4] Celebrated Greek painter of the fifth century B.C.
[5] A mountain-wandering maid,
   Twin-nourished with the solitary wood. [P] [*Dionysiaca,* IX.76.]

Chapter XVIII

CHAINMAIL HALL

Vous autres dictes que ignorance est mere de tous maulx, et dictes vray: mais toutesfoys vous ne la bannissez mye de vos entendemens, et vivez en elle, avecques elle, et par elle. C'est pourquoy tant de maulx vous meshaignent de jour en jour.—RABELAIS, l. 5. c. 7.[1]

THE PARTY which was assembled on Christmas-day in Chainmail Hall, comprised all the guests of Crotchet Castle, some of Mr. Chainmail's other neighbours, all his tenants and domestics, and Captain Fitzchrome. The hall was spacious and lofty; and with its tall fluted pillars and pointed arches, its windows of stained glass, its display of arms and banners intermingled with holly and mistletoe, its blazing cressets and torches, and a stupendous fire in the centre, on which blocks of pine were flaming and crackling, had a striking effect on eyes unaccustomed to such a dining-room. The fire was open on all sides, and the smoke was caught and carried back, under a funnel-formed canopy, into a hollow central pillar. This fire was the line of demarcation between gentle and simple, on days of high festival. Tables extended from it on two sides, to nearly the end of the hall.

Mrs. Chainmail was introduced to the company. Young Crotchet felt some revulsion of feeling at the unexpected sight of one whom he had forsaken, but not forgotten, in a condition apparently so much happier than his own. The lady held out her hand to him with a cordial look of more than forgiveness;

[1] "You men of the other world say that ignorance is the mother of all evil, and so far you are right: yet for all that, you do not take the least care to get rid of it, but still plod on, and live in it, with it, and by it; for which cause a plaugy deal of mischief lights on you every day." Urquhart and Motteux translation.

it seemed to say that she had much to thank him for. She was the picture of a happy bride, *rayonnante de joie et d'amour*.

Mr. Crotchet told the Reverend Doctor Folliott the news of the morning. "As you predicted," he said, "your friend, the learned friend, is in office; he has also a title; he is now Sir Guy de Vaux."[2]

THE REV. DR. FOLLIOTT.

Thank heaven for that! he is disarmed from further mischief.[3] It is something, at any rate, to have that hollow and wind-shaken reed rooted up for ever from the field of public delusion.[4]

---

[2] Brougham was named Baron Brougham and Vaux on November 23, 1830 and was sworn in as Chancellor on November 25. Cf. Guy Fawkes, leader of the Gunpowder Plot of 1605, whose name has become synonymous with conspiracy, anarchy, and civil discord.

[3] As a peer, Brougham had to resign his seat in Commons and move to the House of Lords, at that time a bulwark of conservatism and obstruction. His reformist zeal would thus be stifled.

[4] I may here insert, as somewhat germane to the matter, some lines which were written by me, in March, 1831, and printed in the *Examiner* of August 14, 1831. They were then called "An Anticipation:" they may now (1837), be fairly entitled "A Prophecy fulfilled."

THE FATE OF A BROOM: AN ANTICIPATION

Lo! in Corruption's lumber-room,
The remnants of a wondrous broom;
That walking, talking, oft was seen,
Making stout promise to sweep clean;
But evermore, at every push,
Proved but a stump without a brush.
Upon its handle-top, a sconce,
Like Brahma's, looked four ways at once,
Pouring on king, lords, church, and rabble.
Long floods of favour-currying gabble;
From four-fold mouth-piece always spinning
Projects of plausible beginning,
Whereof said sconce did ne'er intend
That any one should have an end;
Yet still, by shifts and quaint inventions,
Got credit for its good intentions,
Adding no trifle to the store,
Wherewith the devil paves his floor.
Worn out at last, found bare and scrubbish,
And thrown aside with other rubbish,
We'll e'en hand o'er the enchanted stick,
As a choice present for Old Nick,

MR. CROTCHET.

I suppose, doctor, you do not like to see a great reformer in office; you are afraid for your vested interests.

THE REV. DR. FOLLIOTT.

Not I, indeed, sir; my vested interests are very safe from all such reformers as the learned friend. I vaticinate[5] what will be the upshot of all his schemes of reform. He will make a speech of seven hours' duration, and this will be its quintessence: that, seeing the exceeding difficulty of putting salt on the bird's tail, it will be expedient to consider the best method of throwing dust in the bird's eyes. All the rest will be

> Τιτιτιτιτιμπρό.
> Ποποποί, ποποποί.
> Τιοτιοτιοτιοτιοτιοτίγξ.
> Κικκαβαῦ, κικκαβαῦ.
> τοροτοροτοροτοροτορολιλιλίγξ.[6]

as Aristophanes has it; and so I leave him, in Nephelococcygia.[7]

Mr. Mac Quedy came up to the divine as Mr. Crotchet left him, and said: "There is one piece of news which the old gentleman has not told you. The great firm of Catchflat and Company, in which young Crotchet is a partner, has stopped payment."

THE REV. DR. FOLLIOTT.

Bless me! that accounts for the young gentleman's melancholy. I thought they would over-reach themselves with their own tricks. The day of reckoning, Mr. Mac Quedy, is the point which your paper-money science always leaves out of view.

> To sweep, beyond the Stygian lake,
> The pavement it has helped to make. [P]

["Brougham" can be pronounced "broom." *thrown aside . . . rubbish:* Brougham was forced to resign the Chancellorship with the fall of the Whig government in 1834.]

   [5] To foretell or prophesy an event.

   [6] Sounds without meaning; imitative of the voices of birds. From the Ὄρνιθες of Aristophanes. [P] [*The Birds.*]

   [7] "Cuckoo-city-in-the-clouds." From the same comedy. [P]

MR. MAC QUEDY.

I do not see, sir, that the failure of Catchflat and Company has any thing to do with my science.

THE REV. DR. FOLLIOTT.

It has this to do with it, sir, that you would turn the whole nation into a great paper-money shop, and take no thought of the day of reckoning. But the dinner is coming. I think you, who are so fond of paper promises, should dine on the bill of fare.

The harper at the head of the hall struck up an ancient march, and the dishes were brought in, in grand procession.

The boar's head, garnished with rosemary, with a citron in its mouth, led the van. Then came tureens of plum-porridge; then a series of turkeys, and, in the midst of them, an enormous sausage, which it required two men to carry. Then came geese and capons, tongues and hams, the ancient glory of the Christmas pie, a gigantic plum-pudding, a pyramid of minced pies, and a baron of beef bringing up the rear.

"It is something new under the sun," said the divine, as he sat down, "to see a great dinner without fish."

MR. CHAINMAIL.

Fish was for fasts, in the twelfth century.

THE REV. DR. FOLLIOTT.

Well, sir, I prefer our reformed system of putting fasts and feasts together. Not but here is ample indemnity.

Ale and wine flowed in abundance. The dinner passed off merrily; the old harper playing all the while the oldest music in his repertory. The tables being cleared, he indemnified himself for lost time at the lower end of the hall, in company with the old butler and the other domestics, whose attendance on the banquet had been indispensable.

The scheme of Christmas gambols, which Mr. Chainmail had laid for the evening, was interrupted by a tremendous clamour without.

THE REV. DR. FOLLIOTT.

What have we here? Mummers?[8]

___

[8] Groups of young people who go around in costume at Christmas

MR. CHAINMAIL.

Nay, I know not. I expect none.

"Who is there?" he added, approaching the door of the hall.

"Who is there?" vociferated the divine, with the voice of Stentor.[9]

"Captain Swing," replied a chorus of discordant voices.[10]

THE REV. DR. FOLLIOTT.

Ho, ho! here is a piece of the dark ages we did not bargain for. Here is the Jacquerie.[11] Here is the march of mind with a witness.

MR. MAC QUEDY.

Do you not see that you have brought disparates together? the Jacquerie and the march of mind.

THE REV. DR. FOLLIOTT.

Not at all, sir. They are the same thing, under different names. Πολλῶν ὀνομάτων μορφὴ μία.[12] What was Jacquerie in the dark ages, is the march of mind in this very enlightened one—very enlightened one.

MR. CHAINMAIL.

The cause is the same in both; poverty in despair.

MR. MAC QUEDY.

Very likely; but the effect is extremely disagreeable.

THE REV. DR. FOLLIOTT.

It is the natural result, Mr. Mac Quedy, of that system of state seamanship which your science upholds. Putting the crew on short allowance, and doubling the rations of the officers, is the sure way to make a mutiny on board a ship in distress, Mr. Mac Quedy.

MR. MAC QUEDY.

Eh! sir, I uphold no such system as that. I shall set you right as to cause and effect. Discontent increases with the increase of information.[13] That is all.

time performing a playlet about St. George; mummers' plays were popular from medieval times until the middle of the nineteenth century.

[9] A herald in the *Iliad* famous for his loud voice.

[10] Pseudonym adopted during the 1830 agricultural unrest by those who wrote threatening letters to farmers who used threshing machines.

[11] A bloody uprising by French peasants in 1358; the name derives from *Jacques Bonhomme,* the French counterpart to John Doe.

[12] "One shape of many names." Æschylus: *Prometheus.* [P]

[13] This looks so like caricature (a thing abhorrent to our candour),

THE REV. DR. FOLLIOTT.

I said it was the march of mind. But we have not time for discussing cause and effect now. Let us get rid of the enemy.

And he vociferated at the top of his voice, "What do you want here?"

"Arms, arms," replied a hundred voices, "Give us the arms."

THE REV. DR. FOLLIOTT.

You see, Mr. Chainmail, this is the inconvenience of keeping an armoury, not fortified with sand bags, green bags,[14] and old bags of all kinds.

MR. MAC QUEDY.

Just give them the old spits and toasting irons, and they will go away quietly.

MR. CHAINMAIL.

My spears and swords! not without my life. These assailants are all aliens to my land and house. My men will fight for me, one and all. This is the fortress of beef and ale.

MR. MAC QUEDY.

Eh, sir, when the rabble is up, it is very indiscriminating. You are e'en suffering for the sins of Sir Simon Steeltrap, and the like, who have pushed the principle of accumulation a little too far.

MR. CHAINMAIL.

The way to keep the people down is kind and liberal usage.

MR. MAC QUEDY.

That is very well (where it can be afforded), in the way of prevention; but in the way of cure, the operation must be more drastic.

[*Taking down a battle-axe.*]

I would fain have a good blunderbuss charged with slugs.

---

that we must give authority for it. "We ought to look the evil manfully in the face, and not amuse ourselves with the dreams of fancy. The discontent of the labourers in our times is rather a proof of their superior information than of their deterioration." *Morning Chronicle: December 20,* 1830. [P]

14 Brief cases, such as were used by prosecuting attorneys.

MR. CHAINMAIL.

When I suspended these arms for ornament, I never dreamed
of their being called into use.

MR. SKIONAR.

Let me address them. I never failed to convince an audience
that the best thing they could do was to go away.[15]

MR. MAC QUEDY.

Eh! sir, I can bring them to that conclusion in less time than
you.

MR. CROTCHET.

I have no fancy for fighting. It is a very hard case upon a
guest, when the latter end of a feast is the beginning of a fray.[16]

MR. MAC QUEDY.

Give them the old iron.

THE REV. DR. FOLLIOTT.

Give them the weapons! *Pessimo, medius fidius, exemplo.*[17]
Forbid it the spirit of *Frère Jean des Entommeures!* No! let
us see what the church militant, in the armour of the twelfth
century, will do against the march of mind. Follow me who
will, and stay who list. Here goes: *Pro aris et focis!*[18] that is,
for tithe pigs and fires to roast them!

He clapped a helmet on his head, seized a long lance, threw
open the gates, and tilted out on the rabble, side by side with
Mr. Chainmail, followed by the greater portion of the male
inmates of the hall, who had armed themselves at random.

The rabble-rout, being unprepared for such a sortie, fled in
all directions, over hedge and ditch.

Mr. Trillo stayed in the hall, playing a march on the harp,
to inspirit the rest to sally out. The water-loving Mr. Philpot
had diluted himself with so much wine, as to be quite *hors de*

---

[15] Coleridge had given many series of lectures, which, though
generally well-received, were sometimes beyond his audience's compre-
hension.

[16] *I Henry IV,* IV.ii.

[17] A most pernicious example, by Hercules!—Petronius Arbiter.
[P] [*The Satyricon,* ¶104.]

[18] "For our altars and hearths."

combat.[19] Mr. Toogood, intending to equip himself in purely defensive armour, contrived to slip a ponderous coat of mail over his shoulders, which pinioned his arms to his sides; and in this condition, like a chicken trussed for roasting, he was thrown down behind a pillar, in the first rush of the sortie. Mr. Crotchet seized the occurrence as a pretext for staying with him, and passed the whole time of the action in picking him out of his shell.

"Phew!" said the divine, returning; "an inglorious victory: but it deserves a devil[20] and a bowl of punch."

MR. CHAINMAIL.

A wassail-bowl.

THE REV. DR. FOLLIOTT.

No, sir. No more of the twelfth century for me.

MR. CHAINMAIL.

Nay, doctor. The twelfth century has backed you well. Its manners and habits, its community of kind feelings between master and man, are the true remedy for these ebullitions.

MR. TOOGOOD.

Something like it: improved by my diagram: arts for arms.

THE REV. DR. FOLLIOTT.

No wassail-bowl for me. Give me an unsophisticated bowl of punch, which belongs to that blissful middle period, after the Jacquerie was down, and before the march of mind was up. But, see, who is floundering in the water?

Proceeding to the edge of the moat, they fished up Mr. Firedamp, who had missed his way back, and tumbled in. He was drawn out, exclaiming, "that he had taken his last dose of *malaria* in this world."

THE REV. DR. FOLLIOTT.

Tut, man; dry clothes, a turkey's leg and rump, well devilled, and a quart of strong punch, will set all to rights.

"Wood embers," said Mr. Firedamp, when he had been accommodated with a change of clothes, "there is no antidote to

---

[19] Out of action.
[20] A name for various highly-seasoned dishes.

malaria like the smoke of wood embers; pine embers." And he placed himself, with his mouth open, close by the fire.

THE REV. DR. FOLLIOTT.

Punch, sir, punch: there is no antidote like punch.

MR. CHAINMAIL.

Well, doctor, you shall be indulged. But I shall have my wassail-bowl nevertheless.

An immense bowl of spiced wine, with roasted apples hissing on its surface, was borne into the hall by four men, followed by an empty bowl of the same dimensions, with all the materials of arrack punch, for the divine's especial brewage. He accinged himself to[21] the task, with his usual heroism; and having finished it to his entire satisfaction, reminded his host to order in the devil.

THE REV. DR. FOLLIOTT.

I think, Mr. Chainmail, we can amuse ourselves very well here all night. The enemy may be still excubant: and we had better not disperse till daylight. I am perfectly satisfied with my quarters. Let the young folks go on with their gambols; let them dance to your old harper's minstrelsy; and if they please to kiss under the mistletoe, whereof I espy a goodly bunch suspended at the end of the hall, let those who like it not, leave it to those who do. Moreover, if among the more sedate portion of the assembly, which, I foresee, will keep me company, there were any to revive the good old custom of singing after supper, so to fill up the intervals of the dances, the steps of night would move more lightly.

MR. CHAINMAIL.

My Susan will set the example, after she has set that of joining in the rustic dance, according to good customs long departed.

After the first dance, in which all classes of the company mingled, the young lady of the mansion took her harp, and following the reverend gentleman's suggestion, sang a song of the twelfth century.

[21] Undertook.

Florence and Blanchflor.[22]

Florence and Blanchflor, loveliest maids,
    Within a summer grove,
Amid the flower-enamelled shades
    Together talked of love.

A clerk sweet Blanchflor's heart had gained;
    Fair Florence loved a knight:
And each with ardent voice maintained,
    She loved the worthiest wight.

Sweet Blanchflor praised her scholar dear,
    As courteous, kind, and true;
Fair Florence said her chevalier
    Could every foe subdue.

And Florence scorned the bookworm vain,
    Who sword nor spear could raise;
And Blanchflor scorned the unlettered brain
    Could sing no lady's praise.

From dearest love, the maidens bright
    To deadly hatred fell;
Each turned to shun the other's sight,
    And neither said farewell.

The king of birds, who held his court
    Within that flowery grove,
Sang loudly: " 'Twill be rare disport
    To judge this suit of love."

Before him came the maidens bright,
    With all his birds around,
To judge the cause, if clerk or knight
    In love be worthiest found.

The falcon and the sparrow-hawk
    Stood forward for the fight:
Ready to do, and not to talk,
    They voted for the knight.

---

[22] Imitated from the Fabliau, *De Florance et de Blanche Flor,
alias Jugement d'Amour.* [P]

And Blanchflor's heart began to fail,
　Till rose the strong-voiced lark,
And, after him, the nightingale,
　And pleaded for the clerk.

The nightingale prevailed at length,
　Her pleading had such charms;
So eloquence can conquer strength,
　And arts can conquer arms.

The lovely Florence tore her hair,
　And died upon the place;
And all the birds assembled there,
　Bewailed the mournful case.

They piled up leaves and flowerets rare,
　Above the maiden bright,
And sang: "Farewell to Florence fair,
　Who too well loved her knight."

Several others of the party sang in the intervals of the dances.
Mr. Chainmail handed to Mr. Trillo another ballad of the
twelfth century of a merrier character than the former. Mr.
Trillo readily accommodated it with an air, and sang,—

The Priest and the Mulberry Tree.[23]

Did you hear of the curate who mounted his mare,
And merrily trotted along to the fair?
Of creature more tractable none ever heard,
In the height of her speed she would stop at a word;
And again with a word, when the curate said Hey,
She put forth her mettle, and galloped away.

As near to the gates of the city he rode,
While the sun of September all brilliantly glowed,
The good priest discovered, with eyes of desire,
A mulberry tree in a hedge of wild briar;
On boughs long and lofty, in many a green shoot,
Hung large, black, and glossy, the beautiful fruit.

[23] Imitated from the Fabliau, *Du Provoire qui mengea des Mores.*
[P] [*The Priest Who Ate the Mulberries.*]

The curate was hungry and thirsty to boot;
He shrunk from the thorns, though he longed for
 the fruit;
With a word he arrested his courser's keen speed,
And he stood up erect on the back of his steed;
On the saddle he stood, while the creature stood still,
And he gathered the fruit, till he took his good fill.

"Sure never," he thought, "was a creature so rare,
So docile, so true, as my excellent mare.
Lo, here, how I stand" (and he gazed all around,)
"As safe and as steady as if on the ground,
Yet how had it been, if some traveler this way,
Had, dreaming no mischief, but chanced to cry
 Hey?"

He stood with his head in the mulberry tree,
And he spoke out aloud in his fond reverie:
At the sound of the word, the good mare made a
 push,
And down went the priest in the wild-briar bush.
He remembered too late, on his thorny green bed,
Much that well may be thought, cannot wisely be
 said.

Lady Clarinda, being prevailed on to take the harp in her
turn, sang the following stanzas:—

> In the days of old,
> Lovers felt true passion,
> Deeming years of sorrow
> By a smile repaid.
> Now the charms of gold,
> Spells of pride and fashion,
> Bid them say good morrow
> To the best-loved maid.

Through the forests wild,
O'er the mountains lonely,
They were never weary
Honour to pursue:
If the damsel smiled
Once in seven years only,
All their wanderings dreary
Ample guerdon knew.

Now one day's caprice
Weighs down years of smiling,
Youthful hearts are rovers,
Love is bought and sold:
Fortune's gifts may cease,
Love is less beguiling;
Wiser were the lovers,
In the days of old.

The glance which she threw at the Captain, as she sang the last verse, awakened his dormant hopes. Looking round for his rival, he saw that he was not in the hall; and, approaching the lady of his heart, he received one of the sweetest smiles of their earlier days.

After a time, the ladies, and all the females of the party, retired. The males remained on duty with punch and wassail, and dropped off one by one into sweet forgetfulness; so that when the rising sun of December looked through the painted windows on mouldering embers and flickering lamps, the vaulted roof was echoing to a mellifluous concert of noses, from the clarionet of the waiting-boy at one end of the hall, to the double bass of the Reverend Doctor, ringing over the empty punch-bowl, at the other.

CONCLUSION.

FROM this eventful night, young Crotchet was seen no more on English mould. Whither he had vanished, was a question that could no more be answered in his case than in that of King

Arthur, after the battle of Camlan.[24] The great firm of Catch-flat and Company figured in the Gazette and paid sixpence in the pound; and it was clear that he had shrunk from exhibiting himself on the scene of his former greatness, shorn of the beams of his paper prosperity. Some supposed him to be sleeping among the undiscoverable secrets of some barbel-pool in the Thames; but those who knew him best were more inclined to the opinion that he had gone across the Atlantic, with his pockets full of surplus capital, to join his old acquaintance, Mr. Touchandgo, in the bank of Dotandcarryonetown.

Lady Clarinda was more sorry for her father's disappointment than her own; but she had too much pride to allow herself to be put up a second time in the money-market; and when the Captain renewed his assiduities, her old partiality for him, combining with a sense of gratitude for a degree of constancy which she knew she scarcely deserved, induced her, with Lord Foolincourt's hard-wrung consent, to share with him a more humble, but less precarious fortune, than that to which she had been destined as the price of a rotten borough.

[24] King Arthur's last battle, traditionally dated A.D. 539.

THE END

Rinehart Editions